ENDORSEMENTS

THE DELTA TANGO TRILOGY is an in-depth journey of one man as he threads his way through personal problems and the challenge of his harrowing career as a U. S. Border Patrol Agent. His life of trials and sorrows rivals any fiction story today.

–**Clive Cussler**, *New York Times* bestselling author of the Dirk Pitt series

ESSENTIAL AND GRIPPING. *Delta Tango Trilogy* is a heartbreakingly honest tale of the lives that intersect and are forever changed along our bleak and dangerous southern border. This is an important set of novels, not to be missed or forgotten.

–**Margaret Coel**, *New York Times* bestselling author of *Winter's Child.*

USING HIS OWN EXPERIENCE in the U.S. Border Patrol, Christopher LaGrone paints a detailed and intimidating picture of the physical and mental hardships that must be painstakingly endured in order to work as an agent.

–**U.S. Review of Books**

READER COMMENTS

"After reading *Fleeing the Past*, I have a completely new respect for what it takes to become a Border Patrol Officer. I'm looking forward to Book Two: *Felina's Spell* and Book Three: *Moments of Truth*."

"*Fleeing the Past* presents in excruciating, realistic detail the demands of training for the U.S. Border Patrol . . . an uncomfortable but absolutely compelling read."

"I have to disagree with the trilogy idea. I'd rather have a really long book that I can keep reading! I'm ready to read Book 2, and now, I have to wait."

"I'm hooked! I know next to nothing about the life of a U.S. Border Patrol Agent, so this is new reading territory for me."

DELTA TANGO TRILOGY

The *DELTA TANGO TRILOGY* by Christopher LaGrone follows Layne Sheppard from the day he applies to join the U.S. Border Patrol through the rigors of the Federal Law Enforcement Training Center (known as the Border Patrol Academy) and his alternating exhilaration, anxiety, and drudgery as a field trainee, to the often harrowing moments of shift work on the U.S.-Mexico border. Along the way he deals with his own insecurities, a serious drinking problem, the internal politics of Douglas Station in extreme southeast Arizona (where he's assigned) and, for him, the unimaginable: Falling in love with a beautiful girl who was brought over the border as an infant—one of those illegals known as a Dreamer. Through Layne's experiences, life in the U.S. Border Patrol comes alive in ways few Americans can even imagine.

In Book One—**Fleeing the Past**—Layne strives to prove, to himself and others, that his failures of the past are in the past. As he seeks self-respect and self-confidence, he endures the boot camp-like ordeal of the Border Patrol Academy in sweltering New Mexico—punishing long-distance runs and debilitating hand-to-hand combat. During precious free time he meets Felina Camarena Rivera. Both keep personal secrets and pursue plans for escaping them—plans they also keep to themselves, even as their attraction for each other deepens.

In Book Two—**Felina's Spell**—Layne struggles to overcome the politics of the BP's Douglas Station and advance from trainee to regular agent status—to succeed. As he rides with seasoned veterans, Layne gets a first-hand look at the challenges border agents face on a daily and nightly basis and learns realities that agents either accept begrudgingly or surrender to. Felina's clever plan to become Layne's wife seems headed for success, despite Layne's serious drinking problem, when Felina's brother is charged with DUI and deported.

In Book Three—**Moments of Truth**—Layne realizes the inevitable loneliness and fear of patrolling the border without a partner, and pressure from management mounts. While experiencing many "agent adventures," he faces several moments of truth, both personal and professional, among them dealing with secrets Felina has held. She, too, must come to grips with tough choices; can she rely on Layne? They undertake an audacious gamble, and their futures, individually and together, hang in the balance.

THE DELTA TANGO TRILOGY
BOOK TWO

Felina's Spell

THE DELTA TANGO TRILOGY
BOOK TWO

FELINA'S SPELL

A Layne Sheppard Novel

CHRISTOPHER LaGRONE

NEW YORK

LONDON • NASHVILLE • MELBOURNE • VANCOUVER

Felina's Spell

The Delta Tango Trilogy - Book Two / A Layne Sheppard Novel

Published in New York, New York, by Morgan James Publishing. Morgan James is a trademark of Morgan James, LLC. www.MorganJamesPublishing.com

Morgan James BOGO™

A **FREE** ebook edition is available for you or a friend with the purchase of this print book.

CLEARLY SIGN YOUR NAME ABOVE

Instructions to claim your free ebook edition:
1. Visit MorganJamesBOGO.com
2. Sign your name CLEARLY in the space above
3. Complete the form and submit a photo of this entire page
4. You or your friend can download the ebook to your preferred device

ISBN 9781631955457 paperback
ISBN 9781631955464 eBook
Library of Congress Control Number:
2021933921

Cover and Interior Design by:
Chris Treccani
www.3dogcreative.net

Morgan James PUBLISHING Builds *with...* **Habitat for Humanity® Peninsula and Greater Williamsburg**

Morgan James is a proud partner of Habitat for Humanity Peninsula and Greater Williamsburg. Partners in building since 2006.

Get involved today! Visit
MorganJamesPublishing.com/giving-back

To a dream realized
and a legacy preserved

IN MEMORIAM

The unexpected phone call from Nancy came in mid-December 2018.

"Denny, I have terrible news," she said. "Chris died."

And that's how the completion of The Delta Tango Trilogy began.

I had gotten to know Nancy as the person in charge of author events at the Barnes & Noble bookstore on Colorado Boulevard in Denver. Over several years she hosted me each time I had a new book, and we collaborated on several Colorado Authors' League events.

One day, I think it was in 2016, she asked if I would be willing to look at a manuscript written by a young guy who wanted very much to be an author; he needed a professional critique of what he had written.

Sure, I said. I enjoy working with aspiring writers.

Chris LaGrone (the brother of Nancy's sister-in-law, I later learned) was then in his late thirties. He had been an agent in the U.S. Border Patrol for a time and had written a novel based on his experiences.

I read it and was impressed with the quality of his writing and the content of his story. But I told him, "No publisher will ever publish this, Chris, because it's too linear. It's just your character's experiences getting into and going through the Border Patrol Academy, being a field trainee, and then becoming an actual agent." I thought it provided insights the public didn't have, but to make a compelling book it needed more.

"Novels," I told him, "have subplots—twists and turns that make the overall story more complex, and thus, more interesting."

I gave him an example: "You're writing about someone whose job is to catch illegal aliens trying to sneak into the United States. Why not have him fall in love with an illegal? That would complicate matters!" I suggested that he read Helen Thorpe's wonderful book *Just Like Us* to learn what a so-called "Dreamer" faces living in America without legal status.

I also told Chris his main character, Layne Sheppard, needed to have a personal issue to overcome—a demon to conquer. I left it to him to decide what that would be.

Chris proved to be the most coachable writer I've ever worked with. He came back to me some time later with a rewritten manuscript that contained love, conflict, and a demon for the main character. Again, I read it. And again, I was impressed. But again, I saw a problem.

"No publisher will publish this, Chris," I told him. "Two hundred fifty thousand words is too long."

But I offered a suggestion: "We could turn this into a trilogy," I said. "This would break nicely into three books."

Chris liked that idea and saw immediately how to divide his story into three parts. Thus began almost two years of rewriting and editing. Chris would send me chapters as he finished drafts. I'd edit them and send them back to him for revisions. He'd return them to me, and I'd add the finished versions to a growing manuscript file.

We had finished Book One this way and were halfway through the same process for Book Two when Chris informed me that he was going to Argentina in August 2018 to improve his already fluent Spanish and learn more about the Hispanic culture. From Argentina he was to travel to Chile and Peru.

Before Chris left Denver, he finished drafts of all of Book Two's chapters, and we discussed a rough outline for Book Three. His absence allowed me time to focus on a book of my own that I was finishing.

In late October I emailed Chris, asking when he would be returning. "We need to hit it once you are back in town," I wrote.

"I'm in South America for another few months," he wrote back. He was looking forward to visiting the Atacama Desert in Chile, where the thirty-three Chilean miners were trapped underground for sixty-nine days before their dramatic rescue in August 2010.

By early December 2018, Chris had made his way to Cusco, Peru (elevation 11,152 feet), via Lima (sea level). He was headed for Machu Picchu, the center of the Inca civilization of the fifteenth century, high in the Andes Mountains.

"Chris suffered from severe asthma his entire childhood," his mother Sherryl told me later. "It continued into his adult life. Changing altitude quickly when he flew from Lima to Cusco, his body was not able to adapt to the thin air quickly enough."

I can't begin to express how stunned I was when I received that startling phone call from Nancy in December 2018. But, somehow I knew right away what I wanted to do.

"This isn't the time," I began. "But when you think the time is right, please tell Chris's mom and sister (Aimee) that, if they'd like to have the trilogy finished as Chris's legacy, I'll volunteer to write Book Three. I have a good idea where Chris was going with it."

By then I had worked with Chris for more than two years. Over countless meetings I had coached him to develop the story as a three-book series. While Book Three wasn't yet in draft form, Chris and I had discussed it at length. I didn't know exactly how he planned to conclude, but he'd put all of the building blocks in place. And I'd edited enough of his writing to have a good feel for how he expressed things; I was confident that I could replicate his style.

I've never been in the Border Patrol, of course, and know virtually nothing about being an agent. Sustaining Chris's intimate knowledge of life in the Patrol would have been impossible for me. Luckily, I had a source who agreed to provide me with insights into Border Patrol policies and procedures and many examples of an agent's adventures. Thus, I knew I'd be able to fill Book Three with the kinds of true-life experiences Chris related so realistically in the first two books.

Just after the start of the new year, Nancy made sure I knew when and where Chris's memorial service would be held, and said she hoped I would attend. I didn't want to miss it, and afterwards I was thankful I hadn't, because, for as well as I had gotten to know Chris, I had no idea how important writing was to him until I listened to speaker after speaker talk about how badly he wanted to become a successful writer. It drove everything Chris did the last several years of his life.

I knew then what to expect, and a week or so after the service I received an email from Sherryl LaGrone that read, in part: "Aimee and I are very much interested in having you finish Chris's work." A week later his mother and I talked by phone, and in March I met her face to face for the first time, before a Colorado Rockies Spring Training game in Scottsdale, AZ.

The book I was finishing when Chris died was my tenth as an author, but all are non-fiction. I had tried writing fiction almost forty years earlier but decided that, as a career newspaper journalist trained in reporting facts accurately, I just wasn't good at making things up. But I'd edited many novels and had been working with Chris for two years. So, I was willing to take another crack at "making things up"—especially since Chris had done most of the hard fictionalizing: creating characters, setting scenes, and establishing the story arc.

My first step was to finish editing Book Two. I decided to end it five chapters earlier than Chris planned, and use those chapters in Book Three. I also had other material from Chris to build on, meaning at least a third of Book Three is his origination.

From there it was just a matter of answering the recurring question every novelist faces, though it was a new one for me: What happens next?

Chris inspired the answers.

I hope I've honored my friend Chris with the way I completed the story he created, and that my attempt to capture his storytelling style reads like the rest of this trilogy.

—Denny Dressman

ACKNOWLEDGMENTS

MY SON CHRISTOPHER was a successful high school and college baseball player, and like most athletes, most of his focus was on his sport. After graduating from college with a degree in marketing and working in various jobs, he discovered that his true passion was not athletics or marketing, but writing. After uncovering his passion, it became his goal to become a published author. Chris began pursuing his dream earnestly while serving as a U.S. Border Patrol agent.

His loving father Mark, my husband, was a high school teacher and Chris's baseball coach at Arvada West High. Mark, too, loved writing but kept it on a personal level. He encouraged Chris to write what became the *Delta Tango Trilogy*. The two of them would talk daily about their love of words, the challenges of working on the southern border, and the importance of pursuing one's dreams. Mark was Chris's rock.

When Mark died of cancer in 2014, the loss was tremendous for Chris, missing his daily visits with his dad. It was then that the LaGrone family's dear friend, Alan Olds, became Chris's confidant and mentor—and initial editor when Chris began writing his first *Delta Tango* manuscript. Retired from a full career as a highly respected and successful high school English teacher in Colorado, Alan guided and instructed Chris, who'd had no formal writing education. Our family is grateful for all the hours Alan spent with Chris, not only on his novel, but also as Chris's devoted and loving friend.

When expressing thanks, the first person who comes to mind is Denny Dressman, whose role is detailed in the *In Memoriam* section. Without Denny, there may never have been a *Delta Tango Trilogy*. For more than two years, he not only edited Chris's work and helped him develop his novel, ultimately into a trilogy; Denny also became a good friend to him during that time. Since Chris's unexpected death, Denny has become a good friend of mine, a mentor who has guided and instructed me throughout the process of bringing the trilogy to publication. I am eternally grateful for Denny Dressman, a true professional who is also kind and compassionate.

Thanks, also, to Nancy Hestera, wife of my son-in-law's brother, who first asked Denny if he would read Chris's original manuscript. And to Terry Whalin of Morgan James Publishing, and everyone in founder David Hancock's Morgan James family who helped produce this book and the entire trilogy.

It is with tremendous pride, as well as a heavy heart, that my daughter Aimee and I see Christopher's dream realized, and his legacy preserved, with publication of the *Delta Tango Trilogy*. We miss both Chris and his father deeply, but we know that they have been reunited in a better place.

—Sherryl LaGrone

Christopher LaGrone

FELINA'S SPELL

1

AS DAYLIGHT ARRIVED IN DENVER, southbound I-25 intensified an overwhelming sense of loneliness within Layne Sheppard, brought on, at least to some extent, by this momentous departure. He had survived one daunting step of his plan to become a U.S. Border Patrol agent by successfully completing the grueling regimen of the Border Patrol Academy, as the crucible at the Federal Law Enforcement Training Center in miserable Artesia, New Mexico was called. Now, after a week-long respite at his parents' comfortable Denver-area home, he was heading for the next phase of the gauntlet he had chosen to prove to himself that those aimless days of the past several years were indeed in his past. Being home with his mom and dad for those seven days had been a stark reminder of why he was doing this in the first place. Soon he'd begin field training at the Border Patrol's Douglas Station in extreme southeast Arizona, literally a stone's throw from the border of Mexico.

Layne had bought a compact car from a private owner in Denver, and via phone, thanks to help from a trainee-soon-to-become-agent named Ryan Danielson, had secured a place to live in the historic former copper-mining boomtown of Bisbee, Arizona. Somewhat to his surprise, the days back home had flashed by like hours. At the end of the week—also somewhat surprisingly—he happily said goodbye to the Front Range of the Rocky Mountains for the last time. His parents planned on coming to visit early the next year, around mid-February. By then, he hoped, he would be a full-fledged Border Patrol agent.

He set the cruise control on his Honda at seventy-seven miles per hour and leaned the seat back. A man driving an SUV passed by him traveling just a few miles per hour faster, and Layne could sense the man thinking. He was probably on his way to work, concerned with something that most likely didn't involve physical danger or loss of life. He wondered if the man would believe it if he told him where he was going and what he was going to be involved in. As Layne passed through Castle Rock, Denver's most distant bedroom community to the south as well as the largest incorporated town in Douglas County, he tried to imagine what life would be like where he was headed.

His thoughts wandered the way they usually did when he was driving cross-country, but that captivating girl Danielson and his fiancée Marianne had introduced him to a couple weeks earlier—Felina Camarena Rivera—repeatedly intruded on his reverie. He passed through Colorado Springs, Pueblo, and Trinidad, heading toward the New Mexico border, before he reasoned that the timing was close to appropriate to call her. Throughout the past week he had convinced himself that she really didn't like him. Recalling that feeling, he figured it was a no-lose situation; he might as well call. He retrieved from his wallet the folded piece of paper that Marianne had given him with Felina's phone number. As he guided the Honda with one hand, he entered her number on his cellphone. The ringtone repeated several times and he held his breath while he watched the road. On the fifth ring, she answered.

"Hi, how are you? I didn't think I would ever hear from you again."

Girls' voices always sound different over the phone, he thought, then said, "No, no, I wanted to call you earlier, but I didn't have time, packing and all."

"Well, when will you be back in Arizona?" Felina asked.

"I'm on my way right now. I'm on the highway."

"Ryan told Marianne he hooked you up with a place to live in Bisbee. He said he knows a guy at Douglas Station who knows somebody," Felina said.

"Yeah, I got lucky. Ryan is a cool guy. I just have to show up and pay the deposit and the first month's rent."

"Where are you right now?" Felina pressed.

"I'm in Raton, New Mexico. When will I see you again?"

Layne held his breath again, considering that the request might have been premature. The timing was wrong, but he had already said it.

"Well, I'm free next weekend," Felina said with inflection.

"Cool!" Layne was smiling now. "I have post-Academy classes on Fridays, so I have Saturdays and Sundays off until Field Training is over." Layne was trying to sound casual.

"Well, call me when you're settled in, okay?" Felina said.

"I'll call you sometime next week."

"Drive careful," she said. Layne didn't know what to say next, and a few seconds of silence passed before he said, "Okay, bye."

He returned his cellphone to the shift console and felt his grip on the steering wheel relax a bit. He looked around at the terrain as his ears popped. The high altitude, low-mountain landscape of Raton brought back memories of childhood trips to California. The scent of piñon pines caused him to marvel at how a smell could momentarily teleport him back to a specific place in time. But the anxiety of what he was heading toward stopped the feeling in its tracks. He realized that unease had always numbed his nostalgia.

He reviewed the conversation with Felina. He assured himself that he had handled the awkward parts of the conversation smoothly. But the possibility that he might have sounded nervous on the phone troubled him. It was the silences that were too long, when he didn't know what to say. He was thinking too much about himself; he knew better.

Long, solitary road trips always forced him to involuntarily ponder life as a whole. Thinking introspectively was an activity he avoided when he could. What hovered before him was another chance. If he could make it past training, he would earn the self-respect that he craved. But he had entertained similar notions before. He had told himself that he wasn't a loser if he could graduate from college. He'd told himself the same thing about the Academy. Perhaps it was because they were simply milestones, not objectives.

Apprehension over what the field would be like continued to cycle through his thoughts. The yearning to belong was part of what drove him, to be part of a team again—everyone functioning cooperatively for a common good. He missed the esprit de corps, the youthful single-mindedness he recalled from early childhood sports. To be collectively focused on a goal made it easy to meet an opponent or task. But his peers seemed to outgrow that camaraderie frame of mind at the beginning of junior high. That's when he began to notice that some of his teammates were pleased to see him strike out. In adulthood, loyalty and the sense of belonging to a team only seemed to exist between soldiers in combat. He hoped the personnel at the station would look out for one another and have each other's best interests in mind for their mutual benefit, like a team.

Deep into New Mexico he approached a decision point, which pulled him away from his reflections. He wasn't sure which path to take to Bisbee, but for once, the proverbial fork in the road didn't bring on the usual anxiety. Instead, it broadened his vision and he felt a connection to bigger things. The Interstate Highway System exemplified freedom in his view; he could go anywhere he pleased. He eased up on the throttle and felt a radiant anticipation for what lay ahead. The song, "Tequila Sunrise" came over the radio. He turned up the volume; the Eagles' steel guitar had always sounded like Arizona for some reason—like turquoise and silver. It was a profound feeling—a good omen.

He decided to take the back door toward southern Arizona, through Hatch, New Mexico—the road less traveled.

* * * *

IT WAS STILL DARK WHEN Layne awoke from his first night in the place Danielson had helped him secure in Bisbee; 4:30 a.m. came early. But the late-September sun was back and climbing slowly above the crest of the mountains on the eastern horizon by the time he shifted gears and accelerated to the speed limit on the route from Bisbee to Douglas. Only a few other cars were on the road. The engine settled into fifth gear while Layne scanned for a clear radio station through static and the fast-talking Spanish voices of broadcasters on the other side of the border. He had become familiarized with the mechanical feel of his newly purchased Honda during the roughly 900-mile drive from his parents' house. He pressed the button on the steering wheel to set the cruise control at sixty-five miles per hour and twisted his posture to get comfortable for the remaining twenty-minute drive southeast to Douglas Station.

The beginning of his first day in the field as a Border Patrol agent-in-training was less than an hour away.

Being late this particular morning would be catastrophic, and he had set two alarms in case of a power outage during his first night in his fully furnished rental house. But there had been no need; he awoke just moments before his first alarm went off, as if his mind had been counting the seconds since the moment when he drifted off sometime after 1:00 a.m. As soon as he opened his eyes, he found himself longing to be waking up back at the Border Patrol Academy in New Mexico—a paradox he never would have imagined. As it was occurring, the sixteen weeks he spent there only tested the limits of what his psyche could prevail against. But looking back, he realized that despite his constant anxiety and displeasure, it had forced him to become acclimated to the system and routine of federal law enforcement.

As usual, his nervous stomach was not in the mood for breakfast as he began his approach to Douglas Station. He still held out hope that his days of being painfully nervous and worried would someday be over. If he could somehow make it through the six months of field training and tests immediately ahead, the utopia he sought might become reality.

He cleared his mind and once again tried to enjoy a limited period of peace and safety, attempting to block out the myriad concerns that had beleaguered him throughout the past six days. He had competed with world-class athletes in college, and he had earned a degree; it had steeled him, and he wasn't easily intimidated. But he was venturing into an unfamiliar lifestyle; half of his Academy class had been in the military. Although he was an expert with a pistol, he wouldn't have a clue what he was doing when it came to engaging and apprehending aliens. He feared that he would be expected to perform but wouldn't know where to start. In addition to his concerns about the field, he worried that the academic tests to come would be even more difficult than those at the Academy. It would be another nail-biting campaign on multiple fronts.

The week of administrative leave between his Academy graduation and the start of field training had brought on conflicting feelings. Part of him was proud for having set out on his own once again. But since leaving the outskirts of Denver two days before, moving to a different state on such an ambitious undertaking without the supportive presence of family or friends had left him aching with loneliness. The safety net beneath the trapeze was about to be removed. This stage of the endeavor felt like the transition from being an actor playing the role of a soldier in a Vietnam movie, to wading through a rice paddy amidst real enemies and flying bullets. It had caused him to begin to contemplate the difference between the fear of failing and true fear—the fear of final departure from his bittersweet life.

Layne took a drink from a bottle of Gatorade in the console to quench his cottonmouth for another few minutes; caffeine would have only intensified the fidgeting. He realized that he had fastened the Velcro straps of his bulletproof vest too tightly; it was restricting his breathing. But the vest was underneath his uniform top and couldn't be adjusted until he arrived. It was the first time he had worn the body armor since the class of new agents had been measured for the Kevlar vests a month earlier.

His thoughts continued to cycle while his eyes surveyed the road ahead. Coming out of the Mule Mountains, Highway 80 stepped down slowly, like a long staircase, descending west to east into the semi-desert pit of Douglas on the border of Mexico. The orange hill of copper tailings and the collection of rusted mining equipment he passed were the only landmarks he could recall from the station tour almost five months ago, during orientation before the Academy.

Inevitably, his thoughts quickly returned to Felina. It had been only two weeks since he'd met her at Danielson's party, but the memory of that moment still raised his pulse. He longed to be next to her one more time. Latina girls had been accountable for three of four crushes in his youth. He looked at her for a second or two and then looked away, but her olive complexion and dark hair and eyes had sent him on his way to being lost in admiration all over again. In spite of prejudice, he had always viewed it as passable to be with Hispanic women thanks to country songs about Mexican girls and western movies where gringo gunfighters were in love with them. The floral Chypre fragrance of Felina's skin still lingered in his nose whenever she resumed her domination of his smitten thoughts. She had captivated him—the gloss and sheen of her shoulder-length hair, the dangle of her earrings, the light in her eyes amid her eminent lashes. She was far and away the most attractive and alluring girl who had ever reciprocated his attention.

Beyond her looks, her magnetic presence and the aura that surrounded her required him to limit his glances to shorter durations. Layne's desire to impress her by succeeding in the Border Patrol was a continuation of a lifelong sense of inferiority around attractive girls. But the same impulse aroused a fear that she would slip away. Perhaps it was the reason he was already devising a scheme to accidentally show off his new rental in Bisbee to her—the house was less than a quarter mile from the historic Copper Queen Hotel—if only the opportunity would arrive for her to see it. But among countless turn-offs to avoid, it was essential that he not appear as if he were putting forth effort to impact her opinion of him.

He would keep it a secret that, during the seven years leading up to the day he moved into this new home, he had been satisfied simply having a place to sleep with a roof over his head. After four-to-a-room Academy dorms with one bathroom, his rental house seemed palatial. Perhaps its wood floors and brick fireplace weren't as impressive as he thought they were. But he fantasized that she would smile with approval when she saw them, which would validate the pride he felt in his choice. Layne sighed at his hope that a girl like Felina might be sufficiently impressed by his occupation, his choice of housing and his independence that she would actually want to be with him.

In Tucson, meanwhile, Felina was telling herself: *I have to make this work.* It wasn't that she didn't find Layne fun to be around, even attractive. Fortuitously, she did. She just worried what he'd say when she finally revealed to him the secret of her past, that she was one of those illegals they called a "Dreamer." Would he be angry? Would he feel betrayed? Would he walk away? Or would he understand? Support her? Love her?

Could she ever admit to him that, before she met him and quickly wanted him in her life, marrying a Border Patrol agent was the centerpiece of her desperate plan to become a U.S. citizen so she could attend the University of Arizona and eventually become a doctor? Could she ever convince him that she wasn't just using him to get a fiancée visa and thus be in the U.S. legally?

LAYNE TOLD HIMSELF HIS RELATIONSHIP with Felina depended on whether he could handle the increased difficulty of what lay ahead in training. It was bizarre to fathom that he was actually reporting to Douglas Station, one step from becoming a real Border Patrol Agent; surreal that the plan he had devised two years earlier—to start a new life in this way and put years of insecurity and misery behind him—had succeeded thus far. Somehow, luck had seen him through the Academy, but he was fairly certain there would be much less room for error here. One thing he had learned at the Academy was that he had to be realistic about his own restrictions on Friday and Saturday nights. He would implement his most reasonable set of rules: only party on nights when he had the subsequent day off, and beer or wine only, no hard liquor.

The view into Sonora, Mexico, off to his right, looked inexplicably different as he reached the semi-desert flatlands midway to Douglas. The treeless desert mountains in the foreign landscape to the south seemed much more foreboding now that he was responsible for himself. He was seeing with new eyes the expanse of uninhabited desert wilderness, the highway guardrails spanning a shallow wash bridge, and the scanty green mesquite trees and desert sage. The last time Layne had viewed southeastern Arizona, Agent Ortiz was driving the tour group of Douglas trainees in a government van. Ortiz had served as their guardian back then; riding with the other trainees in the seats behind the agent had left Layne feeling like a child. Admitting to himself that he didn't feel measurably wiser now that he was returning for duty caused him to swallow uncomfortably.

Day shift began at 6:00 a.m. Layne had gotten on the road with time to spare, telling himself it was best to arrive at the station early and provide himself a thirty-minute cushion. No one had ever mentioned what the punishment was for being late or unprepared for field training, perhaps because it had never happened. Just like the Academy, there was no missing a day on duty during field training, sick or not. After a car swept past him headed the other way, he went over his mental checklist—although it was too late to turn around. His backpack with every piece of gear he had been issued was in the trunk, next to his duty belt with his holstered pistol. He felt near the pocket opening on his right side and his fingers touched the clip of his Spyderco knife. He was prepared, though he wasn't sure for what.

Layne hoped that his first day of field training would involve nothing more than monotonous orientation: school desks and dry erase boards. His throat became as dry as the desert air and he was unable to swallow when the possibility came to mind again that he might have to arrest an alien today. *Surely, they know we're not ready for that*, he thought.

The butterflies in his stomach fluttered when the Border Fence came into view. He thought that graduating from a Federal Law Enforcement Training Center would have earned him a solid sense of confidence for situations like this. But he had never once succeeded in impressing himself. Making it through the next six months would be the touchdown he had been seeking; surely *that* would change things. If it didn't, nothing would.

Layne slowed to turn onto the driveway that led into the compound parking lot, contained by silver concertina wire atop a shiny new chain link fence. U.S. and Border Patrol flags flanked the gate, hoisted high on separate poles. He turned down the volume on his radio as he drove past rows and rows of green-and-white Border Patrol vehicles with light bars on top, until he found the section for personal vehicles. Other agents were arriving for work and heading to the station entrance from different directions. They walked slowly and unenthusiastically, watching their feet and carrying lunch pails like construction workers on their way to a job site.

Once inside, Layne was greeted by Training Supervisor Salvador

Escribano. It was as if the man was waiting for Layne to arrive. Escribano was in charge of monitoring all of the trainees until they were finished with field training. He wore braces and a blank expression—his body language communicated that he concerned himself with his career path, not trainees.

"Agent Sheppard?" he inquired with a cheerfulness that seemed out of place. "Before you start your first day of field training, I want to ask you if you need help finding a place to stay in Douglas until you have time to get settled."

"Actually, sir, I already have a house that I'm renting in Bisbee," Layne answered. *Odd,* he thought.

"Well, then," Escribano responded coolly, "I guess you don't need my help." The abrupt change in the supervisor's demeanor was obvious. And curious.

Layne briefly wandered the halls with his backpack full of gear until he remembered that the post-Academy classroom was across the hall from the Muster Room that agents now were streaming into. He opened the classroom door and found the familiar faces of a few of his Academy classmates: Runyon, who was Layne's friend despite being a loudmouth, know-it-all, gun nut with a Southern hick accent; Schneider, his body-builder roommate at the Academy; Blair, the self-restrained, studious Mormon; and Melanie Schumer, the token white female, who could show up smoking crack and still wouldn't get fired due to the Border Patrol's fear of an EEOC complaint involving a female. Petite, with blonde hair and an irritating nasal voice, Melanie could be expected to fire at least one snide comment in Layne's direction every day. On top of that, in Layne's view, she thought she was hot.

He entered the room with his backpack over his shoulder and nodded with a smile to Runyon, Schneider, and Blair. Melanie looked away as soon as she saw Layne arrive. They were all sitting in school desks and removing notebooks and writing instruments from their backpacks. He chose a desk near Runyon and set his backpack down next to it, taking off his Border Patrol baseball cap as he took a seat. Five trainees from the training class that followed Layne's were seated in the back row of desks. Not knowing any of them personally, Layne simply nodded. The pistol on his hip made it slightly difficult to sit in the school desk. The magazine cases on the front of the belt and the handcuff case to the rear drastically increased the width of his waist from front to back. And they hadn't even been issued their radios yet.

Carlos Dos Santos arrived a few minutes after Layne, and the reunion of classmates caused him to relax momentarily. Carlos, a pudgy Hispanic (though considerably less so than when they began their Academy gauntlet), was Layne's favorite classmate in the group—a genuine person, agreeable, and altruistic. He was funny sometimes, as well, especially when he was out drinking. Layne admired his unwavering consistency and dependability; he flew under the radar and always ended up succeeding without a trace of ego. Layne sometimes wished he could be like Carlos.

An agent came into the classroom at 6:15 a.m. and began counting heads. Layne and the other trainees sat at their desks, quiet and still disoriented. Layne's heart began to pound, his desperate hope for a mundane shift of classroom paperwork and orientation shattered the moment the agent spoke: "You guys have all your gear with you?"

* * * *

LAYNE'S INTRODUCTION TO VETERAN Agent Erich Schnabel—Field Training Officer Schnabel this day—made him shudder. "We have to un-program you and teach you to be a Border Patrol Agent," were Schnabel's opening words—no hello or anything. "All that bull they taught you at the Academy doesn't fly out here."

Sitting behind Schnabel in one of the Suburbans used mainly for field orientation of trainees fresh from the Academy, Layne shuddered as he stared out his passenger window, wide-eyed with horror, at the streets of inner-city Douglas. He was part of a group of four traveling Main

Street toward its southernmost extent at the southern boundary of the United States. Classes 590 and 592 had been divided into three groups, and Layne was grateful that Melanie had been assigned to a different vehicle. Carlos was riding shotgun, sitting stiffly upright. Only Carlos's presence and the nearness of Runyon sitting next to him was somewhat comforting to Layne. The other trainee, Preussen, hadn't said a word except for acknowledging his presence during roll call.

Preussen was tall and thin, and his head was shaved shiny with a razor as a solution for balding. He had been a cop in the military, a fact Layne knew only from hearing Runyon tease him about being a snitch as an MP. Layne thought Runyon had once again crossed the line, but Preussen had silently ignored the barb. He had graduated from the Academy in Class 592, but Layne hadn't spent any time with him. Layne released his stare just before Preussen looked back at him.

Layne felt as if he were in an American military convoy rolling through occupied Iraq—there were so many suspicious eyes taking notice of their presence. The trainees were on full guard, as they sensed they were behind enemy lines. The scene rendered Layne speechless, numbed by his dawning awareness that reality trumped even his vivid imagination. *If only the politicians could spend a day or two in our shoes,* Layne thought. The Academy seemed like kindergarten now. The magazine in his sidearm was full, his OC canister was live, and his baton was steel. The tour of the station in May was a world apart. What he was seeing made him realize that the initial tour of Douglas four months ago had been limited to the station intentionally, so as not to scare too many of the trainees away before they even entered the Academy.

FTO Schnabel spoke intermittently. "The agents in the field primarily drive those Chevy and Dodge trucks with that holding cell on the back that looks like a camper shell." He pointed to the omnipresent green-and-white Border Patrol vehicles with police lights on the roofs. "The Crown Vics are called Echo Units, and the trucks with the holding cell are called Kilo Units, or Kilos for short."

He was driving passively within heavy traffic caused by the mass of cars entering the country from Mexico through the International Gate.

"Each agent is assigned a star number, which identifies you individually." Schnabel turned to Carlos: "What's your star number?"

"Delta-325, sir," Carlos replied attentively.

Layne could see Schnabel's eyes in the rearview mirror switch their focus to his. "What's yours?"

"Delta-328, sir," Layne responded, trying to sound confident.

"Do all of you know your star numbers?" Schnabel asked with an upward questioning nod of his head into the rearview mirror.

The trainees responded in unison, "Yessir."

"Delta signifies the letter D for Douglas Station along with your star number. The number is in relation to your seniority at the station, I'm Delta-109. PAIC Kramer is Delta-2; he has the most senior number at the station."

Schnabel paused as he checked his mirror to change lanes. "Delta is important in case you're working way out east or west and you run into another agent from a neighboring station at night. The Naco Agents are called Novembers; agents from Lordsburg to the east are Limas. We all use 'Tango' to refer to targets—the Tonks, illegals, drugs—that we apprehend in this job. A Delta Tango is something we're pursuing in Douglas Sector."

The trainees listened without comment, peering out their windows as they processed the information. Layne looked down at his pants; the prominence of the Academy-required ironed seams on his thighs seemed laughably trivial now. Schnabel pointed to the Walmart on the west side of Main Street where the megastore's parking lot almost touched the Border Fence. He acknowledged the store as an important landmark as he rotated the steering wheel to turn left only a matter of yards from Mexico.

No one spoke as Schnabel drove east down 1st Street, parallel to the Border Fence past a Kilo at a static post. The potholed and withered road was only ten yards from the fence to their right. Douglas and Agua Prieta were one city divided by a Border Fence. Citizens of Mexico could be seen going about their daily business through the spaces between the iron pickets of the fence; life south of the barrier seemed to be taking place in a netherworld. To Layne, the lawlessness in the atmosphere made the United States seem under siege; Mexico was fixed on an invasion that was spearheaded through border towns like this one. The Border Patrol seemed to be desperately holding onto possession of the city, in a perpetual standoff with a foreign enemy.

Almost certainly, he had overextended himself by coming here. It made him think about the long chain of events that had brought him to this situation: the string of dead-end jobs, the way his lifestyle outside of work ruined his chances for success, his struggle to fit in socially, his dishonesty during the background investigation, and, what he felt most guilty about, the deceitful way he had wronged Fabiola, his girlfriend of convenience in Denver. Maybe the punishment he deserved wasn't being dropped from the Academy, but rather, landing in this modern-day Stalingrad.

He tried to remember what Fabiola looked like; it had been over four months since she had thrown him out of her Denver apartment in a rage. He should have told her goodbye much earlier, when he knew she didn't cause him the magic tingling sensation he experienced when he first set eyes on Felina. Ah, Felina. He suddenly realized that the situation he had put himself in by choosing to come to Douglas Station made her seem much farther away, as though he were overseas on the front of an urban war while she was back home, out of his control, with an ocean between them. Hopefully she was thinking about him, hopefully he had not misinterpreted her signals. All he could do was call her and pretend only to be curious. To reveal a hint of the infatuation he already felt for her would surely cause her to flee.

Layne snapped back to the present and noticed Schnabel adjusting himself in his seat, one hand guiding the steering wheel, content to drive without comment. Runyon interrupted the silence. "How long have you been an agent here?"

"Eight years" Schnabel said, his voice flat as if he were speaking of a prison term.

"It sounds like you have an accent," Runyon commented.

Schnabel found Runyon in the rearview mirror to analyze him and his comment for a moment, considering how to answer. Then his eyes returned to the road. "I was born in Germany, but I moved to the United States when I was fifteen."

It was strange to be receiving instructions about enforcing immigration laws from someone with a foreign accent. Layne had recognized a slight intonation in Schnabel's voice the moment he first spoke. His behavior and appearance were typical German to Layne, who had spent time in Europe after college. He looked to be in his late thirties, with a jaw and cheekbones that would have accommodated round, rimless glasses. His sandy blond hair was short and tidy, but not Marine short like many of the agents.

Layne had no qualms with being in a foxhole with Schnabel, or any of the other Caucasians that comprised half the agents at Douglas Station. But it was dispiriting to be forced to accept that almost all the rest of the agents were of Mexican descent. He was pleased to be on the same side with the small remainder of non-white agents who were from outlying possessions such as Puerto Rico and Guam. He could sense their unequivocal allegiance to the United States. Their countries' economies benefited from their relationship with the U.S., and they were grateful and loyal. Layne could tell he was not alone being uneasy trusting his life in the hands of agents with ties to Mexico. It was well known that many of them had relatives living on the other side of the border. A dishonest agent could arrange to look the other way for family members crossing illegally, or badge them through somehow. He could read the deception on a lot of their faces.

"Today and most of this week is intended just to be an orientation of the field," Schnabel said, interrupting Layne's pondering. "So just try and get a feel for the AOR, the Area of Responsibility. We don't expect you to know anything yet."

Schnabel drove them in a circle through residential areas while the trainees observed their surroundings. They passed by a "roach coach" food truck and young punks loitering on the sidewalk until they returned to Main Street, waiting for an opening to cross it. Layne looked left to the Port of Entry structure, where Customs Agents were screening traffic coming into the United States and waving people on. A pair of attractive young Mexican girls on the sidewalk were coming from the International Gate on their way to Walmart.

"Check out those chicks," Runyon said casually.

Carlos turned to look. "Wow, that one on the left is top-shelf."

Runyon had obviously gotten a feel for Schnabel's attitude and determined that he would allow such talk, at a minimum. Runyon was always testing the water.

"I give the one on the left a nine and a half; she looks like Selma Hayek," Runyon said as the girls left their view.

"I didn't get a good enough look to judge. I need to see the backyard," Carlos responded. Schnabel smirked slightly as he spoke up. "The agents call those girls K-1s because of the fiancée visa they get when they're engaged to an American. There's two agents from our station married to women they met in processing, when they were fingerprinting them."

"Wow," Runyon said, shaking his head disapprovingly.

"How did they date each other?" Carlos asked Schnabel.

"The guys go down there with their passport on their days off to see them."

He's just messing with us, Layne thought. *How could an agent marry a Tonk?* But he didn't say anything; Schnabel hadn't taken a stance on the issue. And it was awkward talking sexually about Mexican women around Carlos. Layne thought it best to keep his mouth shut around agents until he learned the ropes. He bit his tongue and shook his head in disgust. *What a couple of traitors*, he thought.

Schnabel resumed his commentary. "Agents are concentrated near town, where the highway comes closest to the border. If the aliens cross too far out, away from town, the highway is too far to reach on foot. They could die in the desert before they can make it to a road to be picked up by a load vehicle." Schnabel pointed to ramshackle houses huddled along the edge of town, the majority one-story, dirty-looking stuccos with yards of sand dotted with prickly pear and scattered weeds. Often, the front yards were enclosed by a waist-high cinderblock wall. "Stash houses," he said.

Layne tried to focus. The way the agents were positioned resembled a defensive formation on a football field. Behind a group of stationary line agents were one or two "MITs," or "Mobile Interdiction Teams"— linebackers who roamed back and forth throughout the zone to cut off anything that penetrated the first line of defense. Some things were beginning to make sense.

"They showed you guys sign-cutting at the Academy, right?" Schnabel asked, directing his question to the rearview mirror again.

"Yessir," the trainees responded.

Out of the corner of his eye, Layne noticed Runyon deliberating whether to say something during another pause while Schnabel steered. Layne had learned Runyon's tendencies by now; almost nothing would stop him from inquiring when he was curious. Finally, Runyon said: "Do we search women the same way we search men in the field?"

Schnabel glanced at Runyon then refocused his attention to the road as the right front tire hit a dip that jarred everyone in the vehicle. Then he said, "You're supposed to, technically. It's not just for our safety; it's for the guys in processing. It's unnerving to have to pull someone out of a cell to process them and wonder if they've been searched or not. But most of the guys just run their hands down the outside of their pantlegs and underneath their breasts if there aren't any female agents there to do it."

Runyon nodded with a grin, obviously not receiving the elaboration he was looking for in an answer. Schnabel's sense of humor had not developed from the same environment as his pupils'.

"Just make sure you wear a rubber, Runyon," Carlos quipped, "so you don't give them anything."

Everyone laughed, and even Schnabel couldn't refrain from smiling.

"I'm just asking so I know how to handle it," Runyon explained.

Schnabel said, "No, it's a good question. About a quarter of the aliens we catch are females. Don't hesitate to ask any questions, not just with me but with any of your FTOs. That's what we're here for; now is the time."

Two weeks prior Layne would have eagerly helped fuel a comical conversation about fondling helpless Mexican women in the desert. But now the subject only added intensity to his growing passion for Felina. The thought of touching a Hispanic woman's buttocks and breasts caused him to fantasize about what unbounded intimacy with one specific Hispanic woman would be like.

"Sheppard, how come you haven't put your two cents in today? Are you imagining bad things?" Runyon said.

Schnabel grinned and glanced at Layne in the rearview mirror. Layne couldn't stop himself from blushing, as he knew Runyon had accurately read his mind.

"No, I'm just trying to understand where we're at according to the map," Layne claimed.

"I know it's a lot to take in but just do the best you can," Schnabel told them. "We're short of FTOs because there's so many of you. We're supposed to be one-on-one with you guys." Schnabel pulled over near the Port of Entry and rotated the bar on the steering column to park as he pointed emphatically to the section of fence directly east of the activity at the Port of Entry. Mexicans who lived in the houses near the fence were ready to harbor aliens for money, twenty-four hours a day. Alien smuggling was how the majority of the residents on the East Side made their living. The junky houses and grey unmaintained residential streets comprised a poverty-ridden rat's nest of antipathy. The Douglas population of 17,000 resembled free-range inmates within a penal colony, insurgents who viewed the Border Patrol and Customs Agents as American occupational forces.

"Once the aliens make it twenty-five miles north, they're in the clear,"

Schnabel explained as he continued to drive. "There's no one looking for them up north past our jurisdiction. If they get arrested in a place like Des Moines and the cops determine they're illegal, sometimes ICE will come get them and deport them, but not usually."

"The cops let them go all the time; they never have car insurance," Runyon added.

"So, some of these people walking around might have just jumped?" Carlos questioned.

"Yes, but not everyone is headed north. Some just cross to buy something at Walmart and go back through the Port," Schnabel explained.

The trainees laughed.

"How long do they stay with us if we catch them?" Carlos asked.

"If they don't have any warrants when we fingerprint them, they'll be back in Mexico in a few hours and they'll jump again a few minutes after we put them back. There's just no place to put them."

Layne was in disbelief. *No wonder it's such a free-for-all,* he thought. *What's to stop them if they just get a slap on the wrist?* Again, he thought, *if only the politicians could spend a day or two in our shoes.*

It would have been impossible to envision the reality of this place, Layne reflected. It was an inversion of what the average American thought it was: agents married to illegals, half the agents Mexican, and politically situated, surly, incompetent females on the front lines. He couldn't imagine anything more terrifying than having to work alone at night deep in the desert; yet, it was commonplace. He began chewing his fingernail and noticed a teenage boy walking on the sidewalk who looked furtively over his shoulder at the Suburban then looked away quickly. *It is impossible to tell,* thought Layne, if the young bucks were local or foreign, guilty or innocent. For some reason all of the women appeared to be law-abiding, perhaps because women were more skillful at deception.

But he was unable to concentrate on the task of orienting himself to this place for more than a minute or two at a time. His mind was already five days into the future, fixated on someone who had nothing to do with the ugliness of this place. He prayed she wouldn't change her mind the way the women he had known often did.

FELINA GLANCED TO THE CORNER OF her computer screen and sighed. There were still fifteen minutes left until lunch. She maximized her bids window and continued to appear to be working, but she couldn't set aside what was distracting her. She was still preoccupied with her conversation with Layne the previous Friday. He had called her while he was driving from Denver to Arizona. She was afraid that she sounded too cooperative over the phone. She should've said maybe to his request to see her. She didn't want to seem like a pushover. She needed to play harder-to-get or he might not take her seriously.

She peeked over the top of her cubicle to see the boss's son, Brian, roaming about his spacious personal office, talking on his cell phone. He was laughing while he chatted and made plans. He did nothing all day to contribute to the administration of the company's construction contracts. His workday consisted of personal phone calls and video games like Tetris and Solitaire on his computer. Regardless, he received a larger paycheck than the rest of the employees in the office—he only came to work to appear to have a job. No one in the office had any respect for him. They only pretended to defer to him while in his presence or in front of his dad Mike, the boss and owner.

The boss, "Jabba" as his staff referred to him amongst themselves, had inherited the company. His grandfather founded the profitable contracting business, and it had been handed down from generation to generation. It would belong to Brian one day, when Jabba retired.

Everyone made fun of Brian behind his back, laughing when they imagined him taking over the company. He knew nothing about the day-to-day operation, even though he had been working for the company since high school. Nevertheless, Felina was envious. Money would never be an issue for him. It wouldn't loom in his everyday consciousness like it did for someone without documentation. It was hard to imagine such a life of luxury. Brian would never carry the burden of concern over being short on rent, or not having enough money to eat or to pay for the endless necessaries of life. Best of all, he would never have to worry about being deported.

Felina often dreamt of what it would be like to be an American citizen and have enough money not to worry. What problems could Brian possibly have that couldn't be solved with a big paycheck? And Brian was only twenty-three or twenty-four. Besides the fortuity of being born a rich man's son, he was also white and had been born in Arizona. *People in this country take the basic benefits of everyday life for granted,* Felina thought.

Observing Brian only intensified her desire for her plan involving Layne to succeed. She had worked out all the kinks a month earlier, and it had been just over two weeks since the opportunity to put the plan into action had presented itself. Her best friend, Marianne, had inadvertently sparked the idea at a pool party, and the method in which to proceed had blossomed over the course of roughly a week. The first step had been meeting Layne at the graduation party Marianne had organized at her house for her fiancé Ryan, Layne's Academy acquaintance.

Marianne had mentioned that Border Patrol Agents in remote towns along the border with Mexico often married women who were citizens of Mexico, for lack of alternatives. Initially, Felina laughed when Marianne told her that new single agents found Mexican women in these areas desirable for multiple reasons. Ryan had mentioned to Marianne that many of the agents admired the traditional attitudes that women from the conservative families of Mexico still possessed. They were loyal and took responsibility for domestic duties . . . they made desirable wives due to the culture in which they were raised. They conducted themselves in the manner that women from the United States did in the 1950s; they hadn't been compromised by feminism and modern American society. Although Marianne worked full-time, she, too, embraced the traditional role, though with limitations.

When Felina learned that Ryan had invited a group from graduating Border Patrol classes to a celebration over Labor Day weekend, she saw an opportunity to meet one of Ryan's new agent friends. Part of her plan was to woo him into falling for her and eventually proposing to her. The necessary element of deceit bothered her, but she was becoming increasingly desperate. She rationalized to herself that it was merely a means to an end, and she meant no harm.

Felina was optimistic about her chances of succeeding. She had never been arrested for an immigration violation. As far as the U.S. Government knew, the real Felina Camarena Rivera didn't exist. If she could get one of the young, single agents to ask her to marry him, she could return to Mexico and stay with relatives while the paperwork for the fiancée visa was being processed. It would appear as though she had never left Mexico. After she became a citizen of the United States she could enroll in a university and eventually fulfill her dream of graduating from medical school to become a doctor.

She thought it was cute that Layne was initially shy. But it was his sense of humor that made him easy to like. There were things he said that were so funny that she still laughed when remembering them. She knew at some point she would have to tell Layne that she was born in Mexico. As of now, the way she saw it, she had no choice but to gamble that he wouldn't become angry and turn her in. She became nervous when she imagined telling him that she had been living in the United States illegally since her mother brought her across the border when she was two. Perhaps a fail-safe way to tell him would come to her in time. Her only current solution was to charm him into falling for her to such a degree that he would accept any skeleton in her closet. But if she overestimated his endearment for her it could lead to the end of her life in the United States.

Marianne was the only person outside of her family who knew she was illegal, and even Marianne wasn't aware of her plan. Felina would tell her when the time came; she would have to. But for now, her primary concern was getting the relationship moving in the right direction. She knew she was running out of time. She was twenty-one, and the power that her beauty wielded was certain to expire.

She awoke from her daydreaming to crack her knuckles and put her fingertips on her keyboard, although she knew it would be only a matter of minutes before she was staring into space again, wondering how she would reveal the truth to Layne if her stratagem succeeded to that point.

Jabba would probably be back any minute. Felina looked around to make sure that no one was looking while she dawdled away the remaining minutes to lunch. Her eyes crossed to look at a strand of her black hair. She removed her compact of cheap makeup from her purse and stretched her face and widened her eyes in the mirror. Her dark, toffee-colored eyes were bloodshot; she had stayed up far too late again the night before, searching the Internet for visa information on a laptop that froze every ten minutes. She was repulsed by her appearance this morning.

Her search was partly motivated by the fact that Jabba had cut everyone's health insurance a month prior, everyone except his son's. While she twisted her hair, Felina considered having Marianne pick up some antibiotics for her in Nogales, Mexico next time she went down there to buy duty-free liquor. It was the only thing to do, to have them on hand just in case she came down with strep or swollen glands. Heaven forbid that a serious medical problem arose. Having been uninsured before, she had been turned away from the emergency room for lack of identification. She cringed when she thought about what she was going to do about her female checkups. She despised the free clinics.

If it were not for her ambition and intellect, she would be doing fairly well. Her current position as an administrative coordinator to a contractor was a windfall compared to the menial jobs her parents were forced to endure. Her company couldn't function without her. She worked harder than the rest of her coworkers combined. But her job had no future; she couldn't see herself working here ten years from now. In addition to the loss of her insurance, she had never received a raise. It seemed like all the successful people were in the Air Force and worked at Davis Monthan Air Force Base, or they worked for the Border Patrol. The luckiest of the lucky were white people who were engineers at Raytheon—a socioeconomic level she aimed to reach for security. It seemed like everything else was a dead-end job. There was no in-between.

There was not much more she could achieve without implementing an element of personal deception in her pursuit of fulfillment. She had begun working when she was fourteen, but the documents she used to get the job said she was eighteen. It wasn't a hard sell. She had developed physically at an early age. Her parents had purchased a fake alien registration and a fake social security card for a few hundred dollars on the black market so she could work at Fry's grocery store as a bagger. Her family needed her income to make ends meet. She had been paying federal income taxes ever since, even though she would never collect Social Security for the benefits she had accrued.

Her older brother, Javier, also was undocumented, but content with his life here. He was married with three kids, and his wife was also illegal. He wasn't interested in school, so his immigration status didn't serve as the barrier that it did to Felina. Javier had grown up working on cars and was happy being a mechanic. The owner of the shop where Javier worked was Hispanic and sympathetic to his immigration status. He had long forgotten the one-way journey across the border, of which Felina had fragmented flashbacks.

Felina wasn't sure how long she could hold out. The days when Jabba left his office door open and yelled for her to fetch him coffee were the good days. But the rest were hard to stomach. She felt his lurking presence when he hovered behind her at her desk, breathing down her neck while she was doing bids. He was disgustingly obese, so much so that he waddled when he walked. He didn't think people noticed when he burped, if it didn't make noise. The gaseous, warm odor of summer sausage and cheese churning in his stomach made her gag just thinking about it. And then there were the times when he made inappropriate comments about her while in the presence of men from the field.

The sudden disturbance of the door opening as Jabba returned jolted Felina back into productivity. He didn't say hello, as usual. He was carrying a paper grocery bag and he glanced her way, but Felina pretended to be focused on her computer screen. She knew that if he noticed her not concentrating for even a few seconds, he would stop and ask her what she was doing.

When he closed the door to his office, she returned her gaze to the calendar of beach scenes all over the world on her cubicle wall. She took her cellphone out of her purse and considered texting Layne to see if he had settled without any hassle into the house he was renting. But she decided against it. She needed to remain resolute and wait for him to contact her again. She felt a flush of embarrassment for going too far with him the first night they met. It wasn't her style to drink so much, and she shouldn't have let him do more than kiss her. But he was attractive, and she had convinced herself that it hadn't endangered her chances with him, as long as she proceeded carefully.

She decided instead to text Marianne to tell her that Layne called her. Even though they were best friends, Felina was envious of Marianne, almost jealous. They had been inseparable until Marianne met Ryan. Marianne, who was Hispanic like Felina, had been born a U.S. citizen. She was lucky Ryan was white and from a good family. He was a good guy and about to be a Border Patrol Agent, one of the best jobs in Tucson.

If everything unfolded the way she imagined it, Felina resolved to find herself in the same position someday soon.

4

LAYNE'S FIELD TRAINING UNIT WAS beginning to assimilate and feel more comfortable riding in the Suburban with Agent Schnabel. Runyon had requested to switch with Carlos and was riding in the front passenger seat. Layne and Preussen, the quiet trainee from Class 592, remained in the back. The morning sun created an atmosphere of relative peace, with birds chirping. The city's inhabitants appeared more virtuous, simply going about their daily routines. Management started new trainees on the day shift because it was the least active eight hours of the day. They were able to focus on learning the Area of Responsibility by light of day, with minimal alien activity to distract them. But the monumental task of familiarizing themselves with the Douglas AOR was formidable, creating an undercurrent of dismay as Schnabel continued with orientation.

Today was Thursday. Layne was looking forward to an easy day tomorrow; post-Academy classroom work all day, safe from the possibility of having to interact with aliens in the field. But of greater concern than work was how his plan for the weekend would transpire. As the Suburban entered the city limits, Layne made a final decision not to call Felina until after he was dismissed from class, so as not to seem overly eager to see her. Then he made it a goal to put her out of his mind for the remainder of the shift.

Schnabel drove past McDonald's and Taco Bell on Main Street as he made his way to the line. "I would advise you not to eat at any of the restaurants in town. The employees will spit in your food, or worse," Schnabel warned as he steered, confirming a rumor that Layne had heard.

"Special sauce?" Carlos said, and everyone laughed, even Preussen.

Schnabel was taking them to Juliet, the first static post on the line east of the Port of Entry, at the intersection of J Street and International Road. He waved briefly at the agent sitting in a Kilo facing the fence at Juliet. As they made their way east, they encountered an oncoming Douglas Police squad car. The Hispanic cop behind the wheel looked straight ahead without acknowledging Schnabel as they passed each other. The trainees had been told that the Douglas Police and the Border Patrol hated one another; they routinely flipped each other off when crossing paths. The majority of Douglas Police were involved in aiding the smuggling network that shuttled aliens out of town. A rumor circulated amongst the trainees that two years prior an agent failed to yield to a DPD cruiser with its emergency lights activated, and the cop followed him all the way back to the station parking lot. Supposedly, the cop held the agent at gunpoint when he climbed out of his Kilo.

"Have the cops ever tried to give you a speeding ticket?" Runyon probed. He had been testing Schnabel's boundaries all week.

"Let's concentrate on the AOR," Schnabel replied then responded to Runyon without specifically responding to his impertinence. "I will tell you this: Even when you're off-duty you've got to be careful. DPD will write down the license plate numbers of your personal vehicles. Then they lay-in near bars at night and wait for you to come out drunk and get in your car. They get agents for DUIs all the time like that."

As they reached the end of the alphabetically lettered streets that were perpendicular with International Road, Schnabel began to test Runyon by having him name the streets they approached before their sign was within view.

"Okay, we just passed Alpha, what street are we coming up on now?"

"Delores," Runyon said confidently.

"Good. Alright, what's this next one?"

"It's . . . dang, I can't remember," Runyon admitted.

"Come on! You guys should know these east side streets by now," Schnabel said. "It's Rose." He turned around and headed back west toward the Port of Entry via 3rd Street, three blocks to the north. The radio remained nearly silent; heavy alien traffic wouldn't begin until the sun started going down. As soon as it became dark aliens would begin coming over the fence like ants.

Layne's heart skipped a beat each time the dispatch radio blurted. He took a deep breath and once again did his best to clear his mind of uncertainty over Felina and the radio. Schnabel appeared to be by the book; Layne was hopeful he would restrict them only to geography lessons for the remainder of their two weeks under his tutelage.

Schnabel turned left on Main Street then turned right to enter the Walmart parking lot. He drove on the margins of the parking lot toward the Border Fence and exited the lot through an opening that agents had created by uprooting a concrete divider from the asphalt. The opening was the beginning of a shortcut that dipped through a shallow creek bed and wove through a wooded area next to the Border Fence. The beaten path led to International Road on the east side of the Port of Entry, just west of Walmart. The trainees reached for the ceiling grab handles as the path became increasingly rough. Layne's head hit the ceiling as Schnabel ran over a massive bump, and the wheels continued to fall into holes and bounce over moguls that Schnabel maneuvered to avoid. The west side of Main Street was the antithesis of the east side, devoid of paved roads and residences.

West of Walmart was a weed-infested junkyard, a century-old dumping ground for mine waste and rusted car frames. Schnabel pointed to a giant slag pile that was the capital of the 5-Charlie Zone's vast dumping ground. "The slag" was a black mountain of stony waste material that was visible from a half-mile radius. Schnabel emphasized its significance: "We reference the slag all the time when you're working the west side, so you need to orient yourself and find that landmark on your map of 5-Charlie."

The trainees fumbled through their backpacks to find their maps and locate the zone as it was referred to in the vernacular. Layne had expected to be issued sophisticated satellite photos, complete with legends and scale distances. Instead, what he got could have been misinterpreted as a prank. The maps were Xerox copies of hand-drawn sketches that looked like they had been sketched on cocktail napkins.

The tire ruts through the debris were as rugged as dirt bike trails. Layne hung on with growing anxiety. Radio activity was picking up, ringing out sporadically as the camera room called out aliens coming over the fence near the Port on the east side where they had just been. Beyond the slag pile, the junkyard gave way to fields of desert sage and mesquite. The zones were carved with a matrix of paths that were used for tracking and traversing while in pursuit of aliens trying to make it to the highway.

"The AOR between 6-Charlie and Naco Station is covered by the guys on ATVs and horseback," Schnabel explained. "They're after long-range dope mules and guides leading groups of fifty or more." Layne thought back to those marijuana recovery plaques Runyon had talked about when they first arrived at Douglas Station, as Schnabel drove slowly to allow the trainees an opportunity to learn the positions of static posts that watched the fence. Kilo trucks were spread out a quarter mile apart facing the fence along International Road. The fence faded slightly north and stretched over a hill in the distance, visible for miles like pictures of the Great Wall of China Layne had seen. Schnabel explained that aliens attempted to cross on the west side less often because of the absence of alleys or backyards to hide in.

The remaining twenty miles of sun and dust between them and Naco were covered with desert sage and scattered mesquite thickets. The camera towers off to their right looked like football stadium lights lining the border. The 360-degree rotating cameras surveilled the fence slowly atop hundred-foot-tall towers that stood a furlong behind the line, one every 150 yards. The infrared cameras were joystick-guided by personnel in the Camera Room at the station. They operated them twenty-four hours a day via a wall of television screens. The Hispanic women who often operated the cameras were in the National Guard. In their early twenties, they wore head-to-toe camouflage fatigues with their hair in tight buns. The agents frequently called upon them for assistance in locating groups on the move or hiding.

"West of the junkyard, we need to catch them before they cross the desert between the fence and Highway 80," Schnabel said. "It's about a mile to the highway from the fence right here. If they make it that far, a vehicle can pick them up on the shoulder, and the driver will take them east through Bisbee or north on Highway 191 to Pirtleville."

"There are load vehicles just waiting up there?" Carlos said.

"Yeah, they linger on the highway. They cruise back and forth while they're waiting for groups to arrive," Schnabel explained.

"How does the driver know where to meet them?" Layne asked.

Schnabel looked at him in the rearview mirror. "The driver has a cellphone, and someone in the group has one, usually the guide."

Layne reminded himself to think before he spoke, as he realized the answer was obvious. He was surprised Runyon didn't at least point out his lack of thought.

"I'm going to take you back to the Port and then we'll go to Pirtleville so I can show you where a lot of the aliens are headed," Schnabel informed them. He made his way back east along International Road, weaving through the shortcut between Walmart and the Border Fence. Then he waited for an opening in the northbound traffic on Main Street as a steady stream of vehicles entered the country after being screened by Customs. The steering wheel slid between Schnabel's hands as the tires straightened themselves north on Main Street, and Layne felt himself relaxing the farther they traveled away from the fence.

At the north end of Main Street, Schnabel took them west on Highway 80 for a short distance before turning north on Highway 191. The narrow, two-lane highway through sage-covered desert led them two miles north of Douglas to a satellite establishment of the city.

"This is Pirtleville," Schnabel announced as they passed by a dilapidated fleabag motel sign that had been sunbaked colorless. The motel appeared long since abandoned and had the appearance of withered ruins among blowing dust. The town consisted of trailer parks with decrepit palm trees and vegetation that longed to be rooted elsewhere. Pirtleville looked more like a settlement than a municipality, a reservation for abandoned cars and venereal disease.

Beyond the motel was a graveyard where Schnabel turned with slight reluctance. He rolled through the gates of a double-wide shantytown that was the central neighborhood of Pirtleville, a campground comprised of tumbledown trailers and sagging clotheslines.

"This is the Pirtleville Deluxe Trailer Court. You will be hearing a lot about this place This is the spot where a lot of groups are headed. You will hear agents refer to Pirtleville as 'Whiskey Tango' over the radio." Schnabel paused for a moment as he crept past a broken Big Wheel toy lying on its side. He licked his lips and continued, "When the aliens make it up here, they lie on the floors of these trailers until the heat blows over. Then someone comes to pick them up and take them north, to Tucson or Phoenix. These people charge the aliens hourly rent to lay over here. But don't worry about the highway and Pirtleville yet; I just want to show you what it looks like. The Supervisors put veteran agents on 191 between here and Douglas because of all of the load vehicle traffic."

"These are white people living in these trailers?" Carlos questioned.

Layne, Runyon, and Preussen glanced at one another.

"Yes, unfortunately," Schnabel said.

"Look at that scumbag," Runyon said, pointing to a pale, rail-thin, wasted-looking man in filthy jeans and a wife-beater shirt, glancing at the Suburban then quickly opening the door to enter a trailer. He picked up a dirty toddler, naked except for a sagging diaper, who had been looking through the screen door. The man moved as if he were in a hurry to alert someone about the arrival of a Border Patrol vehicle. Layne often wondered how Carlos felt about members of his own race that were involved in criminal activity. Now Pirtleville gave him some personal insight. These whites were even more embarrassing—methamphetamine cooks and prostitute traitors.

"Does traffic ever slow down?" Carlos asked.

"For a few weeks in June during monsoon. It gets so muddy down by the fence that we back off and stay on the paved streets. It's not worth it to go down there. You just end up getting stuck and somebody has to come pull you out. The aliens can't move very well either. Also, during the holidays; traffic is coming back south during Christmas and New Year and nobody is coming north."

Runyon laughed, "Really?"

"Yeah," Schnabel said. "But they just jump again at the beginning of January to go back to work. The only night you can count on it being slow is Fourth of July."

On the Fourth of July emigrants standing by the fence bothered the Agua Prieta Police while they were trying to watch the annual fireworks display over Douglas. It was the only day of the year when the Mexican police lifted a finger to stop anyone from crossing the border illegally.

Schnabel explained that checkpoints were set up periodically on Highway 191 between Douglas and Pirtleville, but everyone knew it was a waste of time. As soon as the locals saw a checkpoint go up, they called each other to report its location. They simply went around it.

Runyon commented, "I don't see why Washington can't get some tax money together and extend the fence all the way from here to the Chiricahua Surrender Sight. Why don't they just cut out all those worthless programs and funnel some money down here?"

Schnabel shrugged and no one felt like adding anything. Layne reflected on a thought that interrupted his ongoing silent rehearsal of what he would say to Felina the next day. Before he arrived in Douglas, he had imagined border crossers as desperate people motivated to improve their quality of life because of a lack of options. The reality, he was coming to understand, was that at least for many Mexicans living across the border, the illegality of crossing was on a par with jaywalking. Almost nothing was the way he had envisioned it.

Schnabel pulled onto the roadway to head back toward the line. As he began to accelerate, the radio rang out, "Delta-109, 866."

Schnabel unhooked the radio microphone from the dashboard cradle, "Go ahead 866."

"Delta-12 wants FTU to pick up sign in 5-Delta," a female voice from the Station informed Schnabel and his Field Training Unit.

"Ten-four. I'm on route," Schnabel said.

The call spurred Layne's heart to a gallop. He hoped that they only wanted to show something to the trainees as he looked at the others for answers. Schnabel slowed and looked both ways at an intersection on the edge of Pirtleville, then ran a red light with a left turn. The trainees' heads rocked back and forth as he accelerated aggressively and settled in at eighty miles per hour, southbound on Highway 191.

"The FOS in charge of the west side probably wants you guys to see some new sign in 5-Delta," Schnabel announced out loud to overcome the noise. Layne's accelerating pulse caused his mind to go blank. He was only beginning to understand the G-426 Daily Assignment Log and was afraid to ask for clarification. Initially, he thought there was only one Field Operations Supervisor during a shift. But he now realized there were two—one in charge of the east side and one in charge of the west side.

When Schnabel reached the Port of Entry, he zipped around the margin of the Walmart parking lot and through the shortcut again. The trainees held on to the handles on the Suburban's ceiling and bounced in unison as the tires met with dirt again. Layne locked his grip as rocks kicked upward into the undercarriage, clinking while the engine revved. The Suburban ran into a shallow pit and everyone in the back bounced vertically in their seats this time. His head hit the ceiling with such force that Layne heard his neck crunch. Schnabel gripped both hands on the steering wheel.

"I'm driving faster than normal because we don't have much time," he said. "It only takes the aliens about fifteen minutes to make it to the highway from the line in 5-Delta."

Schnabel stepped on the gas again once he reached the straightaway of the warning track on International Road. They skimmed the Border Fence, only fifteen yards to their left, as Schnabel ran through the Suburban's gears. Layne felt trapped aboard a hijacked vehicle, slated for something inevitable that he wasn't yet ready to face. He watched glimpses of Agua Prieta on the south side pass before his eyes through the rusted metal pickets of the fence, like frames of projector film.

The Suburban zoomed past line agents facing the fence, leaving a ribbon of dust like a vapor trail. Despite his speed, Schnabel lifted a finger to acknowledge them and the agents waved back as the dust trail rose and settled in front of them. Schnabel drove for several minutes before the trainees released the ceiling handles as they felt him begin to slow down.

"When we get out, I want you to turn on your handheld radios," Schnabel ordered.

A line agent in 5-Delta had discovered footprints on his section of the warning track directly after a drag. The forward line agents dragged a chain rug behind their Kilo to smooth the dirt on their section of the zone. The National Guard women maintained a log at the station, which the agent referenced to determine that the prints were less than fifteen minutes old.

"You guys all got a full magazine in your pistols with a round chambered?" Schnabel asked into the rearview mirror.

A string of "Yessirs" dribbled out.

"Okay. Let's go."

The trainees dismounted from the Suburban and followed their FTO with timid hesitation. It was apparent by the intensity of Schnabel's new bearing that the west side FOS intended the FTU to pursue the sign and engage the offenders who had created it. Evidently, the FOS had been making his rounds and had happened upon the agent just as he discovered the footprints. As he drove off, the FOS thought to have the new trainees follow the sign to shake up their leisurely day of AOR training. Layne swallowed dryly as he adjusted his duty belt, realizing that his group was being taught to swim by being thrown into the deep end of the pool.

The agent who had discovered the footprints was leaning against the hood of his Kilo with his legs and arms crossed, his eyes masked by baseball sunglasses. The agent straightened himself and looked at his wristwatch as Schnabel approached him. Schnabel walked swiftly to stand directly over a disturbance in the consistency of smoothed dirt on the warning track.

"When did you cut it?" Schnabel asked the agent as he looked down to examine the prints.

"About nine minutes ago, right after I called in my last drag," The agent peered down at the tracks with Schnabel.

Schnabel motioned to the trainees, who had been standing back waiting for directions. "Come take a look at this." The group came forward and knelt down over the tracks. Two pairs of footprints were salient, like fingerprints on powdered sugar. To Layne, they illustrated the story of two people's lives.

"See how far apart the strides are? You can tell they started running as soon as they hit the ground," Schnabel emphasized to the befuddled trainees.

Schnabel walked to the southern margin of the drag, flush with the fence, to turn and ponder the heading of the tracks, gazing north in a hurry. Layne took the pause as an opportunity to look closely at the prints. The patterns of the soles were striped with a Nike swoosh on one set, and a dotted pattern with the logo of the three Adidas stripes on the other. Looking at the prints put him in the aliens' shoes for a few seconds. He wondered how in the world he would proceed and remain in good spirits with a few dollars in his pocket and nowhere to go if he managed to get away. He looked back on the problems he was forced to deal with in his life. Even the most threatening of them had a possible solution. He lacked only the constitution to solve them. He rose from his haunches and looked back, trying to visualize how the pair had scaled the twelve-foot iron fence; a ladder perhaps. The fence was corrugated metal in this section, like a Ruffles potato chip, with nothing horizontal to use as a rung.

"Do you mind if we follow it?" Schnabel asked the agent.

"Be my guest," the agent said with a grin.

Schnabel turned to face the trainees, his microphone clipped to his duty belt instead of his passant like the trainees, causing the coiled cord to dangle and swing when he walked swiftly. He reached for the microphone and brought it to his mouth, "Delta-262, Delta-109."

It was quiet for a moment.

"Go ahead," Delta-262's voice rasped over the trainees' radios simultaneously.

"FTU is going to push from the line," Schnabel said and held the mic at his waist while waiting for a response.

"Ten-four, what are you looking at?"

"Two bodies, striped Nike and the other is dotted."

"Ten-four." Delta-262 cut the transmission.

Schnabel clipped his mic back in place and addressed the trainees. "I remember who the MIT is in this zone from Muster, but if you don't, that's what your G-426 is for. He'll be cutting to make sure they aren't already north of him."

The trainees glanced at one another with silent alarm.

"You ready?" Schnabel asked them rhetorically.

"Yessir," the trainees said, almost in unison.

"Stick close to me. No more than ten yards behind."

They commenced simultaneously like a drumbeat. All at once, Layne felt a bond with his fellows, like brothers in arms. But he wasn't mentally prepared. All of his tough talk in the past about how jackbooted he would be if he were a Border Patrol Agent caused him to feel foolish, inwardly embarrassed. He realized he was not the person he was trying so hard to be. He resisted the sense that he was engaged in a form of savagery. It suddenly sank in that they were tracking humans, like game, partaking in blood sport. The rule of law hovered far away in the Academy classroom, irrelevant here in the arena.

Schnabel gave chase with merciless determination, as if the pair of footprints represented a direct challenge to his personal authority. "They're going for mile marker six," he said, picking up the pace.

The hunt weaved and ducked under mesquite branches and around ocotillo plants at speed close to a jog, too fast to be wary of rattlesnakes and snagging thorns. The locusts sounded like heat, humming in Layne's ears as their boots hustled. He was startled to witness Schnabel transform into a hungry predator at the drop of a dime; he had seemed so indifferent during the tour. After a hundred yards he lost the sign and the trainees caught up to him momentarily. He searched scrupulously at forty-five-degree angles to the left and right of the last print, zeroed-in on the continuance, then resumed like a bloodhound.

Layne followed several yards behind Carlos, struggling to keep up. Mesquite branches whipped him in the face as Carlos brushed them out of the way a few steps ahead. He lengthened his stride to close in and stumbled as prickly pear thorns and chollas clung to his pant legs. The rhythm of the pursuit took on the sound of breathing and twigs cracking.

Out of breath, Carlos stated, "I think they changed direction."

"Those are brush-outs," Schnabel corrected from up front.

The aliens were zig-zagging with desperation to throw off their followers, their advance evidently delayed by the MIT to the north blocking them.

"We must be close enough for them to see us," Layne heard himself say. He was out of breath from nerves and exhaustion as a breeze cooled the sweat on his body.

"Stay with me," Schnabel said. "A minute could make all the difference."

Layne focused on his feet, battling to sidestep pot barrel cactus and prickly pear as sweat dripped off his nose and chin.

Movement became noticeable in the distance. The MIT came into view 150 yards to the north, his Kilo unit kicking up dust as it scurried from east to west.

"I got eyes on you now," came the voice of Delta-262 over the radios. "I haven't cut anything; you must be right on top of them."

Layne tried to swallow between breaths; the aliens could probably hear their radios. His pulse throbbed in his lips and tongue, as he felt everything culminating. The footprints had devolved into a cluster of confusion, illustrating the aliens' apparent panic, step by step, like an abstract painting.

"They're close," Schnabel said with his eyes still fixated on the ground.

He walked in a circle then, glancing to the west, pointed to a thicket of mesquite trees a hundred yards to their western flank. "They're under those trees over there."

Schnabel advanced toward them with the trainees following behind, closing in on the pair as if they were wounded animals helplessly leaving a blood trail behind. Layne pretended to keep up. He could hear himself breathing in conjunction with his heartbeat. Under the cluster of trees lay two young men on their backs, resting on their elbows. To finally set eyes on them was shocking, like stumbling upon dead bodies. They remained so still they could have been mistaken for logs from a distance. Each was wearing what looked like their only long-sleeved shirt; their faces were darkly suntanned.

"Make a circle around them," Schnabel instructed, reaching for his radio microphone.

Both men stared south in a daze. They didn't react to the agents surrounding them, as if they had become catatonic from exhaustion.

"866, Delta-109."

Layne could feel Schnabel's voice vibrate the handheld radio on his hip.

"Go ahead."

"I'm ten-fifteen by two in 5-Delta," Schnabel had planted himself at the feet of the aliens in the shade.

"Ten-four."

The two men stared without blinking despite the immense light beyond the shade. Their Levis, stained with desert dirt, were nearly unrecognizable as blue jeans. Layne could smell their sweat as he glanced at their expressionless faces. Their hair was matted, and their lips were cracked from dehydration. Schnabel leaned over to examine the bottoms of their shoes as if he were inspecting the tires on his car. Layne forced himself to look, as well, comparing the soles to the prints they had created on the warning track. To confirm the evidence in the men's presence felt like an act of dehumanization. Their shoes were devastated, the laces broken and the soles detached. Layne looked around and the others appeared on edge, but in a manner that looked like new authority by proxy. He was unsure of what to do with his hands. He wondered if he was the only one with the need to avert his eyes out of pity. He considered that perhaps callousness was a trait he would develop with time.

"Remember, never turn your back on an alien. Even ones as tired as these two," Schnabel said.

The trainees adjusted their positions to remain facing the two, as if they were inching along the ledge of a tall building.

"Someone order them to get up," Schnabel commanded in a new, stern tone. Layne realized that like most of his white classmates, Schnabel had most likely learned enough Spanish to graduate from the Academy but had forgotten everything down to the basic commands. He was having Carlos issue commands in order to speed up the process and avoid the difficulty of communicating with hand gestures. Schnabel must have assumed that Carlos was the only trainee who was bilingual.

Carlos cleared his throat and muttered, *"Levantense,"* in his officer presence voice from PT.

The aliens complied as they struggled to stand up and manage their balance.

"Tell them to put their hands behind their heads and interlace their fingers," Schnabel continued.

Layne listened carefully to extract the word "interlace" from the sentence that Carlos was about to say.

"Pongan las manos atrás de la cabeza y entralacen los dedos," Carlos ordered.

The aliens placed their hands behind their heads and wove their fingers together. They wouldn't look directly at Schnabel or any of the trainees. They showed no emotion, seeming to have accepted their fate.

"Pay attention. I'm going to show you how we search for weapons," Schnabel said to the trainees. "Sit down!" he said to one of the men, who complied.

Schnabel positioned himself behind the man who remained standing. He grabbed the man's interlaced hands behind his head with his left hand and quickly felt all around the man's torso and each leg with his right hand. The man stared blankly, as his body was jerked in different directions.

"Sit down," Schnabel commanded, when he had finished. The alien sat down, Indian style. "Carlos, go ahead and search the second alien like I demonstrated. Tell this other one to get up."

"*Levantete,*" Carlos said, and the second man stood up.

Carlos modeled Schnabel's search technique.

The group's attention was diverted momentarily to Delta-262 arriving in his Kilo as he skidded to a stop. He put the truck in park and rolled down his window, removing his sunglasses to rub the bridge of his nose.

"*Sientete,*" Carlos said. The alien he was searching sat down with one leg straight and the other bent.

"Let's put them in the back of the Kilo until transport arrives," Schnabel suggested.

Carlos motioned for the aliens to get up, and he stood uncomfortably in charge as the pair began walking toward the back of the Kilo without being told. Schnabel turned the latch on the holding cell of the Kilo and opened the door. The hinges squeaked as he pulled. He motioned for the aliens to get in with his free arm. They ducked and braced themselves on the bumper to climb in. Both sat facing each other on the metal benches inside and looked back at the gawking trainees as Schnabel closed the door and the latch.

To Carlos, Schnabel said, "Make note of the time of apprehension."

Carlos looked at his wristwatch, "Its 1:48 right now, so should I put 1:40, sir?"

Schnabel nodded, and Carlos removed his pen from his shirt pocket and wrote the time on his wrist.

Schnabel explained, "Normally we write them up before transport gets here to move things along, but we don't have our write-ups with us. Carlos, go ahead and radio transport."

Carlos pushed his microphone button and said indecisively, "866, Delta-325."

The reply was received loudly amongst the silence. "Go ahead."

"Can I get transport for two in 5-Delta."

"Ten-four, stand by."

Layne stood by silently in a huddle with the others while they waited. Relief washed over him now that the aliens were locked away. He was trying to look comfortable in front of Schnabel, but he knew he was shaking. Schnabel was too busy with his duties as mentor to notice. "The main thing is to maintain officer presence. Ninety percent of problems in the field are because of poor officer presence. Carlos, you did a good job."

A Border Patrol van arrived, and the driver climbed out, showing little enthusiasm for his duty.

"This is these guys' first week of training, so I didn't have them fill out any G-434s yet. I left mine in my Kilo. Do you have any extras?" Schnabel asked the driver.

The driver looked annoyed and didn't respond. He opened the driver's side door to the van, reached in, and then handed Schnabel a metal clipboard box with forms inside. Taking the clipboard with a curt, "Thanks," Schnabel removed his pen from his shirt pocket and clicked it.

"Okay, guys, I'm going to fill these two G-434's out because transport's got other bodies to pick up. I'll show you how to fill these out in the classroom when we get back." He opened the cell door and said to the aliens, "Give me your IDs." Layne could see arms extend from the cell. Schnabel took the IDs, closed the door and latched it, then wedged the IDs underneath the clamp of the clipboard. He began writing with attentiveness. He looked at a handheld GPS and said, "31.3450 north,

109.5414 west are the coordinates of apprehension." The trainees looked confused as Schnabel scribbled.

The driver opened the holding cell to the Kilo and guided the aliens to the cage in the back of his van. Schnabel clicked his pen and handed the forms and IDs to him.

"Good?" Schnabel asked.

"We're good," the driver said.

Layne looked down at himself. Sweat had soaked the armpits of his uniform top, almost reaching down to his duty belt. He was glad it had happened now that it was over. He became quietly excited by the thought of describing the experience to Felina. She wouldn't be able to help but be impressed. He grinned as he considered how he would portray the situation. He already had begun to contemplate opportunities within the story to embellish his role in the apprehension. But an instinctual voice within urged him to reconsider. Perhaps his goals for their relationship would be better served if he used the situation to display his sympathetic side rather than aim to persuade her opinion of him with bravado. He didn't know her well enough to determine which approach would be more beneficial.

With Schnabel in the lead, the group began walking back to the border where they had left the Suburban. Layne felt dizzy and stunned, but one day closer to the weekend. If only it would turn out the way he hoped, his desired outcome growing more vital by the hour.

5

LAYNE COULD BARELY SIT still in his post-Academy desk. He glanced at the clock above the dry erase board again. There were still twenty minutes left until the trainees were dismissed from Law class. Time was crawling, but at least he was stress-free inside a classroom. As soon as the clock read 2:00 p.m., he would be on his way to Tucson, hopefully to see Felina. He told himself to cherish these post-Academy Fridays out of the field. Having Saturday and Sunday off for the time being was cause for celebration.

The trainees from Classes 590 and 592 had Spanish in the morning, and Law in the afternoon. The classroom was arranged just like courses at the Academy, just like a high school class. He had selected a desk chair in the back row, the same seat he had chosen habitually since junior high. There were five trainees from Class 592 in the room, along with Runyon, Carlos, Greg, and Melanie from his class. Layne noticed that the instructor, Ortega, seemed as ready for the weekend as the trainees.

"Agent Ortega is a Salt Dog," Greg, the trainee who was friends with Melanie, had said before Ortega entered the room and commenced class. "He has every United States code memorized. He's the only instructor I've ever seen that wears that leather flight jacket."

"Post-Academy Instructor is a gravy train gig," Runyon had responded. "It's a whole day out of the field every week. He's pretty slick, though; nobody else has the balls to wear that jacket."

Ortega seemed to enjoy his reputation as a renegade agent. He was cocky, flaunting the one Border Patrol-approved garment that no one else dared to wear, like a Hispanic James Dean. Layne had seen him in the swank jacket earlier in the week, leaning against his vehicle wearing aviator sunglasses. He had charisma, and the same light-skinned appearance as Ortiz. But he was considerably more intelligent than any of the other personnel the trainees had dealt with thus far. He was cagey, seasoned by the border streets. He was eloquent and his explanations were clear and precise. He chose the right words.

"I heard Ortega is dirty; he wants trainees like Sheppard to make it, so his dope gets across the border easy," Runyon stabbed.

Everyone laughed. Runyon had been needling Layne ever since the hotel in Tucson.

Layne brushed off the comment, his pride under wraps on Friday afternoon. His mind was fixated on the clock. He was ruminating over Ortega simply to pass the time.

With about twenty minutes to go before the magical two o'clock, Ortega loosened the collar on his dress uniform and began gathering his materials. He was finished with his teaching for the day despite time remaining in the class.

"You can put your books away now and talk amongst yourselves until it's time to go," Ortega informed the trainees from behind his desk.

They shuffled their textbooks, pens, and notebooks into their backpacks. Before they could whisper to one another, the door opened and Training Supervisor Escribano came briskly into the classroom. He headed straight to Ortega at his teacher's desk without looking at Layne or the other trainees. He appeared to be in his early forties, a few years older than Ortega and most of the agents with whom he interacted at the station. Escribano whispered something to Ortega then left without acknowledging the class.

"I need to meet with Agent Escribano in private," Ortega announced. "No one leaves until two, though. See you all next Friday."

As Ortega walked to the door, Layne noticed that the visit from an administrative agent still caused his pulse to throb. He was still alarmed with fear any time class was interrupted and someone came to speak with the instructor in private. He felt hollow, visualizing Ortega returning to peep through the doorway, saying, "Sheppard, can we have a word with you?" He wondered if declining Escribano's offer to help him find temporary housing would come back to haunt him.

Once the door closed behind Ortega the trainees from both classes began gleefully chatting with one another. Layne glanced at Greg then looked away before their eyes met. Greg appeared to still be pissed at Layne for ditching him at Danielson's barbecue the week before Academy graduation. They hadn't said a word to each other since. Layne had hitched a ride from New Mexico to Arizona with Greg in order to secure living arrangements and attend the graduation celebration that Danielson's fiancée had organized. They had planned on sharing the cost of a motel room the night Layne met Felina, but Layne was powerless to turn down the opportunity to stay the night with her. It became obvious that Greg resented him for failing to follow through on their agreement that night. But Greg was assigned to the other FTU group with Melanie. It was a stroke of luck that Layne had been separated from them; Melanie was still keen to seize any opportunity to say something condescending to Layne.

The loitering clock hands had to cover another fifteen minutes before the weekend could begin. Ortega hadn't come back yet, and Layne's thoughts returned to Tucson. The reprieve from worry was about to begin. It would resume on Sunday afternoon. But it was imperative to make the most of the good time between now and then. There was simply no alternative, almost like a mental block.

"What do you guys think of Instructor Cunningham?" Melanie asked. "He's what, maybe thirty?"

"I didn't expect our Spanish Instructor to be a white guy," Runyon said. "He's kind of a dork. Did you hear him say he passed up the FBI to take this job?"

The trainees didn't seem to completely agree with him.

Runyon clarified, "That's bull; I think he's one of those guys that's dodging the polygraph."

"I think he's kind of cute," Melanie said.

"You must be in heaven with this sausage fest," Runyon said, and everyone laughed. "He said he learned Spanish in Argentina, but he's not a Mormon. I bet he's one of those guys who drinks Coronas with a lime, like Sheppard."

Layne sighed at Runyon's persistence.

"I can't wait until I'm on a unit and in the field," Runyon bragged.

"You're such a Navy SEAL, Runyon," Layne fired back.

The others laughed and Layne felt satisfied that he had scored, even temporarily.

"I like the field," Runyon said simply.

There was no opening to stab at Runyon again. He did seem to take to the field naturally. Perhaps there was some truth to his war stories.

"I heard 562 just took their Spanish Oral Boards," Greg said. He appeared comfortable enough to speak to a group now, graduation from the Academy obviously having improved his confidence.

"I heard that one of the three white guys in the class failed it," Melanie commented. "They forced him to resign. That would be brutal."

Despite the new bogeyman the Oral Boards were becoming to Layne, he was disinterested in discussing them with minutes left until his first weekend as a trainee. His mind had already drifted off on one of its field trips. He was trying to remember what Felina looked like. What filled his memory was little more than a police composite sketch of her, but he knew she was gorgeous. For him, it was rare to be very attracted to a girl and hit it off with her in conversation. He was fairly certain that she wasn't pretending to like him just to be nice.

He put on his hat and checked the clock on his cell phone. It read 1:59, one minute to go. He put his backpack on his desktop and made certain there was nothing left to gather that would delay him even a few seconds.

"What are you guys doing this weekend?" Melanie asked.

"We're playing beer pong at Carlos's house. What are you doing?" Runyon asked with a hint of invitation.

"I don't know yet," Melanie said.

"What about you?" Runyon said to Greg.

"I don't know either," Greg said.

"Come over to my house," Carlos said. "But you have to get bombed with us if you come over. We're playing beer pong until we pass out."

"I bet I know what Sheppard is up to," Runyon said with a growing smile.

Layne felt his cheeks and forehead become warm. He was sure everyone knew about his tryst with Felina. He had come to learn the Border Patrol was a gossip farm. He pretended not to hear Runyon.

"I heard you hooked up with one of Danielson's wife's friends," Runyon persisted.

The other trainees were smiling at Layne and waiting for him to respond. Runyon hadn't teased him over Felina being Hispanic, only because Carlos was present. Layne suspected he was jealous. Runyon strived for women's attention, but he always wound up alone. Women moonwalked away from him. If Greg had told Runyon the truth about what he saw of Felina at the barbecue, then Runyon knew she was hot.

"What do you expect? We've been in prison for four months," Layne said to try to sound modest and get Runyon to back off.

Runyon was apt to keep prodding, but the clock hand moved to two, and Layne, along with everyone in the classroom, picked up his backpack and bolted for the door. He broke off from the group in the parking lot and was the first to pull out and turn left onto Highway 80.

He felt a slow drip of adrenaline inhibiting his weekend exuberance. He considered waiting an hour to call Felina, since she knew that he got off at two. But there was no way he could wait that long. He flipped open his cell phone and found her number in his contacts. He prayed that she was true to her word. He took a deep breath to calm himself. If she detected desperation in his voice, he might scare her away. As the call went through, he felt the rush of female enchantment and tingling passion that he hadn't felt since grade school. It was a new taste in his mouth that came about whenever he was about to talk to her.

"Hello," Felina said.

"Hey, it's Layne," he said with his best effort to disguise his relief that she had answered.

"I know. I can see you on the caller ID, silly."

Don't confirm anything yet, he thought. He told himself to talk to her about her day first; if she knew how crucial her yes or no was, she would keep her distance.

"How was your day?" Layne asked.

"It was rough. I'm tired," Felina said, and her voice did sound tired. *Oh no,* he thought, *she's going to cancel.*

"It was bad, huh?" Layne said as he crossed his fingers.

"Yeah, my boss is this fat jerk, like Jabba the Hut," Felina complained.

His mind drew a blank with questions to ask her and he sensed that the timing was right to attempt the goal of his call. "Hey, I'm almost home. Do you still want to hang out tonight?" he said and held his breath.

"Sure, if you still do," Felina said. She seemed to perk up at the prospect. Layne exhaled.

"I could be up there by six o'clock," Layne said. "I can take you to dinner?"

"That would be fun," Felina said. "Some friends of mine are going to a restaurant for drinks. Want to go with them?"

"Perfect," Layne said. "See you at six?"

"Okay. I'll text you the directions to my apartment."

When he arrived home, Layne couldn't get undressed and into the shower fast enough. The fabric that encased the Kevlar of his bulletproof vest smelled like wet shoulder pads. He unfastened the Velcro straps and quickly unsnapped the keepers that secured his duty belt to his under belt. His radio, pistol magazines, steel baton, Maglite, and handcuffs fell to the carpet with a thud. He felt instantly ten pounds lighter.

Once out of the shower, he stared at the pistol in the holster of his duty belt while he quickly dried off. As he dressed, he removed the loaded pistol from the holster of the duty belt and snapped it, snug, into his concealed carry holster on the inside of his jeans. He smoothed his shirt over the bulge and tightened his belt over it. He couldn't think of anything that would impress Felina more than for her to see his issued gun concealed. He just needed to think of a way for her to see it without appearing that he was showing off.

Layne chose his favorite clothes for this special trip—his best jeans, a black and white bowling shirt, Converse All-Stars, and designer boxer shorts, in case she saw him undressing. He put on a mist of cologne, but not too much, stuffed an extra change of clothes into his backpack and double-checked his pockets for his wallet and necessaries as he locked the door to leave.

His hair was still wet as he headed northwest toward Benson. He shifted gears and settled at four miles per hour past the speed limit. He had been too excited for Tucson to stop for gas in Bisbee. He filled up at the truck stop at the I-10 intersection in Benson, where he bought a "road rocket"—a twenty-four-ounce can of beer for the remaining half of the two-hour drive.

Driving away from the pump, Layne felt a spasm of anxiety and envisioned being pulled over for an illegal lane change and trying to hide the beer. He should've bought a forty-ounce beer with a screw-on cap so he could quickly stash it in his backpack while the Highway Patrolmen approached the car. He would show his badge as a last resort and tell the cop he was packing a loaded gun. He reasoned that a couple of beers wouldn't be enough for a DUI.

As he headed west on I-10, the engine hummed while the sky was beginning to glow dark blue and the sun dashed toward the peaks of the bare desert mountains. It was too inspiring an evening for worry, and he began to foresee ecstasy—dinner with Felina on an outdoor balcony, in the moonlight of a warm Arizona evening.

Water from condensation spilled from the rim of the cold can between his legs as Layne cracked the beer open at seventy miles per hour. The ice-cold liquid tasted like gold, the carbonation tickling the back of his throat. Beer made everything more enjoyable—an enhancement that was mandatory. But he cautioned himself to pace himself in front of her. He didn't want to scare her away by getting too drunk; she probably overlooked the barbecue because it was a special celebratory occasion. He couldn't screw this one up. A girl of this caliber might only come along once before he was too old. He had gotten lucky meeting her; he was starting to believe that she was half of the objective in his grand scheme.

He began to notice saguaros on either side of the highway as he reached the exit for Houghton Road, on the eastern outskirts of Tucson. He used his thumb to open his flip phone one-handed and find the message Felina had sent him while he kept one eye on the road. Even her driving directions were somehow attractive, like neat handwriting. Her apartment was on the other side of the city; he still had twenty minutes before he needed to exit I-10. He dug into his pocket for a stick of spearmint gum to conceal the smell of alcohol. She would probably still be able to smell it, anyway. Women had a keener sense of smell than men. *No matter,* he thought, *she probably knew the Border Patrol's reputation for heavy drinking from Marianne.* Ryan Danielson had drunk as much as he had the night Layne and Felina met, and Marianne was about to marry him.

The sun was setting by the time Layne pulled into the entrance of Felina's apartment complex, although its glow was still visible on the horizon. He could barely contain himself; he nearly skipped on his way through the parking lot. The arid stillness and desert palm trees only enhanced the sensation, like he was on vacation. He walked swiftly, his excitement swelling as if he were meeting her at a prison's gate upon his long-awaited release.

He knocked and counted his string of rapid heartbeats. He could hear and feel someone approaching the door from inside. Then Felina opened the door and her perfume hit him with the wash of air that escaped from the apartment. She greeted him with a broad smile; he smiled and put forth effort to appear reserved. She was wearing a white halter top that skirted slightly below the belt of her snug blue jeans. The color white accentuated her olive skin, and she looked striking, evidence of the time she had spent getting ready. Her shiny hair was arranged into a clever ponytail, displaying gold hoop earrings; even her ears were cute. Glitter on her eyelids sparkled in unison with her immense dark eyes and lip gloss.

Felina welcomed him with a hug and her body heat sent a tingle of warmth up the back of his neck, as his hands fell to rest on the firm fullness of her hips. The density of her breasts pressed and expanded against his chest, forcing him to end the embrace before she noticed the embarrassing bulge that was growing in his crotch. Face to face with her, he couldn't hide his shy satisfaction to be in her presence again, and he looked away just after they made eye contact.

She ended the greeting abruptly. "My friends are on their way to Hotel California right now," she said. "You ready to go?"

She grabbed her purse off a table and took his hand to lead him back out the door, before he could respond or see her apartment.

"Do you mind driving?" Layne asked, knowing that if he had to drive back would put a limit on the amount he could drink. "It took two hours to get up here from Bisbee."

"Sure, I know that's a long drive," Felina said, but the request seemed to bother her slightly. She seemed embarrassed when they reached her parking space. She unlocked an older model Toyota Corolla with fading white paint that smelled like flowers when he climbed in.

Felina's apartment was located near the foothills of the Catalinas, and from the heights they could see almost the entire town as they drove down a main drag of the city. Looking downhill over Tucson, the lights twinkling, he felt surrounded by magic. He was with her and didn't have to work tomorrow; he wished every moment of his life felt like this. He told himself to listen to what she said, then respond, and not to interrupt her. He hated it when people interrupted him. He was ready for another beer.

"How was your first week?" Felina asked.

After deliberating for the better part of twenty-four hours, Layne had come to an intrinsic decision that his feelings for her required as much honesty as he could manage to expose. She wasn't just another girl that he was trying to score with by exaggerating his importance. There was an unprecedented sense of respect that existed the moment he extended his hand to greet her. His deep-rooted fear of embarrassment wouldn't allow him to concede to the inner workings of his mind to anyone, especially her. But he was confident that success would gradually eclipse the shortcomings he had to hide, eventually rendering them insignificant. As he chose his words, he was confident that what had actually happened during the week would show her what she wanted to see in him—that he was morally just, as well as ambitious.

"Eventful. I thought they would ease us into everything, but we had to track down two aliens." He thought that sounded impressive, even though he hadn't done much more than follow Schnabel and the others. But he would leave such details out.

"Was it scary?" Felina asked.

"A little. The part that scared me the most was that it seemed routine, like no big deal to our FTO."

There was silence. Layne sensed that what he had revealed was sufficient for her. She turned on her blinker to change lanes and glanced over her shoulder, the rhythm of the signal blinking pronounced amid the silence.

"Do you think you can do that for twenty years or however long it takes to retire?" Felina said.

It wasn't a question he expected. "I have no choice. There's no turning back now." As he said it, he felt the weight of reality sour the satisfaction of the night. It had begun bothering him that, if he succeeded in training, he might be wasting his life in desolation, while the lucky people lived life to the fullest in bigger cities like Tucson. The impressiveness of the job had to be squared with the fact that he could be locked into a life of hopeless wanting again. He would be attached umbilically to Tucson.

"I've had crappy jobs ever since I graduated from college," Layne continued, "so this is the first good job I've had. My degree is useless. I have to make this work."

Felina seemed to be thinking but didn't comment, and Layne filled the silence. "So, when I was applying, I told myself that I could do anything for the right amount of money and benefits."

But money didn't seem like the fix-all it had a year earlier; happiness seemed more and more like the carrot hanging from the stick.

"Maybe it'll get better after training is over," Felina suggested.

"I hope; everyone says it does," Layne said. He tried to avoid looking at her when she wasn't talking, but he couldn't keep himself from glancing. She was remaining mysterious. She seemed to have straightened the slight curl out of her hair, and the change was beyond attractive to him. Her skin and hair were glowing. He tried not to let her catch him staring out of the corner of his eye. To be involved in her life while she was in her physical prime was intimidating; her femininity and youthful beauty took his breath away. He felt inferior. Only his new status as a federal agent-in-training made him feel nearly worthy of her. She was busy concentrating on driving and didn't seem to notice him looking.

Felina broke another silent interval. "Christine, my friend since high school, is going to be there with her fiancé, Arthur."

"Okay." Layne tried to sound enthusiastic, but the tension was mounting. He speculated that she was presenting him to her chaperone for approval. Girls didn't think guys realized or understood these things. He rarely hit it off with girls' female companions, but it was a good sign that he had reached this level of vetting.

"This restaurant isn't particularly popular with U of A students," Felina advised.

"That's perfect," Layne said. "It's hard to find places to hang out that are age-appropriate. I'm kind of in an awkward age range."

"It's okay; Christine's boyfriend is about your age," Felina said.

The parking lot was full and Felina had to search to find a space. He enjoyed watching her arms and hands struggle to cramp the steering wheel as she bowed her long neck and concentrated. Everything about her was pleasing to look at—down to the length of her French manicured nails.

She parked and they climbed out beneath starlight. Layne smoothed his shirt over the bulge in his jeans where the pistol was hidden as he shut the passenger door. Agents were not supposed to carry the pistol while they were drinking in public. It was supposed to be locked in its lockbox in the trunk of his car; he hadn't been thinking clearly bringing it.

Layne wanted to hold her hand as they walked close to one another through the parking lot. He sensed the restaurant bustling with music and joy. He hoped the atmosphere wasn't too rowdy. From past experience, he feared that some wild and dashing buck might say something to Felina that would require Layne to fight. He regretted not leaving the pistol behind even more. To be arrested under the influence while in possession of a gun would be a quick end to his new career. Layne rushed ahead to open the door for her, and she smiled bashfully.

They approached the hostess stand, but before they were greeted, Felina's friend stood up and waved at them from a table in the center of the dining room. The restaurant's smoky atmosphere smelled like onions and juicy hamburgers. Layne enjoyed the desert Route 66 ambiance the owner had created. He noted the pictures of muscle cars and sixties bands on the walls as they made their way through the clamoring and cheerfulness of the seated guests.

They approached the group and Layne looked to his right to see if the bar was out of view from their table. He was in luck; part of it was.

Christine and Arthur stood up and Arthur extended his palm toward Layne.

"Nice to meet you. I'm Layne." *What a nerd,* Layne thought as Arthur sat back down. Christine's fiancé was white and looked like an engineer or IT person. He wore glasses and business attire. Layne would have to pretend to be interested and to agree with what he was saying all night. Christine was Hispanic, as he expected, but not as attractive as Felina. Her long black hair was plain, and she wore librarian glasses. She wasn't trying to catch anyone's eye. She was the same age as Felina, in her early twenties.

She smiled at Layne out of courtesy, but she seemed less than gracious.

Layne and Felina sat across from them in the two open chairs. Arthur and Christine already had draught beers in pint glasses.

"Layne is a Border Patrol Agent," Felina announced, looking at Layne next to her, and smiling. Arthur lit up with interest at the remark and Christine nodded, her expression indicating that Felina had already told her and that she didn't approve. Layne was learning that a large part of the population, both white and Hispanic, resented his occupation. There was a white concentration of anti-Border Patrol hippies in Bisbee. They gave him the stink-eye at the grocery store every time.

His attention was already focused on the approaching waitress. When she arrived, he ordered a domestic pint for Felina and a Dos Equis for himself.

After the waitress left to retrieve their orders, Arthur asked Layne, "Where do you work?"

"Douglas," Layne said modestly.

"Wow, is it crazy or what?" Arthur asked.

Layne's eyes moved to Christine for an instant. She looked sociable but her eyes revealed a scowl underneath.

"It's not sitting in a cubicle," Layne said.

"So, are you afraid of getting shot?" Arthur asked.

"No, the aliens never have guns. They just have backpacks with their clothes and a toothbrush, things like that," Layne explained.

"They probably have every cent to their name with them, huh?"

"They do." Layne comprehended what that meant for a moment. It triggered a flashback to the footprints on the warning track.

Arthur was enthralled. He sipped at his beer; he hadn't even drunk a third of it yet. Layne could tell that Arthur wanted him to elaborate.

"A lot of them have money belts and they're afraid to give us their money. They're afraid we'll steal it." He could see Felina out of the corner of his eye. She was proud of his title but appeared unsettled by his description of duties.

"Really? That must be stressful. I couldn't do it," Arthur said.

Layne was pleasantly surprised; he was enjoying Arthur's company. He was intelligent and articulate. But the waitress was taking forever to bring their drinks.

"We put a labeled tag on their bags and store them in cubbyholes while they're being fingerprinted," Layne continued.

The three of them listened carefully as Layne went on, as he was prone to do when he was in an awkward social situation.

"I heard that there was an incident where an agent from another station was going through the cubbyholes and stealing all the money, though. So, I don't blame the aliens for being worried," Layne said, to try and gain some approval from Christine. But she only listened and continued to look sour.

Arthur was asking questions and allowing Layne to do all the talking. Layne felt he was expected to maintain the conversation. "But we have to document how much money they have on them on write-up sheets."

"Do they run from you?" Arthur asked.

"Almost every time. The agents near the port chase them like shoplifters every day."

Arthur smiled and nodded. But Layne felt hollow and phony for not admitting his novice level of capability. He looked at Felina and could tell that she was trying to remain polite, but her expression conveyed that she was ready for the subject to change. He considered that she probably felt sympathy for the aliens that superseded her respect for the country's borders. She was most likely in the middle somewhere, like most people, but considerably more intelligent.

Arthur took another sip of beer and looked at Christine. She fetched her large purse from the floor and put it on her lap. She sifted through the contents until she found her cell phone. She opened it up and began thumbing through her text messages. Arthur read her disposition and withheld the rest of his questions.

Layne considered what he had shared with slight regret. Guilt over offending someone with something he said was cause for the nagging regret that often plagued him. He felt the urge to slip away. He advised himself not to use the bathroom more than once, as it might appear strange to Felina.

"I'm going to run to the bathroom," Layne whispered into Felina's ear.

She nodded "Okay," and he excused himself from the table. She was smiling. She seemed to approve of his effort to be friendly with her friends.

He searched the corners of the restaurant for signs of a men's bathroom as he stood up. He headed toward the bar and looked back to make sure he was out of view from Arthur, Christine, and Felina. If the bathroom wasn't in this direction, he would double back like he had been mistaken.

Once he was out of sight from the others, he said hello to the female bartender, who was shaking a metal cocktail mixer. She asked him, "Can I get you something?"

"A shot of Patrón?" Layne unfolded his wallet in anticipation.

"Do you have a tab open?"

"I'll pay cash." He downed the shot and wiped his mouth with his wrist and left a ten. He didn't have time to wait for the change. He headed back into the dining area and tried to look lost.

"Where's the bathroom?" Layne said to the group, feigning exasperation.

They laughed and Arthur pointed to the opposite corner of the restaurant. Felina smiled at him, and their eyes met. Be careful, she's evaluating you, he reminded himself. But he felt his guard slipping, somehow comfortable with whatever judgments she might be making. The warmth of the tequila reaching his stomach made his worrying seem like unwarranted paranoia. The evening was turning out to be the delight he had hoped it would be.

6

LAYNE WISHED HIS FIRST weekend with Felina could have gone on endlessly. But as he sat dazed in his post-Academy desk, the longing to be with her only sharpened the hollow pain he felt in his raw stomach. He had waited too long to taper off and was having difficulty sitting still. He was exhausted yet anxious, simultaneously. He hadn't gotten enough sleep. The grogginess and burning eyes were compounded by the realization that he couldn't remember the last time he had been ready for Monday.

Felina had drawn nearly every blink of his attention. He couldn't stop thinking about her, even now, with the gauntlet in the field waiting for him. She was satisfying to maintain a conversation with. She was intelligent and confident, yet humble and calm. Spending time with her was so fulfilling that her presence limited his liquor intake. Regardless, he drank too much again. He was nearly certain she was unaware that he was intoxicated when he worked to mask the indicators. But he was incapable of reassuring himself that she wasn't on her way to realizing she was out of his league.

The post-Academy classroom was bustling; the other trainees in his group were chatting and reviewing the weekend from their desks. Melanie and Greg were already out in the field with their FTO from the previous week. Ashen-faced, Layne squirmed in his seat looking at the clock. He was already counting down, seven hours and forty minutes to go. He daydreamed about what it would be like to live in Tucson and be able to visit Felina after work. It seemed like paradise.

I would pay fifty dollars for a Percocet right now, Layne thought. Oxycodone was his favorite hangover cure, but they were hard to come by. He would take one just to get through the day, he told himself, then vowed that he wasn't drinking on Saturday night anymore. He was doing his best to keep a low profile; he didn't have the strength to converse with the other trainees. But just as he wiped the beading sweat from his nose with his thumb and forefinger, Runyon turned around in his desk and said, "Hey, Sheppard, how was your weekend?"

Layne winced, forced to participate in the banter he knew was coming. "It was good," he said, while the others turned to look at him, grinning, waiting for a response.

Runyon said, "We know you've been working that Mexican chick from Danielson's party. Did you go deep?"

Everyone laughed.

"No," Layne said as he blushed.

"Don't hold out on us, Sheppard; we know you went to Tucson to shack up," Runyon said.

Layne didn't answer. He looked at Carlos, whose grin wasn't abated by the comment.

In the absence of Layne's response Runyon said, "I struck out again this weekend, so I've gotta live vicariously through Sheppard."

Layne was thinking of what he would say if Runyon persisted, just as a new FTO opened the door and entered the room. He stood at the front of the class with documents in his hand. The dry erase board behind him displayed Ortega's law lesson from Friday. Seeing Ortega's handwriting brought Layne back to a moment during the lecture when there had been only three hours to go until the weekend.

"I'm Agent Cruz," he said once everyone was settled and ready to listen. "I'll be taking over for Agent Schnabel until this pay period is over. He's not normally an FTO; he was just filling in until I was done with my Phase Four trainee last week. We gotta scramble to accommodate all of you since the influx."

Layne put Friday out of his mind and studied Cruz as he referenced his paperwork and glanced at the trainees. Cruz was a dark-skinned, Mestizo

Hispanic of average height and build. He was one of few people that Layne could tell he liked simply by looking at him. He wore a permanent smile, even when he wasn't smiling. He looked good in his uniform, and his affable personality emanated through his laid-back mannerisms as he took his time addressing his new trainees. He seemed enthusiastic, but relaxed. He looked to be about thirty years old, but Layne felt adolescent in comparison. Cruz's experience and maturity embarrassed him, so much so that Layne couldn't maintain eye contact out of shyness.

Cruz glanced back and forth from a list in his hand to his four new trainees while he spoke. "Looks like the other half of the class is already out in the field with FTO Blythe. So, this is Group One? There should be Preussen, Dos Santos, Sheppard, and Runyon, right?"

The trainees nodded their assent. It was only the second or third time Layne had ever heard Carlos' surname.

"How long have you been an agent?" Runyon asked Cruz.

"Six years."

Layne looked at the G-426 on his desktop while his knee bounced. FTO Cruz's first name was Adrian; he was Delta-177. Schnabel's first name was Erich, BPA Erich Schnabel. Their superior positions made it strange to know their first names.

Cruz continued. "Has anyone explained the phases to you guys yet?"

Each shook his head, no.

"FTO Schnabel went over it briefly, sir, but no one has really broken it down for us," Runyon informed.

"Okay," Cruz began. "There are four phases. Phases One, Two, and Three last a month each. Phase One is basically area orientation and an overview of duties. During Phase Two we will be actively engaging and apprehending aliens. I'll be in the lead and you guys will assist me. If you have me as your FTO, I mean."

Runyon started to ask a question, but Cruz cut him off. "You should get a new FTO every pay period. You'll do searches and write-ups in Phase Two. Phase Three, you guys will take turns driving. Your group will serve as a floating MIT in different zones, depending on where the activity is on a given shift. During Phase Three, one of you will perform as an agent would, but an FTO will be right there to assist."

Layne's aching stomach turned as he anticipated the description of Phase Four while Cruz explained, "Phase Four, you'll be alone, one on one, with an FTO. You'll perform like a regular agent would. Your FTO will be grading you the whole time, but he won't help you. You're on your own. We aren't supposed to talk to you during Phase Four unless there's an emergency and your, or your FTO's, life is in danger."

"How long does Phase Four last?" Carlos asked.

"Five days. Eight hours a day. Just hope they put you on day shift when you do it."

Cruz could see nervous anticipation on the trainees' faces. "Don't worry about Phase Four right now. You'll feel a lot more comfortable about it in a few months. You guys got all your gear?"

"Yessir," the trainees answered.

"Meet me in the parking lot in five minutes."

* * * *

CRUZ DROVE THE SUBURBAN more loosely than Schnabel while he headed east towards town on Highway 80. He was sincere about wanting to prepare the group as best he could before they were thrown into duty in the field. Preussen had requested the front seat, which meant tomorrow Layne would have to ask for it or appear unmotivated.

"Ask as many questions as you can while I'm here," Cruz told them. He checked his blind spot before changing lanes. He seemed to be accustomed to people in cars being afraid to pass. They slowed when they saw the Suburban then settled two car-lengths behind.

"Let's go to 5-Delta," Cruz announced abruptly. He slowed and pulled onto the shoulder, then onto a dirt frontage road south of the highway. He was headed for a break in the barbed wire that separated the desert from

Highway 80. He drove across a cattle guard with two clanks and onto the playing field. Preussen reached for his ceiling handle and the others followed suit as they began to bounce.

Once in the desert fields of the west side, Cruz drove the Suburban like a dune buggy. Improvised roads traversed the zones like veins and arteries, which he navigated with second nature. Although they were becoming better at appearing comfortable, the trainees found themselves lost and disoriented again.

"Have you guys done any cutting yet?" Cruz asked, facing the windshield.

"A little," Runyon offered.

"Cutting is ninety percent of what we do. Every surface is cut-able. When I first started, I thought that you could only cut dirt roads. But you can find sign on anything; like when you're looking for dirt or mud on east side streets."

"327 for six," a female voice blurted over the radio.

Cruz reached to the console to raise the volume on the radio. "She's calling out sensors. As soon as aliens come over the fence, there's sensors all over the place."

The trainees nodded. They had heard that the zones in the desert were booby-trapped with sensors like a minefield belt along the border.

"What do the sensors look like?" Preussen asked. It was strange to hear his voice for the first time after a week of silence.

"They're a Frisbee-sized metal disc with a transmitter, buried about a foot underground," Cruz answered.

The trainees listened without reacting.

"Actually, there's two kinds of sensors. Foot sensors, like the one she just called out, and vehicle sensors. The foot sensors are triggered by pressure when something steps on them. The vehicle sensors are magnetic. They go off when the metal chassis of a vehicle goes over them," Cruz explained.

The trainees continued to listen without speaking.

"Did you guys pick up a sensor list at Muster?" Cruz asked.

"Yessir," the trainees said.

Layne labored to unbutton his shirt pocket and unfolded the sensor list. His stomach was causing him to sweat.

"When she calls one out, look it up on your sensor list to get an idea of where it is. After a while you'll know them by heart," Cruz assured them.

The trainees tried to find the sensor code on the list but there were hundreds of them to search through.

"Same with your maps. Unfortunately, the maps suck. Somebody drew those things about ten years ago and they have just been making copies of them ever since," Cruz said.

The trainees reached into their backpacks to find their maps, unsure if Cruz wanted them to reference them.

"Those are the same maps I learned with," Cruz said as he jerked the wheel to dodge holes and bushes.

Layne bent over to unzip his backpack and sifted through the junk to find his stack of maps. They were bent and stained by what looked like fruit punch already.

"When a sensor goes off in your zone, you go and check it for sign. The second number she calls out is the number of hits. But it doesn't mean that's how many bodies went over it."

Cruz explained: "She would say for example, 351 for seven, ten, fourteen, nineteen. It can give you an idea of how many bodies are in a group if the hits are good. But a lot of times it's a coyote or deer," Cruz explained.

Everyone nodded.

Cruz said, "If one goes off nearby, we'll acknowledge it and go check it out."

The sensor codes continued to come in over the radio in the LECA's serene voice. It was like bingo when she called out the three-digit number of a sensor. By the time the trainees located it on the sensor list she had already called out a subsequent code.

After ten minutes of dirt paths and roller coaster dips through arroyos,

Layne tried to concern himself less with bearings and geographic location and more with the tactics of intercepting the fast-moving groups.

"409 for nine," the LECA's voice rang out over the radio.

"That's in 6-Alpha," Cruz said instantly. "Let's go check it out."

"866, Delta-177, ten-four," Cruz said into the radio microphone.

Gravel crunched against the tires as Cruz snapped a quick U-turn to head back north. "You can't learn AOR by me showing you. The only way to learn is when you guys get to your units and you're working groups on your own. Let's get into somethin'." He crossed a cattle guard with two manhole cover clanks and the tires sounded relieved to be back on pavement. He aimed the Suburban west on Highway 80 and gunned the engine as he returned the microphone to its cradle. The trainees braced themselves. Layne began to check his gear as he craned his neck from the seat behind Cruz to see the needle reach ninety miles per hour on the speedometer.

"We gotta get north of 'em before they cross the highway," Cruz shouted over the engine noise.

The trainees held onto the ceiling handles and looked straight forward, expressionless, trying to anticipate what was coming.

"Delta-177, Delta-242," a male voice called over the radio.

Cruz grabbed the microphone without looking as he swerved into the opposite lane to pass a car. He never used his turn signal, even in town. An oncoming car whooshed by just as Cruz straddled the yellow stripes in the road to return to his lane.

"Go ahead," Cruz said into the microphone then rested it in his lap as the spiral cord dangled.

"I just cut that group from the 409 south of the highway and they already made it over," Delta-242 reported.

"Ten-four," Cruz said as he slowed onto the shoulder. He crossed over another cattle guard onto a dirt road that branched off north as they entered a zone above the highway. Rocks clinked against the undercarriage like a hurdy-gurdy as Cruz accelerated over the hard dirt surface. The wide rural road passed under a large electricity transmission tower three cables high as a dust cloud followed them, completely cloaking their view to the rear. But Cruz cramped the wheel and the trainees' torsos shifted to the right and they were headed west again. Layne's mind spun with confusion and his adrenaline pumped with the urgency of Cruz's tone and reckless driving.

"They're moving fast, but we should be north of 'em. You guys get ready. We're gonna have to hurry."

From the moment they left the parking lot, Cruz's frisky demeanor had given Layne the feeling that he wouldn't be satisfied with teaching AOR and sensors for even one whole shift. He was always speeding. It was becoming obvious that Cruz preferred to throw the rulebook to the wind regarding phases before he would allow himself to become bored.

The veins in between the rural roads were mere tire tracks that wound through the desert sage; created by repetition and wear.

"These guys know what they're doing. They must have somebody leading them," Cruz said as he leaned back in the seat to allow himself to reach into his right pocket for something. He glanced in the rearview mirror as he drove. He did a double take, noticing the blank look on Layne's face. He stepped on the brake and the tires made a grinding sound on the dirt until the Suburban slid to a halt.

"Sheppard, you're driving," Cruz said as he opened the door. He read Preussen's nametag and said, "Preussen, sit in the back; I got shotgun."

He got out and left the driver's side door open and crossed in front of the Suburban to get in the passenger seat. Layne felt his heart sink into his stomach, and as he climbed out, he realized that the adrenaline had washed out much of the pain in his abdomen during the previous ten minutes. Layne opened the door and slid into the driver's seat, pulling the seatbelt across his chest.

"Don't put your seatbelt on, sir," Cruz scolded Layne from the passenger seat as he closed his door. "You're gonna get out in a minute here."

Layne hadn't been allowed enough time to panic. The sun caused him to squint as he put the transmission in Drive. He told himself to just get on with it, like jumping into a cold swimming pool. When he pressed the gas pedal, he tried to mimic Cruz's flashy driving to avoid obstacles, having no plan for where he was headed as he guided the misaligned steering wheel.

"Start cutting here," Cruz ordered.

Confused, Layne continued driving north. He was trying to find an intersecting road to turn left on and begin searching a road parallel to the border but had forgotten to roll down his window.

"What are you doing?" Cruz blurted. "Don't you know how to cut, sir?"

"But we're headed north, sir," Layne said.

"Bodies move north, south, east and west, sir. Start cutting right here," Cruz said impatiently. Then he hung halfway out of the passenger side window to get a closer look at the road. Layne drove at moderate speed while his eyes scanned the dirt and sage flowing by on the driver's side.

"There it is; stop here," Cruz commanded as he opened the door while the truck was still rolling.

"I see it over here on this side, too," Layne said, not really seeing anything but the same dirt and rocks he had passed over the previous half mile.

The other trainees dismounted. Cruz moved swiftly to take a closer look at the footprints in the road. The trainees absorbed his sense of urgency as he knelt down to examine the footprints. "It looks like there's about eleven or twelve of them." He knew the sign was good from no more than a glance.

"Over here, you guys," Cruz motioned, leading them to a barbed wire cattle fence. "You see how the bottom wire is bent? That's where the guide held the wire up so the aliens could squeeze underneath it."

The bottommost wire had been bent upward into an upside-down U, so that it was almost touching the parallel wire above it. Cruz pointed to the area under the bend and emphasized the activity that had just taken place there no more than five minutes earlier. The overlapping mess of footprints depicted the guide securing the wire like a fast-moving shepherd, so that the barbs didn't snag on the aliens' clothes after they waited their turn to duck underneath.

"See all the different prints? I count fourteen," Cruz said, an eagerness in his voice.

The trainees stood over the cluster with jaws slackened.

"Did you guys bring your camel packs?" Cruz asked.

Everyone nodded.

"Get them and turn on your radios."

The trainees hopped and wiggled to secure their packs in place and sucked on their hoses to verify a flow of water. Cruz peered with concentration north across a valley of dry sage, mesquite, and ocotillo prongs. This far west, the desert Mule Mountains dwarfed them, dominating their leftward peripheral vision.

Cruz's radio had no microphone cord. He pulled it from its holster and spoke into it like a walkie-talkie as the antenna wobbled. "Delta-295, Delta-177."

"Delta-177, Delta 295."

"I got FTU on that 409 sign; I'm about a mile north of the highway. We're gonna push it," Cruz said.

"Ten-four, I'll try to cut them off by the fork," Delta-295 replied. The acknowledgment was hard to make out through the static; he sounded far away.

Cruz motioned to the group and began to concentrate on the path of footprints. Layne fell behind almost immediately.

Cruz moved like a deer. After 200 yards he said aloud, "There's a kid's shoe in the sign. See it there?"

Layne concentrated on the detail of the path for as long as he could spare the effort. One specific print amongst the herd was only six inches in length and the tread resembled "W" shaped lines with a circle on the heel.

"Those other small ones might be women; they're gonna slow the group down. We can wear 'em out if we haul ass," Cruz said loudly as he moved.

Layne all at once felt conflicted as he stumbled. Perceptually, he had visualized the footprints being left behind by miscreants who were laughing at having duped their followers. But, as the trainees hustled to keep up with Cruz's ferocious pace, Layne couldn't banish from his consciousness now the scene of a woman holding hands with a child. Pulling the child along as they ran. What would incline a woman to expose a child to this madness?

Cruz didn't even bother looking at the ground to track them; he seemed to know where the group was headed instinctually.

The trainees pressed north behind Cruz, never breaking stride as the relentless September sun beat down on them through a clear, oven-like blue sky. Layne was sweating profusely now, working to watch his steps between the sage as he lost his balance and caught himself. His duty belt felt like it was gaining weight. He tried to jog periodically to catch up to the others. Fatigue was now a much more serious burden than it had been when it had weighed him down in PT back at the Academy. He was beginning to understand why they put trainees through such an exhausting regimen. It was difficult to comprehend that this was a job. It felt more like war.

Suddenly Cruz came to a halt. "Hold up a minute. I lost the sign."

The trainees caught up, with Layne straggling in last. He bent over to catch his breath, his hands on his knees.

"There it is," Carlos said, pointing to a set of footprints.

"No, that's two days old," Cruz corrected as he kicked a tumble weed out of the way then bent over scanning the desert floor.

"Here it is. This is brand new," Runyon said, motioning everyone over.

"No, that's not it either," Cruz said from a distance. "That's an agent from Mids. You guys need to know what the tread of our own boots looks like." He took notice of Layne's faintness as he dismissed Runyon's find. "Are you okay, Sheppard?"

Layne was barely hanging on, parched and winded, but he answered, "I'm okay."

Cruz resumed his examination of the ground with a steadfastness that was exhausting just to watch. He scoured the area with a drive that could have been interpreted as wrath, as if he were offended that the aliens had disrespected him by crossing during his shift. Twenty yards northwest of the bird-walking trainees he shouted, "Here they are," and set off again in pursuit as Layne coughed on water from his camel pack hose.

The trainees struggled again to keep pace, and Layne continued to drift progressively farther to the rear. His boots became heavy and he tripped on cactus and fell to one knee before he regained his footing. Cruz glanced to his rear; he slowed down and then stopped. Runyon, Carlos, and Preussen gasped and sucked their camel pack hoses when they caught up. Layne was the last to arrive.

"How do you feel?" Cruz said to Layne.

"Dizzy."

"How much water do you have left in your camel pack?"

Layne sucked on the mouthpiece and pockets of air and water within the hose made a slurping sound. Cruz smiled. He seemed to have known the whole time that Layne was hung over. Before anything was said, Layne made a promise to himself not to drink at all anymore on the weekend. He didn't know what he had been thinking. From his current perspective it was insane to show up hung over to Field Training.

"Delta-242, Delta-177," Cruz spoke into his radio.

"Go ahead, Delta-177."

"Delta-328 is ten-seven, that's going to be about fourteen Golf," Cruz said while smiling and looking at Layne, emphasizing that it was his deficient condition that was responsible for fourteen getaways. Over the radio came whistling of admonishment from anonymous agents. Cruz chuckled. He reached into his pocket, pulled out his cell phone, and dialed with his thumb. "Hey bro," he said as he began to walk, looking at the ground while he talked, "We're about a mile south of the fork. On the 22 Road. Yeah, okay, see ya."

He put the phone back in his pocket, "My buddy's gonna come pick us up and take us back to the truck," Cruz said to the trainees without further comment to Layne. The trainees' faces were red; they were too tired to respond.

A Kilo arrived in ten minutes, and Cruz told the trainees to stand on the bumper as he climbed into the passenger seat. The trainees barely secured themselves before the driver peeled-out. They held on with alarm. The driver, Cruz's friend, drove as fast as Cruz drove the Suburban. Layne clutched the railing on top of the detention cell, afraid of losing his grip. The trainees strained to hang on as the Kilo bounced and sank into holes in the dirt of the 22 Road. Layne tasted dirt accumulating in his mouth and his eyes were forced shut by the trail dust the tires kicked up. He opened his eyes to squint and see the others hanging on for their lives with their eyes and mouths mashed closed. He leaned to look around to the passenger side and could see Cruz's elbow peeking out the window. He was laughing while he chatted with the driver.

"I think this guy driving forgot we're back here," Carlos yelled to his bumper-mates through the dust cloud.

Runyon tried to respond, when his foot slipped off the bumper. His knee bent and he regained his footing as the toe of his boot dragged and skipped on the road for an instant. "I've got nothing to hold on to!" Runyon cried. "This idiot is going like forty miles an hour!"

Cruz yelled from the window, "We'll go back to the classroom and let Sheppard hydrate!"

Layne coughed on dust with his eyes mashed shut while he thought. He had forgotten about the incident at the gun range until now. An expert marksman, he'd rarely hit the target the day after he'd been on a weekend bender while at the Academy, making this the second time he had been divulged in front of others because of his inability to drink in moderation. Nothing was a secret here; he was most likely already in trouble. He grabbed the railing tighter, fearing his sweaty hands might not hold.

He thought of the trainees at the Academy who had been sent home for injuries in PT. Perhaps if he fell, he would have a way out of this and save face, a way that didn't appear to involve failure. But an image of Felina applying mascara in her bathroom mirror came to him between squints and prompted him to soldier on. He was still transfixed by the sight of her belly button and the width of her hips in lacy briefs that accentuated her shape. Losing the job would most likely mean losing her. The memory of her smile was what was keeping him alive.

He knew the onslaught that was coming in the field was going to test the limits of his desire to have her.

AFTER SPENDING ANOTHER SUBLIME weekend with Felina, heading to work when it typically was time to go to bed felt unnatural to Layne. Just the mention of the word Mids—the 10:00 p.m. to 6:00 a.m. shift—conjured up ominous visions of bats and owls. He was amazed at the darkness of the desert highway at night. The stretch between Bisbee and Douglas was uninhabited, its desolation augmented only by the starry sky. The lights of Douglas, a barely perceptible twinkle in the distance, grew slowly larger over the glow of his car's instrument panel. He glanced at the time on the dashboard clock: 9:35 p.m.

His eyelids were heavy and his stomach growled with emptiness, though he wasn't hungry. Compounding the suffering, he had once again drunk more than he had intended over the weekend, leaving his mouth dry and his organs aching. He'd left Felina's apartment in Tucson at 7:30 p.m. and was on track to make it to the station early, but the time cushion wasn't the least bit comforting.

Driving straight through from Tucson to Douglas on his first overnight shift was a mistake he hadn't been able to refrain from making; he had stayed with her until the last possible minute. He regretted not taking a sleep aid around noon—anything to get at least four hours of sleep. Trying to sleep while she was awake had left him with barely an hour of shuteye, but the time that had passed didn't really feel like sleep. He had never heard of someone being late to Muster. Calling in sick wasn't an option, not until FTU was over. One false move would earn him a reputation that would blackball him. Regardless, the thought crossed his mind to turn around.

With heavy eyelids, he did his best to redirect his thoughts in order to prepare himself mentally for his first night in the field. Cruz had covered a significant amount of vital information the week before, and Layne struggled to focus his weary thoughts on what he had tried to impress upon the group. One message was preeminent:

"You will learn the area, and you will know every turn, every mile-marker, and every hill and saddle," Cruz had said. "The reason why you learn this stuff is if something bad happens to an agent, you will know where he's at, and you will be able to get to him. If you guys decide you want to be slugs, and never catch a body, I don't care. But if I'm hurt, you better know where I'm at and find me."

Cruz had taken time off from the field to instill information in the trainees that Layne knew he should retain. Cruz had looked visually bored from the beginning of the classroom work but had selflessly taken on the role of a school teacher even though he wasn't required to. He had spent hours using the whiteboard in the post-Academy classroom, teaching the group the essentials of radio communication. Since the Border Patrol was a branch of the federal government, the service used the same phonetic alphabet as the military. Runyon and Preussen already knew them, but he made sure Layne and Carlos could recite the alphabet from Alpha all the way through Zulu without hesitation.

The ten-codes were equally critical, and Cruz made certain his trainees understood the meaning of the codes that were used with regularity. Layne realized that, much like the subject matter he had studied in college, the countless hours he had spent at the Academy memorizing immigrant and nonimmigrant visas had been a waste of time for real-life activity.

Cruz had also warned them of the pitfalls that agents from the past had fallen victim to. He advised them to use their one pair of handcuffs only on the most threatening prisoners—if the prisoner ran away, the missing handcuffs would need to be explained in a memo. Aliens ran away all the time, but missing equipment could lead to an FBI investigation since, technically, it was classified as an escaped federal prisoner. Likewise,

Cruz warned them never to lie about any event that occurred, regardless of how easy it might seem to hide. To be caught lying was one of few sure ways a career agent could be separated from service.

As Layne drove on, thoughts of the past week waned, and his mind wandered back to Felina as a mirage of her dark eyes shimmered within the headlights on the road. He had begun missing her breath within minutes of her goodbye embrace; the longing for the weekend to go on forever had nearly brought him to tears. The intimacy of gazing silently at one another was heaven. The image of her earrings resting against the olive skin of her neck only protracted the five-day prison term he was forced to serve.

Twenty minutes later, as he settled into place in the Muster Room, he joined the other trainees who knew to sit in the front row, facing forward. Their assigned seating wasn't mandated, but the consequences of not conforming were better left nameless. Veteran agents sat in the back of the room on folding chairs or stood leaning against the back wall. Agents with less than two years of service occupied the tables behind the trainees. Everyone faced the lectern. The agents didn't acknowledge or even look at the trainees, as if they were invisible.

The supervisors sat at tables on either side of their superior—Field Operation Supervisor Benevides. The FOS was at the podium, facing the agents and trainees. They chatted in low voices and laughed quietly. When the clock high on the white cinderblock wall reached 10:00 p.m., the voices in the room abated except for a few suppressed coughs. FOS Benevides cleared his throat and began shuffling through papers at the lectern. One of the supervisors stood up and began distributing stacks of warm paper to the agent in the aisle seat of each row.

Layne put his nose to the G-426 Daily Group Assignment Log to smell the fresh ink as the supervisor returned to his seat and the FOS commenced. "MacInnes and Leslie banged-in, so Messemer, I'm going to have you head over to 6-Alpha tonight."

"Ten-four, sir," Messemer acknowledged from somewhere behind Layne.

"I forgot Leslie threw that party yesterday; I'm sure MacInnes was there—that's his boy. They're probably not feeling too hot tonight." The FOS made a note of the absences with a pencil as he spoke. Agents often called into the Fishbowl with slurred speech from intoxication to request sick leave. Most agents preferred to come to work hung over and sleep in the field so they could use their sick days for small vacations. Knowing such things caused Layne to tell himself that he fit in, though his gut begged to differ. He stared into space, debating himself, until the FOS finalized his adjustments to the roster then cleared his throat. "I'll keep this short, then I'll get to the main issue. No more calling each other regarding traffic using your cellphones. That's what the radio's for. When you're working traffic, you're keeping important information from your unit by having these private conversations over the phone. It's dangerous, and it's a safety issue. Use the radio like you're supposed to. If I catch you working traffic with your phone, I'll assume you don't care what I say up here."

A number of agents readjusted themselves in their seats, and throats cleared subtly throughout the rows. The FOS shuffled papers and continued, his voice deepening into a somber tone. "As some of you have probably heard, there was an agent killed in San Ysidro, California today. There was a Blazer trying to make it back south after a failure to yield, and this agent set up to spike him. The agent was behind some brush for cover and the scumbag saw the trigger cord at the last second and swerved over him. They got the agent to the hospital fairly quickly, but he didn't make it. I was informed he was dead upon arrival."

The room was silent while Layne fantasized about being awarded a medal in front of the room for saving an agent's life in such a situation, the room breaking out in applause as the ribbon was being placed around his neck.

The FOS continued while Layne went on indulging in his daydream. "When drive-through season starts, I want you all to be extra careful when you're laying spikes. If it looks bad, get outta there. I don't wanna be calling your better half with news like that." He paused again to allow time for everyone to imagine the possibility then added, "Nothing that we do here is worth dying for."

Layne was unsure exactly what situation would require spikes, or how to lay them, but he set aside the concern and instead tried to remember where he had put the black stripe pin that they were supposed to wear over their badge when an agent died.

The FOS continued. "You'll notice that the flag is at half-mast. See Delta-76 if you need a black stripe pin for your badge. If I see anyone without it, you're going to be washing the vehicles for a pay period." He shuffled his paperwork again then tapped the pages on the lectern twice to straighten them. He switched gears again, returning to the business of the day. "Traffic has been coming through 5-Charlie the past few days; you know how the trends go. There were nine Golf on Swings today. Make sure you're communicating with each other when you're working traffic. There's no reason anyone should get away if we're working groups properly."

The jargon and references to vague incidents sailed past Layne as he yawned and covered his mouth. He caught himself nodding just as the FOS finished his address. "You guys on the corners make sure you're checking out your long arms. Okay, let's get out there. We wanna radio ten-eight a little early so the guys on Swings don't have to wait for us tonight."

Chairs scooted on the floor as agents rose to head to the equipment counter in the hall to check out their vehicle keys and M4s and begin the shift. Layne and his FTU mates were moving into Phase Three of Field Training, which Agent Cruz had told them meant they would serve as a floating MIT in different zones, depending on where the activity was on a given shift. Layne had survived Phases One and Two and wondered what Phase Three held in store. He would find out sooner than he imagined.

He met up with Carlos, Runyon, and Preussen, and they spotted their latest FTO, a new one named Tipton, almost immediately. He appeared to be looking for them as the other agents waited patiently to pass through the bottleneck at the door. Tipton was tall, roughly thirty years old, and reminded Layne of a football lineman at first glance. Over his uniform top, he wore a green, Border Patrol-issued vest with the letters USBP that held four thirty-round .223-caliber magazines on the breast.

"You guys ready to get out there?" Tipton asked. Judging by his nervous hands, he was trying to play the part.

"Yessir," the trainees responded with what sounded like false enthusiasm.

As the crowd was still funneling out of the room, Tipton looked the trainees over for a moment to see if they were wearing warm clothing. Layne had brought his green hooded jacket but wasn't wearing thermals. Packing for the trip to see Felina had caused him to be negligent about planning what equipment to bring if he chose to drive straight from Tucson. It was evident to Layne that the others had at least gotten some sleep, judging by their mood and appearance.

"Who wants to drive?" Tipton asked.

Carlos volunteered.

"Go ahead and check out the keys and I'll meet you guys in the parking lot," Tipton said.

* * * *

LAYNE OPENED HIS EYES but was unsure where he was for a split second. He found himself looking at the zipper of his green rough gear pants and realized that he had been asleep. Startled, he skipped a breath when he came to and snapped his head upright. He was in the back seat of the Suburban on the right side. He had fallen asleep with his arm hanging out the window, still clutching the pistol grip of his million-candle-power spotlight. Next to him, in the middle, Preussen was half asleep. Runyon was focused intently on the dirt on the other side of the vehicle through the beam of his cutting light. Riding shotgun, Tipton was adjusting the focal point of his beam and hadn't noticed Layne dozing. Layne switched hands to allow his right arm to rest. He aimed his beam to refocus on the dirt beneath the barbed wire fence to his right that skirted Highway 80.

They were headed east, away from the mild comfort of the city lights, searching for footprints. The FTU Suburban was hugging the fence three miles northeast of town, crawling at five miles per hour. Ruts like indented railroad tracks, created by decades of agents cutting the highway fence line, had been worn into the fifteen-yard fringe of the desert shrubbery between the shoulder of the highway and the cattle fence that paralleled it. Carlos held the steering wheel tightly and concentrated on the headlight beams to follow the tracks and maintain a consistent speed. He had to be careful to drive slowly enough to allow the others sufficient time to search for clues of groups sneaking through the blackness of night.

Layne relieved his cramped arm and switched hands again. He pulled slack in the cord and continued scanning for prints, trying to mimic Tipton's technique from the passenger seat in front of him. The high-powered light beam illuminated a hula hoop-sized section of its target like a magnifying glass. Every pebble and twig in the dirt was highlighted as the metal fence posts rolled by at walking speed. Layne's painful nods repeated themselves as his eyes struggled to adjust to the remote darkness away from town.

"We get night differential for this don't we?" Runyon asked from the back seat to interrupt the drone of the engine.

"Yeah, it makes a big difference on your check. Some guys request Mids, just for the pay," Tipton said.

Layne told himself he didn't care if it paid double-time, it was like being water-boarded, trying to stay awake. He looked at his watch, and saw it was only 2:00 a.m. It was as if their watches had fallen asleep in the darkness as well.

"I don't mind working through the night," Runyon boasted. "When I was in the Army we would just be getting to sleep after forty-eight hours straight and they would tell us to gear up."

Layne rolled his eyes.

"Besides, Sheppard, you can't die from sleep deprivation. Eventually your body just shuts down and you pass out," Runyon said.

Despite Runyon's bragging, Layne welcomed a break from the silence. It helped him stay awake.

"You'll notice there's a lot of guys who prefer Mids," Tipton said. "There's an agent—I won't tell you his name, but eventually you'll figure out who he is. He's been here a long time, and he's always on Mids. You're not supposed to have any kind of side job, but he has a gig under the table. He drinks beer all day while he's installing kitchen cabinets, then takes a nap in the evening. Then, he shows up to Muster with a five o'clock shadow and his hair a mess."

The trainees laughed. There was no facial hair allowed except for a mustache. Violating the rule with the slightest bit of stubble meant a memo for almost everybody.

Tipton continued his point. "Anyway, this guy always shows up late to Muster, half asleep, and half drunk. Ten minutes after he radios ten-eight, he's racked-out in his Kilo. He's been in twenty years, though."

The trainees exchanged surprised glances at the story.

"They always put him on the line in 5-Alpha and aliens run right past him. They could jump on the hood and run over the top of his truck and he wouldn't wake up," Tipton said.

The trainees laughed, while they maintained concentration on the focal point of their spotlights.

Carlos continued to drive, concentrating on the tire tracks through the headlights. Layne switched off his cutting light and stretched his fingers. The device was shaped like a ping pong paddle with a cord that plugged into the cigarette lighter behind the console.

"Sheppard, keep cutting," Tipton prodded.

Layne clumsily flipped the switch while it was pointed to the sky and the beam cut through the night and stars like the lights in the Hollywood hills.

"Carlos, you should start honking, too, in case everybody in Mexico didn't see Sheppard's light just now," Runyon joked.

Layne was too tired to retaliate. He bore down and aimed below the barbed wire again. He was painfully exhausted and was considering a trip to a *farmácia* in Nogales in the morning to find a Mexican version of Ambien, or any pharmaceutical that ended in "pam." *If I can make it through tonight,* he thought. He only hoped they didn't run into anything.

"I know, this sucks, but I like to cut the highway on the east side," Tipton said. "When they say that there was ten Golf or whatever on a shift, that's just sign that wasn't accounted for. A lot of groups go right past here and no one even cuts them." His beam zeroed-in on a section between fence posts and his arm lagged behind the progress of the vehicle to stay trained on the spot. "Hold up a second," Tipton said as he motioned to Carlos with his left hand.

Carlos simply let off the gas to stop the Suburban, and Tipton motioned while he concentrated on his focal point.

"Back up a little bit."

Carlos gripped the bar on the steering column and put it in reverse. The engine sounded as tired as Layne felt when it had to backpedal.

"That looks new. I'm gonna get out and take a look. You guys stay in here for a second," Tipton instructed.

Tipton let off the trigger of his cutting light and put it on the floorboard. He opened the door and grunted as he climbed out and shut the door. He walked stiffly a few paces to the fence and pulled his Maglite from the hoop on his duty belt and clicked it on. After a quick examination of the area that had drawn his interest, Tipton clicked off his Maglite and came back to open the passenger door, "This stuff's good. We better follow it," he said in a half-hearted but dutiful tone.

The trainees got out and put on their heavy hooded green jackets and black stocking caps in hurried slow motion. Layne adjusted his cap so that the Border Patrol logo was in the front, offset slightly to the left. The trainees opened the Suburban's hatch to make sure they had the gear they needed, then abandoned the vehicle on the shoulder of the highway.

Layne could see his breath while he paced the fading paint boundary of the highway lane. He stomped his feet to stay warm, his legs felt weak and a light wind numbed his cheeks. Tipton had dialed his cellphone and wandered down the highway twenty yards to continue his conversation away from the trainees.

Runyon approached Layne and said facetiously, "I guess he doesn't care what Benevides says."

Layne nodded while he yawned. "He'll probably switch to the radio once we start following it. I heard that the FOS says that every six months or so and nobody cares."

Tipton started walking back toward the trainees as he ended his conversation and folded his cellphone into his pocket. He came back and gestured to the trainees to follow him as they crossed the highway without looking; they hadn't seen another pair of headlights in several hours. Tipton's classmate at the Academy in Glynco, Georgia, Agent Freitag, was part of the Mobile Interdiction Team in Zone 42, the zone into which the tracks led. There were too many prints to give a description of the shoe treads. Tipton had simply called his friend to say that he and his trainee MIT were pushing a large group and the direction that it was headed. They quickly found where the trail resumed when they reached the shoulder on the north side of the highway.

"They're headed to Pirtleville, right sir?" said Carlos in more a statement than a question.

"Right, ninety percent of the groups that cross out here are headed to Pirtleville," Tipton said.

The trainees clicked on their Maglites and followed the footprints fifteen yards to the barbed wire fence that paralleled the other side of the road, where they crossed over, one by one. Layne stood on the bottom wire where it was attached to the post and gripped the wire between barbs for stability while he straddled the fence. The crotch of his pants caught on a barb, and he unhooked himself carefully before he swung his leg over to land on the other side. He bowed his legs and lifted the crotch of his cargo pants to find a small tear between his legs.

Tipton laughed, "After a while every pair of pants you've got will have a hole in the crotch."

"How many do you think are in this group, sir?" Preussen asked.

"How many did you count?"

"About ten," Preussen guessed.

"There's a lot more than that," Tipton said from the rear. He was allowing the trainees to lead as he observed from behind them.

The march of new footprints weaved through mesquite trees and resumed their course heading west. Layne felt better now that he was moving. The trainees concentrated on the desert floor—their flashlights illuminating the eerie path like four revolving searchlights. They kept their voices low; they might have been right behind whomever they were following, judging by how crisp the prints were.

When they lost the sign, Tipton stayed back silently to allow them to find it. But they were improving daily now and were losing the sign much less frequently.

"Be careful," Tipton said in a stage whisper, a guy saw a mountain lion stalking an agent through the scope truck a couple of weeks ago."

The trainees didn't respond, unable to tell if he was teasing or sincerely warning them. It seemed possible. The infrared surveillance equipment on the scope truck could detect body heat from a range of several miles. Through the scope, the aliens appeared as little yellow dots in the distance, like ants marching slowly. Then the operator could make out the shape of their eyeless faces once they were within a quarter mile. They looked like ghosts in single file. The thought sent chills down Layne's spine and legs—the specially equipped vehicle had been allocated to the west side on this particular night.

After a half mile, the bearing for the Pirtleville Deluxe Trailer Court hadn't wavered by a degree. Headlights flashed like a lighthouse beacon in the distance, then the beams could be seen jarring and changing directions as an oncoming Kilo made its way over the terrain, moving slowly south about three-quarters of a mile ahead of them. The drone of the truck's engine could be heard through the dead calm of night like a train in the distance.

"That must be Freitag blocking for us, right?" Preussen whispered.

"Yeah, that's him," Tipton replied. "He's cutting the second to last road between us and Pirtleville. We gotta reel this group in before they make it to Whiskey Tango." Then, suddenly, Tipton took his Maglite from his belt and accelerated past the trainees. "You guys are doing a good job, but I'm gonna take over the lead so we can move faster, just because of the size of this group." Tipton began tracking at twice the speed the trainees had achieved.

As a consequence of their speed, Layne ceased watching his step so closely, and in his haste kicked a barrel cactus, causing him to stumble. Maintaining his stride, he shined his light on his right foot and saw that several cactus needles protruded from the front of his boot like porcupine quills. He dragged the toe to break them off; there was no time to stop.

Free from the toil of tracking, the simplicity of following Tipton permitted his thoughts to wander and return to Felina's raven hair in a knot while he watched her dressing. The shade of her red lipstick remained in his mind's eye, the taste of it merged with her breath still lingering on his tongue. He imagined curling up next to her and the warmth of her body while she slept. He would put his arms around her, and she would hold his hand without waking up. He secretly enjoyed watching how slowly her chest expanded and exhaled while she was sound asleep. He recalled the smell of her skin for a split second as his boots took long strides and stutter-stepped to avoid prickly hazards in the path.

8

THE SIMULTANEOUS BLURTING OF THE trainees' radios startled Layne out of his yearning dream and brought him back to the chase at hand: "Delta-212, Delta-210."

Tipton brought his microphone to his mouth to answer as he slowed. "Delta-212. Go ahead."

"That group is already past the 66 Road, I'm thirteen right now to Sulphur Springs," Delta-210 reported, indicating that he was en route. There was urgency in his voice and the engine of his vehicle could be heard revving during the radio transmission.

"Ten-four, you got an idea of when they crossed?" Tipton asked.

"I saw the tail end of the group running across the road in my rearview mirror," Delta-210 said. The truck could be heard bouncing and landing as he spoke.

This particular guide appeared to be well-versed in avoiding agents while leading large groups. He had kept his group low, probably laying on their stomachs, while Delta-210 was cutting and blocking on the 66 Road. The guide apparently had tried to wait until the agent was just out of range before moving the group across the 66 Road quickly, but evidently had given the group the green light to run across a bit too early. When Agent Freitag caught that glimpse of bodies darting across the road, he realized he had been outwitted.

"Let's go," Tipton said to the group. He took off and the trainees had to begin running to keep up with him. They brushed branches out of the way and hurdled prickly pear patches. Layne found it difficult to run in calf-high boots, and the weight of his duty belt bounced heavily between strides.

The trainees followed Tipton over the raised dirt of a rural road. From the elevation of the road, the light created by the streetlamps of Pirtleville was visible a mile to the west. When they reached the other side of the road, they held their flashlights low in a hurry to investigate the gravel shoulder to find where the aliens had come out on the other side. There was no time to sufficiently check the road to see if the group had doubled back. Tipton was assuming that the guide was trying to outrun the agents to Pirtleville. The group had crossed perpendicularly. Their prints were on top of tire tracks on one side and had been run over on the other side. Often, when the aliens crossed a road, they would walk with the road for a hundred yards or so then resume their bearing from a parallel course to confuse the agents. Tipton looked briefly at the tracks then brought his radio microphone to his mouth. "Delta-210, Delta-212," he said in a normal tone, then breathed somewhat heavily after he let off the button.

"Go ahead," came the almost immediate reply.

"You got anything yet?" Tipton said.

"I'm cutting Sulfur Springs right now; they haven't come across yet," Delta-210 reported.

"We just came across the 66. We're gonna push them to you," Tipton said.

"Ten-four, I'm gonna see if I can get someone from Simchek's unit to lay-in over by that set of trailers."

"Ten-four." Tipton ended the communication and clipped his microphone back on his passant while he moved. He spurred the trainees to hustle with him.

Layne tried to think like the furtive leader of the group. An experienced guide would most likely be able to slip the group into the harboring neighborhood at the right moment, which was why the additional agent had been called upon. But if the guide was capable of outmaneuvering the agents thus far, he would most likely anticipate a blacked-out agent lying in wait, hidden near the layover spot. From his Applied Authority classes, Layne remembered agents needed to witness aliens entering a premises in order to have probable cause to search. If the guide was successful, the Pirtleville conspirators would intake the aliens, unseen, then they would evacuate their clients gradually over the course of the next three or four days, during shift changes when the agents were distracted.

Adrenaline boosted their stamina, but the trainees were pushing the limits of their cardiovascular capacity to stay with Tipton. Layne's heart pounded but running felt good and helped ease his jitters. Tipton pressed the trainees to catch up to the group while they were trapped, waiting for an opening to sneak into the trailer park.

"We have to be right on top of them," Tipton said from up front.

They could see lights coming from the windows of the first trailers on the east side of the town. Layne watched his boots trade off swiftly in front of him within his erratic circle of light; he and Preussen had fallen twenty yards behind Carlos and Tipton. Carlos appeared to smell blood. Runyon was trailing somewhere in the rear.

"Hold up," Carlos called out from up front as he stopped. He spread his left palm and raised it to the height of his ear. Tipton was somewhere out of sight.

Layne froze. He felt a strange presence. Bushes were rustling.

"Fifteen," Carlos said aloud as he aimed his Maglite from his ear into the bushes to his left at the aliens he had just apprehended.

Layne put his hand on his pistol; the guide could still be with them. He shined his flashlight into the dark to his left, and dust floated through the light beam that reached into the desert. Twenty yards away, his light exposed an area that revealed pant legs from the knee down and shoes protruding from a thicket of sage. He was surprised that he didn't feel panic.

"How many do you see Dos Santos?" Tipton's voice could be heard from somewhere up front.

"I count five," Carlos called out.

Tipton came back within view through the brush. "Okay, guys, start circling the area and bring them in to me here. We'll have them sit down facing north. Stretch your radius about fifty yards from where I'm standing."

Layne approached the pair of legs and tennis shoes he could see. He shined his light on the back of the person to whom the legs belonged. It was a man. The dirt and stickers on his pants and his navy-blue sweatshirt camouflaged him so that he almost blended with the desert floor. Layne could hear breathing and twigs crack directly ahead of him. He shined his light in the direction of the sound and saw the bodies of six to eight others lying face down on their stomachs, as breathless and motionless as statues. But Layne still felt no threat, as if he had located other kids playing hide and go seek.

"I got about ten more over here," Layne yelled back towards Tipton.

"I count twelve over here," Runyon said from twenty-five yards to his right.

"Me too, at least ten," Carlos called out from up front.

"Quedete en el suelo. No te muevas," Layne told the person at his feet: remain sitting and don't move. He looked around three hundred and sixty degrees, then moved cautiously to locate each person. He made sure to find everyone within his portion of the radius before he told them to get up. Only then would he herd them to Tipton.

Each person he came across lay motionless, likely hoping Layne would overlook him or her in the dark. He told each one not to move. He circled the area until he was confident that he had located every person who remained, finally approaching a female, still lying face down, wearing a down coat with a fur-trim hood. His light surrounded her, but she remained still, her fingers coiled tightly in the palms of her hands.

"Levantete," Layne said to her to make her stand up.

She didn't move.

"Te veo, levantete, hace frio," Layne barked. He let her know he could see her, reasoning that the fact it was cold out might persuade her.

She rose slowly to all fours, then stood up and faced him. He struggled to make eye contact with her. He felt suddenly embarrassed by the glaring polarity between his own spoiled middle-class upbringing compared to the desperate circumstances that had forced these people to risk sneaking into a foreign country. The distress was evident in the aliens' despairing facial expressions. He pointed and ordered, *"Camine adelante, muevate al Agente en el Centro. Quedete cerca de yo. En frente."* He was telling them to walk straight forward and move towards Tipton, and to stay close in front of him.

The woman stayed directly in front of him as he moved on to gather the next alien. The others were standing up now without being told. Suddenly, there were twenty people standing all around him. They were lost. They didn't know where to run without guidance. He swallowed and pretended to be assertive.

He looked back and saw one man who had appeared fifteen yards directly behind him. *"Tu, ven aqui. Para te enfrenteme,"* Layne commanded. With all the authority he could muster, he was ordering the man to stand in front of him.

Layne's radio vibrated on his hip. "Delta-210, Delta-212," he heard Tipton call out.

"Go ahead," came back.

"FTU is fifteen by at least fifty here," Tipton said. "We'll bring them back to the 66 Road, about a mile from the fork."

"Ten-four. I'm en route," said Delta-210.

Layne walked his group of aliens towards Tipton. Carlos, Preussen, and Runyon were closing in from different directions with their groups in front of them. Tipton held his radio microphone in his hand, as the flashlights of the trainees made him visible. He looked over the approaching crowd as he walked slowly in a small circle.

"Okay, guys, officer presence. Keep them in front of you. Let's have them form a line. Carlos, you stay in the back. Sheppard, you and Runyon get on that side of them. Me and Preussen will stay on the flanks. After we form them up, we'll walk them back to where we crossed the 66 Road."

Tipton commanded with the absolute confidence of routine. The trainees acknowledged his commands.

"Forme una linea," Carlos called out to the aliens.

The captives moved in quickly to form a line. Layne tried to think ahead to anticipate what Tipton would want him to do. Runyon and Preussen were pointing and motioning, unable to give instructions in Spanish. The aliens had assembled themselves into a column, awaiting further instructions.

"Delta-212, Delta-49," a voice tickled Layne's hip. He could hear Runyon's radio pick up the signal last.

"Go ahead," Tipton said.

"I'll meet you at the 66 Road. I'll have Delta-255 and his trainees there, too. We'll get you some help with that group."

"Okay, let's get them moving. Sheppard, you know what to say?" Tipton asked.

"Yessir." Layne turned to the line. *"Todos escuchen! Vamos a caminar al Camino que ustedes cruzaron diez minutos temprano. Quédense en una Linea. Vamos pues!"*

Tipton and the trainees took their positions and the column began to move to the east. The Unit Supervisor in Zone 42, Delta-49, had ordered the other Field Training Unit and several of his agents to assist Tipton—to prevent any aliens from running south while they were awaiting Transport. Help was on the way to meet them at the rally point. They escorted the column of aliens and arrived at the 66 Road. Tipton moved up closer to the front and said aloud, "Okay, have them sit down. Assemble them into about four or five rows. Carlos, go ahead."

"Seintense, forma cautro filas como así," Carlos instructed as he gestured with his hands.

The trainees pointed and guided the aliens into four rows. Layne looked at his watch as he put on his black Kevlar search gloves. It was almost 3:00 a.m., and colder than it had been when they had first found the sign. He could see his breath in the beam of his Maglite as the aliens squinted and cowered before him. Most of them sat with their arms around their knees.

Layne moved to the front of the group and surveyed the faces of the sitting aliens. They were shivering now that they were stationary. They were wearing whatever they had available to stay warm, coats with the stuffing peeking out of a tear, or several layers of long sleeves. Many of them were wearing hoods, and their clothes were covered with dry grass and stickers. The boys wore skinny jeans and their hair in wide Mohawks with short hair on the sides. The majority of them were men, but there were four females among the group. In the second row was a young woman, hugging a small boy sitting next to her. The boy looked lost and confused by the situation. Layne told himself not to look at them.

Headlights in the distance were closing in from the north and the south.

"Let's just keep an eye on them until everyone gets here. It should just be a couple of minutes," Tipton said.

"Do you think the guide is in this group?" Carlos whispered to Tipton.

"No, he must have seen the Kilo hiding and didn't get a chance to get them through. He knew we were right behind him, so he probably just split. That's why these people just gave up and laid down to hide. You can tell what the guides look like; these are just average Tonks."

In the Academy they had been told that the guides would often blend in and pretend to be one of the migrants once the group was caught. The people in the groups were too intimidated to identify their leader, fearing retribution when they were deported to Mexico. The guides were usually U.S. citizens who had grown up in Douglas and knew every square foot of the Douglas AOR.

"Their guide must have just turned back south," Carlos said. "We got to the spot where we went ten-fifteen about five minutes after we crossed the 66 Road."

"The guide will keep an eye on our Maglites behind him," Tipton explained. "Once we get within a couple hundred yards, he'll TBS [turn back south]. They're like jackrabbits. It's almost impossible to catch one once they turn back south."

It was unsettling to look at the people and realize that their guide had just thrown them under the bus. An alien told Carlos that they had already paid the guide. Layne knew most of them had saved for months to pay the fare. He tried to clear his mind of thoughts about the aliens' lives. He tried not to look at them above the waist; when he did, he could almost read on their faces the circumstances that had led them to such desperate measures. He struggled to shake off the troubling thought that they had failed and lost all of their money on a gamble to try to be happy. He told himself to stop, that they were breaking the law; but his mind moved on to visualize them being put back into Mexico, penniless. Most of them were from far away cities in Mexico, and often times from countries in Central and South America.

Vehicles arrived one after another, within seconds of each other, surrounding the rows of aliens. The trainees turned off their Maglites and dropped them through the hoops on the backs of their duty belts. The headlights of three Kilos and a Suburban illuminated the scene from every direction, and some of the aliens shielded their eyes from the glare while others looked at the ground between their legs. The idle of the engines forced the trainees to raise their voices.

The veteran agents left their engines running as they piled out of their vehicles and gathered to greet one another and begin to socialize. Melanie, Greg, and two trainees from Class 592 joined the trainees, saying nothing, only nodding to Layne and their other classmates.

Tipton resumed control, addressing his group and the other trainees who had arrived to help. "Okay, guys, let's get this group searched. Tell them to put their backpacks, their *mochilas*, in front of them. Search their bags then have them stand up and search them. When they're done, have them sit back down then search the next one. But hurry; we'll call transport when you're about halfway done."

Tipton's colleagues, the other senior agents, had removed M4s from their vehicles and slung them over their shoulders. They lit up cigarettes and continued to smile and joke. The trainees began searching while the agents watched.

Layne picked the first row and searched the backpack that lay in front of a young man, whose expression was one of cooperation. There were clothes and tamales in tinfoil within the backpack. In the small pocket were a toothbrush and toiletries. Layne zipped the backpack closed and told the young man to stand up and interlace his fingers behind his head. He felt something in the man's hip pocket as he ran his hand down his right side to search his body for weapons. He stuck his fingers in the man's pocket as he restrained his hands behind his head with his left hand. He pulled out the cross of a rosary while most of the beads remained in the pocket. Layne pushed the cross back into the man's pocket and told him to sit down.

Tipton stood off with the other senior agents and barked another command. "Agent Freitag has write-up sheets! After we get done searching, we'll write them up; but hurry, just do a once over and have them sit down!" He was trying to sound like a hard-ass, performing in front of the other agents.

"If they're in such a hurry, you would think they might help us," Runyon whispered to the other trainees.

Some of the teenaged boys were less cooperative, rolling their eyes as Layne searched them. He tried to ignore their body language, unsure of how to respond. He was more concerned about the woman with the little boy, and he was trying to stall in order to avoid them. They were now two aliens down the line. *Hopefully Greg will get to her first,* Layne thought.

Next, he came to a teenaged girl with her arms wrapped around her knees. She seemed embarrassed as he stood above her, pushing her dirty hair behind her ear with two fingers when Layne addressed her. She looked up at him bashfully. Her eyes were strikingly attractive. Layne smiled, a reflex, as if they were passing in the aisle at a grocery store. He felt the need to tell her not to be embarrassed, that she was born into these inescapable circumstances, and that it scared him to imagine trading places with her. Curiously, he had respect for her, for doing whatever was within her means to escape her circumstances. But he said nothing, afraid the others might hear him.

He felt awkward telling the girl to get into position to be searched. He told her to spread her legs and he ran the back of his hand from her ankle to her crotch and back down the other leg very quickly—the method he used to search the legs of male aliens.

"Why don't you feel her tits too," a senior agent with an M4 slung in front of him said aloud.

The comment forced Tipton to speak out, "You just grabbed a handful of pussy, Sheppard. What if someone did that to your sister?"

The other trainees all looked at Layne but didn't smile or laugh.

"I used the back of my hand, sir," Layne said.

Tipton stepped from the other agents toward the situation but didn't come close enough to speak in a quieter tone of voice. "It doesn't matter. You don't search females like you do males. Just go on the outside of her legs and around her torso, and don't touch her tits, even though I know you want to, Sheppard."

The senior agents chuckled.

"What are you teaching your trainees, Tipton?" One of the agents laughed, as he flicked a cigarette.

Tipton ignored them and said, "You guys let Melanie search the females."

Carlos said in a low voice so the agents couldn't hear, "That's bull. What if she had knife or something hidden in her underwear?"

"I didn't know," Layne said, and suddenly realized that he had forgotten to search her backpack. He looked back and saw that Tipton and the senior agents were busy talking and didn't notice. *I better do it*, he thought. Layne knelt down in front of her and unzipped her backpack. Beneath a pair of dirty underwear and other clothes were two boxes of tampons. He looked at her, and she blushed.

"*¿Estas enferma?*" Layne said to her, asking if she was sick in order to avoid the specifics.

95

"Es para seguridad," She said, avoiding eye contact, explaining it was for security.

Layne was curious for an explanation but knew she wouldn't tell him the whole truth. He pulled out both boxes and held them up to show Tipton.

"The girls carry those with them while they're crossing the border. They drop them like breadcrumbs as they're coming over," Tipton explained.

"Why do they do that?" Preussen asked as he finished searching a man with his hands behind his head.

"Because there's border bandits that cruise along the fence on the Mexico side. They rob aliens at gunpoint and rape the hotties like her. The girls drop those so the bandits will think they're on the rag."

Layne felt himself turn green as he looked at Runyon, who was shaking his head in disgust.

"That's screwed up," Carlos said.

"I know you would run a red light, Sheppard!" Tipton said, and the senior agents roared with laughter.

When they quieted down, Tipton said, "You guys searched all of them?"

The trainees looked at one another. They had all managed to avoid the woman with the small boy so far. Maybe Tipton wouldn't notice if they weren't searched.

"Let's get them written up and get outta here," the other FTO said, and he and Tipton began passing out write-up sheets.

Layne was relieved to be done searching, but he couldn't expel the images of border bandits from his mind and what they would do if they ran across the woman with the boy. He used his thigh to write on and a quarter inch stack of write-up sheets as a makeshift clipboard. Most of the aliens had Mexican identification cards, and the trainees copied their information into the appropriate blanks of the G-434.

"You guys know, all of those IDs they give you are fake," Tipton said, circulating among the trainees to check on their progress. "They buy them for, like, ten bucks at one of those alien hubs close to Hermosillo."

One of the senior agents heard and added, "Yeah, there's a place that's like a Tonk specialty store. A place to buy supplies and everything they need to cross the border. Like a Camper's World for backpackers."

Layne examined the ID he had in hand and shrugged; it looked real.

"It doesn't matter," Tipton said. "Just write down whatever it says on there. They'll run fingerprints in processing and find out who they are if they've been caught before."

Some of the aliens didn't have IDs. Layne struggled to fill in the blanks on the G-434 when the aliens mumbled their names.

"Hurry up," the other FTO said. "Transport is almost here. Don't worry about spelling or anything else. Those write-up sheets are just like deli numbers when they get to processing."

Layne removed his search gloves. He guessed and filled in the blanks with gibberish. It was difficult to write; his fingers were lethargic from the cold. He looked up and realized the woman with the child was next. They both had to have a G-434 apiece when transport arrived. Greg had timed his stall more effectively and left Layne holding the bag.

When he reached her, he hesitated, taking his time putting the previous sheet under the stack to start two new write-ups. The woman was sitting side by side with the boy, holding him tightly next to her, her right arm around him as if to protect him from Layne. The boy was wearing mittens and a black stocking cap that was too big. The woman, evidently his mother, Layne now realized, had spent her last dime to bundle him up for the journey. His puffy coat was ragged.

"*¿El Niño es tu Hijo?*" Layne asked her politely, inquiring if the boy was her son.

"*Sí,*" she said, shivering with her arm around him.

The boy appeared too confused to be frightened. Layne wondered if he thought that what was happening was a normal part of life.

"*¿Cuántos años tiene el Chico?*" When she was asked his age, Layne expected her to say six or seven.

"Diezyocho," she said, shivering.

"What is she saying?" Tipton wanted to know.

"She says this kid is eighteen years old," Layne said.

Layne turned around to look at Tipton, and it brought the scene into focus. He realized what the woman was seeing. The agents near Tipton were dressed in stocking caps and green hooded coats, leaning against their trucks. They had machine guns slung in front of them; their attitude openly disdainful. The Kilos idled and their headlights flooded the woman's eyes. She cowered before Layne and the agents like they were space invaders.

"Tell her not to lie to us," one of the agents said, as he exhaled cigarette smoke. "Tell her the kid can stay with her and the other chicks in the women's holding cell."

Layne tried to comfort the woman. From her ID, if it was accurate, he saw that she had traveled with her son over a thousand miles from Zapopan, Mexico.

Layne translated to her what the agent said. *"Esta bien si el Niño es Jovencito. Puede quedarle en el Carcel de las Mujeres contigo. No es un Truco, te digo la Verdad."*

"No," the woman said. *"Tiene diezyocho años."* She was trying not to cry.

"She thinks it's a trick. She says he's eighteen. She's got it backwards; she thinks if he's under eighteen they will separate them," Layne said to Tipton, who had come over to determine the cause of the delay.

"Just write something down. No, forget it. Just leave it blank. They'll figure it out in processing," Tipton said.

The first Transport van skidded onto the scene and the trainees handed their stack of write-up sheets to Tipton. The Transport driver grabbed the two-inch-thick stack of write-up sheets as he opened the doors to his van. He began impatiently herding the first row of aliens in, motioning in the direction of the van with his arms and whistling to prod them.

Layne gave up trying to avert his eyes from the woman and her boy.

They would be in Agua Prieta in a few hours, with no money, no food, and no place to stay. He began chewing his fingernail, watching them as the second transport driver arrived and began gathering her row.

Layne's preconceptions about these people were changing with every group FTU apprehended. He felt especially sympathetic towards the women they were encountering, due to their vulnerability. He knew he should consider every alien to be a threat, but instead he found himself treating them in the manner that a foreign aid worker would. He reminded himself never to breathe a word of his concern to anyone involved with the Border Patrol; it might be construed the wrong way. But he couldn't entirely suppress the compassion he harbored. People who belittled the aliens weren't being honest with themselves. They didn't consider the circumstances that people were born into. Ambivalence was leaving him confused, his hatred for Mexican migrants abating more every time his FTU unit entered the field.

9

BEAMS OF YELLOW LIGHT peaked through the blinds into Felina's room as the sun woke Layne from strange dreams of the night before. He rubbed his eyes, squinted at the window, and looked over Felina's shoulder to see if she was awake. She was lying on her side facing away from him, lightly clutching a sheet that was covering most of her naked body. She was still asleep; he was almost positive. He enjoyed the way his feet felt between her cool sheets and thick comforter the instant he woke up. He loved the warmth of her legs against his, even when she neglected to shave them, as Mexican girls often did. The bristles tickled his calves and shins. He could hardly grasp that he was lying next to her for the first few seconds each time he opened his eyes in the morning. But the hot pain in his gut began to heat his face, distracting him from his appreciation of her bare shoulders.

He kept an eye on her as he lifted the covers and inched out of bed slowly. She moved a little and scratched her nose but returned to stillness and slow breathing. He tiptoed in his boxers out of the bedroom, across the warm carpet into the living room, and grabbed his jacket off the couch. Then he stealthily made his way past the bed again and into the bathroom. He closed the door with care and pushed the button lock simultaneously, then hung his jacket on the hook of the bathroom door. Staring at the stranger in the mirror, he was taken aback by the bloodshot condition of his eyes. His irises had turned green this morning from their normal dark brown; caused by toxicity, he speculated. He took two reserved shooter bottles of vodka out of his jacket pocket and set them next to the sink. He flushed the toilet and cracked the seals on both miniature caps while the sound of the water was swirling. Tiny bubbles raced upward to the growing air pocket at the top as each bottle emptied between his fingers. He gritted his teeth with the sting. The room-temperature liquid tasted cold and seemed to make his mouth even more dry. But slowly, the liquor began to overwhelm the pain as he felt its warmth travel to the depths of his stomach.

He brushed his teeth with the toothbrush he had left by her sink the week before, but he avoided looking at himself in the mirror. He sifted through the trash to make space for the empty bottles; burying them underneath maxi-pad wrappers and wadded tissue dabbed with makeup. The wax paper wrappers made a crinkling noise, but the toilet wasn't ready to flush again to camouflage the sound. He opened the door to see Felina turn onto her back and rub her eyes with her fists. Her breasts were exposed now, but she didn't appear self-conscious about their exposure. She was a sight to behold, even when she had just awakened and was without any makeup. He did his best to avert his gaze from her chest and focus on her gleaming eyes as she turned toward him.

"Good morning," Layne said. He sat down on the bed next to her and ran his hand through her messy black hair.

"Good morning." She blinked her eyes several times at the morning light that was filling the room.

"I'm sorry if I was out of line on 4th Avenue last night," he said. "I might have gotten carried away." He recalled a nebulous clip of rowdy behavior on the thoroughfare between bars that he only now realized might have embarrassed her. But he refrained from elaborating; realizing he had apologized the previous Saturday morning.

"Don't worry about it," Felina said, placing her hand on his thigh.

"It sucks so bad down there in Douglas. I just feel like I need to make the most out of my days off." He had repeated this line so many times he had lost count. "But no matter how much fun I have, I'll feel like I fell short when I sit down at Muster on Monday."

He lay down next to her and smelled her hair, which prompted him to think about his own smell. He had forgotten to drink water from the sink to dilute the smell of alcohol coming from his stomach. If she smelled vodka, she would think it was from last night, he reassured himself. But he felt the concentration of morning liquor kicking in, all the way to his fingertips, and his confidence soaring.

"What's bothering you about work?" Felina asked as she yawned.

"There's just a lot of pressure to learn the job," Layne said as he lay beside her, looking at the ceiling beginning to spin.

"Well, you're smart. I'm sure you'll do fine. You've come too far to let up," Felina said.

She didn't offer the sympathetic answer he was fishing for. It sounded like something his dad would say. But the liquor was making him chatty and he took the opportunity to vent.

"Our FTO, Cruz, brought us through the detention wing the other day and there's a cinderblock holding room between the sally port and the processing floor where the jail cells are. It has a polished concrete floor and there was schwag ditch-weed strewn all over the place. The smell hit me as soon as we walked in. It was humid like a greenhouse; they store thousands of pounds of dope behind a chain link fence in there. Only supervisors have the key to the dope cage. There was an agent on his haunches, weighing toaster-sized blocks of marijuana wrapped tight in cellophane on a digital scale. The cartels compress the blocks with a carjack and wrap them so they're hard like a brick."

Layne could sense Felina's interest, so he continued. "Anyway, Ortiz was standing above him with a cup of coffee and some guys from the DEA came into the room to pick up what we'd caught that week. Ortiz is the agent that took us on our tour of the station before we left for the Academy. He's the one who only tries to catch smugglers and ignores aliens on foot. Anyway, these DEA guys were wearing street clothes with their badges on lanyards around their necks. Ortiz said out loud to us, 'Do you know what DEA stands for? It stands for Don't Expect Anything.'"

"Are you serious?" Felina said with a look of astonishment as she sat up with her back against the headboard and pulled the covers over her lap.

"Yeah, I couldn't believe he said it. They were pissed; their faces got so red, and Ortiz was laughing. The DEA comes by once a week to take possession of the drugs, and I guess they chalk it up on their stats when they didn't do anything to catch it. The public sees the stats and thinks they captured it. We drag it through the cactus and stickers, and they take credit for it. But the point is, I just have no idea how to do any of that stuff; like, the procedure after you catch the dope. The DEA paperwork and things like that."

"Well, I'm sure someone will show you how to do it when the time comes," Felina said. She turned to face him directly now, more fully awake.

"Cruz was driving us through town the other day; he's always speeding. We came to a stoplight and I looked over to the lane next to us, and Ortiz was in full uniform driving an old minivan with his shades on. He didn't even see us; it looked like he was turning the knob on the radio to find a station."

"Why was he driving a minivan?" Felina asked as she brushed her hair back behind her ear, a habit that Layne found familiar and encouraging.

"He had just seized it from an alien-smuggler. Cruz told us Ortiz doesn't like chasing foot traffic. He just hides in different places all day and catches people picking up aliens. It's how he entertains himself, like fly-fishing. There's a whole section of civilian vehicles in the parking lot where he and this guy named Darmody keep them. It's like their trophy case until the cars get auctioned. Some of them are brand new cars. Cruz told us Ortiz drives a Dodge Neon into the field that he uses as bait while he pretends to be a smuggler. Sometimes he uses a truck—the aliens hop in the back of the truck and lay down and he drives them to the station."

Layne expected her to laugh but she only grinned a little.

"Oh, gosh, those people are probably still making car payments on a car they don't have," Felina said.

"When he catches a smuggler, he takes their cellphone and answers the calls that come; he knows all the Spanish lingo and codes they use."

The strength of the liquor was becoming intense because of Layne's empty stomach, the euphoria making him feel like a storyteller. He could tell he had Felina's attention, so he continued.

"They all look the same; they all wear a black or navy-blue hooded sweatshirt with cactus stickers and twigs all over them. The girls all have dark coats with a fur lining on the hood. They look like they've been wrestling around in a barn. Their hair is all messed up and matted with dirt and sweat. One of the boys was wearing a Michael Jackson t-shirt and Runyon cracked a joke about it. But Cruz told us not to laugh at them, because they're so poor that a lot of their clothes are hand-me-downs from a long time ago."

Felina frowned and turned away from him to hide her reaction. He could see that his description of the aliens' clothing had upset her. Layne's inhibitions had vanished again, and only the release of his thoughts would satisfy the euphoria. Against his better judgment, he continued. "They had their *mochilas* laying in front of them, so their property was ready to be tagged and stored. Before I entered the service, I thought we would at least zip tie their wrists, but we don't. Most of them are docile and demoralized."

Felina got up abruptly. "I'll make us some coffee," she said.

When she stepped out of bed, she turned her back to him and gave him a chance to admire the small of her back and buttocks in the boxer shorts she had slept in. She opened a dresser drawer and put on a red University of Arizona t-shirt to walk to the kitchen, which caused him to consider that perhaps she was trying to escape his bluster. Even worse, maybe she suspected that he was still drunk, or had recently become drunk.

Layne lay with his eyes shut and his fingers interlaced on his chest. He wanted another shot of vodka but had intentionally kept only two tiny bottles in reserve as a method of self-governance. To sneak a drink from her barely touched bottles of Apple Pucker and Fireball in the kitchen would be too risky until she took a shower. But girly liquor was too easily detected by a female sense of smell, which was why he chose vodka. Someone had once told him it was the best booze to drink while driving, because purportedly, it was the most difficult for cops to smell. But perhaps it was a fallacy, and Felina was attempting to sober him with caffeine because his blabber was making her uncomfortable.

After five minutes speculating about what she was thinking, Layne sensed her come back into the bedroom and he opened his eyes to see her carrying two cups of coffee. She carefully handed one to Layne and warned him not to spill it as he sat up. He thanked her and received the cup, holding it with two hands as he sipped. She had overloaded it with flavored creamer so that it was lukewarm and tan in color. Tasty creamer was just one of the amenities of her apartment that he enjoyed; like the exfoliating, scented soaps and shampoos that he liked to sample when he used her shower.

"What were you guys doing there, in the sally port?" Felina asked as she sat next to him and puckered to blow gently on her coffee. He suspected she was resuming the conversation in order to be polite.

"Cruz just brought us through there to show us the procedure. He did a weapons check while we were there. He just did a press check on our guns to make sure we had a round chambered, and he sprayed our OC pepper spray to make sure the canister was still pressurized. That red smell made me nauseous; it brought me back to the drills at the Academy," he said. She nodded, pretending to understand. "I think he didn't feel like chasing traffic and was trying to think of something to do. He was taking us to our post-Academy classroom to teach us the phonetic alphabet and the ten-codes for radio communication—you know, Alpha, Bravo, Charlie."

"What are you afraid of?" Felina asked suddenly. She had sat down on the edge of the bed and propped up the pillows, careful not to spill her coffee. She eased herself against the headboard, her legs crossed in the lotus position and her eyes directly on him now.

He was surprised by the question. There were so many fears that he had to rank them in order to narrow his answer. "You mean about the station?"

"No, I mean about life as a whole." She took a sip from her coffee, peering over the rim of the mug, waiting for his answer.

No one had ever asked him this question, and he felt curiously relieved to answer her. "I've been afraid my whole life, since I can remember. I was always sick with worry. When I was little, I felt like the really bad things in life were always going to end up happening to me, starting when I was about eight or nine."

"You poor thing," Felina said. There was genuine sympathy in her reply. She reached out and touched his bare shoulder, their eyes meeting before she lowered her hand.

"It's not just that I'm scared," Layne said. He took a deep breath. "The other night we were tracking a big group of aliens. We trapped them and they were all lying on their stomachs trying to hide. When we had them sit down in rows to write them up there was a mother with a little boy in the group. She was trying to tell me her kid was eighteen years old because she thought we would let him stay with her if he was of age. But she had it backwards. I've never seen anyone so scared; it still bothers me."

Felina covered her mouth, and tears began to well up in her eyes.

Layne said, "I know; she had no money, but somehow they'd made it all the way to Agua Prieta from Guadalajara. I couldn't conceive of what she was gonna to do when they deported her and her son right back to AP. There are so many predators there; no way is someone gonna help her." Saying it aloud disturbed him. He could only imagine the sub-human miscreants that would zero in on the two of them wandering the streets of a border town in desperation.

"Oh my goodness." Felina began to cry. She was still covering her mouth. Layne had already seen her tear up at the sad parts of movies, so he knew that she had a sympathetic heart. Her distress intensified his own regret and the sense of helplessness he had felt when encountering a protective mother and frightened child.

"I feel terrible for having anything to do with it. The other guys could care less; they were laughing and telling me to hurry up while I was trying to help her," Layne struggled to say. He could tell he had upset Felina with the story and considered that perhaps he shouldn't have shared what was troubling him with her. But it was too late, so he continued. "I was gonna try and slip her some money; whatever I had. I think I had about forty dollars in my wallet. But if anyone would've seen me slip it to her . . . I don't know what they would've done; everyone at the station would've heard about it within twenty-four hours. But I should've risked it when no one was looking. She might've been able to get a room and some food for the boy for a couple of days; or bought a bus ticket. I feel really guilty, even though I was only doing my job."

Felina set her coffee on the nightstand and put her arms around her legs, then she put her chin on her knees. "I'm so sorry, Layne," she said as tears ran down her cheeks and she wiped them away with her forearm.

"I'm sorry I didn't do anything. I think about her and the kid every day. I wonder where they are."

Felina didn't say anything. She sighed deeply. The tears had stopped, but she continued to hug her knees and stare straight ahead.

"I feel like I'm balancing on top of a house of cards; every little thing feels like life or death. I'm afraid of running out of money and having no place to go," Layne admitted.

Felina turned her head and observed his fixated stare. She gathered herself and said, "So am I. Everyone is afraid of that, baby."

Layne cracked a grin that she couldn't see. He looked at his folded hands and said, "Whenever I get any money together something comes along and takes it. Like, I got a photo radar ticket in the mail and there's a picture of me at the intersection of River and Ina, and in the picture, I'm drinking a beer just as the camera snapped the shot."

"What? Shut up," Felina smiled and wiped her tears away.

"Just kidding," Layne turned to her to make sure she appreciated the joke. She was smiling broadly and laughing. There were red circles around her eyes.

"What are you scared of?" Layne asked her. He reached over and ran his palm up and down her thigh.

"I'm afraid I'll never get to go to college and will have the same dead-end job I have now when I'm fifty." Her smile went away as she said it.

"Can't you get financial aid?"

Felina looked away and said, "I don't have the money to quit my job. Financial aid alone wouldn't be enough."

"You do belong in college; you're smart. If I make it through training maybe I can help you somehow," Layne said.

"You're so sweet," Felina said. She seemed slightly embarrassed about discussing her lack of money.

Layne leaned over and kissed her on the cheek while she stared at her coffee.

Felina moved on from the subject of money to end the momentary awkwardness between them. "You're very intelligent, Layne. I'm sure you're going to pass the Spanish Oral Boards, and all of this'll be behind you. You're just going through a rough patch right now. I've never doubted that you'll succeed. I just worry about your safety sometimes."

"Don't worry too much. The aliens never have guns, and with the smugglers, it's just a game. They know the rules. If they get away, they make money. If their dope gets caught, they lose it. It's not personal. It's hard to explain, but they're not going to kill a federal agent to save some dope. Every time I've heard of someone getting killed it was an accident," Layne explained.

"Be careful, though," Felina said and she touched his face.

"I will, but some stuff does kinda scare me." Layne got up and raised her blinds. He looked out the window at the palm trees and desert mountains. There were things on his mind that he was holding back. He had no patience. He should've waited for an opening at Tucson Station. He could've been here with her every day. He would be behaving better, he told himself, because he would be happier with his surroundings. But he might not have met her in the first place if he had waited for the opening.

Felina observed him and continued sipping her coffee. He could feel her thinking and watching him. She started to say something but seemed to think better of it just after she said, "Layne." He glanced back at her but returned to gazing out the window without asking her to finish her sentence. He feared that she was contemplating asking him something about drinking. She only started a sentence with his name when she wanted to discuss something he didn't. So, he said the first thing that came to mind to sidetrack her train of thought before she had a chance to gather the courage to say what she wanted to say. He hoped what he was about to tell her was intriguing enough to postpone whatever it was she wanted to tell him so she would say it in a text message, to allow him time to answer it tactfully.

Still looking out the window, he said, "To be honest, I don't belong down there. But admitting that to myself is like admitting that I'm not a man. A few weeks ago, two ICE Agents in Douglas were doing a sting to catch some guys who were smuggling coke through the Port of Entry. It must have been ingenious, because even when smugglers get creative and put dope in the gas tanks or inside the tires, the Customs dogs at the Port still hit on it."

Felina asked, "So what happened?"

"These two ICE agents in an unmarked car tried to corner this smuggler's truck on the east side. But the smugglers slipped away, and during the chase the ICE driver lost control of the car and crashed and rolled over. The agent riding shotgun was hurt pretty bad. He broke his arm. The smugglers circled back and drove by, laughing. They were taunting the ICE agents, who were upside down in the wreck. Then the smugglers drove back across the border into Mexico through the Port. They're two local Mexican scumbags from Douglas."

Deflecting any uncomfortable inquiry that she might have been contemplating was working. Layne could tell by the way her eyes became wider that Felina was eagerly waiting to hear the rest. So, he continued.

"So, last week ICE got a tip that these guys were gonna be back in Douglas in a different car. I heard that two hard-looking white dudes from ICE came to the station in jeans and Pantera t-shirts, carrying nine-millimeter MP-5 submachine guns slung over their shoulders. Some of those ICE guys were Rangers and commandos in the military before they started working for ICE. They ordered the National Guard girls in the camera room to turn off the cameras on the east side; I guess they were driving an unmarked Dodge Charger. These two ICE agents evidently intercepted the smugglers over by the airport. The smugglers tried to get away and the agents chased them. When the agents caught up with these two guys, they sped up next to the left side of smuggler's car and the ICE agent riding in the passenger seat of the Charger unloaded a thirty-round magazine into the driver side door and window."

Felina's mouth dropped open, but Layne couldn't tell if she was fascinated or disgusted. The story was disturbing to him, being that he was immersed in the environment where it had taken place.

"The smuggler's car crashed into a light pole and the driver got out and tried to run, but he was shot through the stomach. The passenger was hit, too, and couldn't get out of the car to run. The ICE guys let the driver stagger about a hundred yards before he fell down, and one of the agents grabbed him and dragged him back by his hair. He almost bled out. The agents yanked the passenger out of the car and kicked the crap out of him, and I think he eventually died from the gunshot wound and the beating. I heard the driver is in the ICU. No one is supposed to talk about it. I heard about it from Carlos. Management never mentioned it in Muster."

Layne considered telling her about the agent who was run over in San Ysidro and explaining that the attack was partially motivated by retribution, but he decided not to cause her any more worry than he already had.

Felina looked concerned, like she was still visualizing the story. "Promise me you'll be careful down there, Layne. If you feel like you might get hurt, just back away, even if you think it won't be good for your reputation," she said.

* * * *

LAYNE DELAYED LEAVING UNTIL the last minute on Monday, then sped through Tucson to make it to the highway where he could make up time. He had suffered through the weekend blues until there was no time left. As he ran red lights making his way toward I-10, he worried that if he ran into any kind of delay, he might not make it to Muster on time. He wondered why he was incapable of being kind to himself so he could arrive to work hangover-free with time to spare, to eliminate the stress in his shoulders. He felt as low as he could feel while still being able to function—like he hadn't seen the sun in several days. He felt starved, but not hungry. He was unrested and paranoid. The drive that was putting distance between him and Felina was when a drink would help the most. It hadn't been feasible all day. His abdomen ached like an ulcer was flaring; he wasn't rested enough to go to work, but he had no choice. When he was sick from drinking it seemed like the symptoms would never subside. He couldn't see a future for himself. He feared that Felina was figuring him out and growing tired of his irregular moods; that she was shopping for someone else.

He recalled Felina walking him to his car and the last hug with her just before he got into his car to leave. He had almost cried, and he knew she had seen the desperation on his face. He couldn't help looking weak in front of her. She had begun stroking his back when he wouldn't let go of the embrace. It was the sincerest and needed hug he had ever had. But she seemed out of reach, even while she was in his arms, as everything that gave him comfort slipped away to grey. He wanted to stand guard over her; he had no choice but to trust her. He didn't sense that she would do anything to damage their relationship, but he knew that because of her looks she was probably hit on at least once a day. The fear that she would find someone with more money that she liked better was constant.

He noticed his hands shaking as he switched his grip on the steering wheel. As he weaved from lane to lane to hurry past cars, he told himself, *next weekend I'll taper off better—if I can make it there.* To go back to the trench was difficult even when he was feeling well. *Who knew what he would be into in three hours,* he thought as he shifted gears onto the I-10 ramp at high RPM. There was not much traffic; the lucky ones weren't going anywhere, and the rest were already where they were going.

If only they knew how lucky they were, punching in for their mundane jobs on Mondays, he muttered.

LAYNE SAT DAZED IN his post-Academy desk chair, idly reading the dry erase board from the previous Friday. The trainees had just finished attending Muster, and Layne's FTU group was told to gather in the post-Academy classroom. He was weary and sluggish from the repetition of his life as he was currently living it. As a matter of course, the previous week had been predictably drawn-out while he yearned for the clock hands to accelerate toward Friday. Once it finally arrived, he wished the hands would revolve in slow motion. But the weekend was over in a flash. Two days and two nights with Felina simply weren't enough to sustain an endurable mood come Monday. Before the past weekend began, he had committed himself to cutting his alcohol intake in half. But once the liquor entered his bloodstream, such limitations seemed ridiculous until the following morning. He was incapable of enforcing his own rules after the first beer.

Once again, he suspected that Felina was on the verge of confronting him about his incessant partying. He had seen the look in her eyes when he arrived with his customary twelve-pack. But perhaps he was overanalyzing her behavior.

He took three ibuprofen tablets and returned the bottle to his backpack as he tried to get comfortable in his desk. His stomach was boiling and sweat began to bead on his forehead. The other trainees seemed to notice his jumpiness, or perhaps his perceptions were wrong again. His sleep cycle was completely malfunctioned now. It was 2:30 p.m.; in making the transition from midnight shift to swing shift, he had left himself with little sleep yet again. The proper timing to sleep for Swings was to go to bed not later than 3:00 a.m. and wake up around 11:00 a.m. He had passed out around 2:00 a.m. but awoke two hours later and ended up staying awake watching the ceiling fan spin while Felina laid with her back to him in a coma-like sleep. When she finally awakened, he wanted to spend as long as possible with her. And so, he had failed to carve out time to drive across the border and find a *farmácia* that sold Percodan or Tafil without a prescription. Even at the expense of insufficient rest, he couldn't bear to set aside an hour that could be spent with Felina.

A new agent was standing at the head of the class. But, before the classroom had settled enough for the new agent to speak, Training Supervisor Escribano came in to address the class for him. Without hearing the agent mutter a word, Layne already sensed he was fundamentally different than the FTOs like Cruz that had guided them through Phases One and Two, or Tipton, who had led them on that eventful MIT adventure with the woman and young son that upset Layne so. This guy was white, looked to be about twenty-eight years old, and appeared to be someone who was a proud weightlifter who never worked out his legs. With paperwork in hand, Escribano stood next to the agent and introduced him. "This is Agent Ashlock. He'll be your FTO for the rest of Phase Three. He knows the law, and he's got two years of experience, so pay attention to what he tells you."

Ashlock initially had his arms crossed then put them behind his back during Escribano's introduction. He was fair-haired and above average height. He appeared to be confident but currently out of place. He looked to be unaccustomed to being in front of a group, in the same manner that Tipton had. His discomfort was magnified by being the focus of the room while Escribano lauded him.

When Escribano finished the introduction, he leaned over and said something into Ashlock's ear then announced, "I need to talk to Mr. Ashlock in the hallway for a moment." Layne took notice, and alarm triggered the tingling in his extremities and brought him back in time to the Academy with unpleasant déjà vu. The paranoia was exacerbated by the routine of his Monday discomfiture.

"This is his first time as an FTO," Runyon said, once the door closed behind them. "I heard some agents talking crap about him before Muster the other day." Specifically, he'd overheard agents referring to him as a snitch when they were talking amongst themselves.

Layne was in no condition to find gossip entertaining. Everything would be depressing until at least Wednesday, especially negativity. The feeling made even simple tasks seem impossible.

The training classes arriving at the stations across the United States border with Mexico were so numerous that management was becoming desperate to assign enough Field Training Officers to instruct them. Four trainees per FTO was already a stretch; it meant that individual trainees riding in the back of the vehicle sometimes missed vital information. Now management was forced to ask for volunteers to instruct the trainees. Often that meant agents who were deficient in education skills. The main incentive to volunteer was to receive weekends off and gain favor with management. But agents who volunteered were looked upon by their agent peers as boot-lickers, which compounded the difficulty of finding FTOs to manage the flood of incoming classes.

Despite the stigma, Ashlock had volunteered to help; he was already unpopular with the rest of the agents anyway. Layne had heard his name called out during attendance but didn't know what he looked like until now. Ashlock customarily sat in one of the folding chairs against the back wall during Muster. Agents around him either moved or looked like they wanted to move when he sat down.

Runyon continued reporting his observations but stopped in his tracks and pretended to have been studying Spanish the moment Ashlock opened the door to come back into the classroom. Layne's fear of reprimand passed—it was obvious that Escribano wanted only to pass along information of an administrative nature.

Ashlock stood in front of the dry erase board with his hands in his armpits, contemplating what to say. He was having difficulty looking at any one trainee for more than a few words.

"Were you in the military, sir?" Runyon asked in an attempt to relieve the tension.

"No," Ashlock said. Before Runyon could ask another question, Ashlock made an impatient gesture with a facial expression and continued, "I don't really care for classroom work. I like to be chasing traffic as much as possible."

"I'm with you on that," Runyon said.

"Which one of you wants to drive?" Ashlock asked. He was itching to get out of the station. Everyone looked at one another except Layne, who looked at his desktop and held his breath.

"I'll drive," Runyon volunteered.

Ashlock read Runyon's name tag and said, "Okay, Runyon, go get the keys from the equipment counter and I'll meet you guys in the parking lot in ten minutes." He turned and headed out the door. Layne took a deep breath and began gathering his gear. He could barely conceive making it to midnight but had no choice but to press on.

* * * *

THE SUN MELTED OVER the horizon as the hostile partisan faces of downtown Douglas glared at the Suburban passing by. Ashlock sat, arms crossed, in the passenger seat while Layne and the others quietly occupied the seats in the rear. They were still cautiously probing Ashlock to determine the subjects of conversation he would allow. In absence of their usual prattle, the trainees were paying close attention to the developing radio traffic that signaled the beginning of Swings. The aliens south of the fence often took advantage of an arriving unit's vulnerability during shift change to make their moves.

"866, Delta-127," came over the radio in a static burst.

"Go ahead, Delta-127," the law enforcement communications assistant's female voice replied.

"Ten-eight," Delta-127 reported.

One by one the agents were checking in for the swing shift. Ashlock reached over and raised the volume on the FM radio. "I hate this song," he said as he found one of the few radio stations available. The trainees looked at each other, visibly forming opinions about their new FTO. "But, there's only two radio stations; I just have to suffer."

"Do you have satellite radio when you're in the field, sir?" Carlos asked.

"No, that's for agents who wanna sit on their butts all day," Ashlock responded cynically. No one had anything to say in response, and they drove on.

Layne didn't like the songs on the radio, either. He wiped the sweat from his forehead when the others were distracted by an attractive Mexican female who ignored their gawking as she moved along the sidewalk. Layne glanced at her then looked away. The girl's figure only reminded him that guys were probably doing the same thing when they encountered Felina, and there was nothing he could do about it.

Layne did his best to make himself inconspicuous in the rearmost bench seat on the left side. Despite his attempts to focus, Layne was helplessly dreaming of cradling Felina's warm body in her bed. But dream is all he could do. He found himself once again suffering through Monday, mentally and physically, counting the hours until she was in his arms. He wasn't certain how much longer he could maintain this cycle.

As the sun finished its descent, the remnants of its light turned the clouds a heavenly salmon pink against a baby blue desert sky. Layne didn't find any comfort in the delightful horizon; he could feel the activity on the south side of the fence percolating. He shielded his eyes from the fading sunburst and longed for it to stay. When it was gone, he knew the restlessness behind the fence would boil over. He couldn't be in worse condition for his first night on Swings, and he prayed for non-activity that he knew was unlikely at best.

As if he had been reading Layne's mind, Ashlock said, "You'll find out on Swings that once it gets dark, the aliens start coming over like ants."

No one responded. They had already been warned about the intense alien activity on Swings. As soon as the glow of dusk succumbed to darkness, it was a race for the line agents on the east side to chase after the aliens and catch them before they could make it into the houses just north of the fence. For an agent on Swings assigned to 5-Bravo, it was a nightlong search of dimly lit streets, alleys, and backyards. Agents and flashlight beams were ordinary nighttime sights for residents who lived east of Main Street.

Layne pressed deep into his abdomen and rubbed his liver while he remembered bits and pieces of the weekend. He had been more careful not to reveal any indications of his surreptitious liquor consumption to Felina. Regardless, she seemed suspicious. If he could make it to Friday, he planned on not drinking at all, so he could show her he was capable.

"Drive to Juliet and find a spot a couple blocks north of line," Ashlock ordered Runyon. "We'll serve as a floating MIT."

The trainees looked out their windows at the locals arriving to park in their carports after work. Most of the houses were fortified with bars on the windows.

"They should just bulldoze this whole dump; it's tough to work Juliet during Swings," Ashlock commented with disgust. He wasn't withholding his personal opinions the way other FTOs did. Layne realized his choice of location was intended to make driving as difficult for Runyon as possible. There were a lot of agents at the station who preferred Swings because there was constant action; remaining busy made the shift go by faster. Nearly every night the LECA and National Guard girls were keeping track of a dozen groups on the west side while the agents struggled to round them up. Crack agents like Darmody patrolled the highway for the load vehicles that cruised back and forth, waiting to gather the groups that had breached the line agents and MITs.

"Can we go over to 4-Charlie tonight?" Runyon blurted, interrupting the silence.

Ashlock stared at him from the passenger seat for an extended period before answering, "No, I'm still deciding where I want to go. We'll stay in

5-Bravo 'til I make my decision."

The trainees returned to tentative silence.

"Did your other FTOs let you choose where you wanted to go?" Ashlock asked.

"Some of them," Runyon said.

"Which ones?" Ashlock asked.

Runyon paused, concentrating on the road, but Ashlock was looking at him, waiting for an answer.

"Cruz," Runyon said, reluctantly. He had kept his eyes on the road, but he felt required to glance at Ashlock for a moment when he answered. Ashlock shook his head slightly, obviously suppressing the urge to criticize Cruz.

"What else did they let you do?" Ashlock wanted to know.

"Tipton let us study for a few hours here and there," Runyon said. "We have our Spanish Oral Board coming up. My Spanish is terrible."

Runyon looked over to see how Ashlock would receive his admission.

"You guys are gonna have to study on your own time. I want to be working traffic as long as I'm doing this," Ashlock said, looking over his shoulder at Layne and the others in the back seat to make his point. Runyon concentrated on driving while Preussen and Carlos looked at Layne with discontent.

Layne was trying to remain optimistic. He considered that Ashlock was trying to project the image that was expected of an FTO. He told himself to give Ashlock the benefit of the doubt. Maybe he would be more like Cruz once he settled in.

"Where are you from?" Layne asked him.

Ashlock looked at him through the rearview mirror and took a few seconds to respond.

"New Jersey."

"What city?"

"Jersey City." Ashlock was already visibly losing patience after only a few questions.

"Have you ever been to Atlantic City?" Layne asked. He had always wanted to go there, and it was the first place he thought of when someone mentioned New Jersey.

"It's a dump," Ashlock snorted, and Layne sank back into his seat.

Ashlock redirected to the business at hand. "They said in Muster there was something like seventeen Golf on Days today. Those guys on Days are a bunch of slugs. They show up and don't do anything; that's why they want that shift. There should be no more than one or two getaways per shift."

The trainees had heard Tipton complain about other agents, but it was understood that the information was not to be disseminated. Ashlock didn't seem to care if anyone leaked his views into the sewing circle of gossip that Douglas Station had turned out to be.

"676 for eight," the LECA said over the radio.

Ashlock grabbed the radio microphone from the dashboard, turning down the FM. "866, Delta-267, ten-four," he replied, then turned to the trainees. "Let's go get that. I wanna get into something."

"That sensor is over in 6-Alpha isn't it?" Runyon said.

"You don't know?" Ashlock said condescendingly while he stared at Runyon.

Runyon reached for his shirt pocket, leaving one hand on the wheel.

"I'll look it up," Carlos offered.

Ashlock didn't offer assistance, visibly annoyed while he waited for someone to tell Runyon the location of the sensor.

Carlos unfolded his sensor list and quickly located the correlating number with his pointer finger, "It's in 5-Charlie."

"Hurry," Ashlock said as he leaned sideways to take his radio from his hip and switch it to the west side channel. "That sensor is usually good when it hits."

Runyon turned left quickly then stepped on the gas to cross Main Street.

Ashlock sighed. "That was a stop sign."

"Did I do something wrong, sir?" Runyon was losing patience; he could reach a point where he would rebel.

Ashlock said, "Just stepping on the brake doesn't constitute a stop. And are you planning on using your turn signal tonight?"

Runyon was gnashing his teeth.

"I don't know what your other FTOs have been letting you get away with, but while I'm in the vehicle you need to obey the traffic laws unless we have the emergency lights on."

Runyon gripped the steering wheel tightly and said nothing while his face changed color. Ashlock's mouth opened to continue his critique when the radio squawked, "Delta-267, 866."

Ashlock looked puzzled. He unhooked the microphone, "866, Delta-267."

"Delta-9 needs you to go to 5-Alpha. There's a group on the diagonal road that they need help with," the LECA relayed.

"Ten-four." Ashlock hooked the radio microphone back in its cradle on the dash while muttering to himself, "I just ten-four'd that sensor. I guess they're just gonna let it go?" He sulked for a moment then looked at Runyon and said, "Go ahead and drive over to the diagonal road."

Runyon drove past Mexican men and women with Border Crossing Cards who were leaving Walmart. They were laden with plastic shopping bags, en route to the walkway back into Mexico before the danger of night set in on the streets. Runyon performed a U-turn in the Walmart parking lot and backtracked over Main Street, careful to obey traffic signs and posted speed limits.

The remnants of the sun's light had faded to black when they arrived where the group had been apprehended among the sage and mesquite area of 5-Alpha. Through the headlights, the trainees could see the aliens sitting in rows, while several agents leaned on the hood of one of their Kilos and conversed. Two Kilos remained idling with their headlights on to keep light on the prisoners.

Preussen had barely said a thing all evening, but he was the first to notice and announce, "They haven't even started searching them yet. It looks like they haven't even searched their *mochilas.*"

Runyon parked and left the engine running while Ashlock exited the Suburban and ordered the trainees to remain in their seats as he shut the door. They watched with interest as Ashlock approached the indolent agents. He appeared as though he was consciously trying to project an image of authority by his artificial gait. The agents turned their backs to him as he approached. Runyon rolled down the front windows and turned off the engine so he could hear what was being said.

"I wanna see 'em trash this clown," Runyon said.

"Me, too; what a butthead," Preussen added.

Layne was too ill to care about what was occurring.

"What do we got here?" the trainees could hear Ashlock say.

One of the agents looked over his shoulder to answer while the others continued talking.

"We need your trainees to search this group and get them written-up, pronto," he said. "We haven't called transport yet. Tell them to use Delta-190 and Delta-214 for the apprehending agents. The batteries are dead on my GPS, so just use this spot for the coordinates. We caught 'em about three-hundred yards toward the line." The agent then turned around and resumed his conversation.

Ashlock pretended not to interpret the snub and turned around to walk back to the Suburban. He knew the trainees were watching. He opened the passenger side door and said, "Okay, let's get this group searched and written-up. I'll call for transport. Use this spot for the coordinates."

Runyon started the engine again and left the headlights on. The trainees opened the doors, climbed sluggishly out of the vehicle and stretched their legs. Layne followed suit and noticed his hands quivering as he put on his search gloves. They each picked a row of seated aliens and commenced with the monotonous routine. The agents paid them no mind and continued exchanging comical stories.

Layne's core throbbed a poisonous pain and his fingertips were partially numb, but his stomach was too raw and empty to vomit. He had become seasoned with this part of the job by Phase Three; he only hoped that searching this one group would be the only task required of them this evening. He would feel better tomorrow, he told himself.

One by one, Layne and his companions performed a cursory search of the aliens' backpacks, followed by the required pat-downs. They periodically glanced in Ashlock's direction to determine if he was noticing their lackluster application of search procedure. He was standing awkwardly by himself near the Suburban, away from the other agents, trying to appear comfortable as an outcast. Several of the agents lit up cigarettes, and as they stuffed their lighters in their pockets, they peeked over their shoulders at Ashlock and burst out in laughter. Ashlock pretended not to notice and repeatedly checked his watch while averting his eyes from them.

As the trainees continued down the rows of the captured to prepare them for transport, Layne noticed that Ashlock had walked even farther away from the other agents. Ashlock unclipped his microphone from his passant, and the trainees heard him over their own radios say, "866, Delta-267."

"Go ahead," the LECA replied.

"Can you arrange transport for nineteen in approximately ten mikes?"

The LECA gave a positive response, and Ashlock returned his microphone to his shoulder and took his cell phone out of his rear pocket. He peered at it to kill time.

"These gloves are a pain to wear while you're searching," Preussen complained.

"Would you rather go bareback?" Carlos said as he sat an alien down.

The comments made Layne wonder how much English the aliens understood.

"You'll be glad you're wearing them if you find a needle in one of their pockets," Runyon said. "These gloves are sweet. They're Kevlar." The alien he was searching looked straight ahead at nothing while he was being patted down. He flinched a bit when Runyon touched his crotch. "This must be a form of hazing," Runyon whispered, nodding his head toward the agents entertaining one another.

"Yeah, like a Phase Three tradition or something?" Carlos suggested in a hushed voice.

"They're just screwing with Ashlock; it's got nothing to do with us," Runyon said.

"It's pretty nasty. They should at least help us a little bit. There's nineteen in this freaking group," Preussen said.

Carlos was standing over two female aliens who looked drained mentally and physically from their journey. What do we do with these two chicks? Melanie isn't here and I don't wanna search 'em."

"Hold on; let me see what they look like," Preussen said, standing over the girls to look them over. He made a gagging gesticulation and said, "Never mind, just leave them."

Runyon and Carlos laughed.

"If they have switchblades in their snatches the guys in processing will just have to swashbuckle with them," Carlos said, prompting more laughter.

"Hey, this guy's got some pills in his front pocket," Runyon called out, holding up a bubble pack of Mexican pharmaceuticals.

Layne took notice.

"Anything good?" Preussen asked.

"*Acetaminofeno,*" Runyon struggled to read from the packet.

"That's Tylenol," Carlos translated.

Runyon stuffed the packet back into to alien's front pocket and sat him down.

Carlos looked at Ashlock to make sure he was still out of hearing range. "I'm draggin' today. If you find any that say *anfetamina* let me know."

They laughed and Layne joined them briefly, as best he could.

The apprehending agents flicked their cigarettes and dispersed to climb into their Kilos and drive off. One of them drove by Ashlock slowly and smiled at him before he sped off.

"So, they're just gonna leave us with this group?" Preussen said.

"Looks like it," Carlos said.

Runyon finished searching one of the last aliens in his row and said, "These people aren't carrying anything. I'm tired of searching these Tonks for lint. I bet when they run their prints, they've all been caught at least fifteen times, though. Darmody doesn't search anybody. He just throws their *mochilas* behind the seat of the transport van and herds them in."

Runyon had taken a special interest in Darmody and Ortiz because of their stature, which in turn piqued Layne's interest, especially in the mysterious Darmody. They had both been in the Service over ten years. The latest buzz was that Darmody and Ortiz had surprised and apprehended another group of fifty or more aliens while trying to net a load vehicle. Without searching the group, the pair had herded the aliens into processing to the annoyance of the supervisor in the Fishbowl whose unit had processing duty that pay period.

"I bet the people in processing appreciate fifty unsearched aliens with fifteen minutes to go in their shift," Carlos said sarcastically.

"C'mon Bro, like an alien's gonna take someone hostage and force their way out of the station with a Swiss Army knife," Runyon quipped.

Carlos shrugged; it was never a good idea to engage Runyon in an argument. He was too well-informed and too well-versed in procedure.

The trainees finished searching and writing-up the group. With the other agents gone, Ashlock approached the trainees. "Standby for transport. They should be here any minute."

But twenty more minutes passed. With the transport van nowhere in sight, the trainees set eyes on Ashlock since he had taken responsibility for radioing the request. He finally gave in to the tension and removed his microphone from his passant, barking: "866, Delta-267."

"Go ahead," the LECA said.

"Can I get an ETA on transport for the bodies in 5-Alpha?"

"Standby Delta-267, transport is en route," The LECA replied. But the National Guard girls could be heard laughing in the background before she cut the transmission.

11

LAYNE'S HEART POUNDED AS his hands gripped the steering wheel of his Honda. He was disoriented to time when he checked the clock on the dashboard, which read 7:09 p.m. He was fairly sure it was Saturday night. The feeling reminded him of instances when he had awakened somewhere and been uncertain if the twilight was dusk or dawn.

He found himself driving through Tucson on his way out of town with several oncoming cars on Ina Road flashing their lights. His heart skipped a beat, as he realized he had been driving for ten minutes with no headlights. He quickly switched them on and flashed a glance at his rearview mirror. He exhaled, his six o'clock clear of cops. He wasn't thinking straight. He cursed himself—he had lost his head again.

He had recently noticed that Felina had hidden all the liquor from her modest bar. He didn't think she would notice the bottles' levels diminishing, since she rarely drank. But she must have, so he had acted as though he hadn't noticed that the bottles were gone. But he had planned ahead for this weekend and brought additional shooter bottles in case he needed them.

The weekend hadn't gone as planned. He had anticipated smiling and laughing the way people did in television commercials; drinking cabernet from burgundy wine glasses and embracing Felina in the moonlight. Such moments didn't seem enjoyable without a buzz. And to his delight, the evening had begun in the manner in which he had hoped. But everything had unraveled. He had tried to make it too pleasurable and had lost control. Felina had found him unconscious after he fell into the bathtub with his pants and boxer shorts around his ankles. Evidently, he had lost his balance while trying to pee, and had tripped backwards into the tub and hit his head. Felina heard the crash and came to see if he was okay, and found him, along with an empty shooter bottle lying on the floor. He had been allowing her to think he was only drinking beer.

The loop of the dreadful incident from an hour before began to replay itself over and over in his memory without intermission while he tried to stabilize his driving. It began with him opening his eyes to see Felina standing above him covering her mouth with tears in her eyes. She was sobbing before he awoke and it confined her voice to a whimper until, finally, she shrieked loud enough to penetrate his stupor.

"Layne, wake up, Layne!" The way she cried his name was a sound he knew he would be incapable of forgetting.

It was all she could say before the sobbing resumed, and she walked into the living room to collapse on the couch with her face in a pillow. He clambered out of the bathtub and pulled-up his underwear and pants to follow her.

"I must have hit my head," Layne tried to explain. But she was weeping like a mother who had lost a child, and he surrendered any hope that he could convince her that it was an accident that didn't involve his weakness.

"Felina, I'm sorry. I fell and hit my head. I'm sorry!" He was fighting back tears himself because of the dismay he had caused her. "I'm okay," he pleaded with her.

"No, you're not," she said between breaths. "You've done stuff like this before that you probably don't even remember."

The vodka dampened the realization of what was occurring, but regardless, he didn't want to her to go into detail about events that had escaped his memory. He didn't want to conflict with her in this circumstance, either. It was a moment of abject horror that would become another remorseful memory he wished he could go back and change with time travel.

"Remember when you had bruises on your arms, and you couldn't figure out how you got them?" Felina had asked between breaths.

Layne vaguely remembered, but he nodded his head as if the memory was clear. It was one of hundreds of fragmentary flashbacks that mysteriously had no semblance when the weekend was approaching. Like clockwork, on Fridays, he felt so exuberant and judicious that the recurrence of such an incident seemed impossible.

"That night you were just like you were tonight. Out of it. It scares me," she said as the loop continued.

Layne looked at his feet, unable to face her. "I'm sorry."

Felina gathered herself a bit. "I don't want apologies," she struggled to say. "Please, I'll make some coffee. But as soon as you sober up, you need to go."

He tried to reach for her hand, but she pulled it away. He could see the tears return as she rolled back onto her stomach.

He dressed without saying anything, grabbed his backpack and left.

"Layne! Don't drive like that," Felina said as he opened the door to leave. But he ignored her.

Once in the car, he didn't blame her for kicking him out. He needed to change, but he feared that it was too late. He feared he had run too far to get home. He could feel Felina pulling away, like all the women he had ever attempted a relationship with. The possibility that he may never see her again was something he knew would be unbearable come morning.

Layne returned to concentrating on the steering wheel and the road. He would go home and get a good eight hours of sleep, then call her in the morning to make it right. He didn't have any Valium. Anything justified taking one when he had them. *I should have saved them for emergencies like this,* he told himself; he would have paid a hundred dollars for one as he merged onto I-10 East.

Layne knew he wouldn't be able to sleep without help once he made it home. He decided he would stop at a Circle-K in Sierra Vista and pick up a pint, strictly to calm down and be able to sleep. Then, starting tomorrow, he was done, he promised himself. If trouble at work wasn't sufficient motivation, the thought of losing Felina would be—or nothing would. He was tired of the sleepwalking incidents; it wasn't worth it. He would rather be bored and safe, he told himself, than enjoy himself and be regretful.

Suddenly, he became aware that his headlights were almost straddling the yellow line on the shoulder of the interstate. He jerked the steering wheel to return to his lane but overcorrected and nearly lost control. He realized he was still completely drunk. The adrenaline the incident had brought on had sobered him initially, but it had subsided a bit and now his blood alcohol level skewed his center of gravity. He told himself to stay at the speed limit and keep his hands at ten and two. To pull over and park somewhere to sleep would be just as perilous; police often did security checks on people they found sleeping in cars at gas stations. It was best to stay on the highway and pray he didn't run into a sobriety checkpoint.

Layne tried to reassure himself that everything was recoverable. But he felt an emotional cramp every time the audio clip of Felina's voice waking him up repeated. The feeling made him panic. He knew he had done something so shameful that he wouldn't be able to smile in the morning when the booze wore off. He needed to know tonight if everything was alright before he could sleep. He forced himself to speed dial Felina's number on speakerphone, hoping to activate her voicemail so he could speak his mind without interruption.

On the third ring, though, he heard, "Hello." Felina's voice indicated that she had calmed down, but her nose was still stuffy.

He had to switch gears faster than he preferred. "Hey Babe, I'm so sorry. I'm done drinking." She didn't hang up, so he continued. "I promise; I'm done drinking around you."

He could hear her breathing and she finally said, "Don't make promises you can't keep."

"I can't believe I did that." His words escaped from him like he was out of breath.

Felina let them hang in the air for a while, and Layne could hear her breathing still.

"After you got here you drank three beers. Then you went in my bedroom and didn't come out. I was waiting on the couch for you. I paused the movie." There was another long pause before she continued, "How many shots did you do in the bathroom?"

"Let's just forget about it, okay?" Layne pleaded. "I don't want to think about that ever again."

But she wasn't going to let it go. "I took your car to the store the other day, and you had empty mini bottles of Absolut in the console."

He responded almost instantly. "Those are from a long time ago. It doesn't matter because I'm not doing it anymore. I'm so sorry, Babe; this is it. I'm not drinking anymore. How about I call you tomorrow? I'm driving."

He could almost hear Felina thinking. "Okay," she finally replied, and there was another pause, as if she were considering saying something more. But instead, she hung up, and he didn't know what to think. The past seven years had been one pathetic apology after another; he had run out of things to say. He told himself to cease his introspection, but his mind skipped a beat and descended into the fear that he might sink to such a depth that he would be lost within himself for days, even weeks.

When he was honest with himself, he was surprised she had put up with him this long. He didn't understand why she liked him; he didn't even like himself. He considered that perhaps she had overlooked his behavior at times because she was waiting to see if he could overcome field training. With the money he would be making as a career agent, she might put up with anything.

By the time he was halfway between Tucson and Benson he was still trying to reason the incident away. Felina, Fabiola, the other women—none were able to understand. When the warm glow of the liquor kicked in, he was the person he wanted to be while the buzz lasted. He viewed the world rationally and accepted his place in it. He stopped trying to make sense of everything. He was unbound, and the pragmatic person within was set free. He wasn't so mad at his enemies; they weren't so bad. He stopped cursing the people who had wronged him and stopped complaining about incidents that were unfair and weren't his fault. He didn't dwell on the mistakes he had made in the past. He became serene and felt comfortable in his own skin; he didn't feel useless. His self-concept was clear, and his ego was justified. When he was drunk, he was grateful for what he had. He ceased obsessing over financial security and guarantees about the future. He lived in the moment. He could handle situations with people that he otherwise would avoid until forced to.

The highway stripes in the headlights continued to stream by as he caught himself dozing off. The two-hour drive back to Cochise County was difficult enough without the agony of intense regret gnawing on him. There was a chance that this reckoning would set him straight, but an equal chance that his resolve would fade once again. He feared that in five or six days he might conclude that he had exaggerated the incident and blown it out of proportion.

With time, he could convince himself that he was a hypochondriac.

MUSTER BROKE AND THE agents lethargically rose from their chairs to begin the shift while the FOS gathered his papers from the lectern. It was evident which agents were assigned to processing by the displeasure they wore on their faces. Layne's group waited in line for their turn to exit the Muster Room and follow Ashlock down the hallway to the Fishbowl. For the trainees, an entire swing shift to practice processing inside the station was a welcomed change after weeks of flashlights, cactus stickers, and aliens' armpit odor. When the alien floodgates opened at dusk, Layne and his companions would be comfortably sitting behind a computer with the aliens already caught. His FTU group was to spend every other shift on the processing floor for a pay period until they were competent in operating the computer applications that managed aliens in custody.

Physically, Layne felt better than normal for a Monday, having been frightened away from nursing his hangover all day Sunday. His thoughts raced nevertheless, and physically he was simply less jittery than normal. The lingering shame he felt combined with dreadful speculation about Felina's plans for their relationship left him preoccupied. He told himself repeatedly to be thankful for the memory of the bathtub incident that still made him wince. He hoped it would serve as a reason to resist that he could always reference when a beer seemed harmless. The fear of losing her was an effective motivator. He had spoken with her over the phone three times since the incident and he sensed that her disappointment was gradually receding as time passed. Still, he feared that it indicated she was giving up on the relationship.

Maintaining an abstinent mindset had proved to be the great struggle of his life. It was easy to quit directly after a disaster, when the fear was strong. It was when the repercussions settled and life became tolerable again that the battle of reason resumed within. Experience made him aware that with enough time he would block out or rationalize even the most appalling of improprieties. He would convince himself that the idea to quit had been made under duress. A sense of well-being and an opportunity for celebration was all it would take. Then, his resolution to achieve only a buzz would seem perfectly sensible. It was the gradual deterioration of logic that was disturbing, like losing sanity. After seven years of this ailing cycle it was grim to realize there was only one hope remaining, the hope that Felina would make the difference this time.

He couldn't wait to show her that he had quit. He thought she would be giddy to see that he was honoring the promise he had made. But just like a song stuck in his head, concern that she was planning to leave him played constantly in the background.

The agents assigned to processing gathered in the confines of the Fishbowl for a briefing before they entered the processing floor. The first agents to arrive sat in rolling chairs and the rest formed a semicircle, standing around a dry erase board. Layne and his group stood near the back. Together with the supervisor in charge of the unit assigned to processing, Supervisory Agent Calavera, the agents surveyed the list of prisoners in isolation cells who needed to be handed over to the contractor by the end of the shift. The whiteboard listed the Hispanic surnames of the prisoners in red and blue marker in columns headed by the cells where they were being detained. Each isolation cell listed the name of its occupant in black marker.

When Supervisor Calavera finished briefing his unit, he said aloud, "Alright, let's get to work. I wanna see every one of those bodies outta here with an hour to spare." Agents and trainees first removed their duty weapons from their holsters and secured them in the lock boxes next to the thick steel door that led down three steps onto the processing floor.

Layne pinned his lockbox key to his shirt pocket and turned his radio knob to the processing radio frequency as he followed the herd. The agent in front of him didn't hold the door for him and it closed before he could grab the handle. His keycard was stowed in his right shirt pocket and he touched his chest to the sensor, which beeped; the electronic lock clicked and freed the heavy steel door. He was the last to step through and the door closed with a clang behind him, sealing in the aroma of latex and stinky blue jeans. The atmosphere inside processing overcame him; it was like a hospital during a night shift. The buzzing of overhead lights amid the quiet created a dismal atmosphere for the plodding workers and detainees.

His stride changed as he passed by the first cell full of prisoners. He was not yet accustomed to being in the presence of people being held against their will, irrespective of whether they deserved it or not. It was different than the field. Here, the aliens were like animals in cages. They wanted out, regardless of having no refuge to seek, nor the means to seek it. The filthy worn-out men and women behind Plexiglas stared blankly at the agents, never making eye contact, instead looking through them. He made a conscious effort to shield himself from the sight of their transparent misery. Their hopelessness seemed contagious.

Layne made his way around the semicircular processing floor past an agent spitting a stream of tobacco juice into a Mountain Dew bottle while he logged-in at a computer station. Layne located Carlos, Runyon, and Preussen; their eyes met his, but they had nothing to say to one another. They were gathering at a computer station with Ashlock, who spoke and behaved as if the trainees were a burden and a chore. "As you can see, the processing floor is divided by gender," he began. "Males on the right, women on the left." He pointed to the corridor in the center that divided the male and female sections of the floor. "That hallway leads to the holding room where the drugs are stored, then out to the sally port. As you know, the six ISO cells are in that hallway. We can lock down either men or women in them."

Layne glanced down the corridor to which Ashlock was referring. The ISO cells were preferable to deal with because the agents didn't have to look at the prisoners inside unless they chose to. At eye level, there was a small observation window where the lone prisoner inside could be viewed. When an alien's fingerprints were referenced against the FBI Database and produced a "hit," the alien was removed from the general population. The prisoner was then placed into the tiny cell while the agent who entered the fingerprints completed the necessary paperwork for the prisoner to be prosecuted. The ISO cells were also reserved for United States citizens who had been caught smuggling humans or narcotics.

After Ashlock finished with his explanation of the processing operation he directed his attention back to the computer monitor and fingerprinting apparatus on the counter. He motioned with his head and long neck to a holding area to the far right near the Fishbowl entrance. "That cell over there is for OTMs, which stands for Other Than Mexican." The term brought a smile from the trainees, even Carlos. The prisoners from countries other than Mexico had to be separated from the rest of the prisoners because they had to be transported by bus to Phoenix. From Sky Harbor Airport they were flown back to their country of origin. The prisoners from Mexico were simply led through a gate near the Port of Entry back onto Mexican soil. Once back, they were free to choose a different location along the fence to cross over for another try as soon as the opportunity presented itself.

On the whiteboard, under the category of OTMs, were separate cells for "Guats," and "El Sals." Of the prisoners from Guatemala and El Salvador, the Salvadorans were the most common. Aliens from Honduras and Brazil arrived in processing but not nearly as often.

Like a junior high bully, a white agent moved inconsiderately between the trainees and claimed the computer station that Ashlock was preparing to log in to. Ashlock pretended to not be offended and redirected the trainees to an unoccupied station where he entered his password with a sullen frown. "ENFORCE is the program that stores and cross-references fingerprints with the FBI Database. It's the primary application we use in processing," Ashlock explained. He took a write-up sheet from the stack that had just been delivered by a transport driver.

Every hour or so the transport driver delivered another group of aliens from the field, guiding a column of female and a column of male prisoners into the "unprocessed" cell of each side. The aliens were forced to decide whether to sit on the concrete benches or stand and look through the Plexiglas at the agents working to get rid of them. There was no goal being pursued; everyone was detached and dispassionate.

Ashlock waved a write-up sheet in the air and gave Layne a dirty look as he spoke. "You're only going to deal with the basics tonight. I'm gonna put you guys with an agent so you can observe. Help them out if they ask you to, and maybe we can try and put a dent in RFD-1, the male unprocessed cell."

The pace at which the agents worked was driven by the speed at which the capacity of the cells was being reached. In addition to the growing population inside the cells, motivation for the agents to hurry was provided by the unit's supervisor. He knocked on the Fishbowl window periodically to prod an agent who was slacking.

Ashlock directed the trainees to find an agent to pair up with and observe. They dispersed and began tentatively searching the semicircular processing floor for a station with an agent who looked approachable. Runyon strayed in the same direction as Layne and introduced himself to the first agent he saw logging in to a computer. Layne moved on indecisively to the next station where he saw an agent with a broad back maneuvering the mouse to prepare the windows on his monitor. He approached the agent tentatively and said, "How's it going?"

The agent turned to face him and Layne stutter-stepped, realizing he had inadvertently selected Agent Darmody to be his processing mentor. Layne did his best to hide his dismay as he extended his hand to shake. Darmody grinned sincerely and reached out to reciprocate the greeting. His meaty hand felt calloused and dutiful, and he responded graciously, "Pretty good. You need someone to partner with?"

"Yeah, we're supposed to watch an agent fingerprint aliens."

"Alright, pull up a seat," Darmody said. "My name's Adam, by the way."

"I'm Layne; nice to meet you."

Layne hesitated to place an extra tall chair next to Darmody. He considered making up an excuse to choose another agent, but nothing seemed plausible without time to think. He recalled the multiple warnings he had received about interacting with Darmody in the field. But he considered that they were in processing, and the potential harm lay in becoming involved with Darmody's tendency to meet with trouble while outdoors.

Layne pretended to be unaware of his notoriety or who he was. "I thought I saw you on Days when my group was with FTO Schnabel?"

"Normally I am, but I'm building a deck at my house and I requested to be on Swings for a pay period so that I have enough daylight."

Layne wondered how he had failed to notice him in Muster. Darmody sat by himself in the briefing room. Ortiz was his only known friend. The agents gave him a wide berth so as to have nothing to do with him, especially in the field, where working alongside him might lead to a firefight or vehicle rollover. Every day, he took detailed notes like Muster was a college class even though he had been in ten years. None of the other agents even took out their memorandum notebooks. They just sat with their arms folded and stretched out, legs crossed like briefing was an ethnic sensitivity workshop.

Layne rotated his eyeballs to view Darmody's profile. He was around forty years old, and weighed about 240 pounds with a slight potbelly, but the rest of his body was dense. He had a thick neck and large forearms—he looked like a cement truck driver. He wore short-sleeved uniform tops year-round, and his duty belt carried the bare minimum of equipment. Other agents carried a multitude of tactical equipment—double-action switchblades, extra pistol magazines, even vests that carried four thirty-round M4 magazines.

Layne looked over his shoulder to try and determine if anyone had taken notice of his choice of tutors.

Supervisors and their units were routinely angry with Darmody when he was working the field. Every other day he would herd three-dozen aliens into processing like an elementary school teacher leading a field trip, and the agents working the computers were forced to fingerprint them all. The supervisors in the Fishbowl kicked chairs and threw things, being responsible for the added workload of handling fifty additional bodies halfway through the shift.

Darmody took a drink from a Pepsi bottle and screwed the cap back on as he entered the data of a write-up sheet into the fields on his monitor with concentration. Layne had left his house hastily and had forgotten to pack his evening sack lunch. He had been eyeing the packages of peanut butter crackers and juice boxes arranged on the back counter since he passed by them when the shift began. He walked over and selected a box of grape juice and grabbed a packet of orange-colored crackers and returned to look over Darmody's shoulder while he chewed. Darmody was still referencing his green memorandum notebook for his list of passwords.

Darmody heard him chewing and turned to grin, "Don't eat too many of those. They're for the aliens. I don't care, but someone will hassle you for it."

Before Layne could apologize, Ashlock was standing behind him. "What are you doing?"

"I didn't know we couldn't eat the crackers. He told me; I know now," Layne said.

Ashlock started to say something, then shook his head and walked back to his computer station with an exaggerated sigh. Darmody continued typing and didn't react to the confrontation. He glanced to make sure Ashlock was gone then looked over his shoulder and said, "You forgot to bring your lunch?"

"Yeah."

"You can have half my sandwich. My wife made it and I'm not that hungry."

Layne hesitated for a moment, then with surprise said, "Thank you."

Darmody reached for a brown paper bag and unrolled the top. He removed a Ziplock sandwich bag and handed it to Layne. The bag contained half a sandwich that appeared to have been prepared by a woman. It was thick and complete with lettuce and tomato, and it crunched with freshness and the taste of mayonnaise when he bit into it.

Darmody spoke while he transferred the last of the data from a write-up to the computer, "Yeah, we give the snacks to the aliens while they're waiting, but only if they tell you they're hungry."

"Okay," Layne said as he chewed.

Darmody moved the mouse pointer to click finish and rose from his tall chair and reached for the box of latex gloves. "Go ahead and get a pair of latex gloves from that box over there on the countertop. You aren't allergic to latex, are you?"

"I don't think so," Layne said as he finished the last bite of the sandwich.

"If your hands break out in a rash, make sure you tell a supervisor right away." Darmody's rubberized hand separated a write-up sheet from his stack and peered at it as he began to move. "Follow me," he said while still reading.

Layne followed him to the cell labeled RED-1, which was filled with disoriented men who had just been brought in from the field. Darmody drew his radio from his hip and spoke into it. "Open RED-1, please."

Instantly, the door buzzed and clicked, and Darmody swung it open using his right foot and shoulder as a doorstop.

"Camarena," he shouted into the cell while he double-checked the write-up.

A round-faced, short Hispanic youth stood up from the concrete bench, and Darmody pointed him toward his computer station. Layne took notice of the boy's surname—it was the same as Felina's. He looked as if he had just been roused from a park bench by the police. All the aliens seemed to be wearing navy blue sweatshirts covered in plant fibers and stickers. The boy stopped midway to the computer station, uncertain of where to walk. Darmody directed him with a tap on the shoulder.

The boy didn't notice Layne staring at him. The names that agents scribbled into the designated fields of the write-up sheet tended to be recurrent. Layne was fond of Felina's last name because he enjoyed the combination of sounds required to pronounce it, but moreover because of its uniqueness. It made him wonder if the boy was possibly a distant cousin. Darmody remained standing and clicked continue until a screen appeared that was waiting for a fingerprint. He watched the screen for guidance as he used his two gloved hands to sequentially scan the boy's fingertips. Darmody's behavior was the antithesis of what Layne had expected it to be. Other agents like Ashlock were exulting in front of the aliens, but Darmody treated them respectfully. He gently selected the correct finger the screen requested. "I'll do the first couple so you can see, then I'll have you do some," he said.

Darmody finalized the fingerprinting with the pinky of the boy's right. Then he aimed the webcam at the boy with one hand and clicked the mouse at the right moment with the other to photograph him. "Okay, now that his information is entered, we put him in BLUE-1. That's for the aliens who've been processed."

Layne nodded with study.

"As long as no arrest warrants come back, the transport driver will take him and the rest of the guys in BLUE-1 to the fence and deport 'em, or whatever you wanna call it."

"Catch and release?" Layne said.

"Exactly," Darmody smiled.

Layne followed Darmody and the alien to the BLUE-1 cell, and Darmody radioed the Fishbowl to open the door. When the door clicked, he pulled it open and guided the boy into the cell with twenty other men waiting to be freed. Then he quickly returned to his station to begin another write-up. Layne had to hustle to keep up with him. Darmody was always in a hurry, watching his feet while he moved briskly through the hallway. He said excuse me when he needed to get by, and Layne was surprised by his courtesy and willingness to explain. Most of the other agents would scarcely look at a trainee or say hello to one.

Darmody scanned over the information of the next alien then turned to ask Layne, "You wanna try one?"

"Sure," Layne said, with uncertainty. Darmody handed him the sheet and approached the holding cell. He radioed the cell door operator, the door buzzed, and he pulled it open.

"Duarte," he read aloud. An older man in a denim jacket and blue jeans stood up after a pause. He looked like someone who had been in processing before. Layne realized that the man must have forgotten the name he claimed when he was caught. He escorted the man to the computer station where Darmody demonstrated fingerprinting the man's right hand. The man remained expressionless as he was utilized for demonstration.

"Go ahead. Do the left," Darmody said.

Layne avoided eye contact with the man as he maneuvered to press each of his fingertips to the laser glass. He watched the image of the print arrive on the computer monitor. When the image of the fingerprint was clear and within the boundaries of the computer screen, he clicked the left mouse button, and the print was either accepted or rejected.

Darmody allowed him to fingerprint the next detainee and handle ENFORCE without assistance. The task temporarily kept his mind off the problem with Felina, and he felt a new bounce in his step as he repeated the procedure with a half dozen write-up sheets from the stack. By the third one, Darmody had left him entirely on his own and had begun processing a separate stack of write-up sheets on the next computer station over.

The processing transport driver returned just as the BLUE-1 cell reached capacity. He escorted the group of processed aliens through the corridor towards the sally port. There they would be loaded in a van and driven to the Port of Entry and shoved back into Mexico without even a slap on the wrist to dissuade them. Agents often scanned an alien's fingerprints and learned they had previously been caught thirty times. Layne glanced over his computer monitor at the aliens being herded back out the way they had come in. The boy who shared Felina's name was last in line. Layne wondered again if there was any relation while he observed the boy and considered asking her. It caused him to think of another question, and he asked Darmody: "Have you ever had anyone request asylum?"

"Once or twice. It's usually people from communist countries. But they never get it." Darmody picked up another write-up and suggested Layne do the same, nodding toward Calavera in the Fishbowl. Supervisors didn't care if one of their agents didn't catch a single alien in a year. They were only concerned with how efficient an agent was with prosecution files because of the time constraints supervisors were under pressure to meet.

Suddenly, Layne's attention was diverted to an agent struggling to control a young female alien in her early twenties, who was physically resisting placement in an ISO cell.

"What's going on?" Layne asked Darmody.

"Her prints came back with warrants," Darmody said.

"What a commotion," Layne remarked. "It distracted the whole room."

Agents kept an eye on the disturbance while they continued working. In a voice louder than usual the agent radioed, "Open ISO-3 please." The ISO cell door buzzed and opened a crack behind the agent and the petulant young woman. The agent grabbed her by the arm. He opened the door to put her in, but she dug in her heels and was grasping his shirt sleeves and he was unable to force her into the cell.

Someone radioed for help. "Fishbowl, we need Supervisor Calavera's assistance on the floor please."

Calavera burst onto the processing floor and quick-stepped toward the corridor in long strides. In Spanish he pointed and ordered the woman to get in the cell while he was still approaching the situation. She was hysterical now, flailing at the agent and crying, then sitting down in protest. Layne could see the veins bulge in Calavera's neck. He grabbed her by an arm and pulled her to her feet. Then he began forcing her into the cell. The woman clutched his shirt, her cries became screams.

"Get in there, now!" he shouted in English as he kicked her the rest of the way into the cell, using the sole of his boot, and shut the door quickly behind her. He straightened his uniform top and complained to everyone who was watching. "Why do I have to deal with this crap?"

Everyone focused on their keyboards and typed. Calavera began walking angrily back toward the Fishbowl. Layne had been watching with his eyes, not moving his head. He remained busy on the computer. As Calavera walked by to return to his nest in the Fishbowl he said to Layne, "Did you like that, Sheppard?"

"I wasn't paying attention, sir," Layne replied.

"Atta boy," and he gave Layne a slap on the back of his shoulder on his way to the door. Layne glanced at Ashlock, who was a couple stations over. He glared at Layne. After a couple of seconds of eye contact, Ashlock rolled his eyes and returned to looking over Runyon's shoulder.

FELINA AND MARIANNE WAITED in line at the concession counter for popcorn and sodas before they entered the movie theater. They still had ten minutes before their movie started. In the line next to them were two Hispanic men in their early twenties that they could tell were hoping to get the girls' attention to initiate a conversation. Without speaking of their admirers, Marianne and Felina made an effort to ignore their ogling while they continued their conversation.

Marianne was more talkative than usual. Her mood had grown noticeably more cheerful since Ryan had returned home from the Academy several months prior. Felina was slightly jealous of her happiness. She wished Layne was stationed in Tucson so she could see him on a daily basis, too. Equally, she wished she could influence him to be as well-behaved as Ryan was.

"Is Ryan working tonight?" Felina asked as she glanced at Marianne's engagement ring, which she frequently flaunted.

"Yeah, he's working the swing shift this pay period," Marianne said enthusiastically.

"Oh, that's not bad. So, he'll be home around midnight?" Felina asked.

"I wish! He has to drive all the way back from Sasabe. He won't be home until about one thirty in the morning." Sasabe is a border hamlet about seventy miles southwest of Tucson.

"I've been wanting to see this movie since I saw the preview," Felina said. "I couldn't get Layne to see it with me; he always wants to go to Fourth Avenue to go to the bars."

Marianne looked at her ticket stub; it read, "Sisters of the Moon." She hadn't seen the preview, but she trusted that she would probably enjoy it if Felina had chosen it.

"Why didn't he want to see it with you?" Marianne asked as she checked her purse to make sure her wallet was still inside.

They moved up a place in line and Felina said, "He said it sounds like a chick flick."

Marianne laughed. "I can't get Ryan to go see anything with me either, unless it's a Jason Bourne movie."

Felina eyed the boxes of candy beneath the counter glass while she was ordering. But she looked away and instead restricted herself to a medium popcorn and medium Diet Coke. Marianne ordered the same before the clerk could ring up Felina's order separately.

"I'll pay," Marianne said. Felina protested, but Marianne grabbed her wrist and wouldn't allow her to take her wallet out of her purse.

As the usher tore their tickets, Felina fantasized about one day being able to go shopping all day, then going to a movie, and afterward going to dinner at any restaurant she wished. She wouldn't bother looking at the prices on the menu and would order whatever sounded delightful. She visualized the gold that the credit cards in her wallet would contain if she were a doctor.

The two of them found seats in the center of the theater; there were only nine or ten others waiting for the previews to start. The overhead lights were still shining down on the theater and there were only advertisements showing on the screen without any sound.

"So how is it going with Layne?" Marianne asked in a hushed voice as she selected one of the butteriest pieces of popcorn from her bag.

"It's going okay," Felina said while she put her purse under her seat.

"Just okay?" Marianne asked, with her brow furrowed.

"Yeah, he kind of misbehaved the other night," Felina said in a morose tone.

"Oh, no. What happened?" Marianne's tone was sympathetic.

"He just drank too much and passed out," Felina admitted.

"Oh," Marianne said. She sensed it would be invasive to ask for details at this moment.

"Yeah, but I think he's under a lot of pressure. He says training is really hard," Felina said as popcorn crunched in her closed mouth.

"Ryan says it's hard, too. It's because they keep switching their shifts, so they know what it's like to work at night," Marianne said.

"That's what Layne says is hard, too. He can't sleep when they switch him to Mids. He hates Mids the most." Felina was still deciding whether or not to share details about her issue with Layne.

"Maybe it'll get better after he's done with training," Marianne offered.

"I hope so, but I've noticed a pattern developing since I met him." Felina said.

"Are you thinking about breaking it off?"

Felina thought for a moment before she answered. "No. Whatever is wrong with him, I want to fix it. He said that he isn't going to drink around me anymore."

"Do you believe him?" Marianne asked.

"Yes, I think he'll try; he was really upset," Felina said.

Marianne didn't say any more, knowing that nothing she could say would persuade Felina to change anything in regard to a relationship with a guy. She sensed that Felina was beginning to have feelings of endearment towards him that would be difficult to interfere with. The lights in the theater dimmed and they could see the beginning of the film being projected and hear the sound crackling.

Marianne whispered in her ear, "Maybe you can get him to marry you. You know what that would mean."

Felina smiled and whispered back, "I've already thought about it."

Marianne smiled with excitement and whispered, "Seriously?"

Felina grinned and nodded.

"When are you going to tell him about everything?" Marianne asked, looking behind them to make sure they weren't bothering anyone with their conversation and that no one was listening.

"I don't know; when the time is right, I guess. It doesn't feel right just yet," Felina said thoughtfully.

"What do you think he'll do?" Marianne asked with interest.

"He likes me a lot; I can tell. I think he'd be surprised, but I'm not sure exactly how he would react. He might get mad." Felina thought about what she had stated. She had given the thought of telling him considerable consideration. But her initial suspicion about his habits had been confirmed, and the problem took precedence.

"If I tell you something, you've got to promise me you won't tell Ryan," Felina whispered to her.

"You know me, honey. I won't say anything," Marianne said.

Felina watched the transition from the end of one preview to another and took advantage of the noiseless interlude to quickly say, "I might as well tell you what happened. We were watching a movie, and he got up to go to the bathroom. A few minutes later I heard a crash, and I went to go see if he was okay. He had the door locked, but if you push hard on the door it'll open. I found him passed out in the bathtub and there was a shooter bottle on the floor."

"Oh, honey, so he was drinking hard liquor in the bathroom?" Marianne said with wide eyes.

"Yeah, vodka," Felina said reluctantly.

"You need to have a talk with him," Marianne said pointedly.

Filling her mouth with popcorn to let that comment sink in, Marianne then added: "Ryan said that everybody in their class knows he has a problem. I never mentioned it before because I didn't want to overstep my bounds."

"Oh, no! Poor guy," Felina said. Slightly embarrassed, she turned away from Marianne to pick at her popcorn. She assumed that people had already noticed, but the information still upset her. Layne hadn't shared much about the Academy except the curricular obstacles he had to overcome to graduate, especially in PT.

"Have you tried talking to him about it?" Marianne asked.

"Just a little bit during the incident," Felina said, as she sifted through her popcorn pensively.

Marianne paused while she thought carefully about how to continue the conversation. They had begun to lean over and talk in one another's ear to overcome the sound of the previews. Then she said, "I know it must be hard. But maybe you should talk to him about it without accusing him of anything, you know, so he doesn't feel like you're doing an intervention on him."

Felina nodded. "That's what I've decided to do. I just haven't had the guts to go through with it yet. I don't know if he'll deny it or how he'll react. He's already having a hard-enough time. I don't want to make it worse and ruin his weekend. He cherishes his weekends because he suffers so much during the week."

"I know it must be hard, sweetie," Marianne said sympathetically as the movie began.

"It is."

14

AS LAYNE SAT WATCHING the FOS step up to the podium to begin Muster, he looked behind him but didn't see Ashlock. He didn't think much of it. *Hopefully he's not here. Time will go by faster if he's not breathing down my neck,* Layne thought.

As the bathtub incident began to fade into the past, he was feeling more confident that his relationship with Felina would return to the way it had been. He could tell by the sentiment in her voice that she had forgiven him, even though she hadn't said so. Her changing attitude toward him was improving his outlook on things, and there was a skip in his step. Regardless, he remained adamant about his decision to quit drinking.

The FOS started Muster with attendance as Layne quickly checked his uniform for blemishes. He was wearing the same uniform top as the day before, but with clean pants. The pants he wore the night before had dirt around the ankle area from being in the field. He had re-ironed the shirt with a once over, using lots of steam, avoiding the pockets. He felt secure; he hadn't seen anyone scolded for a sloppy uniform since he left the Academy.

After Muster broke, the unit assigned to processing headed down the hallway to the Fishbowl for their daily briefing. Those assigned to the field hurried in the opposite direction through the hallway to get in line at the equipment checkout counter. Layne had been in the field the previous night but was back in processing this shift. While he stood waiting with arms crossed, Layne looked through the Fishbowl glass and saw Ashlock already on the processing floor, standing by a computer station. He seemed to be suppressing a grin when he made eye contact with Layne.

Supervisor Calavera arrived a few minutes late and clapped his hands together as he stepped through the door. Taking his first glance at the names on the dry erase board, he said, "What are we looking at tonight?" It was as if he were perusing a poker hand he had just been dealt. To make up time he quickly assigned the prosecution files in the isolation cells to his preferred agents and concluded the briefing with enthusiasm. The unit began to unlatch their pistol holsters at the lock boxes and line up to enter the processing floor.

Layne unlatched his pistol and waited his turn to claim a lockbox. He followed his FTU group through the steel door and down the steps as he pinned his lockbox key to the left pocket of his uniform top. He walked toward the center of the room, ignoring the aliens in his peripheral vision who were staring at him through the Plexiglas. When he made eye contact with Ashlock he knew instantly that something was wrong. Ashlock appeared anxious to see him. Before Layne reached a conversational distance, Ashlock burst out with, "Do you have something to tell me?"

Layne thought, *Yes, I have something to tell you. I wish that someday I will find out that you got your head blown off in the field.* But instead Layne responded with, "No, I have nothing to tell you." He considered that perhaps he had made a clerical error entering an alien's information into ENFORCE two nights before—the last time they had been in processing.

"Where's your notebook?" Ashlock asked, speaking down to him with a gratifying smile.

Layne stopped dead in his tracks. Frantically, he unbuttoned his shirt pocket. He realized in an instant that there was less bulk in his right shirt pocket than normal. He quickly patted his other pocket in hopes it was there, but it wasn't. "I must have left it at home," he said, desperate for a solution. He thought there was a chance he had left it on his nightstand with the receipts and junk from his pockets.

Ashlock smiled and held up a green pocket-sized memorandum notebook that he had been hiding behind his back. "An agent on Mids cut it in 6-Alpha last night. He turned it in to his Supe' and the Supe' turned it in to Escribano."

"I'm wearing the same top from yesterday," Layne said. "I usually leave all my stuff in the pockets. I didn't even know it was gone."

"Do you know what this means?" Ashlock wasn't smiling now, his glare dour.

Runyon, Preussen, and Carlos went to computer stations and pretended not to hear when they realized what was happening.

Layne felt hollow with distress. "I don't know how I could've lost it."

"We gotta go talk to Escribano," Ashlock said as he motioned with his pointer finger for Layne to follow him back through the steel door. They began to walk together while Layne looked at the floor, trying to remember when he had taken the notebook out of his pocket. His FTU group had spent the shift in the field the night before. But he couldn't recall ever taking the notebook out of his pocket the whole night—or being in 6-Alpha, for that matter. He only used the notebook for his computer logins and passwords; he rarely touched it in the field. It mostly contained scribblings and his useless notes from Muster. He only flipped through the airplane drawings and other doodles to find the page where he had recorded the logins. He really only referenced it when he was in the computer room checking his email, or to log in to ENFORCE in processing and the FBI Database.

When the two of them reached the door to Escribano's office Ashlock stopped him with a stiff-arm. "Wait out here. I'll tell you when we're ready for you." Then he turned the knob and opened the door enough to slip in sideways, closing it carefully behind him. Ashlock was giddy with anticipation. Despite his slim entry, the door had opened just enough for Layne to see Escribano sitting at his desk, facing the door. They had made eye contact, and Escribano communicated with his austere brow the trouble that Layne's folly had created. Escribano was at the end of his Day Shift—Layne surmised that he must have continued into overtime to deal with the predicament. The swelling magnitude of the situation left Layne's extremities numb from disbelief about what was occurring. He could only speculate about the degree of punishment that would be imposed for failing to secure sensitive information like his FBI Database password.

He began to pace as the possible repercussions snowballed in his mind. He realized he might as well not even call Felina again if he were fired. He couldn't conceive of her wanting him without his gold federal badge, working as a nobody somewhere for a meager paycheck. He would simply tell her he had sincerely adored every moment with her. He would explain that he wasn't certain he could carry on; that there was nothing left for him.

Escribano opened the manila folder on his desk and glanced to make sure the door was closed so Layne was unable to hear their conversation. Ashlock sat in a chair against the wall to the left of Escribano's desk. Ashlock attempted to conceal the excited satisfaction in his posture and leaned back after briefly being hunched over with all his fingertips touching one another in anticipation. He had been in Escribano's office earlier to touch base with him about Layne's situation. "What did he say when you asked him where it was?" Escribano asked, focusing with tired concentration on the pages within the file while he waited for the information.

"He said that he left it at home. Then I showed it to him, and he said he didn't know it was missing," Ashlock replied.

"Do you think he didn't know it was gone, or do you think he knew and was going to try to cover it up?" Escribano said.

"I don't think he was going to tell anybody when he realized it was missing," Ashlock answered.

"Did he try to log in to ENFORCE and realize it was missing?" Escribano asked as he closed the folder and looked at Ashlock.

"No, sir, I asked him if it was gone before I had him log in to a computer," Ashlock said.

"You should've waited for him to try to log in to ENFORCE." Escribano said. "Then we would know for sure if he was going to lie about it. All we can do is speculate now.

"How's he doing in processing?"

"He's real slow, sir. He seems to not be all there," Ashlock said.

"So, he hasn't made any improvements since you started last week?"

"He was worse at the start. He shakes sometimes and I can't figure out if he's on some kind of medication or what's wrong with him. He doesn't pay attention; it's like he's on another planet."

Escribano opened the folder again and flipped through the pages to a quiz that Layne had failed in October. It was the only classroom test that Layne had failed.

Escribano couldn't figure Sheppard out. There was something wrong, but he wasn't sure what it was. He still hadn't learned all of the AOR, which seemed like one of the simpler aspects of the job. But he wasn't dumb. He couldn't be; white guys who learned to speak Spanish as fluently as Sheppard were usually exceptionally smart.

Escribano ran his finger down a page of the performance evaluations while Ashlock sat quietly.

"He has a ninety-eight percent in post-Academy Spanish, and Cunningham said his accent is exceptional—unheard of. I heard he was one of those guys who studied in Mexico and lived with a Mexican family. He has a bachelor's degree."

Ashlock dismissed the information with a scowl.

"And they say he's unbelievable with a pistol. He's been near a perfect score every time he's 'qualled.' He's better than the Firearms Instructors," Escribano thought out loud.

Ashlock's face continued to sour and he started to speak, but Escribano cut him off. "But you say he's terrible in the field, that he doesn't know where he's going or what he's doing." Escribano looked for confirmation from Ashlock, who nodded 'yes' several times in response.

Escribano pushed himself back from the desk. He joined his hands behind his head and closed his eyes to make some sense of the situation. He was getting the feeling that the other FTOs weren't reporting Layne's deficiencies in order to avoid controversy. But he knew that Ashlock wasn't going to let anybody pass FTU that he didn't approve of—certainly not during his first stint as an FTO, and maybe never. Ashlock had no concept of how to make things run smoothly for an administrator, Escribano thought. The inability to overlook negligible deficiencies caused more headaches than necessary.

There was a reason why everyone hated Ashlock. He believed there was a genuine war raging on illegal immigration, and that he was the only agent in the station qualified to help fight it. Escribano considered Ashlock a fool and a weasel, but he had dropped this problem in Escribano's lap. If Ashlock had let it go, he could've, too. But now there was paperwork because Ashlock submitted a memo about it without being instructed to do so. Escribano was concerned about a promotion he had applied for. If he was awarded the job at the Academy and Layne got into trouble or killed somebody in the field, the FBI would want to know why he had allowed Layne to pass FTU with this memo in his file.

He opened his eyes and brought himself forward to his desk. "I can't figure out what's wrong with him."

Ashlock responded, "Me neither. Sometimes he's real nervous and jumpy, and sometimes he's relaxed and staring off into space. Agents in my unit have seen him frisk a woman inappropriately . . ." Ashlock seemed eager to continue, but Escribano held his hand up again to show that what he had stated was sufficient. Layne was too astute academically to wash him out at the Spanish Oral Board. Escribano would just have to figure out a way to get rid of him. Perhaps he could talk him into quitting.

"Go ahead and bring him in," Escribano said to Ashlock.

Ashlock disguised his satisfaction with an expression of diligence as he stood up to open the door and instructed Layne to come into the office and sit down.

Layne had given up pacing and leaned against the cinder block wall facing the office. He sensed that the door was about to open. He couldn't hear the sound of anyone talking inside any longer.

Ashlock cracked the door open and told Layne to come in. Layne pushed the door open slowly and peeked in before stepping all the way through the doorway. Escribano was sitting at his desk and didn't look anxious to see him.

Layne sat in the chair in front of Escribano's desk as Ashlock sat back down at an adjacent chair with his back against the wall. Layne refused to look at him. Instead, he focused on Escribano's braces and lips while he talked.

"Mr. Ashlock has written a memo that will go into your file, about your incompetence regarding the lost notebook," Escribano began. "You understand that you're only an intern and that you're under a microscope every day until your probation is up two years after your EOD date back in May."

Layne sat forward in his chair to plead his case. "Sir, I didn't even know that my notebook was missing until I came into processing and he told me." Layne couldn't utter Ashlock's name. "I wore the same uniform top as I did yesterday, and I didn't check my pockets before I left home today."

Escribano considered the explanation before speaking; his intuition told him that Layne was telling the truth. "Mr. Ashlock said you lied to him and said nothing was missing."

"He asked me if I had anything to tell him. I didn't know what he meant," Layne defended. "I didn't know the notebook was missing until he showed it to me."

Ashlock sat idly, shaking his head slightly.

"Well," Escribano said, his braces gleaming, "There's a discrepancy then." He turned to Layne's accuser. "Mr. Ashlock, you will document that in another memo." Ashlock stiffened and sat upright, ready to speak on his own behalf, but once more Escribano quieted him with a gesture. To Layne he said, "He claims you said you left the notebook at home and it wasn't missing. I need you to write a memo also, Mr. Sheppard."

Layne felt himself caught in a trap, and as if by survival reflex, further explanation poured out. "If I knew I lost it, I would've had to tell somebody to reset my passwords. I can't remember all of them. If I knew it was missing, I would've told someone as soon as I realized it. I would've had to;

I wouldn't have been able to log in. We have about nine different logins."

Escribano finished browsing through Layne's folder. "So, let me get this straight. Agent Ashlock thinks you knew you lost it and tried to lie to cover it up, until you realized it was found by another agent."

Layne responded without hesitation. "I only had a few seconds to contemplate what happened. If I had known I lost it, I would've said so right away. How else would I explain why I needed someone to look up my logins and some of the passwords?" Layne couldn't help himself from looking over at Ashlock, who disgusted him. He felt anger and frustration swelling. Layne fantasized about torturing him with power tools. He had to take a deep breath to refocus on Escribano.

Escribano tapped his pencil on the file and leaned forward, his elbows on the desk. "As a member of the union you have the right to union representation because management is requiring you to submit a memo. Agent Ortiz is waiting outside if you want to speak with him."

"I do," he said. Escribano gestured permission for him to get up, and Layne nodded at him as he rose to leave. As Layne turned to exit, Ashlock said, "Make sure you use spellcheck."

Layne kept walking without acknowledging the order. For all of the stories he'd heard about Ortiz, and the exposure he'd had when Ortiz drove them from Tucson and gave them a tour of Douglas Station before they went to the Academy, he was finding out only now that Ortiz was the head union steward.

When Layne opened the office door, Ortiz was already standing in the hallway, waiting. "I know generally what happened. I just wanna know what you said to Ashlock," he said. Ortiz looked excited, and in a hurry to enter the office.

Layne explained what had happened, sticking to the exact wording of the conversation as best he could recall it.

"Okay, go ahead and wait out here for me," Ortiz said just before he stormed into the office. He didn't close the door behind him.

Ortiz walked directly to Ashlock in his seat and pointed down at him to put his finger in his face. "What is this crap?"

Layne was taken aback by the ferocity of the attack. Ashlock looked up at Ortiz with stupefied horror. Escribano stared straight ahead, awkwardly caught in the middle. Layne repositioned himself in the hallway so as not to appear to be eavesdropping; he had no idea that union reps routinely dealt with management in this way.

Ashlock panicked, his mouth falling open a little. He muttered, "He lost his notebook with all his passwords in it."

"You weasel. He lost it in the field. What makes you think he was going to try to cover it up?" Ortiz was yelling, his voice echoing throughout the station hallways.

"He told me he left it at home," Ashlock pleaded, stunned by how quickly the situation had come over him.

"Because he didn't know it was gone," Ortiz yelled. "People lose stuff all the time and don't figure it out until they need it."

"He can't even take me to the four corners when I ask him to," Ashlock whined.

"So, what! He's a trainee. He took you to the vicinity," Ortiz yelled. Layne could only see Ortiz's broad back now. His arms were bowed like he was preparing to punch.

"Well, he doesn't know what he's doing," Ashlock shot back.

Ortiz was stabbing his finger in Ashlock's chest now. Layne could see Ashlock's neck turning red like the onset of a rash; he was on the verge of crying.

Ortiz took a step back as Ashlock cowered lower. "I've been hearing about your petty crap for two years now. All you do is talk trash and screw with people like Sheppard, you sorry malcontent. If we were on the streets, someone would knock you on your sorry butt."

Ashlock shrank into his chair, raising his left arm as if to defend himself against an imminent blow.

"What you got him doing now?" Ortiz yelled.

"I told him to write a memo."

"He ain't writing no stinkin' memo, you weasel."

"Okay," Ashlock cried, unable to say more without choking up. Ortiz whirled around and stormed out of the room, putting his hand in the small of Layne's back as he passed, directing him down the hallway.

When they were out of earshot, Ortiz grinned and faced Layne. He seemed to have been waiting for an opportunity to destroy Ashlock.

"I chewed him out. Listen, this isn't a big deal. You should've said right away that you lost your notebook. People have lost them before. All that happens is they reset your passwords. Even if it got into the wrong hands, someone would have to get into the building and get onto one of the computers to do anything anyway."

Layne pleaded, "I did. I only had a few seconds to figure out what I thought happened. I wasn't trying to hide anything."

"I know. You just got unlucky getting that pansy for an FTO," Ortiz said.

Layne felt a wave of relief that perhaps he was not in as much trouble as he feared.

"Don't worry about it," Ortiz said. "Just write in a memo exactly what you told me but let me look at it before you submit it to management." He patted Layne on the back. "If anything else happens, come and get me."

Layne went directly to the computer room and began working on the memo. He had only begun typing the header when Ashlock walked in. His face was still flushed; he was visibly humiliated. He had to take a moment to gain his composure before he spoke. His voice had almost become a whisper.

"Don't worry about the memo right now," he said. "You can go to the training room and study for the Oral Board. You're going back to Mids and repeating Phase Three. You're getting a new FTO tomorrow."

With that, Ashlock turned and left the room.

LAYNE SAT WITH HIS hands folded and elbows resting on one of the two front-most tables in the Muster Room. He sat stiffly upright and his knee bounced while he examined the details of the G-426 Daily Assignment Log for the overnight shift. He found his name listed alongside BPA Launius, another agent he had heard stories about but had never interacted with. He didn't turn around to see who had arrived as the agents began to fill the room behind him. He felt as if all eyes were upon him. He suspected that everyone in the room knew about the incident with Ashlock and why it had transpired. He was in limbo, not appearing to blend in anymore.

Carlos, Greg, and Melanie were all on track to be assigned to a line unit; they hadn't upset the flow of things. They would most likely have no problem overcoming the peril of the Spanish Oral Board Exam. Carlos and Greg were safe because they were sound academically in Spanish, and Melanie's gender, he was certain, assured that she, too, would graduate from Field Training without a hitch. Runyon was the only other trainee at the station from Class 590 that had cause for concern. The subjectivity of the exam was intended to allow management to discriminate regarding the personnel they would be dealing with during their tenure.

For Layne to get back on track, he would have to right a wrong and appear to fit in again. He was determined to ride out his sentence and successfully repeat Phase Three. He told himself that it simply would be like being held back a grade. He was somewhat confident that Ortiz had repaired the road to his objective and made it navigable again.

It was his first time being one-on-one with another agent. Because Layne was being made to repeat Phase Three, Escribano had no choice but to put him alone with another agent who was not an FTO because of the shortage in training personnel. Layne would have to endure Phase Three in the manner that Phase Four was to be conducted—by himself.

When Muster broke, Layne looked around the room for his new FTO as everyone rose. He knew who Launius was from Runyon's admiration of him. He had pointed Launius out to Layne on several occasions. Launius was from Michigan, as was Darmody. For some reason, all of the charismatic white agents seemed to come from Michigan. Launius had a reputation for being a tough guy with a mercurial temper and a hatred of aliens. Layne scanned the room and spotted him waiting patiently in line for his turn to squeeze out the door. Launius was slender and hard, in his mid-thirties. He had been a paratrooper and was a combat veteran of several military conflicts, including Iraq, according to Runyon. He was next in line to exit the room and was looking over the shoulder of the agent in front of him. He didn't appear to be looking for Layne.

Layne approached him from the side and said, "Hey! I guess I'm with you tonight."

"You *think* you are," Launius said promptly, then faced forward again.

Confounded, Layne didn't know how to respond. He wandered to the back of the line with his head low as Launius and the rest of the herd poured out.

The last of the agents slung their M4s over their shoulders and pushed the horizontal bar on the door to leave the station while Layne watched. He lingered in the hallway, unsure of what to do. For lack of a better idea, he decided to head to the computer lab to surf the Internet until morning. If Escribano asked him what he had done all night, he would tell him that Launius wouldn't allow him to come along. But just as he logged into his email, he heard a voice from the doorway behind him.

He turned around; it was Launius.

"Sheppard?" Launius asked curtly, but with a forgiving smile.

"Yes, sir."

"I talked to my supervisor. I guess you *are* riding with me."

Layne stood up, pushed in his chair, and slung his backpack full of gear over his shoulder to follow Launius through the hallways on their way to the parking lot. Layne had to hustle to keep up with him; Launius was moving fast and wasn't toting any gear. Once in the parking lot, Launius located the parking spot where the Kilo he had been assigned was parked. He disregarded his seatbelt, and Layne followed suit as he climbed in to see Launius was already turning the key in the ignition.

With his arm between his legs, Launius fought impatiently to adjust the seat to his leg length as he whipped around to the personal vehicle section of the parking lot. He put the Kilo in park and left his door open with the engine running as he got out. He reached into his pocket for his personal key ring as he walked to an older model Honda and removed a Border Patrol duffel bag from the passenger side. He threw the bag into the rear seats of the Kilo and hopped in, speeding off before his door was completely shut. The confusion in the Muster Room had caused them to be late getting to the field.

Layne wondered how much Launius had heard about him. Judging by the initial shun, Layne suspected he had heard something negative and perhaps sided with Ashlock in the feud. But as Layne continued to observe him, Launius appeared instead to be in the process of forming an unbiased opinion. His uniform looked like he had never once ironed it; there was no trace of a crease behind or through the center of the Customs patch on his right shoulder. And it looked like he wore a hat so as not to have to comb his sandy hair. When facing him, Layne noticed that the bill on his hat wasn't rounded uniformly and sat crooked on his head like a left-handed pitcher. He had rugged good looks, a narrow jaw, and narrow features.

Launius reached behind himself to retrieve a satellite radio from his duffel bag while neglecting his path through the parking lot. Once he arranged the device on the dash, he chose a preprogrammed Metallica station that began blasting the moment he found it. The music was piercing as he drove by the vast fleet of white and green vehicles with red and blue light bars. A Field Operations Supervisor just back from Swings had just parked in his personal space and was exiting his Kilo as Launius approached at high speed. The FOS failed to look and see if anyone was coming and stepped directly into their path as he was returning to the station. He glanced at the oncoming vehicle, and Launius stepped on the brake to come to a complete stop in order to allow the superior to stroll leisurely in front of them without hesitation.

"Walk slower, you fat slug," Launius said as he waited for the agent to make way. The FOS appeared to perceive the message intuitively and watched his feet as he stepped up on the sidewalk. Once he was out of the way, the FOS turned to watch as Launius peeled out of the parking lot to the theme of "For Whom the Bell Tolls."

Once they were on the highway heading toward the line, the lights of the city twinkled in the distance, briefly reminding Layne of the beginning of a night with Felina in Tucson. But the fierce music clashed with recollections he enjoyed of watching her tilt her head to one side to remove her earrings while she looked at herself in the mirror.

"Escribano wants me to take you to cut sign out east, but I don't feel like it tonight," Launius said aloud in the middle of a guitar solo.

"Where are we going?" Layne had to raise his voice to ask.

"We'll be another MIT in 5-Alpha."

Layne looked straight ahead and nodded with despair—5-Alpha was the epicenter of alien traffic within the city. It was a hornet's nest at night—located on the eastern most outskirts of the residential area where every apprehension was a foot race. Launius reclined in his seat, guiding the steering wheel with one arm straight. The dispatch radio was overpowered by the heavy metal as the lights of the city grew imminently closer. Launius didn't seem to be paying attention to the radio activity, but Layne couldn't ignore it.

"Bodies coming over at the Yellow S," a National Guard woman warned.

"Two coming over at the Wooden Cross."

"Another one going into the junkyard," a second camera operator blurted.

The cameras switched to infrared at night. In 5-Alpha during Swings and Mids the agents at static posts witnessed bodies coming over the fence in plain sight. The aliens ran full speed across a 100-yard dirt field to reach hiding places within the first residences on the American side of the border. The 5-Alpha field reminded Layne of a high school football field on Friday night. Gas-powered generators that pumped electricity into giant spotlights ran from dusk to dawn, illuminating the Border Fence like a preordained crime scene.

It was 12:23 a.m. as they turned off of Main Street to enter the menace of the East Side darkness. The dimly lit residential streets were ominously vacant—despite all of the radio activity while they were still on the highway. The aliens had simply taken advantage of another shift change. Attempts to get by the line agents at the front seemed to come in coordinated waves; transport was kept busy in patterns. Launius guided the Kilo past defunct vehicles with flat tires and corrupted youths delinquently heading inside for the night. The molded, ranch-style stucco houses looked abandoned, with dirt-and-weed front yards contained by property boundaries made of waste-high brick walls. Layne glanced at the green cursor on the radio transmitter waiting to blurt as Launius turned the music down to make his approach. It felt like Halloween under the faint light of the dying streetlamps and absolute quiet in the air beneath the stars. Only the faraway sounds of a train and a barking dog were detectable.

Launius slowed as he prepared to put the vehicle in a covert location facing the Border Fence. He suddenly became overcome with concentration—precisely putting the Kilo in the most advantageous ambuscade position. He killed the headlights prematurely for stealth and leaned forward with his chin over the wheel. His eyes became meticulous as he rotated the wheel to bump over the sidewalk curb and drive carelessly through someone's front yard as he made his way. He weaved between two houses and entered a hidden alley with only a few inches of clearance for the side view mirrors. He crept methodically, like loading the spring to a trap. "I know a good spot to lay-in for these sons of bi—," he said with virulence as he looked through the windshield.

The brakes gently squeaked to a halt at the southernmost end of the alley just to the left of a dumpster, and the dreaded field was suddenly completely beyond them. Launius forced the bar on the steering column to park and the engine relaxed into idle. The Border Fence seemed to breathe as it loomed in the array of generator lights. Their position gave them a complete view of the field and fence from a location malevolently hidden in the shadows.

"See that generator?" Launius pointed to one of the machines twenty-five yards to the south, and Layne gave it his attention. It vibrated with a lawnmower noise that could be heard inside the cab of the Kilo as it emitted visible heat that tried to mix with the cold of the surrounding late December night air.

"They're gonna be referencing that when they call it out over the radio from the camera room. The Tonks will be coming right past us to get a ride to Pirtleville, so they can hide with those turncoats."

Layne nodded to show that he understood.

"They're gonna be coming over right there," Launius said as he pointed to a spot on the fence. He grabbed the microphone from the dash and called in, "Delta-101, ten-eight."

"Ten-four," a woman's voice responded, followed by a bleep.

Layne observed without comment as Launius returned the microphone to its cradle. The smell of gasoline from the generator penetrated the cab through the heater vents, enhancing the sense of lawlessness in the expanse in front of them. He sensed his pulse in his neck as it plateaued at an elevated rate. He cleared his mind of any hope that the night would be uneventful. The aliens who crossed through 5-Alpha in the middle of the night were swift and aggressive, which Launius seemed to enjoy like a sport. Layne's hands gripped one another. The aliens who preferred to cross through this zone wore sleeve and neck tattoos. They didn't fall passively into enemy hands like the family groups that crossed on the desert fringes of the city.

After fifteen minutes of silent waiting, Launius twisted his torso to reach into his duffel bag and retrieve an energy drink. He cracked the tab on the can and puckered his lips to slurp the foam from the rim. Layne looked at a camera tower and thought of the camera room. He knew they would most likely spend much of the time waiting, and it felt awkward to sit next to each other and stare at the fence without saying anything to one another. He hesitated for a moment then said the first thing he could think of. "Have you ever worked the cameras?"

Launius looked at him with a look that was neither glad nor annoyed that Layne had spoken. "A couple times. It's so boring. It's torture; you don't wanna do it unless you have no choice."

Layne said, "Yeah, it looks boring staring at those monitors all night."

Launius turned back toward the fence and took a pull off his energy drink. "It's supposed to be just the National Guard chicks in there. Most of the guys you see in there wearing regular clothes are either injured or they've had their guns taken for getting in trouble."

"What kind of trouble?" Layne asked.

"It's probably good you asked. If you get charged with domestic violence for slappin' your wife around, they take your gun away. Even if you didn't do it, they take your gun until you get convicted or acquitted. They take it if you get a DUI, too; most of those guys got busted driving drunk. You gotta be careful drinking, even in Sierra Vista. I won't even drink a beer in Douglas. The cops write down our license plate numbers and lay-in for us outside of bars."

"So I've heard," Layne said. "Crap."

"There's a guy in there right now that was working on the fence crew extending the Border Fence in Nogales. Everyone wants that detail 'cause there's barely anyone supervising you. People just screw around the whole time and never pound a nail all day. Plus, they get like a forty dollar per diem on top of night differential pay. Anyway, this guy was crossing over into Mexico during their lunch hour to bang some Mexican chick every other day."

"On the clock? Are you kidding me?" Layne said.

Launius grinned and slightly shook his head in condemnation. "He was leaving at lunchtime and parking at businesses near the Nogales Port of Entry. He was leaving his gun and badge in the glove compartment of his truck then walking through the Port to go see this chick. Then he'd come back through with his passport like he was a regular dude."

"What was he telling the other guys on the crew?" Layne said.

"He was tellin' 'em he liked the *tacos al pastor* on the south side. People do go down there for lunch just to get cheap food. But I wouldn't have the balls to do it during a shift. Crossing the border on the clock is automatic termination. It's one of the few ways a career agent can get launched, immediately."

"That guy's crazy," Layne said.

"He's an idiot. He's got two kids and a big mortgage payment. I heard he hasn't told his wife yet. Those house payments would be murder; there's no other job around here that pays enough to cover that note."

"What would you tell your wife if it was you?" Layne said.

"I'd say I got caught beating up an alien or some bull," Launius said.

"Who tipped-off the station that he was doing it?" Layne said.

"I guess he parked at a Burger King a few blocks from the Port. The fence crew drives those same unmarked white Ford trucks the Sensor Unit drives. The manager at Burger King noticed the truck sitting there a few times and had it towed for trespassing. When he got back, he couldn't find his truck and he panicked and reported it stolen. But the tow company saw that it had government plates and called the station."

"You gotta be kidding!" Layne said, wide-eyed.

Launius chuckled momentarily. "Yeah, management checked with Customs in Nogales and the records showed his passport coming back through after lunch. He's screwed. They got him dead to rights. He's just waiting in the camera room for his paperwork to go through, separating him from service."

Layne stared at the fence in disbelief.

"Don't do any stupid stuff like that and they can't fire you. And don't ever let anyone think you're a snitch for management," Launius said.

"The guy just couldn't resist that taco," Layne said.

Launius laughed hysterically. He started to say something, but the laughter hadn't subsided and he struggled to say, "I'm glad I'm married, living around here, man." He reached out and turned the volume up on the satellite radio a notch to absorb "The Shortest Straw." The live wire electricity in the guitar strings irritated Layne's already heightened pulse. He squirmed in his seat while remaining still. Launius's irascible personality exteriorized the violence in the drums and cymbals as he nodded with the beat.

At the end of the song Launius turned the volume back down again. Layne picked up the conversation to sooth his nerves. Most of what he had learned he had retained from conversation; in turn, he had a litany of questions to pose.

"Do you ever go to AP?" Layne asked.

Launius read a text message on his cellphone as he answered. "I used to, but not anymore. It's too risky. You get wasted and go to a strip joint and they'll say you owe a stripper a thousand bucks for a lap dance or something. Then they'll throw you in jail if you don't have the money on you."

The thought reminded Layne of his trouble in Ruidoso. He cringed at the recollection of the whole ordeal—the dim memory of being at the racetrack then waking up unable to remember what happened after he cashed a winning ticket on a 26-to-1 longshot. It was like letting go of the wheel on the highway. He banished the thought from his mind, but it was followed by the sound of Felina waking him up in the bathtub. He told himself to utilize those scary memories the next time he was close to caving in and having a beer. He quickly thought of a question to provoke comedy to scramble the thoughts. "Do you think if you went to AP and a hooker stole your Passport you could jump over the fence and get back here and get away?"

Launius nodded his head with a smile. "Easily. I'd jump right over that spot right there." He pointed to a section of pickets in the Border Fence that were a different shade of brown than the rest. "I'd jump here in 5-Alpha and run full speed until I made it to 15th Street."

Layne laughed and nodded in agreement.

Launius said, "I would try to get a mask or something, though, for the cameras. These guys wouldn't even get out of their trucks if you just kept running." He gestured to indicate all of the agents in the vicinity around them. Despite his tension, the image of Launius sprinting across the field wearing a Bill Clinton mask was so funny that Layne couldn't help from laughing.

Launius elaborated. "The mistake the aliens make is they try to stop to hide and we cut 'em and find 'em. If you keep running, no agent is gonna keep following you. I won't walk-out a single."

Launius leaned back in his seat and looked like he was becoming bored. Layne continued to stare at the fence, and the scene with the lights and the generators reminded him of seeing Checkpoint Charlie and the Berlin Wall on the TV when he was a child. Launius fluffed up his hooded jacket to use as a pillow and rested his head against the driver's side window. "I'm goin' to sleep now. Wake me up if anything happens."

"Okay," Layne said.

With one eye open Launius added, "You have to stay awake. You haven't been in long enough to sleep yet."

"How long do I have to be in before I can sleep, too?"

"Two years. Once you're a career agent you can get away with it." He yawned and situated his head to find a comfortable position. Within minutes his mouth was ajar, and he began making small sleeping noises. Layne admired his soldier mentality, in part for his intelligence and ruthlessness when confronting an enemy. He seemed able to simplify a situation so as to eliminate confusion and stress. He accepted his role in the world; his conscience wasn't a cross to bear—his aim wasn't convoluted by morality. These were attributes Layne sought for himself.

Launius slept for several hours. It was astounding; he seemed capable of disregarding radio traffic from other zones while in R.E.M. sleep. Near 4:00 a.m. Layne was still wide awake, his eyes still trained on the fence through the windshield of the Kilo, the nearby generator humming with an occasional miss in the background.

The fence was different on much of the west side. It was corrugated in some sections, made of smooth new metal in others. On this side, close to the Port, the barrier was constructed like a picket fence made of iron, so images on the Mexican side were visible, like a silhouette behind a shower curtain. It allowed him to stare into the abyss of Agua Prieta. Everyone seemed to be asleep down there.

The stillness was broken by a vehicle emerging from the dark streets. It pulled up abruptly to the curb on the Mexican side of the fence, and two people climbed out. The sound of the car doors shutting penetrated all the way into the cab of the Kilo, the noise delayed and muffled by distance. The pair clung to the fence and began to climb with considerable speed, like spiders. Layne's heart pumped a burst of adrenaline through his extremities, and regretful thoughts of Felina in the bathroom finally dispersed. The driver and someone in the passenger seat stepped out and watched them ascend. Personnel in the camera room had not yet reported them over the radio. Layne sat up in his seat. He did his best to hold fast, he could almost hear his heart beating now. The group looked like the type that taunted and yelled obscenities about agents' mothers from the other side of the fence. Still, he remained silent and motionless. Nothing more than his mere awareness that something was occurring alerted and woke Launius, who opened his eyes and unfolded his arms while remaining low.

"You see something?" Launius asked in a voice just above a whisper.

"A car pulled up. It's still there; two guys are climbing the fence. Do you see them?" Layne whispered.

"Where?"

Layne guided his vision with a pointer finger. "There's two guys staying behind with the car."

The cameras still hadn't seen them.

Launius reached for his door handle while his eyes continued to monitor the pair. "They can't see us. Okay, get out real slow and don't make any noise closing the door."

Layne's body flooded with numbness. He could discern by his expression that Launius was exhilarated by an opportunity for ambush.

"Someone disabled the dome light in this Kilo; we're good," Launius whispered as he remained hunched over, stepping out discretely The door hinges creaked a tad as he delicately closed his door. "Don't turn your radio on," he said just before it shut.

Layne opened his door a few inches per second. The ball of his right foot made a slight grinding sound beneath his boots on the gravel as he put it down to step out. He put his weight on it slowly, until the sound settled. He shut the door delicately and only the spring-loaded click of the inner hook made a sound as he let go of the door handle. His green insulated vest felt warm on his back and chest while the cold penetrated through the long sleeves of his uniform top and chilled his arms. He looked across the hood of the truck at Launius hunched over in delighted anticipation, his expression barely visible in the moonbeam. Launius motioned with his fisted Maglite to get down, then he waved Layne in his direction. Layne looked and saw that the aliens were running and were already halfway across the field coming north. They were headed to an area of tall grass and weeds fifty yards to the east, in front of a flanking chain-link fence on either side of the opening to the alley. The aliens' path would take them through the backyards of a series of houses directly east of the Kilo's hiding spot—the first properties on the United States side of the border. Once over the chain-link, the aliens would be difficult to track down throughout the fences and other boundaries of the squalid neighborhood.

Layne struggled to keep pace with Launius as they pressed the lateral angle on the pair to cut them off before they reached the cover of tall grass before the fence. Layne closed in behind him as they hugged the backyard fences of the houses between the alley and the aliens' objective. Waist-high grass concealed their advance. They ran hunched over gripping their Maglites like guerrilla soldiers, keeping low to avoid being seen by the lookouts with the car behind the Border Fence.

The runners still hadn't seen Layne and Launius closing in on the tall grass to cut them off. Judging by the way they moved and the way they had arrived, the aliens were local miscreants from AP—habitual crossers. Launius only once turned around to see if Layne was close behind. Layne's mind and heart were moving too fast to prepare mentally for a confrontation he expected would lead to hand-to-hand combat. He wasn't ready but had no alternative. Launius appeared to dwell in this state of mind. Layne asked himself what he would do when they resisted? Spray them with OC, or hit them with the baton? Or should he draw his gun? He concluded that he would tackle one of them and reach for his handcuff case, but he wasn't certain or decided.

Just before the tall grass there was a ten-foot swath to cross that was without cover and exposed the agents to the lookouts' field of vision. Layne could hear the aliens' footsteps coming closer and toward them. Then, just when they were no more than twenty-five yards from colliding, a two-fingered whistle coming from the scouts behind the Border Fence pierced the night. The aliens reversed directions and sprinted back towards the Border Fence as if they had bounced off of a wall. Launius gave chase and Layne followed, running at eighty percent of his maximum speed. He feared that the obstacle of the Border Fence would slow the aliens down enough so Launius could snatch one of them off as they tried to climb. Layne would have to grab the other one. He would have to start throwing punches immediately, but the cameras were recording the whole engagement.

Through jarred vision, Layne watched the pair leap onto the fence and struggle to gain footing. They put their shoes between the spaces in the iron slats, using them as vertical rungs to climb. Layne could hear cursing and yelling from the scouts behind the fence along with his own breathing as he ran. As he closed on the pair there were thuds on the ground all around him and clanging against the fence. Layne and Launius both let up their speed. Layne realized the thuds were rocks being thrown at them from the scouts behind the fence. Launius drew his pistol fifteen yards short of the fence while he slowed. The rock throwing ceased. He quick-stepped to within five yards of the pickets and aimed his weapon at a scout through the space between two pickets, just as the pair of aliens reached the top. The young man stood frozen, without the slightest movement of even a finger.

Layne arrived directly after. He could see the body and face of the other scout clearly now through the space between two slats. His hoodlum appearance looked as though he were capable of any crime. Layne drew his pistol and modeled Launius, aiming at the face of the scout that was exposed to his line of sight. Time seemed to freeze and there was complete silence. It was strange to see the expression on a man's face above the sights, Layne thought. It was the first time he had ever aimed a gun at a person, and his arms and hands resisted zeroing the sights on the man's nose. The scout exhibited an astonishing look of fright Layne had never seen upon a person's eyes and mouth before. The young man in his sights was paralyzed by a motionless obedience that only a loaded firearm could demand. Peculiarly, Layne saw the entirety of the man's life from birth to this moment pass before his own eyes. He prayed that the group would retreat without any sudden movement. The two aliens at the top of the fence leaped. They met the ground simultaneously, landing in Mexico with their legs bent like shock absorbers. The group turned their backs slowly and cautiously as they returned to the car and it sped off into the dark streets of the hinterland.

BY 5:30 A.M. SUNLIGHT WAS beginning to peek over the shallow mountains on the horizon, signifying the approaching end of the shift and a return to relative safety. Layne rubbed his eyes and resumed his gaze at the Border Fence through the windshield. Launius was sound asleep with his mouth wide open in the driver's seat. The spotlights had shut off automatically ten minutes earlier. He watched one of the agents from the nearest static post to the east approach in a Kilo and park next to the generator. The agent climbed out of the vehicle sluggishly and walked with stiff legs to turn off the generator's engine. Layne observed him and continued to stew over the encounter with the nefarious aliens and their rock-throwing lookouts. The scene had been replaying itself, interrupting his preoccupation with the Felina predicament and his vow to remain abstinent from alcohol for the time being.

Launius tussled in the driver's seat as he tried to readjust his sleeping posture and get comfortable with his makeshift pillow. He smacked his lips and pulled the bill of his hat low to shade his brow from the rising sun. But he was unable to keep his eyes closed. He gave up and became restless as he sat up in the driver's seat of the Kilo. "This is all bullcrap. You realize that by now, don't you?" He seemed to have already forgotten about the guns-drawn encounter with the aliens three hours earlier.

"What do you mean?" Layne asked.

Launius pointed at the fence towards the Port of Entry. "Everything that's going on here is just for show. The kingmakers behind the scenes who really control the government want as many Tonks to get away as possible."

Layne wasn't sure what meaning to take from his observations. "What are we doing here then?"

"The government has to appear like they're trying to keep all these people out. If they could get away with it, they'd get rid of us and just leave the border open. But it would be too obvious, and people would protest. The way they have it set up now, it looks like they're doing the best they can. But the aliens can get in if they really want to. That's why they're allowed unlimited tries. And the general public thinks we're doing the best we can 'cause the media is controlled, too, and won't report the truth." Launius turned to put his jacket behind the seat.

"You mean the bigwigs want illegals to come over so rich people can have their lawns taken care of for cheap?" Layne said.

"No, it's a lot more complicated than that. Don't you ever wonder why they don't build a continuous fence, and why they don't throw anybody in prison down here?" Launius asked.

"Yeah, but I just figured it was politics and I would understand once I was in a while," Layne said.

"You can't see the big picture yet. Have you noticed how most of the guys who've been in more than four years don't even try to catch anybody?" Launius said.

Layne didn't respond. He looked at the fence and tried to connect the dots. He could sense when someone was telling him the truth, and what Launius was revealing was deeply disturbing.

"You saw that earlier—the guys in this zone are all veteran agents—we were the only ones who put out any effort."

Layne became even more confused.

Launius grabbed his Maglite off the dash. "They don't try because there's no point. Why waste your energy when they're just gonna get VR'd and try again in a few hours?"

Layne remained unable to respond intelligently.

"Most everyone figures out they're wasting their time after about four years. But not everyone knows why," Launius said.

"Why would the people in charge want the aliens to get away?" Layne asked with an addled look on his face.

"Because they want as many of these people in the country as they can get. They wanna create a poor victim class and cause chaos so society is begging for help. Then they offer help, but only if we agree to new rules. They create the problem, so we'll accept their solution that has stipulations in it, like less freedom—like the Patriot Act."

"I heard we let 'em go 'cause there's not enough room in jail to put 'em all."

"Come on," Launius said, "you've seen those outdoor camps that guy in Maricopa County, Sheriff Arpaio, builds. They could build enough of those so the aliens would be scared to try. The way it's set up now, there's no consequences to keep 'em from jumping."

"But it would take a lot of money to build a wall and bring the National Guard down here," Layne said. But then he considered the price of invading countries like Iraq. He had difficulty understanding why the government spent so much money overseas when there were so many problems at home.

"If it was a bank we were guarding, they would tell us to shoot anybody who came near it. You don't think the government has enough money to stop them?"

Layne tried to solve the riddle before Launius told him the rest. He thought for a moment then said, "But it doesn't make sense. It costs a lot of tax money to support all these people. Why would they want them to come into the country illegally?"

"Because these people are as poor as it gets. As soon as they make it in the country, they have four anchor babies and get on welfare. Then their kids do the same thing. They don't care how much it costs; we pay for it with our taxes. They want as many people as possible to get used to depending on the government to survive."

Layne's confusion spiraled.

Launius continued. "They let them vote, and they vote for candidates who will give them more free stuff."

"So, they don't build a wall because Democrats want their vote?" Layne asked.

"Yeah, but it's not just to get elected. Democrats, Republicans—they're all on the same side. They just pretend to argue, like professional wrestling. They just can't change everything all at once. They do it incrementally, so no one notices. That's why the Border Patrol has no morale; there's no objective," Launius said.

Layne gave up. "Why do you try so hard then?"

"Because I hate Mexicans," Launius said matter-of-factly.

"That's why?"

"That and I don't want to feel like I'm ripping off taxpayers by doing nothing. At least I run after people. Most guys won't even walk fast. You'll see."

Layne adjusted his duty belt, more awake now with the sun, as he tried to digest what Launius had told him. Layne considered telling him about his concern over the Ashlock situation and its significance in regard to the Spanish Oral Board Exam. But he refrained, uncertain if such openness would be beneficial. He reminded himself that Launius was his FTO.

Launius scratched his bed head and yawned. Then he put his cap back on and put the truck in gear. The engine rumbled slowly out of idle as they lurked out of the alley and into the field Layne had been staring at all night. The light of day made the landscape appear to be a different place. It appeared civilized now. Launius selected a beaten path towards the Border Fence as dry grass brushed the truck's undercarriage. The sun had removed their cover. So Launius made their presence known, intending to deter any further attempts to breach their stronghold by remaining visible. He drove to the southeastern corner of the zone and turned west, parallel to the Border Fence, driving along the warning track. He waved at the agents locked in static posts as they passed by.

"They told you not to drive too close to the fence, right?" Launius asked.

"Yeah. So that people can't hit your truck with rocks."

"It's true," said Launius. "I've seen new guys come back to the station with the front windshield smashed because no one told them." He scanned the fence line as they rolled. "There's no one here right now who looks like they'd throw anything at us."

He veered left and drove directly next to the fence only five feet away so that someone on the south side would have to heave a rock like a jump shot to hit the Kilo. "All the scumbags are gone. These people don't look too bad," Launius said as he surveyed desperate groups of soon-to-be aliens through the pickets.

Dawn's early light brought the border world to regular life again. From the passenger seat Layne could see through the fence, all the way into the city streets of Agua Prieta. People were driving to work and going about their daily routine. Passing by the vertical slats in the fence created the jumpy illusion of an old film projector, and Layne took in the early morning stirrings on the Mexican side of the border like he was watching a silent movie. They passed a group of mostly women peering through the fence, anticipating the vulnerability of the line during shift change— waiting for the right opportunity to find a way through. Launius stopped and rolled down the window and said to the group, "Don't try again until six-thirty when my shift is over, okay?"

A few women in the group seemed to understand some English and nodded in agreement. Launius sped off to continue following the warning track west along the Border Fence. He drove another hundred yards then slowed when he spotted another group of people waiting to make their move. He stopped next to the gathering of people and made the same request to the confounded faces peaking between the slats in the fence.

17

FELINA WALKED ALONG THE sidewalk next to Marianne as they passed by the university bookstore on their way to the center of campus. Their surroundings inspired them, and they intermittently reminisced of their childhood plans to attend the University of Arizona. The two were making their way along a busy street that bordered campus. The lampposts bore cardinal red pennants with the iconic capital A—the university's red, white, and navy-blue logo that was symbolic of Tucson and the University. Felina's sense of longing to be a student here flared anytime she came to this part of town—the part of town that revolved around the U of A. She had been friends with Marianne almost as far back as her memory could recall, and she couldn't remember a time when she wasn't enchanted by the ambiance of the campus. But as much as she hungered to be a student, she never felt like she fit in with the type of people who were fortunate enough to be students here.

Parking spaces along the street were occupied by spotless new Mini Coopers and BMWs that gleamed in the sunlight. Even the bicycle racks looked sumptuous with the new mountain bikes stored in them. The bicycles had wide tires and expensive-looking locks securing them. The students wore designer sunglasses and appeared to have money. And they seemed to know intuitively that Felina didn't, just by glancing at her. Felina was wearing large round-rimmed sunglasses that cost less than twenty bucks. She self-consciously tucked her hair behind her ear with two fingers and looked at her feet when she felt someone looking her up and down judgmentally. Felina and Marianne were the only ones without backpacks, which magnified their alien appearance. They were two of very few Hispanics in the area.

Marianne was there simply to accompany Felina on another tour without a guide. Marianne's interest in college had fizzled by her senior year in high school, and her job as a bank teller had caused her to postpone further education. She doubted that she would ever try to attend, even if Ryan would support them both when he reached the GL-11 pay scale.

They continued to reminisce about their adolescent years as they entered campus along a pathway. Touring campus had been a favorite activity throughout high school when they were tired of the malls and lacked money to go to the movies. But Felina was more determined than ever to make the dream of graduating from the U of A come to life now that meeting Layne had made it conceivable. Experiencing the campus felt different this time; it didn't seem merely like a dream anymore. She imagined herself carrying a cup of Starbucks coffee on her way to the library to study for a test, and the vision now seemed like something that could possibly come to fruition—if the rest of her plan succeeded. But her daydreaming was impeded by thoughts of how she was going to express her concern over Layne to Marianne, and how to be vague about her description of events so as not to prompt a critical reaction. She had decided not to bring up certain bathtub details again. Felina's primary motivation for inviting her confidential friend on this walk was much-needed catharsis.

A student on a skateboard rolled past them wearing headphones, and the feeling that she didn't belong here grew stronger with every subsequent person who made eye contact with her. She tried to avoid looking directly at anyone, feeling that students were wondering why they were there—whether or not they, in fact, were. Boys with fulfilled, confident expressions secured their backpack straps with their thumbs and made their way with a gait of superiority. They didn't take a second look at Marianne or Felina. It was rare that Felina didn't draw attention from boys her age, but they seemed to be so accustomed to seeing attractive girls that the two of them were nothing more than faces in a crowd.

White sorority girls wearing shirts with Greek letters across their breasts flipped their hair arrogantly as they passed by. Felina felt conspicuous and wondered if the girls' snobbish looks were due to their disapproval of her modest clothing labels. Or perhaps they thought she looked overweight. Nevertheless, Felina couldn't help but feel slightly jealous of their lifestyle.

"These girls are so spoiled. They don't even realize how good they have it. They look like they're complaining even when they aren't talking."

"I know; they probably all drive brand new SUVs and gas up with daddy's credit card," Marianne answered.

Throughout junior high and high school Felina and Marianne secretly referred to conceited white girls as "Jennifers" when criticizing them, because so many of them, or so it seemed, shared the name Jennifer. The female students on the U of A campus appeared even more spoiled. They were wasting their parents' money as they constantly talked on their cellphones, laughing and gossiping carelessly while the books in their backpacks were still wrapped in cellophane.

"If I had the opportunity to go to school here, I wouldn't waste it partying and missing class like I bet these girls do," Felina said. She fantasized about trading her worries of being caught in the country illegally for their concerns over exams and grades.

Everything looked clean and tidy on campus. Many of the academic buildings had been built in the 1920s, and their age was evident by their architecture. They had been constructed of light red-colored bricks that were almost pink after decades of exposure to the desert sun. Felina resisted the urge to examine the statues and bronze sculptures they passed. She knew Marianne would grow impatient without saying so while Felina read every plaque. They walked a considerable distance without saying anything, and Felina considered the timing right to bring up Layne's troubles. But instead she procrastinated and told herself she would bring it up when she was ready—when she could weave it tactfully into a conversation they were already having. Marianne, too, was growing uncomfortable with the silence and said, "Me and Ryan are gonna start trying for a baby after we get married. I mean, if he passes all the BP tests, knock on wood."

Felina's eyes lit up and she looked at Marianne with her mouth open. "Really?"

"Yeah, we talked about it the other night," Marianne said proudly.

"What do you want, a girl or a boy?"

"I'm hoping for a girl, but Ryan wants a boy," Marianne said, visibly trying to hide her satisfaction to appear modest.

Felina felt envious despite her personal vow not to dwell on womanly desires until she had reached her career goals. With a baby, she might as well clear her mind of college or medical school or a career of any kind. She had noticed that Marianne was beginning to put on weight and suspected she might already be pregnant. But Felina would never point out such a thing. She now suspected it was because Marianne was confident that she had Ryan under her thumb and didn't have to compete with other women anymore.

They were approaching the central campus mall where two pathways the width of a city street were separated by fifty yards of freshly mowed grass. The mall looked like it was a quarter mile in length. Identical equidistant palm trees with enormously wide trunks lined the outer perimeter of the walkways; it always reminded her of pictures she had seen of the Champs-Élysées in Paris. The massive trees fit perfectly within the length and breadth of the mall. Masses of students traveled the mall and picnicked on the green. Felina imagined herself on her way to class during her last semester of her senior year, already accepted into medical school. She would enjoy every minute of college. She would be delighted to study at night after years of being yelled at by Jabba and fetching him coffee. She sighed and said, "I wish I could go here so bad."

"I know you do, honey," Marianne said. "Someday."

But Felina was closer than she ever imagined she would be. If only Layne could clean up his act for her and make it through training. She realized that she not only wanted him to succeed for the advancement of her agenda, but primarily for his own wellbeing, with or without her.

She knew she would be gambling everything; she wouldn't blame him if he wanted nothing to do with her when she told him the truth. She wouldn't blame him for turning her in to ICE for deceiving him, either. Nevertheless, she fantasized about coming through Customs with her fiancée visa and planning her class schedule.

Marianne was growing bored but didn't want to cut their promenade short if Felina wasn't ready to head back to the car.

"Is it going better with Layne since we talked at that movie?" Marianne asked optimistically.

"Not really," Felina admitted. She was glad that Marianne had brought it up. She thought it would make what she had decided to tell her sound more lighthearted.

"Oh, honey, that's no good," Marianne said with concern.

"I know, but he's going through a lot." Felina knew she'd made that excuse before with Marianne, and herself, but she couldn't help it. "He's special to me," she continued. "I've never met anyone like him. He says things that are so funny that I laugh again when I think of what he said a few days later." She laughed, recalling one of his jokes.

"Do you think he suspects anything about you?" Marianne turned to ask her.

Felina took her time answering. "I don't know."

"Do you think you're ever going to tell him?"

"It depends if we're still together when he passes training—if he passes. I don't think he would ever turn me in, even if he was mad at me. I'm not worried about that." She nearly mentioned the drinking issue but couldn't.

"What do you think he would say if you told him the truth?" Marianne asked. They'd had this conversation before, in the movie theater, but she couldn't resist bringing it up again.

"I don't know how I'm ever gonna have the guts to tell him," Felina demurred.

They moved past a set of stairs, and a young man carrying a backpack by one strap grabbed the railing and chop-stepped up the stairs on his way inside one of the buildings. He looked like he was late for class. Felina watched him jog to the building and pull the door open to rush inside then said, "That's not really what I'm worried about."

"What are you worried about?" Marianne asked.

Felina sighed and forced herself to say, "His drinking. He drinks a lot more than I first thought."

The statement piqued Marianne's interest. She looked at Felina again and in a deflated tone said, "Really?"

"Yeah, he was hung over the other day and he looked like he was about to cry when it came time for him to go back. He loathes Sunday afternoons," Felina said.

Marianne didn't say anything, waiting for Felina to continue.

"He told me he came to the Border Patrol to clean up his act so he would be accepted by society. But when I first met him, he told me he drank harder at the Academy than any other time in his life," Felina said.

Marianne nodded, "Ryan did, too. I think they all do because it sucks so bad; they were there for four months."

"Yeah, but I don't think Ryan ever drank this much. Layne doesn't admit how much he drinks. He might not even realize it. He usually forgets a lot of Friday and Saturday night. He tries to stay good in front of me, but after the first two or three beers he doesn't stop until he passes out," Felina said.

"Is it affecting your relationship?" Marianne looked at Felina to ask while they walked.

"Yeah, I worry about him, and he's embarrassed. I want him to get help. I think he likes me enough that if I ask him, he will. I think he probably has childhood trauma that's causing it, and it'll really help if he talks to someone about it."

"Do you think you can get him to take it easy?" Marianne asked.

"I don't know," Felina said. She began to look at the cement pathway directly in front of her while she walked.

"That's not all I'm worried about."

"What else?" Marianne asked.

"I think he's wondering why I haven't introduced him to my parents yet. He knows they live in Tucson." The issue was visibly perturbing to Felina.

"Has he asked about them?" Marianne asked.

"Yeah, but not about meeting them. I can tell he's wondering why I haven't brought him to see them, even though he doesn't say it."

"You don't want him to meet them?"

"I do; it's just that they're so . . . *ethnic*. He's not dumb. He'll be really suspicious when he realizes they don't really speak English. I wouldn't let him meet them until after I tell him."

Marianne thought about possible solutions for a moment.

"He knows how important they are to me," Felina said. "I'm afraid he thinks I don't let him meet them because I don't take him seriously. His parents live in Colorado, so me meeting his parents is a non-issue for him right now."

"I wouldn't worry about it right now," Marianne said. "Guys don't want to meet parents. Maybe he thinks it's because he knows you think he wants to avoid meeting them."

"I hope so," Felina said.

"What are you gonna do about him drinking?" Marianne asked.

Felina sighed again. "I think I'm gonna ask him if he'll talk to a counselor about it or something."

Marianne nodded and they were both quiet for a moment while they made their way across the tile walkway that led to the Arizona State Museum. After they walked fifty yards without speaking Marianne said, "Have you considered the possibility that he might not pass Field Training?"

"Yes. If that happens, I don't know what we'd do. I don't want to think about it unless it happens because it's out of my control. Why, did Ryan tell you something?"

"Ryan heard through the grapevine that he got in trouble or something," Marianne said timidly.

"He told me," Felina said. "He said he lost his notebook with all of his FBI logins and passwords in it. He said he basically got held back a phase. But he says if he passes the Spanish Oral Board, there's nothing they can do to him; they have to put him on a unit. It's just another situation where there's nothing I can do about it. If I worried about everything he's involved in and all my problems, too, I'd lose my mind."

"I know what you mean," Marianne said.

"I had the strangest dream about Layne the other night," Felina said. "It was one of those dreams that you remember and think about the rest of the day. It doesn't happen very often."

Marianne responded quickly with curiosity. "What happened in the dream?"

"It was black and white and there was no sound to it. It didn't make sense; it's hard to explain. It wasn't chronological," Felina said.

"I've had those," Marianne said.

"Yeah, we were standing face to face in an empty parking lot. He was about to go back to work after a weekend we spent together. He was wearing his dress uniform and the look on his face was so sad. I wanted to hug him, but I couldn't for some reason that I didn't understand. He really wanted to stay with me," Felina said.

"That's so sad," Marianne said.

"The sun was going down really fast. I could see it moving. I sensed that Layne had to be gone before the sun was below the horizon. He walked away, and it seemed like I would never see him again. So, I started yelling for him to come back so I could make sure we made plans for the future. But he couldn't hear me; it was like I was yelling under water and my feet were stuck to the ground so I couldn't run after him."

There were meanings to the dream that Felina didn't want to share with Marianne just yet. It made her realize there was no way around Layne; Felina had met her match. He was the person who caused her to stare blankly. He was the first thing she thought of when she woke up in the morning.

"I've had dreams like that," Marianne said again.

"Yeah, but it was weird. It went backwards. We were back at the barbecue at your house when I met him. I was waiting for an opportunity to introduce myself to him, but I couldn't catch up to him because there were too many people in the way," Felina said.

"Was I in it?" Marianne said.

"I don't think so, but it was definitely at your house. I couldn't reach him to introduce myself and I ended up in the same parking lot, but he wasn't there. I screamed his name. It felt like he exposed every part of himself to me and I was holding back. Like he deserved to know everything. I was holding a bouquet of roses that he gave me to try and talk me into being with him. He was trying to tell me to trust him, that he would accept me as I am. But it was too late for some reason." It reminded her of slow dancing with Layne to a song he loved. She liked to touch the back of his neck and feel his chest against her cheek, when she could hear his heart beating. She liked the shape of his back and the smell of his neck.

"Well, it was only a dream," Marianne said.

"The ending was the weirdest part," Felina said. "I was alone in the parking lot and there was a car honking at me, but I couldn't tell from which direction. Right then I woke up and realized the car horn in the dream was my alarm clock waking me up."

18

JUST OVER EIGHT HOURS remained until Layne's tour on Mids with Launius was over. Layne grasped the passenger side ceiling handle of the Kilo as the truck plunged and jounced through the darkness near the advent of morning along another beaten path. Launius had taken advantage of his freedom by looking for trouble abroad as opposed to remaining stationary and reinforcing one particular zone in town again. Layne looked again with gratification at the text message on his cellphone from six hours earlier. Felina had asked if he was alright and told him to be careful. It was all he needed to revitalize his spirit. He saw himself conquering the Oral Board while Felina waited for him with open arms until he returned to her in triumph. But the scene with the rock-throwing aliens continued to intermittently replay itself in his thoughts.

"Do you think anybody will ask us about the aliens we drew-on at the fence?"

"Maybe Escribano. Nobody else who matters cares. If he asks just tell him exactly what happened; we didn't do anything wrong." Launius showed no concern as he steered with one hand.

"Alright."

Layne felt like Launius was his only friend in this strange environment. He told himself he would gain friends if he could prove himself by graduating from field training. On this night, final victory seemed within his grasp—if only he could find a way to overcome the Spanish Oral Board.

The barbed wire together with the repetitious clank of their tires rolling over cattle guards seemed never-ending as groups of cattle revealed themselves by the reflection of their curious eyes in the headlight beams. The Kilo lumbered through another far-east zone that was foreign to Layne but was habit pattern to Launius, until eventually they came to a stop at yet another cattle gate. There was an arch above the gate with a symbol welded to it that Layne recognized as being significant from early in training. He opened his door and walked toward the gate through the cold dust that lingered in the headlights. They had been on the move all night, cutting for sign and checking sensors, looking for a group to track.

Layne removed his list of combinations from his shirt pocket and searched with his Maglite for the Brennan Ranch west end gate listing. Once he removed the lock, he walked the twelve-foot gate to the other side of the road. Gravel crunched beneath the tires as Launius rumbled by. Once the truck was clear Layne walked the gate closed and made sure to secure it with the padlock. Then he jogged towards the truck's red taillights through the dust cloud and exhaust, anticipating the warmth of his seat. Launius was already rolling forward before Layne had climbed in completely.

"You made sure you locked that, right?" Launius said.

"Yeah, I double-checked it."

"You gotta make sure you're extra careful with any of these ranches that border International Road. Especially this guy, Brennan; he's a jerk. A couple years ago some Mexican on Swings left one of his gates open and about sixty of his cattle got out. Brennan parked his truck on that walkway right in front of the entrance to the station and marched straight to PAIC Kramer's office to chew him out. The guy that left the gate open had to round up all the cattle—off the clock."

Just as Launius finished the anecdote the headlights of a vehicle heading toward them appeared. Launius said, "Crap, it's him; that looks like his truck. He must be on his way to town. He eats breakfast at that cafe on Main Street every morning at five o'clock."

A new heavy-duty Chevrolet truck with dual wheels on the rear axle slowed as it approached them, and Launius began rolling down his window. Both vehicles came to a stop once the driver's side windows were flush. The driver rolled down his window and rested his arm on the door. He seemed to know who Launius was and offered an upward nod.

"What's goin' on?" Launius greeted.

"Just gettin' somethin' tuh eat," Brennan said.

Layne leaned to his left to get a clear look at him. Brennan was wearing a Carhart jacket with a flannel shirt underneath, and a camouflage baseball cap that bore an archery logo. There was a high-powered rifle with a scope in a gun rack mounted on the roof above him. He looked to be about fifty years old and was overweight, with a round face and double chin.

"What are you guys up to?" Brennan asked with low energy.

Launius put the transmission in Park and rested his elbow on the steering wheel. "Just checkin' a sensor."

Brennan nodded slowly then said, "Was it the 454-3?"

"Yeah, it went off about ten minutes ago," Launius said.

Brennan's speech sounded slurred; he rotated the bar on his steering column to put the truck in Park. When he turned to face Launius again his eyes were slow to catch up and refocus. "That might've been me; I was over there earlier," Brennan said. He turned to face forward and took a long pull from a silver can until his cheeks became full.

"Alright, I'll check it out, just in case," Launius said.

Brennan didn't respond; he was staring straight ahead now, teetering slightly. Layne sensed that Launius was in a hurry to move on.

"Well, we better go check that out. It might be good," Launius said.

"Later," Brennan said as he put his truck back in gear.

Launius drove off before his window was completely rolled up. "He's bombed. I'm not checking that sensor; I just didn't wanna talk to him anymore."

"Was he drinking a beer?" Layne said.

"Yeah, he had a twelve-pack of Coors Light in the console. He must've been spotlighting coyotes all night."

"Animals or humans?" Layne asked seriously, hoping it would be taken as sarcastic banter.

"Animals."

"How does he know where our sensors are?" Layne said.

"He's got a scanner. He watches where the Sensor Unit plants 'em. Just try to avoid him. I didn't think we'd run into him. He causes problems for us; a couple years ago he caught some Tonks crossing through here. They tried to keep going north and he pulled a shotgun on 'em. He held 'em at gunpoint until agents got there."

Layne could taste the cold beer as he visualized Brennan drinking it. "How does PAIC Kramer put up with that guy?"

"He just tries to ignore him until he has to deal with him. A lot of people think Brennan's involved with runnin' dope through his property." Launius glanced at his side view mirror then accelerated and said, "Let's get outta here. This road veers north to Highway 80; once we get there, we'll just cut the highway all the way back to town."

The radio had turned to crickets; the receding glow of city lights sparkled on the horizon behind them, like Las Vegas from a distance. At night, this far east, Layne felt as lost as the aliens after their guides abandoned them. He could see that Launius was losing interest by the fatigue he wore on his eyes and brow.

"I'm tired. I'm gonna let you drive," Launius said.

Launius parked and they crossed through the headlights to switch places.

"Start cutting once we get on the highway, it's only about a half-mile from here," Launius said as he situated himself in the passenger seat.

Eventually the rising sun allowed Layne to turn off his handheld spotlight and put it behind the seat; the end of the shift was on the brightening horizon. Border Patrol vehicles had worn deep ruts in the dirt shoulder of the highway that ran parallel to the wire fence he was investigating for disturbances. The grooves guided the steering like railroad tracks as they crept along. The tires straddled brush and cactus that made rhythmic pings and clinks on the oil pan beneath the truck. Launius was able to ignore the racket somehow. His hat was tilted to shield his eyes from dawn, and he remained semiconscious as his head swayed from side to side against the window when the truck bounced and fell in holes.

The relief of morning light allowed Layne to scan the horizon in every direction. Images of Felina had been drifting in and out of his mind for almost seven hours while he stared at the focus of his spotlight. After he turned it off and put it behind the seat, he rubbed his eyes with his fists. The calf muscle in his right leg was cramping as a result of maintaining minimal pressure on the accelerator in order to sustain a slow enough speed to search effectively.

Suddenly, every bit of brush in a hundred-yard radius was flattened by overwhelming wind. He was overcome with confusion momentarily until the unmistakable sound of a turbine helicopter engine became apparent. Launius uncrossed his arms and snapped to alertness. His hat fell off and his hair made him look like a woodpecker. "What's happening?"

"There's a helicopter flying around above us."

"Well yeah, but what are they doing?" Launius said, his brow wrinkled.

"Unit on the ground, Omaha-327," the radio rang out with the pilot's voice.

Launius grabbed the microphone angrily. "Go ahead," he said, concealing his irritation.

"There's four bodies fifty yards to your south."

"Ten-four, I'm thirteen," Launius replied, to notify the pilot that he was en route.

Layne stopped the truck, and as they opened the doors to climb out, he shielded his face with his sleeve from the cyclone-like slipstream that propelled stinging dust and debris against his cheeks and hands. The two of them struggled through the rotor wash to scale the barbed wire fence south of the highway shoulder. They straddled over and began to weave through thickets of mesquite that veiled their view of the desert on their left side.

They brushed away mesquite branches for twenty yards until they came to an open space that was spotted with ocotillo and barrel cactus where four aliens were pinned down by the helicopter. The group saw Launius and Layne approaching and made a move to escape, but the helicopter banked to cut them off, following like a shadow hovering one hundred feet above them. When the aliens saw the agents closing in less than twenty yards away, they stopped and glanced at the helicopter, then raised their arms in surrender. The helicopter's engine was deafening, too loud for voice commands to be heard so Layne motioned to the aliens with his palm to get down on their stomachs as dust swirled around them. Once the pilot witnessed the aliens under control, the helicopter lifted its tail and sped away to the east like a dragonfly.

With the noise of the helicopter declining in the distance, Layne voiced his commands, now coming to him through second nature. *"Quédense en las Panzas, acuestense!"*

The four of them dropped to their knees and then to their stomachs. They were all young men who appeared to be in good physical condition. They looked up at Layne and Launius from the pushup position.

"Sientense uno al otro hacia el Norte." As he ordered the group to sit and face north, Layne turned to Launius. "Is that bad, that I didn't see them?"

"Not really," Launius said. "There was too much cover between us."

Layne noticed that Launius was observing the aliens with more caution than usual. "Customs must have run across them on their way to New Mexico or something," Layne said.

"Maybe." Launius seemed to be eyeballing the group with study, walking in a complete circle around them. "Be careful what you say. They probably speak English."

Layne tried to assess the situation himself. Usually groups out away from the city were more diverse, with women and sometimes youngsters. These four were all young bucks.

"Handcuff that one right there," Launius said, pointing to a sharp-cheeked, firm young man who seemed to be looking around for an opportunity to run.

"Arrodillense," Layne said, and all four complied, rising to their knees. They appeared to be in their early twenties and resembled the rock-throwers in 5-Alpha. Layne interpreted the jeopardy of the situation and his jaw clenched as he unsnapped his handcuff case. He tried to calm himself, but he didn't know what he had gotten into; it felt off. He fumbled to remove his cuffs as he saw Launius put his knee and all of his weight in the back of one of them, pinning the man's face in the dirt. He was forcefully applying handcuffs to the cagey youth in the center, who carried himself like their leader. Launius maliciously pulled the man back to his knees by his shirt collar and the man spit dirt from his lips. "Too tight," the man complained in broken English.

"Shut up," Launius snapped and clicked each cuff an additional notch tighter as he engaged the double-lock spring with his handcuff key.

Tension was throbbing within Layne's chest. He realized they lacked handcuffs for two of the young men. He pulled the cold metal rings from the case above his right rear pocket and let one dangle from the other. He bent over and applied them to the alien next to the leader. He was careful not to hear too many clicks which would indicate that he had made the cuffs too tight. He noticed the alien's fingernails were caked with dirt and his palms were calloused and cracked. Layne used the post on the rear of his handcuff key to push the double lock spring until it snapped in place. He noticed his hands shaking as he repeated the procedure on the second cuff, all the while keeping track of the two unrestrained aliens out of the corner of his eye. He prayed they would remain compliant. Launius was examining the shoulders of their shirts. They all wore dark long-sleeve t-shirts, with layers of clothing underneath. Layne looked closer and realized that all four had bloodshot eyes and dilated pupils. They appeared to be not completely cognizant of what was occurring.

Launius reached out and plucked beige fibers from the shoulders of their cotton shirts and said, "They've got burlap fibers all over them. And they've all been sampling; just look at them." Layne told himself he should've noticed it immediately. They looked like they had been working with a thresher, and they were either wild-eyed or out of it.

Launius leaned his cheek to one side and pressed the button on the microphone clipped to his shoulder passant and radioed the supervisor in charge of the zone, "Delta-26, Delta-101."

"Delta-101 go ahead."

"Yeah, we're directly north of Brennan Ranch near the Mason Wash and 80. We're fifteen with four bodies and it looks like forty-six," Launius reported, indicating that they suspected that drugs were involved.

"Ten-four, I'm en route. About five Mike's." the supervisor replied as the transmission broke abruptly.

The aliens wouldn't look up at Launius or Layne. Their eyes remained trained on the ground in front of them.

"Ask them where the dope is," Launius told Layne.

Layne thought about the appropriate term to use for marijuana. He had heard people use two different words to describe it. It was formally called *"Marihuana,"* but Mexicans usually called it *"La Mota."* The negative connotation branded such terms in his memory. *"Donde escondieron la Mota, cerca de aqui?"*

The aliens shook their heads sideways, still avoiding eye contact. *"No hay,"* they muttered. All four wore sweatpants made of sponge cotton material with elastic around the waistband and ankles. They were the same sweatpants Layne wore as a kid to practice sports.

"Look at their sweatpants," Layne said. "Those are old-school."

"It's so they can move faster. They're all beat now, though. They're worn out from lugging dope all the way up here. Go ahead and search 'em," Launius said.

Layne stood them up one by one. He searched the two who were not restrained first, using the routine method. He used two hands on the handcuffed aliens, who both stumbled to maintain their balance. He pulled a marijuana roach from the leader's pocket and put it to his nose. "He just smoked this; you can smell it. They must have been saving it for the way back."

Layne studied the group while they waited quietly for the zone supervisor to arrive. Smugglers were referred to as "mules" in Border Patrol jargon. They took the risk of delivering the dope while their cartel employers stayed in Mexico and collected the majority of the profits. Mules seemed to instinctively sense when they were being followed—they were stealthy, foxlike. When agents were on their tail, they often dumped their cargo and disappeared back south like jackrabbits before agents ever came within reach. They seemed to be capable of outsmarting even the dogs— German Shepherds or Belgian Malinois—that the Canine Units used to track them. Often the dogs would lead agents to bales of marijuana that had been jettisoned days or weeks before by mules avoiding capture. It was extremely rare to capture mules and their dope simultaneously.

Layne could see the roof of an arriving Kilo as it pulled up on the shoulder of the highway behind Launius's vehicle.

"It's the MIT in this zone," Launius said. "He probably heard us over the radio."

They heard the agent turn off the engine and exit the vehicle. A Hispanic that Layne didn't recognize emerged from the mesquite and quickly climbed over the barbed wire fence. He was wearing short sleeves and his black search gloves. He wore his green bulletproof vest on the outside of his uniform top. To be permitted to do so was a right earned at some indistinguishable point during exposure to Border Patrol. He carried an M4 slung beneath his right armpit that swayed when he walked. Dark wraparound sunglasses masked his identity. Agents seemed to be circling the situation like coyotes zeroing in on a wounded rabbit.

The Hispanic agent stood next to Launius without speaking.

"They must have sidestepped all the sensors and dropped off their dope somewhere. They were on their way back south when the helicopter spotted them," Launius explained.

Layne considered that the mules knew where every sensor was located, which explained their covert arrival. He remembered Tipton explaining that sensors had to be relocated routinely. Deviants from the south side, who were the people the sensors were meant to deter, mysteriously knew where they were located within hours of reactivation.

"They aren't gonna tell us where the dope is. Let's wait for Tomlinson to get here," Launius said.

"You guys asked them?" The Sensor agent had arrived as Launius was talking.

"Yeah, they said they didn't have any," Layne said.

One of the unrestrained aliens whispered something into the ear of the young man next to him, then smirked to himself.

"*Cállete,*" the Hispanic agent said, telling him to shut up.

The smirker shook his head slightly in defiance and grinned as he rolled his eyes.

"Tell that guy to get up," Launius said to Layne.

Layne pointed to the man. "*Tú, levántete.*"

The alien's grin disappeared, and he looked like he regretted drawing attention to himself. He pretended not to understand and remained on his knees. Launius's face turned blood red and he walked around the row and approached the man from behind. Then, without warning, he leaned down and snatched the young man into a vicious headlock, pulling him upright in a craze.

Launius was a head taller and the man's feet struggled to find the ground. Layne's heart pounded as he glanced at the Hispanic agent to gauge his response. He kept his eyes on Launius, expressionless through his sunglasses. Layne averted his eyes for a moment, but he couldn't help but resume watching.

The man's face was turning purple and his eyes bulged with deathly panic. He clawed at Launius's bicep and forearm while his legs flailed, but he was helpless to loosen the chokehold as he struggled for his life. He gasped, trying to speak but emitted only a hoarse cough. "Okay, okay," he bleated, but could say no more. He was seconds away from losing consciousness. The strength began draining quickly from his resistance and his legs were becoming limp.

The two handcuffed mules in the middle kept their eyes trained on the ground in front of their knees. The unrestrained man on the other end of the row turned his head left to watch the struggle with terror. The Hispanic agent approached him from the front and raised his M4 to his hip, one-handed. He pointed the rifle directly at the mule so that the barrel was touching his forehead.

"Quieres morir, puto?" the agent said, asking him if he wanted to die.

The man put his hands up slowly to his ears.

"Mire al pinche Suelo," the agent warned him to remain looking at the ground. He lowered the rifle and proceeded to handcuff the man.

Meanwhile, Launius had loosened his grip on the man he was choking, releasing him and throwing him forcefully to the ground so his head bounced off the desert floor. The man lay on his stomach as though he were listening to the ground as he gasped deep breaths of terror while a scrape on his temple began to bleed. He gathered himself on all fours and cried quietly. There was a moment of dubious silence and stillness. The mule returned to his knees without being told to and the Hispanic agent used his second set of handcuffs to secure him. All four prisoners remained handcuffed with their hands behind their backs, motionless, with their heads down.

Layne could hear another vehicle arrive on the highway behind the mesquite trees. He heard the bushes rustling and SBPA Tomlinson came striding leisurely to join the group. He was a stocky forty-year-old man with combed sandy blond hair who didn't wear the green cap. The brass bars on his collar flashed in the sunlight as he approached. He had removed the microphone cord from his radio, and he pulled it from his hip holster. He spoke into it like a walkie-talkie, eyes wandering while he waited for a response.

"Where are we? The Mason Wash?" Tomlinson asked, not needing a reply. "Go ahead and put these guys in your vehicle, Chavez." He seemed to know exactly what had occurred by the scrape on the mule's temple, and he couldn't have cared less.

"Ten-four, sir," Chavez replied to his unit supervisor. He helped the handcuffed mules to their feet and led them toward the parade of vehicles on the shoulder of the highway behind the mesquite. He raised the barbed wire fence so the prisoners could roll underneath it.

"Let's let the new guy have this one for his stats, what do you say Launius?" Tomlinson said.

Launius nodded with a devious grin.

Oddly, the farther southwest they walked, the more visible the vehicles on the highway became. Layne looked back over his shoulder to watch Agent Chavez locking up the mules. He was helping them climb into the holding cell of his Kilo. The mules were having difficulty balancing themselves with their hands cuffed behind their backs as they stepped up on the bumper. The last mule to enter the cage appeared to turn and say something to Chavez, who tripped his leg and pushed him so that he fell sideways. His cheek met with the asphalt. Then Chavez kicked the mule in the ribs, and the wince traveled all the way to the agents. Launius and Tomlinson pretended not to hear it. Layne turned away quickly; if asked, he would say he hadn't seen it.

Tomlinson sported a sly grin with Layne by his side. They began to circle the area while Launius watched. In less than a minute Tomlinson homed-in on footprints leading southwest—some of them no more than a slight mark, too inconspicuous for Layne to make out on his own. The sign had been brushed out in segments, but the attempt to conceal it had been done in haste and left a broken trail that Tomlinson followed with regularity. The trail meandered west past a windmill next to a stock tank and led them one hundred fifty yards to a waist-high arroyo that ran north and south. Layne no longer felt in danger now that Tomlinson was in charge, and the search took on the feeling of an Easter egg hunt.

"The mules bring the dope north and they usually stash it close to a road," Tomlinson explained with a southern California accent. He lost the sign momentarily but relocated it after a few seconds. "That way they can throw it into the back of a truck and drive it into town in a hurry."

"So, they put it by a dirt road but close to the highway?" Layne asked.

"You got it. They don't want to be on one of these dirt roads too long with dope in their truck," Tomlinson said.

Layne began to disregard obvious hiding places and instead considered where he would stash dope if he were the one leaving it for someone to pick up. Probably somewhere its location could be described with simple instructions and prominent landmarks, he reasoned. Tomlinson seemed to already know where the stash was hidden, but he was keeping it to himself in order to force Layne to find it without guidance. The tracks they were following led into the arroyo. Tomlinson waited behind and watched Layne, seemingly entertained by a trainee's stumbling about.

The gully was overgrown with brush, and Layne gave up looking for footprints. He walked twenty yards north along the bank and noticed a pocket within a thirty-degree northwest turn in the wash. The pocket looked like a den of some sort, where an animal had once burrowed and lived. But, he noticed, the area had been disturbed by what appeared to be unnatural forces. Dried creosote brush covered the pocket and looked out of place. It stood out like a plaster patch, a slightly different shade of white that did not blend into the rest of a wall. He waded into the brush of the arroyo and removed the creosote brush, uncovering four burlap potato sacks with ropes attached. They were stowed in a cluster in the pocket of the bank.

He smiled broadly and looked over at Tomlinson, who was already grinning. Layne stepped away from the pocket and pumped his fist in celebration. His first thought was the beginning of a plan about how he would swagger and boast about his trophy to Felina. He was certain she would be astounded and impressed.

"What are you waiting for?" Tomlinson said. "Call it in." He looked like a proud father.

Layne unclipped his microphone from his passant and pushed the button, "866, Delta-328.

"Go ahead Delta-328."

"I'm ten-forty-six at the Mason Wash." Layne reported narcotics in custody with elation.

"Ten-four, good job," the LECA said. She didn't sound impressed.

Layne dug in and began pulling the sacks out. His forearms strained to dislodge the heavy sacks from the pocket. He swung one over his shoulder and carried it out of the arroyo and dropped it on the bank. From their labels he noticed the burlap sacks were manufactured by a potato company in Mexico. "They have to weigh about fifty pounds apiece," he said to Tomlinson, who stood above the arroyo, watching him recover the bags.

"That's about right," Tomlinson replied. "They weigh about as much as those guys can carry. "How many you got?"

"Four, sir." Layne dragged the last sack into a clearing.

Launius and Chavez had been lagging behind and arrived to assist them.

"Go ahead and help him carry these bales back to the trucks," Tomlinson told them.

Each grabbed a sack of dope.

"I can't believe they can carry these all the way up here. How far do you think we are from the fence?" Layne asked.

"I don't know, several miles," Launius said.

"They must use these ropes as backpack straps." Layne had hoisted his bag onto his shoulder and struggled with its awkwardness.

When they arrived back at their vehicles, Tomlinson signaled for everyone to hold on a minute. "Before you guys load them into the truck, let's get a picture with the new guy." The four of them arranged the sacks neatly and stood behind them. Tomlinson assembled them with guidance like a photographer: "Chavez come in a little bit closer to the middle. Sheppard, go ahead and kneel over the bag in the center." He fiddled with the viewfinder for a moment then aimed the camera and it flashed several times.

Layne's excitement heightened in anticipation of showing off the photos to Felina.

"Good one. I'll email these to you, Sheppard."

"Thank you, sir," Layne said. It was rare to feel any satisfaction. He felt warm inside, like he was an essential part of a team. Especially because Tomlinson had learned his name from his name tag. He fantasized that Felina had witnessed the seizure.

Tomlinson and Chavez helped load the bags into the holding cell of Launius's Kilo before evacuating the area. Layne and Launius were left standing at the rear of their vehicle as Layne closed the latch on the holding cell. Their shift had ended more than an hour earlier, and it would be at least another hour before they finished writing their reports after getting back to the station. Several vehicles had swept by. Layne did a double-take and said, "Hey, that red truck has driven by three times since we brought the dope back." He pointed west down the yellow stripes of the highway to the tailgate of the truck growing smaller in the distance.

"What kind of truck is it?" Launius said.

"A red S-10; there's a Mexican chick driving it. She keeps slowing down; I just thought she was a lookie-loo at first."

Launius grunted slightly, "It's Burnadette Trujillo. Her crew was probably gonna pick up the dope—scandalous bi—."

"Who is she?" Layne said.

"She's a local dope and Tonk smuggler. She gets about five hundred per run to take dope and aliens to Phoenix." Launius didn't seem the least bit interested in her in lieu of his newly acquired responsibility over the dope and the already extended shift.

"We should do something," Layne said, still ardent and confident from his achievement.

"What are we gonna do to her? Arrest her for watching us? She's a U.S. citizen," Launius said with a receptive look, expecting Layne to repeal the comment.

Layne shrugged.

"I guess we could pull her over and gang-bang 'er," Launius said sarcastically, then felt clownish for speaking without thinking.

"Hurry up," Launius said, heading for the driver's side of the truck. "We gotta take this dope back to the Sierra Papa. I don't wanna be filling out forms until Swings."

Launius took the keys from Layne and burdensomely climbed into the driver's seat. As Layne closed his passenger side door, he could tell Launius was still worked up over his assault on the mule. He checked the side view mirror on Layne's side and merged onto the highway in a hurry.

"You about choked the life outta that guy," Layne said tentatively.

"Don't take anything off Tonks," Launius said emphatically. "If you give 'em any slack, word will spread on the south side and it'll just keep getting worse. Next thing you know they'll start arguing and running south when you take your eye off 'em. You gotta make an example outta one once in a while." He was driving much faster now. He stepped on the accelerator and looked at his watch as they raced for the station.

"We gotta hurry up and get this dope weighed and get the DEA paperwork done. We can't leave until it's done, and it could take a couple hours. That's why Tomlinson let you take credit for it; nobody cares about stats. No one wants to do the paperwork for it. The dogs on the Canine Units find bales lying around all the time because agents will pretend they didn't see it and walk right past a hundred pounds."

"Did you see Chavez face plant that dude on the highway? I couldn't believe that," Layne said.

"He deserved it," Launius said.

"It just surprised me, that's all," Layne said.

"Those Mexican agents hate Tonks worse than we do. They think scumbags like those guys we just caught make 'em look bad," Launius said.

"You think Tomlinson knows?"

"I don't know," Launius said. "Make sure you don't tell anybody anything you saw. Don't ever let people think you're a snitch. If agents don't trust you, they might leave you hanging when you're in a tough spot and need help."

Layne recalled the hypothetical situation presented to him in his Oral Board at the Rocky Mountain Hotel in Denver when he was still trying to get accepted into the Border Patrol Academy. He remembered how important loyalty was in that interview. But he also thought about the warning Cruz had given his trainee group just a few weeks earlier to never lie. And now Launius is telling him to never be a snitch. The contradictions were obvious.

"I won't tell anyone," he said after pausing longer than he should have, to think. "If anyone asks, I'd tell 'em I was out looking for the weed and didn't see it."

"Good. Sometimes those Tonks will tell when they're getting processed. If they have a supe' that goes by the book, it might become a problem. If anyone asks, just say you didn't see anything."

"Do you think that dope load had anything to do with Brennan?" Layne asked. "We were directly north of his ranch; the mules must have passed through where we were earlier."

"Makes you wonder, doesn't it?" Launius said. "Brennan steered us away from that sensor, and those mules sidestepped all the others. How'd they know where the sensors were?

"The Cartel is a billion-dollar business," he continued. "It has an unlimited amount of funds—no red tape, no policy. They just say, 'You: Go talk to the rancher and buy him off. We don't care what it takes. If it takes a hundred grand, we don't care. A hundred grand is nothing.' How do you catch a rancher on his own land letting mules through, even if it's illegal?"

"Dang," was all Layne said.

19

LAYNE GLOWED TO BE holding hands with Felina in such a setting as they window-shopped the storefronts in what appeared to be the hippie capital of the world. It was mid-morning on Saturday in Bisbee; soon it would be Christmas. The sun on Layne's face and shoulders had been a constant the transparent, low-traveling clouds seemingly incapable of obstructing the morning's warm rays—as they browsed their way uphill along the narrow sidewalk of the old mining town's meandering primary commercial street. It was remarkably narrow; it augmented the cramped feel of small nineteenth-century shops in adjoined buildings with facades facing the street. The antiques and creaking wood floors within the Victorian structures enriched the boomtown ambiance, creating the feel of a Frontierland attraction in Disneyland. The lights and Christmas decorations gave it a Currier & Ives look—even without the snow, which fell only on rare occasions and made the news when it did. The older men who operated many of the establishments looked like goldpanners, and their women, who sold eccentric trinkets and cotton candy, resembled witches.

Felina looked more striking than ever, and Layne spent more time secretly observing her than he did inspecting the items on display in the windows. She was wearing tight jeans that accentuated her hips, and a white camisole with a long-sleeved white sweater over it, buttoned only part way to expose the front of her tank top and the separation between her breasts. In the past, Layne had been embarrassed to hold hands with girls in public; it caused him to blush with self-awareness when people took notice. But Felina was exceptional. He was proud to display her, while simultaneously self-conscious about his worthiness. Her eye-catching physical beauty was enhanced by her perceptive choice of words when she communicated her curiosity. He grinned with satisfaction while observing her as she examined antique metal toys and western jewelry in the display windows.

Layne enjoyed the sense of security he felt roaming in broad daylight, surrounded by elderly and foreign tourists. He felt apprehensive when he was out with her at night in Tucson while in the presence of rowdy young men with their inhibitions removed by alcohol. Fourth Avenue at night was one setting where he wasn't contented by her capacity to draw attention. But today he felt impervious to challenging insults from jealous peers. He was sober and armed with his duty pistol concealed beneath his shirt. The locals his age here knew he was an agent and kept their distance.

It was refreshing not to be hung over. Years earlier he invariably was glad on Saturday and Sunday morning when he had refrained from drinking the night before. But beginning about the time he turned twenty-one, those mornings had become few and far between. Most of the rare abstinent weekend nights had occurred when he was sick, or when he had something important scheduled the following day with family and was lacking the pharmaceuticals necessary to ease the hangover symptoms.

He periodically glanced at Felina in search of a reciprocating smile. But he began to suspect that the preoccupied headspace she had been in the last time he saw her remained. Normally she wasn't moody; she only became angry when she had reason. Wondering what it all meant, he fell in behind her, single file, to allow oncoming pedestrians to pass. Asian families with cameras, and tourists from European countries, paid them no mind. The foreigners were too fascinated by their surroundings to take a second look at them. But the locals couldn't overlook Layne. After briefly examining Felina, they glared at him as they drove by.

The twenty-something youth among the local population wore dirty dreadlocks and tie-dyed clothing and looked like Deadheads. Their primary reason for remaining in Bisbee was to work in the illegal drug trade and take advantage of the demand for methamphetamine and marijuana in Cochise County. Many of the Bisbee locals made a living selling only hallucinogens like LSD and magic mushrooms to their neighbors. It was unusual to see them on Main Street; they rarely traveled among the window-shoppers. Their hatred of law enforcement was no secret, and they held a special aversion toward immigration officials. They stared daggers the way local boys in college towns did when Layne was an athlete. The feeling of being hated for simply being himself typically resulted in Layne driving thirty minutes west to Sierra Vista to do his grocery shopping.

Layne looked at Felina and grinned, "It's fun looking at this stuff isn't it?"

She responded with a restricted smile. "Yeah, I can't believe I've lived in Arizona all my life and have never been here." Then, relaxing her pensive demeanor slightly, she said: "Can you tell me about this place and its history—be my tour guide?"

Layne inwardly beamed at the opportunity to impress her with what he'd learned about Bisbee in the short time he'd lived there. He'd driven past the Lavender Pit Overlook almost daily on his way to Douglas, and he had stopped a time or two to read the markers. That alone gave him enough to show off, he thought.

"They called Bisbee the Queen of the Copper Camps," he began, "after copper ore was discovered in the Mule Mountains around here in 1887. In the early 1900s it was one of the largest copper-producing areas in the world, and Bisbee was Arizona Territory's largest city; Arizona didn't become a state until 1912. Mining continued until 1975. After that Bisbee became an artists' colony, a hippie hangout, and a place for tourists to visit.

"On the way out of town, on the way to Douglas, there's a huge pit that's become a tourist attraction. It was actually three different surface mining operations between 1917 and 1974. It's four thousand feet wide, five thousand feet long and eight hundred fifty feet deep at its deepest point. It's called The Lavender Pit after the general manager of the Phelps

Dodge mining company, a guy named Harrison Lavender. He died in 1952 and by 1954 they dedicated the place to him."

Layne felt good about his little spiel, but what he thought would engage Felina's interest failed to draw the reaction he hoped for. He pretended not to notice Felina's generally preoccupied state of mind and avoided the topic he suspected was responsible for it. He was selective about what to mention so as to avoid accidentally shedding light on his difficulties at work. At the same time, he was absorbed in careful consideration about the right Christmas gift to surprise her with as his eyes scanned Indian beads and turquoise bracelets. Despite the underlying tension, Felina took in the surroundings with wonder and pleasure. He could tell that she was setting aside her unresolved issue with him until the window-shopping was finished.

He attempted to savor every second but felt time ticking away again. As much as he appreciated feeling well, he remained unfulfilled. Friday and Saturday nights seemed to go to waste if they were not spent partying. It was never a desire to be drunk again that caused him to return to drinking after he had quit. It was boredom and distorted rationalization that he fell victim to; recreation was boring without, at least, beer.

They passed by a cozy patio restaurant enclosed by an antique metal railing that showed a century's wear. An older couple sat at one of three tables with pilsner glasses of light beer in front of them; scarcely a sip had been drawn from their frosty glasses. Layne fixated on the carbonation bubbles traveling upward the length of the glasses to join the diminishing foam at the rim as he slogged by. He fantasized about rubbing elbows with the guests and surveying the menu, turning to the back to consider the ale and lager that was available on the old-fashioned taps. His mouth watered as he felt his resistance waning. A thought came to mind to devise an excuse to separate from Felina for ten clandestine minutes so he could slam a pint of draught beer. Then he realized that without her presence he wouldn't have put up a fight, and one beer would turn into fifty. His heart raced at the realization, and he looked to the sky to force the thought from his mind as the sun swirled its arm-warming heat.

Felina seemed to be satisfied with only walking and window-shopping without the intention of buying anything. He knew that she lacked spare money to buy an item that was non-essential to her survival, but she was too embarrassed to admit so. The realization reminded him that if he bungled this attempt at a career, the days of handholding with Felina would most likely become just a memory.

Layne and Felina remained connected to one another, passing by historic landmarks and Bed & Breakfast houses surrounded by cypress trees. They continued to trudge steeply uphill along the confined sidewalk that wound up and around the canyon hill, hugging the facades of Victorian saloons and candy stores that sold saltwater taffy.

Layne switched his grip on her tiny hand so that their fingers were interlaced. Her hand was pleasantly warm, and their palms continued to sweat against one another. His plan was to continue avoiding in-depth conversation and carry on touring the main commerce strip until they worked up an appetite. He was looking forward to ending their holiday tour at the restaurant in the historic Copper Queen Hotel. He tried to return to his "tour guide" persona as they approached it.

"Let me tell you about that grand old Victorian landmark," he said. "That hotel opened in 1902 and has NEVER closed. Really. The entry doors don't have locks, so they've been open for more than a century. Phelps Dodge needed a place for investors and company bigwigs to stay when they came to Bisbee to see the mines, so they built this place. It had seventy-two rooms, with a *shared bath* on each floor. Supposedly," he added, pausing in an attempt to build suspense then finishing with sinister emphasis, "*it's haunted.* They say three ghosts live there."

"I don't like ghosts," Felina said, giving Layne an opening to chivalrously declare: "Fear not! This Border Patrol Agent will protect you."

Felina's divine presence and his playful response distracted Layne from the quandary in which he found himself at the station involving his transition from field training to a regular unit. But the disapproving looks from the locals that owned the shops were beginning to overshadow what serenity existed. It reminded him that conflict seemed to follow him wherever he went.

Layne's calves became fatigued from walking the incline as they swung their arms together slightly. Silver and turquoise Indian jewelry attracted his attention from the periphery, and he stopped to peek into an alluring jewelry store while their hands remained joined.

"You want to go in here?" Layne asked her.

"Sure," Felina smiled, then she released her grip on his hand. Layne's hand seemed to miss hers as soon as she let go.

The door handle to the shop was cut from a tree trunk, and the door was surprisingly heavy. Layne had to pull with the majority of his weight to open it for her. A cowbell dinged as they entered, alerting the long-haired proprietor of their presence. He took notice, the sound of his grinder motor winding down. He came out from his workshop in the back of the store but failed to greet them. He wore horn-rimmed glasses and had a grey ponytail that took several rubber bands to manage; his braid reached all the way to the belt loops of his overalls. The shop smelled like leather and the electric motors of jewelry tools. It was cool inside.

Felina wandered with interest to one of the display cases while Layne put his hands in his pockets. He smiled briefly and politely in an attempt to greet the owner on his way to stand next to Felina.

"Let me know if you have any questions," the jeweler said in an unwelcoming tone as he looked Layne over judgmentally.

Layne could sense the man attempting to determine if he was a Border Patrol Agent. He considered that perhaps the guy might grant him clemency for being in the company of a Latina. Layne looked away from the jeweler's stare and leaned in and put his chin on Felina's shoulder, looking over her to see what items beneath the lighted glass of the display case interested her. The smell of her neck would linger for days in his mind after he had to say goodbye to her.

She was looking down at Indian jewelry that seemed to embody the geographic environment and history of the Southwest. Layne's eyes narrowed down the items and reverted back to a pair of silver earrings that caught his eye. They were the size of peas with a round turquoise stone in the center that he could visualize dangling from her ears. Just then she turned to look at him. She seemed to have become aware of his attraction to her hair being up and was wearing it so. She continued to stare over the display and Layne kissed her cheek and pinched her waist.

"Can we take a look at those?" Layne said to the jeweler. He wouldn't maintain eye contact with Layne for more than a moment.

The jeweler reached into his pocket and retrieved a ring of keys. He divided the keys and pinched a small one, then unlocked the display case from the back. Without looking at Layne, he pointed to a turquoise necklace, then a stick pin, until Layne succeeded in directing him to the earrings. "Those ones," Layne said.

The jeweler carefully handed them to him, and Layne put them in Felina's hand. She smiled a shy smile and pursed her lips to conceal her delight. She leaned her head to the side to remove the earrings she was wearing and set them on the display case. Layne grinned with anticipation. She tilted her head to the side again to put the posts of the earrings through her ears and fiddle with the backs to secure them. While he waited, Layne admired statically charged strands of hair at the top of her neck that were too short and had become detached from the clip that secured her tresses. They remained suspended adorably without purpose. Once the earrings were in place, she bashfully turned to model them. He was breathless and didn't ask the price; it was of no consequence.

"Merry Christmas," Layne said as he motioned to her to keep wearing them and paid the long-haired shopkeeper.

They walked hand in hand toward the Copper Queen, disinterested in the shops they passed due to their growing appetites. Layne was hoping that the gift he had bought Felina would dissuade her from bringing up whatever it was she was contemplating.

"Those earrings look good on you, Babe," Layne said.

"Thank you, I like them," Felina said.

He was hoping to get her to elaborate.

"Would you rather eat somewhere else, Babe? You don't seem too excited about the Copper Queen."

"No, this place we're going to is fine." Then Felina sighed as she said, "Layne, this is hard for me to say, but I need to talk to you when we get home."

The adrenaline blast that had stunned him off and on for the past nine months bolted down his spinal column and tingled in his extremities. He tried to camouflage his panic, but he could feel his face flush with heat, which caused his forehead to shine with dew sweat. He became frustrated and said, "Come on; don't tell me that now. How am I supposed to enjoy lunch with that hanging over my head? Just tell me now." The way she had put it sounded like she wanted to break up. He couldn't conceive of how he would carry on if she did. It seemed like dying. The sparkle in her eyes was what kept him alive once it was time to go back to the front.

"I'm sorry Layne, I didn't mean to make you mad. I just want to tell you something."

He considered that perhaps she was pregnant, and some of the tension released. He sighed and said, "Just tell me now so I'm not worried about it."

"I want you to get help with your drinking," Felina said abruptly.

Layne looked away, too embarrassed to make eye contact with her. His anger only intensified until he was steaming. Several long seconds passed before he was able to respond, "But I haven't had a drink in weeks."

"I know you haven't, and I'm proud of you. But I think that it's been hard for you with everything you're going through with BP. I think that something bothers you from a long time ago that's part of what is causing you to drink."

Layne continued walking, unable to speak. He looked at the sidewalk in front of his feet, then at the store windows to his right side as they continued to descend down the canyon hill. *Anything to avoid looking at her*, he thought. He knew she was waiting for a response, but his pride wouldn't allow him to submit to her while the insult was fresh. He knew the bathtub incident would continue to haunt him; he had known it when he saw her crying. He had believed she thought he was a normal person until that night.

Felina said, "It's not that big of a deal Layne. Marianne said Ryan told her the majority of the agents at Tucson Station drink way too much. He even said he thinks some of them drink at work. He says it smells like vodka in the room whenever they have their Muster meeting. I know the things you see and have to deal with can't help."

"Can we just not talk about it anymore today, please?" Layne grunted. He feared that she would tell him that she thought he would most likely start drinking again, and he might say something he couldn't take back.

They stood awkwardly silent next to each other on wood flooring in front of the hostess stand, waiting to be seated. Felina took her purse off her shoulder and looked through it for something, apparently to make sure her wallet was inside. Layne stared at an authentic mine cart and a pickaxe that were on display in the restaurant along with other pieces of mining equipment. Whoever designed the place, he thought, had done an excellent job creating the ambiance of an 1800s mining town.

The uncomfortable silence between them continued as they were seated. Layne customarily chose to sit directly next to her in a booth, but today he sat across the table from her. He immediately buried his face in a menu and pretended to be occupied by the choices, even though he had previously stated that he planned on ordering his favorite mussel soup. Felina glanced at him periodically to see if she could get him to make eye contact with her, but he resisted, childishly. She knew from past experience that it was best to allow him time to cool off before she attempted to break through and converse with him.

But the issue was pressing. She put her menu down and said, "Layne, will you talk to me, please?"

"What?" Layne said impolitely while his eyes remained trained on the page he was turning.

"It's not a big deal. A lot of people seek help for private issues they're having. You don't have to try to be macho all the time. I like you when you're yourself."

"You've been with me; you've seen that I haven't had a drink for several weeks. You don't think I can keep it up?" Layne said.

"I know you can, honey," Felina answered. "But I think there are things that bother you that you need to address and work out. I think it causes you to drink."

Layne began to respond when the waitress interrupted him to take their drink orders. Layne ordered a Diet Coke for Felina and an iced tea for himself. But beyond the waitress his eyes became fixated on beer taps at the bar where a woman in her forties was sitting on one of the tall chairs and eating a celery stick that had come with her Bloody Mary. He could taste the vodka-soaked celery on his tongue as the stalk crunched between his teeth. After the waitress collected their menus, his eyes moved on and allowed him a taste of each individual draught beer on tap, then the liquor behind the bar.

Felina regained his attention and said, "I would go see a counselor in a heartbeat if I could afford it. There are things that cause me to question myself that I would like to get help with—things that damage my opinion of myself. You've got the best health insurance available."

Layne knew he was going to have to placate her or she would eventually leave him. But his pride wouldn't allow him to submit to her now while he was angry. It was impossible. He said, "I'll go as soon as everything settles with BP, and I won't drink between now and then, okay?"

"Okay," Felina said.

20

MUSTER BROKE AND LAYNE stood up from his accustomed front row seat as the agents in the room pushed in their chairs and made their way to the line at the door. It was the last day of the five-day final evaluation, and if he was deemed adequate, Layne would be working by himself come Monday. The Spanish Oral Board would be the last obstacle in his way. He was scheduled for Day Shift during this pay period, and this was the beginning of his last day on Phase Four with Agent Cruz as his FTO. Cruz was leaning against the back wall, talking to one of his Hispanic agent friends from El Paso. Layne stood before him awaiting instruction, but Cruz ignored him for a moment before eventually saying, "Go get the keys from the equipment counter and meet me in the parking lot." Then he continued the conversation he was having.

Layne felt something was not right, but with false confidence he reassured himself that he was simply being paranoid. This was the first time he had gone more than a few days without alcohol for the past seven years. He considered that his foreboding was perhaps a withdrawal symptom of temperance. He checked out his assigned keys, and on a whim, did a U-turn in the hallway and decided to check next week's schedule in the Fishbowl, even though he didn't expect to find his name listed anywhere. He walked tall as he maneuvered through agent traffic coming the other way. Agents weren't eying him with the look of condemnation over the loss of his notebook the way they had previously. He assumed their change in attitude was due to his performance with Launius at the end of Phase Three.

Layne faced the bulletin board and ran his pointer finger down the list of names. As expected, he couldn't find his name among any of the line units. Instead his eyes glanced to the subheading for the Field Training Unit. Puzzled, he found his name and realized that Escribano had already assigned him an FTO to repeat Phase Four instead of leaving him off the schedule until Cruz submitted his evaluation. The rest of his classmates had remained unscheduled while their Phase Four evaluations were underway.

Layne found his assigned parking space and loaded his gear into the Kilo while his attention was elsewhere. With intense preoccupation he checked the Kilo's tires and filled up at the gas pump located in the center of the lot. Then he returned the vehicle to its parking space. With nothing else to do in preparation for the shift, he sat alone in the driver's seat and continued waiting for Cruz, whose chatty personality kept him in the station five minutes longer than the other agents. Layne fantasized momentarily. He was able to imagine what it would be like to leave the parking lot alone on his way to his assignment in the field. But the thought was fleeting. Instead, he wondered how benevolent and patient Felina would remain were he to become jobless.

His objective still seemed within his grasp. Nonetheless, he never seemed to be able to focus on a single worry; they always came in groups to overwhelm him. The politics that governed the Spanish Oral Board Exam frightened him. He feared he might freeze up under the intense pressure he anticipated. But he reminded himself he had once gone over a month without speaking English while in Mexico. It had been lonely not being able to wholly express himself, and the memory of the feeling overcame him momentarily. He felt much the same today—the rest of his classmates had already been assigned to units and seemed to have separated themselves from him.

Cruz startled him out of his reverie when he opened the passenger side door and began loading his gear into the truck. He was carrying his Border Patrol-issued green duffel bag over his shoulder—the attractive accessory was issued only to career agents. Layne envied the bag the way he had a high school letter jacket while he was in junior high. He admired how

Cruz always wore his green insulated vest with the long-sleeve uniform top and carried only the bare minimum equipment. Watching him, Layne felt like a child yearning to be a rock star.

"I just checked the schedule for next week and Escribano has me with Tipton for Phase Four again," Layne said, broaching the subject that was weighing on his mind. "Have you already turned in your final evaluation for me?"

"No, I can't submit that until this afternoon when we're done. Are you sure he already has you down?" Cruz shimmied his torso as he lifted his duty belt to reposition it before he got in to sit down in the passenger seat.

Cruz's answer only elevated Layne's concern, "Yeah, I'm sure."

"Wait here," Cruz said, reopening the passenger door. "I'll be back in a few minutes."

Layne's anxiety swelled as he watched Cruz head back into the station through the side view mirror. He had been hoping for a simple explanation that alleviated his worry.

After fifteen minutes he saw Cruz in the side view mirror, returning through the parking lot. Layne could tell that he was bearing bad news by the way he carried himself. He watched his feet and seemed lost in thought as he walked. Layne watched him in the mirrors until he opened the door and climbed in.

"What did he say?" Layne said as soon as the door opened.

"He said that Ashlock started a paper trail on you and that he can't pass you from FTU until you pass the Oral Board because of it," Cruz appeared indignant as he situated himself.

Layne couldn't withhold his outrage over the news, "That's bull." He pounded the steering wheel with a hammer fist, and a brief honk came out. "Ashlock wrote that memo because he's a hater."

Cruz acknowledged Layne's disappointment but kept his gaze forward, out the front window. "I told him I was the most experienced FTO and that he was going around me. But he said there was nothing he could do."

Layne blurted an expletive. Unless he passed the Spanish Oral Board, he would have to repeat Phase Four several more times with other FTOs that weren't as friendly as Cruz.

"He wouldn't have told me, but he could tell I was angry, so he panicked and told me. It was heated. That weasel Ashlock pressed that memo," Cruz said.

"Why can't Escribano just ignore it?" Layne whimpered.

"He can't. It's in your file. If Cabrera was still the Training Supervisor, he would just throw it away. He didn't care about petty things like this. But Escribano is bucking for promotion. He's trying to be an instructor at the Academy." Cruz looked over at Layne and shrugged his shoulders to confirm that there was nothing he could do.

Layne said, "What if I pass the ten-month, though?"

"That along with a passing grade on Phase Four means you're done with training. You won't be Escribano's problem anymore. But he's not putting you on a unit until that test is over," Cruz said. "They're gonna be gunning for you big time at headquarters for the Oral Board. I'm sure Escribano will send along a message with Cunningham for them to give you the axe. But if you can speak Spanish, it'll be obvious what they're doing. I just don't know.

"Come on, we better head out."

Layne started the Kilo and maneuvered through the parking lot, heading down the driveway through the gate toward the highway.

"You know, screw this. I'm not doin' squat today," Cruz said as he tucked his G-426 into his shirt pocket. "I'm gonna give you a perfect score in every category this evaluation, just to tweak him. What's the point of doing anything?"

"Yeah, screw it," Layne agreed.

"Let's go to Walmart and look at chicks," Cruz suggested.

Layne followed the highway toward Main Street as he fantasized about getting even with Ashlock and Escribano. He couldn't force the resentment to settle. "I can't believe he's still screwin' with me. Did you know that I caught forty-six the other day with Launius?"

"Yeah, I heard," Cruz said.

Layne felt compelled to share details he found interesting because they dovetailed with the theory that Launius had shared with him. "I called the U.S. Attorney and asked him if he wanted to prosecute. The guy said, 'Great job, son.' He asked me if we caught the mules carrying the dope. I said no, but they had burlap all over them and we backtracked them and found it. Two hundred twenty-six pounds! I had just weighed it. The U.S. Attorney said that it wasn't enough weight to devote resources to. He said the docket's all backed up."

"I think it needs to be 500 pounds to prosecute," Cruz said.

The threshold for quantity only further validated the view Launius expressed the previous week. But Layne had decided not to bring up the conversation with anyone, even Cruz. He didn't want to sound crazy. He didn't know if anyone else had similar beliefs. Instead he said, "When we ran the mules' prints, one of the guys had a sexual assault in South Carolina. He probably raped some chick out there, and they still let him go."

Cruz's mood seemed somber. "He probably wanted to get prosecuted, so he didn't have to go back to Mexico."

"Why?" Layne asked, surprised.

Cruz looked over and explained the obvious: "Because they lost the cartel's dope. *Sicarios* will probably blow those guys away to make an example, so other people are more careful."

Layne steered the Kilo into the Walmart parking lot and found an empty space away from the mass of cars near the entrance. Their parking space was less than forty yards from the Port of Entry, facing the incoming walk lane from Agua Prieta. He turned off the engine and the two of them observed the queue of Mexicans with border crossing cards and visas waiting to pass through.

A Walmart employee wearing a florescent orange vest struggled for leverage to push a centipede of shopping carts past them. Layne avoided looking directly at him, embarrassed about what he was doing.

"Look at this chick," Layne said, pointing towards a pair of girls headed their way. "We gotta wait for her to go by so I can get a look at her from behind in the side-view mirror." He expected Cruz to chime in with a witty remark. But his mood was still somewhat restrained because of his confrontation with Escribano.

"You know, these people here are normal," Cruz said. "The ones who come from a decent background have enough money to survive and they just come here to do business. They follow the rules."

Layne picked up on Cruz's mood and agreed.

Cruz continued, "The ones we catch are the poorest of the poor. Most people aren't interested in crossing illegally."

Layne had noticed that the young men and women from Mexico who crossed through the Port of Entry with border crossing cards were scrupulous about their appearance. The men all wore Puma shoes and designer jeans, and molded their hair into the same wide Mohawk with gelled spikes. He enjoyed observing the way the girls matched the color of their eye shadow with the color top they were wearing. They reminded him of Felina. The way they prepared themselves was the essence of what he found most attractive about women. He could smell Felina's perfume thinking about it. The girls who walked past possessed the same keen sense of attention to detail that she did. Glitter sparkled on their eyelids when they blinked; they were exotic and alluring to him.

"That chick right there is as K-1 as it gets. It's indisputable," he said, pointing to a girl who was returning her documentation to her purse while she waited for her companion to be admitted into the country by a Customs official.

"I'll have to wait and see when she gets closer. I can't call it from here," Cruz said.

"We better search her for weapons before she goes into Walmart." Layne pointed at her as the pair of girls approached from the front.

"Don't point," Cruz said as he pretended not to be looking at her. He spoke with a mouthful of tortilla chips and prepared to wash it down with a liter-size glass bottle of Mexican Coca-Cola.

Layne felt suddenly restless. "I can't take much more of this. It's hard just to sit here and watch them—that's why I don't go to strip joints. It's like torturing yourself." He started the engine and pulled out of the parking lot onto Main Street. Cruz continued eating and didn't concur or object.

He drove purposeless throughout the east side streets, ignoring any traffic that came over the radio. Making the watch hands move was more laborious than it seemed, he realized. To consume time, he began following vehicles with Sonora license plates, but only those with female drivers. He unexpectedly came to a stoplight alongside a soccer mom driving a minivan and surveyed her without much effort to be indiscernible. She sighed, and it was apparent that she wanted him to pull ahead of her. But when the light turned green, he accelerated sluggishly, she quickly lost patience and drove faster to escape his lecherous gaping. He took notice of her Arizona license plate and laughed to see that it read, "NO1MOM."

"Let's pull her over. She's got huge tits," Layne said excitedly.

"No, don't."

"I'll run her plates then," Layne said.

Cruz shrugged with uncertainty and Layne grabbed the radio microphone and said, "866, Delta-328."

"Go ahead," Lori, the woman performing as LECA, responded.

"Can I get a twenty-eight, twenty-nine on a Dodge Astrovan?"

"Ten-four."

"Arizona Plates: November, Oscar, One, Mike, Oscar, Mike," Layne said with a grin. Even Cruz was smiling.

"Ten-four, standby."

More time passed than Layne had expected, and he became anxious after thirty seconds had passed without response. He began to rethink the stunt, taking his situation concerning management into consideration.

The LECA's voice burst through the radio, "Negative on the twenty-eight, twenty-nine, no warrants."

The two of them broke out laughing and the tension released. Layne continued driving aimlessly. "Where should we go now?"

"Let me think," Cruz said as he rubbed his chin and wiped the corners of his mouth.

"Let's go all the way to the New Mexico Border and back," Layne suggested.

"Nah, that's too far."

"Let's go eat breakfast at that restaurant in Portal," Layne tried again.

"Sounds good. I didn't eat anything this morning," Cruz said.

Layne headed northeast out of town on Highway 80, but just as he settled in and set the cruise control on seventy miles per hour, the voice of Lori, the LECA, came over the radio: "All available Units, ten-ten, shots fired approximately one mile south of Pirtleville on 191. Repeat, shots fired one mile south of Pirtleville on 191."

Layne's spine tingled as if he had heard the emergency broadcast signal for a tornado warning back home.

"Pull over, let me drive!" Cruz commanded.

Layne slid to a stop on the dirt and gravel shoulder, and they got out and passed one another in front of the Kilo, like a Chinese fire drill, to trade seats. Cruz cramped the wheel left, glanced quickly in both directions and did a U-turn. Layne clinched the grab handle on the ceiling; he had never seen Cruz this alarmed. As he tore off back toward town, Cruz reached down to turn on the emergency lights and activate the siren. Cars coming toward them pulled over to the shoulder of the road as he raced past them. He was pushing the truck to its limits.

"I've never heard a ten-ten in six years," Cruz said loudly over the engine noise.

Layne held on as they accelerated, "What's going on?"

"It's gotta be Darmody, he's MIT Pan Am today." Cruz said aloud. "That guy's crazy. They told you to avoid him whenever you can, right?" Cruz was focused on the road ahead, his face thrust toward the front windshield as the engine raced.

"Tipton told us he's a trouble magnet and to stay away from him whenever he's working traffic," Layne shouted. They sped past vehicles in their lane that had pulled over halfway onto the shoulder after having seen the flashing lights in their mirrors. In an instant Layne became conscious of the power their authority wielded and felt more important than he ever had before.

"He's right," Cruz shouted. "He's a good guy. He's the best agent at the station, probably in the whole BP. But the guy finds trouble. You don't wanna get involved with that. You just wanna show up and make the routine plays then go home. You don't wanna get in gunfights or anything."

"Darmody's a beast," Layne said as he envisioned Darmody calmly changing magazines amidst the chaos of a gun battle.

Cruz was approaching the intersection of Highway 191 and slowed to turn right and head north to the scene. Ahead of them, Border Patrol vehicles were leaning to one side in mid-turn onto Highway 191, coming at high speed from other directions with their emergency lights flashing blue and red. Layne gripped the ceiling handle with both hands and his torso swayed to the left side as Cruz made the right turn and stomped on the gas to follow the others.

"Maybe there's still a shootout going on?" Layne speculated out loud as he press-checked his pistol to ensure that there was a round chambered.

"I doubt it," Cruz said while he concentrated. The engine sprinted as they passed confused civilian vehicles with their brake lights on, looking for a place to get out of the way.

"It'll be over before we get there," Cruz said aloud.

Layne's heart was thumping as he held on and visualized the two of them barricaded behind the hood of the truck, taking selective shots at smugglers during a standoff. For some reason he wasn't concerned about his own safety. Perhaps he was inspired by Darmody—he was like a Border Patrol Agent action figure that Layne would have played with as a child. But before he could enjoy the shootout fantasy, Cruz began slowing rapidly to a stop. A quarter mile long traffic jam of civilian and police vehicles, all with emergency lights flashing, blocked the roadway.

Cruz rammed the Kilo into Park, and they jumped out and climbed onto the roof of the truck to attempt to see what was going on ahead. A red emergency medical helicopter had landed at the front of the gridlock with rotors still spinning. A Border Patrol Kilo was coming back toward them from the front, driving on the dirt outside of the shoulder to avoid the column of stationary vehicles.

"Hey, it's Sepulveda. I know him," Cruz said.

They climbed down from the roof of the truck and Cruz flagged him down. Sepulveda stepped on the brake when he recognized his friend. He looked like he had seen a ghost as he rolled down his window.

"Was it Darmody?" Cruz asked with urgency, the concern evident in his voice.

"Yep," Sepulveda said.

"What happened, bro? Did you see it?"

"I got there right after," Sepulveda said. "Darmody's Kilo was parked about 100 yards behind a red twin-cab Chevy truck."

"What happened?" Cruz asked.

"Evidently, Darmody knew it was a load vehicle and pulled it over. I heard he told the driver to turn off the engine and give him the keys, and the guy started arguing with him. So Darmody reached in and tried to take the keys out of the ignition, and the guy tried to take off. Darmody's arm got caught in the seatbelt and the truck started dragging him, so he pulled out his gun and shot the guy so he'd stop. He got him through the chest. There's blood all over the windshield."

"Are you kidding me?" Cruz said.

"There were aliens packed in the back cab. The bullet went through the seat and missed this girl's face by a couple inches." Sepulveda was visibly dismayed and psychologically affected by what he had seen.

"Is the guy dead?" Cruz asked.

"The paramedics tried to revive him, but he's done. Darmody's still up there talking to the PAIC." Sepulveda looked at Layne and then back at

Cruz. "Didn't you guys hear the twenty-eight, twenty-nine, about twenty minutes ago?"

"No, we were out east on a different frequency," Cruz said. Layne kept quiet.

"Watch your back," Sepulveda warned, and then he moved on.

Cruz motioned to Layne, "Let's go back. There's nothing we can do." He resumed his seat behind the wheel. Layne took one more look ahead then hopped back in the passenger seat. Cruz turned around and headed back into town.

"That's crazy," Layne said.

Cruz seemed just as concerned as Sepulveda now. "That's why you call in a twenty-eight, twenty-nine, before you pull somebody over. So even if there aren't any warrants, the station has a record of the license plate. Also, so everyone stays off the radio. So they don't tie it up until the agent radios that he's Code Four."

"I can't believe Darmody isn't hurt, if the guy was dragging him," Layne said. "He's like James Bond . . . 007."

Cruz laughed. "See what I mean? You really wanna get dragged by a truck and barely escape with your life?"

Layne shook his head.

Cruz added, "You're supposed to touch the trunk or the tailgate of the truck with your bare hand before you approach the driver. That's so if you get blown away, the cops'll be able to match your fingerprints to the getaway vehicle for evidence."

"I can't believe he blasted somebody," Layne mused, trying to contemplate what had happened.

"He's done it before. He shot some dude about three years ago," Cruz said.

"Did he kill that guy, too?"

"No, but the guy was in the hospital for three months. I think he's paralyzed from the waist down. The guy was a sleazy alien smuggler from Pirtleville," Cruz said.

"Dang."

Cruz said, "You're supposed to take a week or two off to clear your head if you're involved in something traumatic like that. Darmody was back at work the next day, taking notes in Muster like it was just another day." Cruz seemed to still be stunned. "I wouldn't be surprised if he's at work tomorrow, driving up and down 191. He's so salty that when a vehicle is coming toward him in the other highway lane, he can tell if it's good just by glancing at it."

Layne's fascination with Darmody continued to evolve. He was like a droid—a righteous sociopath. Layne wished his courage and temperament mirrored Darmody's. He was able to remain mentally balanced, heel to toe on the fulcrum, regardless of what happened to him. The incident overshadowed his anger at Ashlock and Escribano for the time being.

He couldn't wait to tell Felina about it.

LAYNE SLUMPED LOW IN his seat, with his arms crossed on the table in front of him, as he continued to look straight ahead. He was surrounded by the bustle of the Muster Room five minutes before the start of the swing shift at 2:00 p.m. He tried to be invisible as he separated a photocopy of the G-426 from the stack that was handed to him, then passed the stack to the trainee sitting to his left. It was obvious that the trainee had just arrived from the Academy. Layne intentionally missed the opportunity to make eye contact with the new guy so he wouldn't have to introduce himself. The first question unacquainted trainees asked one another was their class number. Layne preferred to avoid explaining why he was still on the Field Training Unit while the rest of his class and those in the class behind him already were assigned to regular line units.

Layne studied the G-426 but couldn't decode the motive for Escribano switching FTO Cruz from day shift to Swings in order to repeat his observation of Layne during another week of Phase Four. Perhaps it was to send a message to the both of them. Layne surmised that Escribano had scheduled him for Swings in order to demoralize him by attempting to further disrupt his sleep cycle. But Layne didn't understand why he was involving Cruz. Maybe Cruz truly was the only FTO who was both available and qualified to conduct a Phase Four evaluation and Layne was overanalyzing the situation. Layne stared at the dry erase board in deep thought as Figueroa, the FOS in command of the shift, began taking roll. Layne glanced at the clock high on the wall to realize it had turned 2:00 p.m., and the agents had all settled in to fill the room behind him.

"Bettany."

"Here."

"De Andrea."

"Present."

"Pirkis."

"Here."

"Sheppard."

Layne stared at his folded hands on the table in front of him and said "here" as though he were trying not to wake a baby in the next room. He deduced that many of the agents had probably heard his name as the subject of gossip. But they probably didn't know who Layne was by sight, so they were using roll call as an opportunity to identify him. His sleep-deprived eyes continued to scan his copy of the Daily Assignment Log to remain busy while he waited for roll call to end. Even after the FOS finished taking attendance, Layne felt as if all eyes remained upon him. It felt identical to the alcohol issue at the Academy. There was nothing more embarrassing than trying to pretend that everything was normal when those he interacted with, both friendly and hostile, knew for certain that it wasn't.

Here at the station, it was the way the agents looked away when it was time to make eye contact that bothered him. He feared that they were aware of the pitfalls and booby traps Escribano was arranging for him at the Spanish Oral Board Exam. He felt beset on all sides. The mounting pressure of the exam was compounded by his awareness that it was the final hand in this high-stakes game to turn his life around that he'd been playing for two years. He would be all-in, with every last chip to his name on the table—the highest-value chip being his relationship with Felina.

After Muster broke, he found Cruz in the back of the room; he had been leaning against the wall as usual during the briefing. "Go get the keys from checkout. I'll meet you in the parking lot," Cruz told him, then quickly resumed his conversation with another Hispanic agent from El Paso.

Layne waited in line at equipment checkout behind Carlos, who greeted him but avoided conversation. Layne didn't blame him. He considered that it might be hazardous for Carlos to be seen interacting with him.

This time, Cruz arrived at the assigned parking space only a few minutes after Layne. He loaded his gear in the cab of the Kilo and climbed in as Layne watched him with his hands already on the steering wheel. Agents were getting into their vehicles all around them. Layne waited for Cruz to completely shut the door before he began speaking, in case anyone could hear them.

"Are you pissed he put you on Swings with me?" Layne asked.

"Not really. As long as it's not Mids. It's a change of scenery. I've been on Days for a long time," Cruz stated.

"You gave me almost a hundred percent on my evaluation, right?" Layne asked optimistically.

"Yeah, like, a ninety-five," Cruz said.

"It doesn't matter. He's gonna have me repeat until I take the ten-month in a couple weeks. No matter what you put on the eval, he's gonna have me do it again with another FTO next week. He's just hoping he can get me to quit with shift changes every week."

"I think you're right. At first, I thought he might put you on a unit, but I underestimated him. I've never seen a bigger CYA guy in my life. Just be ready for a curveball when you take that test."

"What I don't understand," Layne continued, "is why he switched the schedule. He had me with Tipton on Mids. Then he changed me to Swings with you. I don't get it."

"I don't get it, either," Cruz said. "He's just hoping he can get you to resign. All I can say is don't quit. And pass the ten-month. If you can pull that off, you're on a unit. There's nothing he can do; you passed Phase One, Two, and Three, and I passed you on Phase Four. If you get above a seventy percent on the ten-month, you graduate from training. I don't know what else to tell you.

"You know how it works, right?" Cruz continued. "The whole test is conducted in Spanish. They'll ask questions in Spanish, and you have to respond in Spanish. Your responses should indicate that you comprehend Spanish. Make sure you use the right tenses of the verbs and have person agreement. You know, me, you, us, all of us, etc."

Cruz's friendly voice lifted Layne's mood a bit and he started the Kilo. "What do you want to do this week then?" he asked Cruz.

"I'm getting bored just screwing around. Let's get into something. It'll make it go by faster." Cruz grabbed the ceiling handle and situated himself into his seat.

Layne settled in at sixty-five miles per hour on the highway, heading southeast toward Douglas. Despite the confusion of his internal clock, his normal curiosity functioned because of his affinity for Cruz.

"They keep talking about drive-throughs in Muster. What's that all about? No one ever explained it to me."

The subject seemed old and worn out to Cruz. He appeared to still be mulling over the situation with Escribano. Finally, he answered: "The cartels load pickup trucks with marijuana and put a tarp over the bed. Then they sneak across the border way out in the desert and drive it into town. Drive-throughs are called Tangos, in our sector, Delta Tangos."

Layne remained mystified and continued to press Cruz for a more detailed explanation. Cruz explained that the Mexicans routinely stole half-ton pickup trucks from Phoenix and Tucson and brought them back to Mexico. The smugglers loaded a thousand pounds or more of brick marijuana into the bed of the truck then drove across the border far out east or west of town where the agents were spread thin. The sections of the border where they chose to cross were fortified by no more than tumbledown barbed wire with rotting wood fence posts. In many places, the smugglers didn't even need to cut the wire to breach the fence because the barbed wire was already lying flat on the ground. To new agents, it was astounding that this was the only obstacle that the richest country in the world erected for border defense. It made Launius's theories about the border seem not so ridiculous.

Cruz explained that Tango season corresponded with the Mexican marijuana harvest. When the dope was ready to be delivered to distributors on the American side of the border, the mysterious trucks began to appear. The trucks customarily made their runs after midnight, blacked-out. Except for the headlights, every light in the truck was disabled—from the taillights to the dome and dashboard lights. They turned off their headlights upon crossing the border in order to travel with complete stealth. Like foxes, many of them routinely snuck into town without ever being noticed. After they delivered their cargo, they reactivated their lights and returned to Mexico through the southbound lane at the Port of Entry, like any other vehicle. If an alert was issued across the border to be on the lookout for a particular truck, the driver would return to Mexico via the same route over trampled barbed wire by which he had arrived.

Although the agents knew the truck's destination was typically in 5-Bravo, the drivers still seemed to be virtually impossible to catch. Their goal was to arrive unseen to the residential streets east of the Port of Entry, where a garage and crew were on standby, ready to swiftly unload sometimes up to a ton of dope. If they suspected that agents were aware of their presence, they would lay over for the night, safe with the truck stored in an anonymous garage until the heat blew over. If they arrived without a tail, they returned to Mexico immediately. After it was delivered, the marijuana was apportioned and gathered by a separate fleet of smugglers who transported it to Phoenix, Los Angeles, and Albuquerque, from which it was distributed nationwide.

Layne checked his rearview mirror and kept the speedometer at sixty-five. "I can't believe they have the balls to try that with all of us here."

Cruz instinctively looked in the passenger side view mirror when Layne checked behind them, then responded. "They're pros; they do it for a living. They're the guys who drive big trucks around in Mexico listening to that accordion music all the time."

"What about the Mexican cops; don't they notice anything?" Layne had heard rumors about their involvement in trafficking.

Cruz confirmed his suspicions. "Those drivers are working for the cartels. The cops aren't gonna do anything to them."

"I heard in Muster the other day that Mexican cops reported finding a stolen truck from Phoenix abandoned in AP," Layne said with puzzlement.

"They steal trucks from up here and use them a few times, then they ditch them in AP somewhere. The Mexican cops just report it so it looks like they're trying to help. But they're never gonna give us any useful intel or they'll get killed," Cruz explained.

Layne visualized the trucks being efficiently loaded within secret garages in Mexico, preparing for their missions like bomber pilots from clandestine takeoff strips. The scenes he imagined emulated World War II movies he remembered, involving high-risk aerial missions. Naively, he had thought of a McDonald's drive-through when the trucks were mentioned in passing during Muster. But after he heard Cruz's explanation, a charismatic concept of the drivers blossomed in his mind. Layne became quiet with fascination. The pilots of the mysterious trucks were nestling themselves into a special place within his imagination—a realm of unrivaled mystique among Spitfire pilots, Pony Express jockeys and Steve McQueen. Once they were there, they would never leave. He stared into space while he continued driving south down Main Street.

Cruz interrupted his stargazing. "I don't wanna be by the port tonight. Let's go to 5-Delta."

Layne cut behind Walmart and drove west on International Road. Despite another week with an FTO, and his departure from Border Patrol becoming a more realistic possibility, he lost himself in the moment and felt in charge. He waved confidently at the line agents, one by one, as they passed by the static posts of the west side.

Layne didn't want to annoy Cruz with too many questions, but he couldn't let the subject of drug smuggling drop. "What else do you know about the drive-throughs?"

Cruz seemed willing to continue discussing the topic. "I've heard they're professional race car drivers from Spain. They get paid, like, ten grand per run."

"I'll bet they're good, huh?" Layne goaded.

"Yeah, they're good. It's almost impossible to spike 'em. They dodge stop sticks like whiffle balls."

Layne grinned and became more enthralled the more Cruz gratified his interest. As they drove, they passed agents standing next to generators and their Hollywood lights, waiting to turn them on when day fell to night in a few hours.

"What gets me is: All those agents against one driver?"

"It's not that simple," Cruz replied, looking past Layne in the driver's seat, checking activity behind the pickets of the Border Fence. "We aren't even supposed to be chasing them. And a lot of times they're getting help from up here."

"What do you mean?"

"There's agents working for the south side," Cruz explained.

Layne gave him a skeptical look.

"You'll notice it when someone bangs-in at the last minute. It leaves the zone short a position. As soon as the unit goes ten-eight, a drive-through will go right past that section of the zone."

"So, the guy who bangs-in calls the guys on the south side and tells them?" Layne had a multitude of questions and was trying to select the most interesting aspects.

"No, the guy who bangs-in probably has nothing to do with it. It's someone in Muster. As soon as the supervisor lets the unit know they're missing a guy, anyone in the room could send a text message to the south side and let them know which zone and what part has a position missing."

"So, the dirty agent is like the quarterback using an audible." Layne was proud of his analogy.

Cruz changed his tone to emphasize an important point. "You know that you're not supposed to chase them in a vehicle, right? For liability?"

Layne repeated what he remembered from briefings in Muster and instructional videos at the Academy. "If the vehicle doesn't yield to emergency lights, then you're supposed to break pursuit and turn around 180 degrees." He didn't completely understand the scenario that the FOS was referring to when he mentioned the pursuit in Muster, but he remembered what was said because of the way the FOS had phrased it: "If you crash into a minivan full of kids and screw yourself up chasing somebody, not only will you be sued, you'll be lying in a hospital bed with no pay and no health insurance because you'll be fired."

Layne recalled hearing a chase during the first month he had arrived. One night he heard agents pursuing a vehicle over the Mule Two frequency when his group was with Tipton. The agents were frantic over the radio, rushing to direct other agents to block the path of whatever they were chasing. It sounded like the fray of radio communication during combat. Layne had been so new to border occurrences that he didn't understand what was happening. He hadn't even realized it had anything to do with dope.

Cruz said, "The agents chase 'em because they don't want the south side rubbing it in their face that the dope is getting through. It's an ego thing. But the only way to stop 'em is to lay-in somewhere and spike 'em."

When Layne thought about what Cruz said, it made sense. The only effective defense against the renegade vehicles was to deploy stop sticks, or as they were sometimes referred to, "stingers."

"Did you get to see that video where a Highway Patrolmen shows how to deploy the stop sticks?" Cruz asked. "The demonstration was in a parking lot with orange cones."

"Yeah, it reminded me of the movie *Jackass*," Layne said. They both laughed.

Layne recalled watching a video in which a Highway Patrolman wearing a helmet was driving a Crown Victoria test vehicle and another cop threw stop sticks under the car when he drove by. There was a boom and the test car instantly sank a foot and screeched to a halt amidst smoke and noise from the friction of the rims on the pavement. After the stunt was complete, the Highway Patrolman explained the mechanics of the stop sticks while the test car lay slouching behind him, crippled. The stop sticks were a pair of triangular shaped boxes approximately four feet long that were attached to a cord. Inside the boxes were tire shredders that look like jacks from the children's game. The multi-pointed spikes were hollow and when the car's tires ran over the box, it collapsed and the spikes inside penetrated through the tread and detached, which deflated the tires like hypodermic needles.

"I bet it's touchy, layin' those mothers," Layne said, anticipating more entertainment.

"Oh, it's sketchy" Cruz said. "The key is stealth; they didn't show it good on the video. You hide the box behind a bush or something then you lay the trigger cord across the road, so the guy driving doesn't see anything until the last second. When the vehicle gets close enough, you pull the boxes under the tires."

Cruz seemed to secretly share Layne's fascination with glory, at least in the abstract. His enthusiasm for discussion prompted Layne to stargaze again. He was forever chasing his lifelong aspiration; the Border Patrol endeavor was just another shot-on-goal in the grand scheme. If he could manage to be impressed with himself to a certain extent, he believed he would reach a level of self-respect that would negate any character flaw, and eliminate self-loathing forever. It was the utopia he had been striving for since his athletic career ended.

"Like a trap," Layne said. Just the word "spike" stimulated his heart. But it seemed more dangerous than skydiving.

"It's the easiest way to get killed, though," Cruz warned, as if he had been reading Layne's thoughts. "Some guy got killed in California a while back throwing spikes." Cruz looked away, trying to recall the details.

"I remember that," Layne told him.

"You gotta make sure you got plenty of cover. You hide the spikes on one side of the road and get down low on the other side, on your stomach." Layne was looking at Cruz while he spoke. "Then you've gotta have the balls to wait 'til the front tires are only a few yards from the cord. Then, you yank the stop sticks under the tires and, peace, you can get all four tires if you're good."

Layne nodded as he visualized himself yanking the stop sticks under the tires of a vehicle driven by a notorious smuggler. The hair stood up on his arms when he imagined the respect he would earn from the agents at the station, even those in management.

"The problem is, the driver always swerves when he sees the cord and, sometimes, he runs you over. It's risky," Cruz continued. "Most of the guys who've been here for a while won't lay spikes. Even when one drives right past 'em. And a lot of supervisors won't even authorize using them because they don't want the responsibility if something goes wrong, like if the driver loses control and hits another car or flips and gets hurt or killed. Whatever happens is on us as soon as we use the spikes."

"Have you ever seen someone get one?" Layne asked.

"I heard Ortiz has. They say he's done it a couple of times. He's been here so long that he knows where they're headed. He lays in somewhere where he has time to camouflage the sticks and everything. He's got the timing down cold, so he yanks the cord at the right moment."

Layne had overheard Ortiz bragging about spiking a vehicle one time. His storytelling mannerisms and hand gestures made it look like fishing with a fly rod, and he made the strikeout signal an umpire makes when he bragged that he blew all four tires out. But he went on to say that he was amazed that the truck made it all the way back to Mexico on rims with sparks flying in its wake. The drivers of the renegade trucks seemed to possess superhuman powers when avoiding capture.

Layne imagined a medal of valor being placed around his neck on a podium in an auditorium somewhere as the audience rose from their seats and broke out in applause. The scenes he visualized inevitably led the focus of his musing back to Felina. He imagined her proudly clapping with tears in her eyes as he was being awarded. Imaginary scenes of his mind's design dated back to the far reaches of his childhood memory. The splendor that fueled his imagination was often the adornment of a girl who wouldn't notice him, someone he felt inferior to. In the dreamlike scenes, his heroism earned him the love of the girl and usually ended with him marrying her. As he drove and Cruz remained quiet, Layne realized that Felina was the first crush he'd had on a girl since he was in college seven years prior. This was the first situation in his life when the girl he desired was actually within his reach, and the spectacular scenes he visualized to sweep her off her feet were actually viable.

But the reflection of Felina's face in his mind's eye prompted the return of reality, and the dream became dreary with fright. Actuality made lucid the seemingly impenetrable barrier that was the Oral Board Exam—the dream-killer that would likely stop him just inches shy of victory and true romance. He could feel his pulse in his lips when he imagined the pressure he would be under when the class arrived at headquarters in Tucson next Friday morning. To stand a chance, it was imperative that his sympathetic aunt should come through one last time with an envelope containing Valium. The envelope was supposed to arrive within the next two days. Without the drug, he would invariably panic, and his mind would go blank the moment he ran into the slightest bit of difficulty during the exam. There was no way to know what measures Escribano had taken to stack the odds against him, and a thought came to him that turned his stomach.

"Are you feeling okay man? You look pale," Cruz said to Layne with concern.

"I just feel queasy all of a sudden," Layne said, and sweat began beading on his brow and his upper lip. He let off the gas pedal and slowed down to twenty-five miles per hour and considered stopping.

"Don't puke in the truck; if you feel like you're gonna hurl, just stop," Cruz said as he kept an eye on Layne.

"I'll be alright," Layne assured as he accelerated back to forty-five miles per hour to continue west down International Road. A thought had come and gone that caused him to briefly become nauseous. He put forth effort to remain positive, but he couldn't completely hold back thoughts about what he would do in the event that he didn't pass the exam. It was the consequences of failure in relation to Felina that had made him ill. He had only begun to conceptualize how he might manage to maintain his relationship with her; it was this thought specifically that had made him sick. He simply couldn't fathom how he could succeed in holding on to her without the means to impress her with money or a uniform.

It was deflating to think of trying to woo her while he was employed in a low-paying, unexceptional job without prestige or glamour. He realized he had no reason to believe his relationship with her involved prerequisites. He simply believed there had to be something special about him to be worthy of her, based on his past experiences with attractive women. Women as gorgeous as Felina seemed to be perpetually searching for a higher profile catch with more resources.

Layne's dismal glimpse of his possible future caused his mood to further decline. It led him to imagine reading discontent in Felina's attitude once he was an ordinary person. It would prompt him to begin saving every dime he could put away in order to buy her a gift that might make her smile—something that might persuade her just to stay with him a while longer, until her goodwill was exhausted.

He forced himself to change the subject in his mind before his thoughts wandered too far into the dark and caused his mind, in addition to his stomach, to become ill. Devoting too much thought to such bleak subject matter could cause him to lose his ability to choose not to think about certain things.

Mercifully, the shift ended a few hours later without incident.

LAYNE SAT DOWN FOR Muster in the same seat he had been sitting at for the past month. He quietly looked behind him at the agents standing around in small huddles waiting for the briefing to commence. They were laughing and chatting like they were at a cocktail party; word of another Tango during Mids had aroused their storytelling enthusiasm. They were recounting previous drive-through chases to each other, using their hands as models like fighter pilots—depicting how they had been out-turned and out-sped by the aces from south of the border.

Layne looked at the clock and saw that the FOS was running a few minutes late. He felt much better tonight after a solid eight hours of sleep. His eyes and alertness had almost returned to normal. He had made a run to Nogales that morning and picked up thirty Tafil at a seedy *farmácia* within walking distance from the Port of Entry. Tafil is a controlled substance used to treat anxiety and panic disorder which, he knew, could cause paranoid or suicidal impulses and impair judgment and other functions. But he felt the benefits outweighed the risks.

During attendance, when the FOS came to his name, he said, "here" a little bit louder than the night before. No one seemed to be paying any attention to him; perhaps he had been paranoid, and no one really cared about his status. The G-426 listed "stop sticks" next to the names of the agents who were required to take them into the field. The trainee next to Layne told him that the drive-through activity had escalated during Mids the previous night, and the supervisors on Swings wanted the front-line agents in their units to have the weapons readily available.

The FOS cleared his throat and began: "As you guys have probably heard, there were two more drive-throughs on Mids last night. Those of you that've been here a while know that this happens like clockwork around this time of year." He cleared his throat again. "Make sure you guys are communicating out there. Remember the pursuit policy." Layne noticed the younger agents in the rows to his left exchanged glances.

"Use your radios and try to anticipate where they're going. It's always safety first. The most important thing is that you go home to your families in one piece after you punch out. It's not worth getting killed over some dope. I know you guys don't want anyone showing you up, but don't forget rule number one. Now, let's have a safe evening."

The young agents rose quickly from their seats and the veterans resumed their conversations as they took their time making their way to the door. Layne found Cruz against the wall again. He was talking with an agent who ignored Layne's presence. Cruz acknowledged Layne momentarily before resuming his conversation. "Go ahead and get the keys from equipment and check out stop sticks."

Layne promptly claimed a place in line to leave the room and funneled out with the rest of the agents.

Behind the equipment counter was a burly agent in his late thirties with a high and tight haircut and police mustache. He gave Layne what he took to be a disapproving look as Layne signed for the keys and stop sticks. Layne gathered his keys and a drawstring bag containing the stop sticks as the agent behind the counter looked over his shoulder to serve the next in line. The stop sticks looked like a camping equipment bag for tent poles. He put the bag under his arm and noticed that many of the agents had checked out M4s and twelve-gauge shotguns due to the increase in activity near the fence.

He found Cruz in the hallway and asked, "Should we check out an M4?"

"No, they're a pain in the rear to carry. And I don't want to leave one in the truck when we get out. I hate locking it down." Cruz was always practical.

"They're light, though, don't you think?" Layne was hoping he could get him to change his mind.

Cruz only shook his head; he wouldn't budge. He had said before that they seemed light at first but they became heavy after carrying them a while. He also complained that the magazines were a "pain in the ass" to keep track of. He could tell that Layne was disappointed, so he explained that in six years he had never heard of anyone firing an M4 in the field on purpose.

Layne cleared his mind of the M4. He found the letter and number that marked the parking space of his assigned Kilo, and they loaded their gear at the same time and climbed in. Cruz shared his frame of mind on this evening: "Let's try to spike one of these guys. Let's go to that same spot we were in the other night. I think I know an intersection where they might come north." He directed Layne to head to the northern most parallel road in 5-Delta, just south of the highway in the center of the zone. Layne felt motivated for the first time as they left the parking lot. He realized he had never been in fear for his own safety. He was only in fear of making a mistake, and how others would react to it. He was most afraid of being embarrassed.

On the drive to 5-Delta, Layne's confidence began to decline as he began to think about what would occur. If he was successful in spiking a vehicle, he didn't know what the subsequent procedure was. It didn't even say what to do in the video. The drivers behind the wheel of the drive-through trucks wouldn't just put their hands up and surrender after their vehicle was immobilized. They would almost certainly run. He could picture the two of them, him and Cruz, in pursuit. What came next was not so clear. It wasn't a situation that he could improvise like every other situation he had been involved in. He concluded that he would draw his pistol and tell them to get on the ground, like he had seen on television.

* * * *

LAYNE AND CRUZ SAT WAITING in their fixed hiding place. After several hours of non-activity, they had exhausted topics of conversation and Cruz busied himself by text messaging back and forth with his wife. He smiled each time a message came back. Layne was envious; he romanced over sharing such a relationship with Felina. He admired the unity of a man and woman who were fiercely loyal to one another.

The radio had been eerily silent except for sensors going off ten and twenty miles out in the eastern and western boundaries of Douglas Station's Area of Responsibility. The starry night was peaceful, and he could almost see the universe revolving around the earth. If there was going to be any action tonight, it would have to happen in the next hour. He began to relax, although not enough to completely quell his usual vacillation and brooding over the worst-case scenarios his mind could ideate involving Felina and the Oral Board Exam.

While Cruz continued to titter over his phone in the passenger seat, Layne's thoughts shifted to imagining what it would be like to throw spikes under a drive-through truck. The stop sticks were on the floor of the cab, tucked behind him. He admired the potency of such a weapon, but he couldn't ignore the inherent danger in their use. If something did come their way tonight, he told himself that he had the option to inform Cruz that he didn't feel quite ready to take part. To withdraw from an engagement at the last minute because of uncertainty would be understandable, he reasoned. He had no experience. But he hoped it wouldn't come to that. It was important to him that Cruz respected him because of the fairness Cruz had shown him thus far.

The lights of Douglas and Agua Prieta twinkled a few miles to the east. Cruz folded his phone closed and leaned to his left side to put it in the right cargo pocket of his pants, having run out of methods in which to counter the boredom. Layne dwelled within the idle of the truck engine and the stars while his nagging concerns continued to make their rounds.

Suddenly, amongst the silence, they both realized Cruz's phone was vibrating and blinking in his pocket just as he was buttoning the pocket closed. Agents always kept their phones on silent and vibrate so the ringer didn't give away their position when they were laying-in, hiding in wait. Cruz read the caller ID with a slightly puzzled look for a moment before he unfolded the phone to answer. "This is Adrian Cruz."

Layne observed him with minor curiosity.

"Yes, sir. Tomorrow at 14:30? Ten-four, sir, I'll let him know," Cruz said. Then he pressed the red button on the keypad and folded the cellphone shut. He turned to look at Layne and said, "That was Elizalde; he's the supervisor on the west side tonight. Escribano emailed him and told him to make sure someone tells you you're supposed to be in Escribano's office tomorrow afternoon at 2:30."

"Okay," Layne said.

"You gotta start checking your email, dude. You're supposed to check it twice a day. I guess Escribano emailed you and you didn't respond. That's why he had a Supe on your shift let you know, so he can make sure you know about it."

"Ten-four," Layne said. "I wonder what he wants?"

"I have no idea. Just make sure you've got your stories straight in case he tries to cross you up and say you lied to him. He's a weasel like that," Cruz said.

"I know he is," Layne said with vitriol. "I can't even stand to look at him with those adult braces. He's always quietly trying to move up the ladder by throwing people under the bus. If he was cool, he would've brushed out that notepad crap with Ashlock. He's gotta know what a suck-up that guy is. I really think Ashlock's queer by the way he acts around certain guys. And it's not just me; I've overheard other agents saying he's a pillow-biter."

"Do you know how Escribano got that position?" Cruz asked.

"No, what happened?"

"Did you hear about that supervisor that got fired about three years ago, Ronin?"

"No, I never heard."

"When he was a supervisor in the field, he would drive around checking up on agents who were writing up groups. He'd cherry-pick the hottest alien chick in the group and he'd tell the agents he needed to talk to her to get intel. Then, he'd take her somewhere and tell her that if she blew him, he'd let her go north."

"He wanted a Bravo Juliet?" Layne said.

Cruz laughed uncontrollably and Layne joined him. Just watching Cruz's laughter was funny even if he hadn't heard the joke. The two-word phonetic acronyms the Border Patrol and Military used for radio communication clarity always seemed to magically delineate the term they represented.

Laughter caused Cruz to struggle finishing the story. "Anyway, he was picking up a different girl a couple of nights a week. But one night he let this chick go, and she got caught again by some different agents farther north. When they were writing her up, she told them that she'd already talked to their boss and he said she could go free if she waxed his Vader."

Layne began to shed tears of laughter. "Holy crap! That's ruthless. What an idiot, though. He never considered that these chicks might get caught again?" Layne had heard plenty of agents joke about K-1s, but he had never heard of anyone actually taking advantage of them.

"The agents told their Supe, and they took her to the station to talk to their FOS," Cruz continued. "The FBI eventually did an investigation. Turns out, after Ronin cast a pearl, she spit it in her hand and wiped it on the back of the seat. The FBI did a DNA test on the seat of his Kilo and it was ball game for this dude."

"The guy got blown-up CSI style," Layne said. "That's the craziest story I've heard yet. What happened to him, Ronin?"

"He's gettin' his *you know what* bored out in prison. He's doing five-to-ten. That's rape, dude." Cruz paused a second to allow Layne a moment to process the story. "Anyway, Escribano had been a regular agent here for a long time, like ten years. He wouldn't accept a Supe position at another station because he didn't wanna move his kids. So, when Ronin got fired,

Escribano picked up his job. Then, about six months ago he took over as FTU Supervisor."

The radio console between them lit up and a female voice interrupted their conversation: "Units on the west side, drive-through in 6-Charlie."

Layne's heart beat to quarters. He sat up straight and looked to Cruz for instructions.

"Stay here. It may not be headed our way." Cruz held his hand up and cocked his head to hear any further information. "Let's just wait and see."

In the distance they could see the entirety of front-line agents activate their emergency lights. A string of flashing red and blue was visible, the lights rotating like lighthouse beacons along the border miles to the west. Cruz prevented Layne from touching the switch to activate their emergency lights and instead instructed him to stay blacked-out while they moved closer to the line. Layne put the truck in gear and followed a beaten path through the desert grass, utilizing only moonlight.

After thirty seconds the first update came over the radio as the Kilo bounced and jarred. "He's headed down the line, headed into 6-Bravo now!" An overwrought agent broadcast like a distress signal from a remote location, then silence.

"He's coming this way," Cruz said.

"Where should we lay-in for him?" Layne's mind was functioning strategically while he could feel his heart pounding.

"On the 5-Charlie road in that one mesquite thicket." Cruz pointed towards a cluster of mesquite trees about fifty yards ahead that offered cover for their Kilo. "I'm betting they turn north there." He pointed to the intersection of the east-west International Road along the Border Fence and the northbound dirt road that they were approaching.

Layne could anticipate what Cruz was thinking. The vehicle would need to take a route into town that was clear from the view of the cameras if it was to lose the agents. To succeed, they would need to cease traveling east, hugging the border, and head north, above the front-line agents. There were too many agents near the port. Cruz was guessing the driver would make the turn at the eastern boundary of 5-Delta and travel north on the road that served as the boundary between 5-Delta and 5-Charlie.

Cruz pointed out a dirt path that led to the thicket.

"I can't see anything," Layne said with his face pressed toward the windshield.

"Go ahead and turn on the headlights until we stop," Cruz said.

The truck bounced on rocks and dipped in holes as the headlights lit up tall grass they trampled. The radio was going wild with chatter from agents in pursuit of the outlaw vehicle.

"Hide the truck behind those trees," Cruz instructed, pointing out a pair of desert willow that offered the best cover. Layne parked north of the trees so that the truck was only partially visible from the road. They dismounted and turned their handheld radios on. Layne reached back into the truck and pulled the seat forward to retrieve the bag with the stop sticks from the cab, while Cruz, perched on the doorframe, looked back west over the cab from the other side of the truck.

Updates chimed over the radio every fifteen seconds about the course of the truck. With heart thumping, Layne came around the Kilo and joined Cruz, scanning westward through the dark. He spotted what looked like a quarter-ton pickup about a half mile away, speeding along the warning track directly next to the Border Fence. The dust it kicked up rose upward through each generator light that it passed along the fence.

"Hurry, they're coming!" Cruz took off toward the bushes. Layne plodded along behind, the awkward bag of stop sticks tucked under his arm. He overtook Cruz, ran to the opposite side of the road, then fumbled with the drawstring and jerked the stop sticks from the bag. He could hear the humming of the truck's engine growing louder. Nervous sweat beaded on his forehead and dripped from his nose, chilled by the night air.

Cruz spoke into his handheld radio, "Agents on International Road, Delta-328 and Delta-167 are laying-in on the 5-Charlie Road with a stinger."

No one acknowledged his broadcast. Layne laid the stop sticks down behind a bush, trying to remember how Cruz had advised him. He scurried backward toward the other side of the road, hunched over as he backpedaled, laying the trigger cord as he hustled. Layne had expected Cruz to position himself close to the road but instead he set up twenty yards to Layne's rear.

Once behind the bushes and on his stomach, holding the handle to the cord in his right hand, he looked back to check with Cruz. He was laying on his stomach, barely visible within the desert grass. He pointed to the truck coming closer. The flashing emergency lights of two separate vehicles could be seen trailing fifty yards behind the pickup, like Boss Hog's deputies chasing the General Lee. The Border Fence and the warning track that the truck was navigating were a hundred yards to the south of Layne's position. He felt his heart beating against the Kevlar vest mashed between his body and the earth. The pickup's engine could be heard charging as it approached the T-intersection where Cruz had gambled that it would turn north.

Out of nowhere, Layne realized that he must look like Wile E. Coyote arming an ACME trap in anticipation of the Roadrunner speeding by. In the same instant he realized that a poor performance could cost him his life. He would have to hang on to his composure and force himself to wait until the last second to pull the cord, like a game of chicken, or he might be run over. The thought slowed his senses and he began to cycle through the possibilities that the moment held. It was worth the risk; respect was almost worth dying for. He imagined telling Felina about this adventure; she would be so proud of him. He realized that if he succeeded in capturing the truck, Escribano would be forced to abate. Word would assuredly reach the examiners at Headquarters before the exam. They would pass him even if he didn't speak a word of Spanish after such an exploit. He realized he could win at this moment.

As the truck closed in, he envisioned a glorious scene in the Muster Room. He saw himself crowd-surfing over the rest of the agents—if he could pull it off.

The radio belted out a new message, "He's coming up on 5-Bravo now." Then a short burst of static before silence again.

Layne could hear the truck within their presence now. He felt his scalp tighten like a drumhead in anticipation. The palms of his hands were sweating. His perceptions shrank to a single physical sensation: the ache in his clenched right hand that held a nylon cord tethered to the stinger across the road.

The pickup engine roared in a rising key as it approached. It was not slowing down to turn. Then the engine whine lowered as the pickup blasted through the intersection and on into 5-Bravo, Layne and Cruz stood up and brushed themselves off.

They waded through the grass to meet halfway between their positions. Cruz looked relieved that the truck hadn't come their way. Layne was also secretly relieved as it struck him what he would've been risking his life for: 1,000 pounds of ditch weed that really was less harmful than most of the prescription drugs in the average American's medicine cabinet. Together, Layne and Cruz stared silently to the east for several seconds. The truck could be heard faintly shifting gears in the distance as thousands of stars twinkled above. The radio chatter dwindled to silence, and finally the truck was declared Golf.

The mercenary driving the truck must have read their minds.

23

FELINA CRAMPED THE WHEEL when she spotted a parking space next to a showroom-floor-new Ford F-250 twin cab pickup truck with temporary plates. The boss's son, Brian, had just bought it, even though he had no need for a truck. Felina scoffed as she pulled her emergency brake and glanced at the time on her car stereo. She turned off the engine in a rush and put her keys in her purse as she opened the door to get out. She was in such a hurry that she was wearing sweatpants and a hooded sweatshirt with tennis shoes instead of her usual work attire. With the door open, she looked at herself in the rearview mirror to make sure she was at least presentable. She didn't have time to put on makeup, and her hair was still wet.

"Screw it," she said to herself.

She got out and shut the door on the move, quickly pulling the straps of her purse over her shoulder while she walked with long, quick strides. She glanced at her watch; it was 6:03 a.m. As long as she wasn't five minutes late, she would be okay.

When she opened the office door she dashed in and glanced toward Brian's office window. The women she worked with were huddled around his computer monitor, drinking coffee from Starbucks with their backs to the door. By the way they were engrossed, she assumed they were watching another blooper video. Brian was the only one she had to worry about seeing her come in late; the other women she worked with were disinterested. Jabba couldn't see the door from his office. She was nearly certain she had gotten away with it. If Jabba said anything about what time she clocked in she would blame the construction on Fort Lowell for her tardiness. His anger was less intense when he discovered she had been late after the fact.

She walked softly but swiftly to her desk and glanced over her shoulder to make sure the others hadn't come out of Brian's office yet.

She sighed and set her purse on her desk then moved the mouse and logged into Windows before she sat down. Then she double-clicked on the icon to open her bids. She sat down and her stomach growled. She had set her alarm for 4:30—p.m. instead of a.m.—by mistake, and had awakened just in time to shower, put clothes on, and leave.

As soon as she became settled, she heard her cellphone vibrating in her purse. She ignored it. She considered that it might be Layne on his way to the station for post-Academy; if it was, she would text him back on her first break. If not, he would call her back when he was dismissed from class.

Thank goodness it was Friday. At 3:00 p.m. she planned on going home and getting her things and driving to Bisbee to stay with him again; she couldn't wait. She already had her clothes and things packed, but when she woke up late, she forgot the bag when she darted out the door. She had been looking forward to seeing him all week now that she had told him what she needed to and had gotten it over with. He appeared to be keeping his word to her. She stared at her keyboard, motionless, thinking about the broad smile he would give her when she pulled into his driveway. He made her call him when she was five minutes away so he could wait on his front porch for her. She thought it was cute. He would be standing at her driver's side window so he could hug her as soon as she got out of the car. Then he would carry her things inside.

She forced herself to stop daydreaming. She had to get to work to be able to show Jabba she had completed at least five bids by the end of the day, in case he checked. She stood up and looked around the room. Jabba's door was open, indicating he was in his office. It sounded like he was on the phone buying something that had nothing to do with the business. He took money out of the company budget to buy classic cars and other toys for himself. He balanced the books by not giving his employees a raise. If she was lucky, she would get a stocking with candy and trinkets as a Christmas bonus instead of a large check like others in her industry did.

Just as she forced herself to begin typing and concentrating, she heard her phone vibrating in her purse again. A disturbing feeling came over her that the second call meant something was seriously wrong. She peeked over the walls of her cubicle to make sure neither Brian nor Jabba were lurking nearby. Then she sat down and opened her phone to see that both missed calls were from her mom. Her heart jumped out of her chest and her leg began bouncing the moment she saw who was trying to reach her. The calls were a sign that something was wrong; there was no other explanation for two calls in less than five minutes. Alba, her mom, never called her at work. Felina put both elbows on her desk and texted with both hands quickly to her mom, *"¿Que' pasó?"*

She prayed that someone wasn't dead as she waited for the phone to vibrate and light up with a return message. She thought of stepping outside to call, but she had already been late. Her mom barely knew how to send a text, but she would try if she had to. After several long minutes, the phone lit up and vibrated with a new message. Felina held her breath as she opened it. The message simply said, in jumbled words, that her brother Eduardo was in jail.

"Oh no," Felina gasped, covering her mouth with her palm and beginning to cry quietly. She knew her mom was desperate to notify her because she needed to go to the house to help the family pool their money, hopefully to pay a bail bondsman.

She stood up and pulled herself together. She wasn't sure what to say to Jabba, but she had to go. She thought of leaving and calling him on her way to her mom's house, but Jabba could be unreasonable if she left without informing him. She was going to have to approach him and wing it.

Felina took a deep breath and walked straight to his office as the other women she worked with headed to their desks from Brian's office. They sensed a serious disturbance in the atmosphere and allowed Felina space to pass by without intruding with inquiry. The door to Jabba's office was wide open; it fed his ego to allow the employees to hear him buy and sell stock out loud over the phone.

She stood in the doorway, but Jabba didn't acknowledge her. He couldn't tell that it was important because he wouldn't look directly at her. He was talking on his desk phone and laughing about something, holding the phone with his right hand and looking away from her while spinning a plastic top on his desk with his left hand. He put the toy aside and moved his computer mouse to bring up his computer screen. He clamped the phone between his ear and his shoulder to free his hands so he could type and locate a picture on the Internet of whatever he was prattling to his friend about buying. He was enjoying another conceited discussion with one of his spoiled, adolescent-minded associates.

He continued pretending he didn't notice Felina standing there as he laughed and made plans. She gathered that it was a boat he was buying, by talk of Patagonia Lake. She knocked on the open door with her left hand and he looked at her by moving his eyeballs. When he perceived the state she was in, he grabbed the phone from his shoulder and put it to his chest so his chum couldn't hear. "What's up?" he said with his receptive look—eyes wide and mouth slightly open.

"I've got a family emergency I've got to take care of," Felina said. She was a fidgety, nervous wreck, and Jabba could tell that her dismay was sincere.

"Are you going to be back today?" Jabba asked her politely.

"I don't know," Felina said, holding back tears.

"Okay, see you Monday, I guess," Jabba said. He put the phone back in its hands-free position and said, "Okay, sorry about that. I'm looking at it right now."

Felina said, "Thank you, Mike," and he turned to nod at her briefly while he was in mid-sentence.

Felina raced home as tears streamed down her cheeks. It seemed like her whole life had been one continuous crisis. It didn't seem real that this lifestyle of living on the edge, paycheck to paycheck, could possibly end someday soon. She realized her life had always been like this, with brief intervals of joy and serenity every now and then. She was overwhelmed with concern about what would happen to Eduardo. If his situation was manageable, she worried that whatever needed to be resolved would take time, and she would have to cancel her plans to be with Layne this weekend. But what reason would she give him?

She pulled up in front of her parents' house and jogged to the front door as quickly as she could. Her mom's sister and brother were already there.

Felina hugged everyone, and her *Tía* Lupe, filled her in with the details about what had happened. Her aunt spoke Spanish. When Felina grasped the situation, she went to sit at the kitchen table by herself. She collapsed into a chair and cried in her palms. The others discussed the problem in a state of distress and thought out loud to try and come up with a solution. Felina was too distraught to participate in the brainstorming. The desperation and sorrow in their voices was terrifying. Anguish seemed to be more consuming to her when it was being expressed in Spanish.

Her brother Eduardo had been pulled over for driving drunk at 2:00 a.m. the previous night. He had been arrested by the Pima County Sheriff's Department. He was driving his Blazer the wrong way on Ina Road, and when the police pulled him over, they administered a Breathalyzer test. Felina wasn't sure if he was still using his fake Mexican driver's license. He and she had purchased their documents from the same seedy source on the south side of Tucson. She reasoned that he wouldn't have shown the fake to the police if he knew he was drunk. But when they searched him, they might have found it along with another Arizona driver's license with a different name. If he had been pulled over for speeding, the Mexican driver's license was usually sufficient, and the police would've simply written him a ticket. But arrested for a DUI, they would've searched his truck after they handcuffed him. Felina shuddered to guess what they might have found.

Eduardo didn't get a chance to make his phone call until 5:30 a.m. He called a friend and requested that his confidant pass on the message to his family that he was in jail. Eduardo avoided calling his mother directly so as to not alert the authorities about the location of his family in case they wanted to pass the information on to Immigration and Customs Enforcement—ICE. Eduardo's friend didn't call Alba until about the time Felina was on her way to work. The plan was to raise money to pay a bail bondsman if Eduardo was being held by the Sheriff's Department. But while Felina hurried home, the family received word that the sheriff was turning Eduardo over to ICE Agents because the police had discovered his immigration status.

Felina continued to sob uncontrollably, her mind racing. He had never been arrested before. The police must have realized that he was illegal when they searched his truck. They would have fingerprinted him, and now he would have an immigration record. It was a disaster. Since he was in the hands of the immigration authorities, the Sheriff's Department must have finished booking him and handed him over for an immigration violation. It was inevitable that he would be deported back to Mexico. Depending on how much money he had, he could make it to Magdalena, Sonora, and stay with their grandparents until he could be put in contact with people who could sneak him back across the border.

Family members feared they might never see Eduardo again. Felina's aunt and uncle had their arms around her mom. They were both holding her simultaneously and rocking back and forth in a huddle to try to calm her. Her dad was out on the back porch drinking whiskey from a pint bottle. He wouldn't speak. He hadn't said a word since Felina arrived; she wasn't sure if he knew she was there.

Felina knew Eduardo drank every night, but he usually stayed home so that he wouldn't get into trouble. If he did go out, he would have someone else drive. If something ever happened, he could tell the police that he left his wallet at home. He spoke English as fluently as Felina, and no one ever gave him a second look. But if he had been driving while intoxicated, he would have left himself without any means of escape. What could he have been thinking? They would need to identify him if he was stopped while driving, and if they suspected him of being drunk, the Mexican driver's license wouldn't suffice.

She was imagining the worst when her cellphone's ringtone shattered her silence. It was Layne. He must have been on one of his fifteen-minute breaks between classes. She was unsure of what to do. The news of Eduardo's arrest had come so late that it hadn't left her time to think of a plausible explanation as to why she had to cancel her trip to Bisbee. It was agonizing to watch her cellphone continue to ring while she knew that Layne had no idea what was happening on the other end. She couldn't answer; she would have to let it go to voicemail. Her face frowned back into tears and she wiped her eyes with the back of her hand. She wished she could confide in him and get ahold of herself with his support. He would make her laugh and she would feel better.

She couldn't talk to him while she was fraught. He would suspect by her emotional condition that the problem was more serious and complex than she let on. She would wait until she calmed down to return his call. But she needed to modify what had happened to Eduardo, so the story was presentable to Layne as a reason to cancel their plans. She would simply tell him that Eduardo was arrested for driving under the influence and omit what happened afterward with ICE. Layne wouldn't expect to talk to her until around 4:00 p.m.

She didn't know what else to do but call Marianne. She stepped out the front door and began walking the sidewalk toward the end of the street as she dialed.

"What's wrong?" Marianne knew something wasn't right immediately when Felina greeted her.

"My brother got arrested last night for a DUI," Felina said. She was going to summarize the whole situation in one breath, but she broke down before she could finish.

"Oh, sweetheart, are you okay? Do you want me to come over? I'll leave work and come right over, okay?" Marianne said sympathetically.

"No, don't leave work. I just wanted to tell you what's going on because you might know what to do." Felina took a deep breath. "Pima County is turning him over to ICE."

Marianne knew that move meant he would be deported. "It's okay honey; it happens all the time. Eddy can get right back across and he'll be home in a few weeks. Don't worry."

"I know, but Pima County booked him. Border Patrol will see it when they fingerprint him and throw him back in jail. He'll only have one try to get through." Felina broke down again as she finished.

"That's not gonna happen. It's gonna be okay; trust me," Marianne assured her. "He can easily get through near Nogales. If he gets caught, they'll just put him back and he can try again until he gets away and makes it back. They won't prosecute him for a DUI. It has to be something violent; they don't have room in jail if it isn't."

"Are you sure?" Felina asked.

"Positive. Ryan says the only people they'll hold for prosecution are people who have sexual assaults in the United States. DUIs are nothing. They must not even be charging him with it if they're turning him over to ICE," Marianne said.

"Okay," Felina said sniffling. She felt guilty using information Marianne had obtained from Ryan. He had no idea about Felina's secret.

"Aren't you supposed to go stay with Layne tonight?" Marianne asked her.

"Yeah, I was gonna leave around five, but I can't go now. I need to be here for my family. I'm gonna tell Layne I'm staying here to raise money to bail him out. But we're gonna have to get some money together so we can get it to Eduardo in Mexico somehow, so he can make it to my grandma's house in Magdalena."

"Definitely, but what are you gonna tell him?" Marianne asked.

"I don't know. He called me and left a message. He has post-Academy today, so he probably called me on his break."

"How sweet," Marianne said.

"I know." Felina's nose was runny, and she sniffed and laughed while crying.

Marianne was waiting for her to say something, and Felina finally said, "I don't know what I'm gonna do."

"What are you gonna tell him about not going down there?" Marianne asked.

Felina thought for a moment. "I don't know. I don't wanna lie to him. He'll know I'm not telling the truth. He'll wanna know why I'm so upset."

Marianne didn't say anything.

"Maybe I should just call and tell him," Felina thought out loud. "I'm tired of being secretive, it's exhausting. But I really think I need to tell him face to face. I'm just gonna have to make something up when I call him today; I'm not ready, not with all this going on. I'll apologize later and explain that I had no choice because I didn't wanna scare him and I wanted to tell him in person."

"Are you sure you'll be ready?" Marianne asked.

"I'm not sure. I need a few days to think about it." Felina began to cry again. "I'm so overwhelmed, I don't know what to do."

"Don't worry, it will work out honey, I promise," Marianne said.

LAYNE SAT IN ONE of two chairs available that faced the desk of SBPA Escribano. It was the third or fourth time Layne had been summoned to his office since he arrived at Douglas Station in September. It was 2:05 p.m. Layne had come straight to his office directly after being dismissed from post-Academy. Layne stared at the wall, then at his hands clutching one another—anything not to look at Escribano's face. Everything about him was repulsive. Escribano was wearing reading glasses low on the bridge of his nose. He pretended to be absorbed by whatever he was jotting down in order to make Layne wait. It was obvious when he was acting. He did this each time Layne had come to see him. Layne suspected Escribano made him wait needlessly so Layne would feel as though he wasn't important enough to be dealt with punctually. It was to display his superiority.

Layne briefly looked down at his uniform, realizing he had forgotten to take it into consideration for this meeting. There was a visible crease in his pants, but there was a hot sauce stain near his right front pocket from lunch that his pistol holster covered when he was standing. When he was sitting, he managed to conceal the stain with his elbow. He feared Escribano might order him to write a memo about his uniform not being in order. Or that he hadn't shaven well enough—anything to add petty depth to his training file for future use. He did so to build a case against a trainee so the information could be passed along to the examiners at the ten-month Oral Board. Layne suspected Escribano secretly hated white people but was careful not to allow it to be recognizable.

To avoid accidental eye contact, Layne gazed at pictures on the office walls while Escribano pretended to finish the paperwork on his desk. A new FTO roamed in and out of the office, performing various administrative tasks. He looked to be aware of the awkward silence that existed between the Training Supervisor and his unyielding subordinate, slowing the second hand on the wall clock.

Layne had resorted to twiddling his thumbs by the time Escribano finally moved his paperwork aside and took a deep, laborious breath. "I'm going to have you on Mids for Phase Four again starting Monday," he finally said. His braces shone when he spoke, and he could only manage to maintain eye contact for a few seconds at a time. Layne wasn't surprised by the news. He had come to expect the result being unfavorable to his wellbeing whenever Escribano was involved with a decision about his existence at Douglas Station. Escribano's methodology seemed to be to do whatever was within his power to make sure Layne operated on insufficient sleep. Equally, it was imperative that he hide any of Layne's accomplishments such as the drug seizure, while highlighting any mistakes he made—like the Ashlock incident.

Layne focused on a portrait of Escribano and his obese wife on the desk while Escribano continued his attempt to demoralize Layne into resigning. The way he slightly puckered his lips to conceal his braces when his mouth was closed was irritating. "I'm going to have you riding with Agent Tipton next week for Phase Four. He's a veteran agent and he knows the law. So, study your maps and make sure you have an updated sensor list. On Friday you need to be here at zero six hundred to go to Headquarters in Tucson to take your ten-month."

Layne throttled his anger over having to repeat Phase Four again and asked, "Sir, what was Cruz's recommendation for me based on my evaluation this week?"

Escribano's face became red. "You need to show me that you're ready to be on your own."

The wandering FTO was within earshot behind Escribano and was looking through a drawer of a file cabinet. He pretended to be disinterested in the conversation but remained hovering close enough to make out what was being said.

"I think I've made the necessary improvements, sir," Layne said.

"Mr. Cruz said you've made improvements. But you're inconsistent, and I don't think you're ready to be on your own yet." Escribano continued to move papers about his desk, paying more attention to them than to Layne.

"Yes, sir. If I pass the ten-month next Friday, what unit am I going to?" Layne asked in an attempt to read Escribano's reaction.

Escribano grinned deviously as his eyes remained focused on reshuffling his papers. The second hand ticked off a slow second before he answered. "You'll be assigned to Liemer's unit."

"Okay," Layne said, as if he had accepted a challenge to try and find a way to sidestep the trap Escribano had laid for him at the exam.

Escribano retained his grin as he looked up and said, "ten-four?"

"Ten-four," Layne said. He rose from his seat and put his cap back on as he turned to leave.

* * * *

FELINA SELECTED LAYNE'S NAME and phone number under her list of contacts and put her thumb on the button to place the call. She noticed she was trembling slightly. She was sitting in the center of the rickety porch swing just outside the door of her parent's house. It was 2:30 p.m. and the afternoon had turned cool and overcast. She found it difficult to sit still, but she was far from being in the mood to swing. She had been rehearsing what she would say to Layne since her conversation with Marianne ended that morning. She told herself she would call Layne at 2:15 p.m. But she had been procrastinating and hadn't gathered the nerve.

In the upper right corner of her cellphone screen the time read 2:33 p.m. Layne was probably on his way home from post-Academy by now. She took a deep breath and almost mustered the courage to press call, but failed at the last moment. She told herself just to clear her mind and stop thinking about it and do it. She was hoping to reach his voicemail. She would leave a message and sound moderately upset and disappointed. She had only one attempt. It would look strange if her name was on his caller ID from a missed call and there was no voicemail. It would look like she was afraid of something.

She got up from the swing and decided to walk and talk, hoping that movement would relieve the painful tension in her chest. She made her way down the driveway towards the sidewalk and made up her mind to call. But just before she pressed the green phone button, a thought intervened that told her to consider texting him instead. Perhaps she could avoid sounding rehearsed by having him read what she had to tell him instead. Sounding nervous, distraught, or insincere could require more explanation than she had prepared for. He might ask her a question she hadn't anticipated, which could lead to stuttering. A text message would give her time to consider her responses and avoid mistakes.

She dreaded hearing the disappointment in his voice. She didn't think he would ask for many details, but he would expect to hear a general explanation. She changed her mind again and decided she had no choice but to call. A text message would come across like she was hiding from him because she lacked an acceptable explanation. It was lying to him that caused the anxiety. But she reminded herself that she had done nothing wrong. She had no choice but to lie to him for the time being.

She took a deep breath and unfolded her phone again. She went over again what she had silently practiced saying to him so she wouldn't make a mistake that would require her to tell the whole truth to make right. She wiped her tears with the back of her hand and calmed herself so the problem would seem like an inconvenience she was obligated to deal with instead of the calamity that it truly was. It was lying to him on the weekend that he deemed special that troubled her.

She thought about the adages that scolded people for lying that she had heard while growing up. But whoever popularized them was hypocritical or wasn't being realistic. She tried to tell the truth whenever possible, even when it was inconvenient, or time-consuming, or expensive. Her Catholic upbringing told her that it was what God expected of her. But there were circumstances when telling the truth wasn't beneficial to anyone. She thought about when she shopped with Marianne when they tried on clothes together. Marianne often came out of the fitting room wearing a dress or something she had no business wearing. She usually asked Felina if she looked fat in whatever she was trying on. Felina always lied and said no, she looked cute. She lied in order to be kind and preserve their friendship. Felina realized she had to lie every day in order to be polite.

She took a deep breath and tried to clear her mind. She had to tell him something for the time being. Everything she planned to tell him was true; it was simply incomplete because it had to be. She opened her phone again and found his name in her contacts. It was simply listed as "Layne." She pressed send and put the phone to her ear and stopped walking to begin pacing along the sidewalk instead. After three rings she prayed it would continue ringing so she could leave a summary message and tell him to text her back because she would be occupied. But between the third and fourth ring he picked up and instantly said, "Hey, Babe."

Felina hesitated for a moment then said, "Hey, Babe. How are you?" She could tell by the time it took him to respond that he knew there was a problem. He must have determined so, judging by the emotion in her voice.

"Are you okay?" Layne said with concern she could feel.

"No, Babe, I'm not." She broke down a little but gathered herself. "We had a problem last night."

"Oh no, what happened?" Layne said. He sounded extremely disappointed, as she dreaded he would be.

Felina stopped pacing and stared at a crack on the sidewalk. She was standing next to a dying palm tree and a rusted car by the curb with the majority of its paint worn off. As she answered, she realized she had never seen the car move since she was a sophomore in high school. "My brother was driving drunk last night, and he got arrested."

"Oh no," Layne said.

There was a pause between them for a moment.

"He's in jail and we're trying to find a way to bail him out," Felina struggled to say. She was down to the last bit of strength that was preventing her from breaking down into tears.

"I'm sorry, Felina," Layne said.

"I'm not gonna be able to come see you this weekend," she told him.

Layne didn't say anything for a few seconds, and Felina felt the need to give reasons why the trip wouldn't be practical. "We've got to find a way to come up with the money to pay a bail bondsman to get him out."

"Who's holding him?" Layne asked.

Felina sniffled through her runny nose and began walking again and watching her feet, the hard part seemed to be over. "He got arrested by the Pima County Sheriff's Department."

"If it's a matter of money maybe I could loan it to you guys," Layne said.

She hadn't anticipated him negotiating a way to see her in this way. The only rebuttal she could think of in a believable amount of time had to do with pride. "You're so sweet, honey, but I couldn't ask you to do that." She realized there was no way around causing him to become increasingly suspicious about why he couldn't come into contact with her family.

"It's not a big deal; you guys could pay me back whenever you get it," Layne said.

"Layne, that's too much. This isn't your problem. Besides, you may need that money—it's in the thousands," Felina added, hoping the amount she came up with would deter him.

"Well, if you change your mind, I could pitch in," he said.

Felina could sense him backing off. She knew his pride wouldn't allow him to go so far as to appear desperate.

"Okay, I'm gonna miss you this weekend," Layne said. "I guess I could just hang out with Runyon and Carlos. I should be studying for the ten-month, but I know I won't."

"Please don't go out drinking with them," Felina blurted then regretted saying it.

"Don't worry," Layne responded, hiding his shock. "I won't let you down."

She could tell he was downcast by the way the spirit had departed from his voice and the diminished speed at which he spoke. It caused her to be overcome with guilt. She was only concerned with preventing herself from crying until she hung up. He would wonder why she was so despairing over her brother's DUI and skipping a weekend with Layne. He knew she was disappointed about not being able to see him before the ten-month exam, but not so much as to break down crying over it.

"I'm gonna miss you, too. But I'll see you next weekend after you pass the test." Felina managed to say.

"I've never wished for anything more than to see you and tell you I passed," Layne said. He sounded like he was also on the verge of tears.

"You will," Felina said.

AS HE TRUDGED SLUGGISHLY OVER the Border Patrol emblem inlay in the hallway floor, Layne glanced at his watch and saw that it that read nine minutes before ten o'clock. His eyes were dark and sunken from insomnia. Fear of the Oral Board Exam, less than forty-eight hours away, in tandem with the lingering anomalies in Felina's story, had made certain that he stared at the ceiling for six hours while sunlight peeked through the blinds. His blessed aunt had come through once again, and a much-anticipated letter arrived containing three Valium within the envelope. They could've allowed him to sleep comfortably before his Wednesday night shift—his last before the Oral Board. But it was a must that he saved them for use on Friday.

He opened the Muster Room door to a roomful of newsy conversations, like a high school classroom before the teacher arrived. He had been paired with Agent Tipton to repeat Phase Four for the fourth time, and tonight was his final night before the big test. Tipton was perpetually on Mids because he preferred it. He was the offensive lineman-looking FTO in charge when Layne encountered the mother trying to protect her young son.

The clock reached starting time and the muttering in the room faded into stray coughs and silence. Field Operations Supervisor Shields cleared his throat from the podium and said, "It looks like everybody's here tonight; good." He looked back and forth from his G-426 to the roomful of agents to make sure he hadn't overlooked an absence. "There were two drive-throughs simultaneously on Swings a few hours ago. There was one on the east side that came over through 4-Bravo and another in the west,

265

in 6-Alpha. The one on the east side turned back south after a couple minutes, but the one on the west side wanted to play. No one could get an opportunity to spike him and he eventually TBS'd [turned back south] on the west side somewhere about twenty minutes later. So, all you guys that are marked down—make sure you're not leaving for the field without your stop sticks. I mean it."

The FOS thumbed through his stack of documents to find his next talking point and moved on, but Layne couldn't hear him. He had ascended into one of his body-tingling fantasies to escape his list of worries. The drive-through report set adrift in his mind a visualization of glorious scenes in which he was the prevailing hero. He imagined Linda the LECA and the military women in the camera room plotting his position on an immense map table with croupier sticks. Layne was in and out of communication with them while he was struggling to stop a drive-through vehicle. The top personnel at the station held their breath as he prevailed to save the country in an epic climax. He returned to the station in triumph where a mob of agents had gathered to congratulate him and carry him on their shoulders.

He came to and heard the FOS say, "The last issue is about time sheets. Make sure everything is filled in and accurate if you wanna get paid. Your supervisor has better things to do than correct your mistakes. I don't know about y'all, but I don't wanna do this crap for free. Alright, let's get out there." The FOS evened his papers on the lectern and chairs scooted as the agents began to rise.

Layne re-examined the night's G-426 as he stood up. He was surprised to discover that he had been assigned an up-to-date Dodge Kilo with the new Hemi V-8. By now he had become accustomed to missing radio knobs and sunflower seeds scattered on the dash of an overused Kilo with the steering wheel out of alignment. Agents like Launius treated their vehicles like horses. Layne had become satisfied simply receiving a Kilo that didn't have a half-flat tire or chew-spitter in the cup holder. The only explanation was the supervisor who drew up the G-426 must have been in a hurry and assigned him the new truck by mistake.

Layne slowly made his way through the mingling to meet up with Tipton.

"Should I check out stop sticks?" Layne asked.

"No, I don't think we'll need 'em."

Layne retrieved the keys from checkout and headed out the door back into the night beneath the parking lot lamps where agents were strolling to their vehicles. He toted his cutting light and backpack full of gear in search of the parking space where the new truck was located. When he found it, he opened the door and the aroma of new interior struck him. He felt a sense of added responsibility as he fastened his seatbelt and put the key into the ignition.

Tipton opened the passenger door and climbed in to situate himself. When Layne turned the key in the ignition, he felt a rumble through the seat that vibrated the side view mirror as he backed out.

As they turned onto the highway to leave the boundaries of federal property, Tipton said, "Take Highway 80 all the way past town. We're gonna lay-in way out east tonight."

"To where?" Layne wasn't sure how far they would be going.

"Just keep driving east. I'll tell you where to stop. I wanna go to a place near mile marker seven," Tipton replied.

Tipton sat facing forward, patiently and without speaking during the drive through town. The lack of conversation caused Layne to notice the occasional burnt-out bulbs in some of the streetlamps that lined Main Street until the road grew dark when it became Highway 80 again. As they were leaving the northeastern outskirts of Douglas, Layne couldn't remain silent any longer. "Why aren't we going to the line?"

"Because I have an idea. I'll tell you when we get there. You take your Oral Board on Friday, right?" Tipton said.

"Yeah."

"Then I'm just babysitting you until you take your test, and there's no point in evaluating you with a clipboard all night. So, we're gonna do something productive instead," Tipton said.

Layne maintained a speed of sixty-five miles per hour as they traveled the barren, two-lane highway east out of Douglas. He was forced to begin concentrating, the worn-out road hadn't been resurfaced in decades. The broken yellow lines that separated the lanes were inconspicuous under the bright beams of the headlights. Seen through the side view mirror, Douglas was becoming a faint glow in the twinkling distance. He began to bear down and read the green mile marker posts. After mile marker six, he looked at the digital odometer to measure a mile and anticipate where to start slowing. When the reflection at the top of the next marker post flashed in the headlights, Tipton said, "Okay, start slowing down here. It's a couple hundred yards ahead on the left side."

Layne slowed and tried to anticipate Tipton's intended destination.

"Okay, turn here."

Layne rotated the wheel left to pull into a small clearing that he realized was a dirt rest area that had been created to make room for vehicles to pull over.

"Pull in there and turn around so we can see cars coming from the east," Tipton instructed.

Layne nodded and circled the lot to turn around and face the highway perpendicularly on the right side of the rest area as if to head back to town.

"We're gonna lay-in here," Tipton said.

The lot was enclosed by brush and mesquite trees, which gave them complete cover from vehicles coming from either direction. Puzzled, Layne pushed the bar on the steering column into Park and the truck settled into rest.

Tipton looked at him expectantly and said, "Kill the lights."

Layne turned off the headlights, and the highway that passed before them was barely made visible by starlight.

"How far south is the border from here?" Layne said.

"About six miles."

He was confused. They were positioned as if they were setting up a speed trap. He could just see the highway over the hood of the truck, the bumper was only a few feet from the pavement.

"Blackout," Tipton said.

Layne turned the knob beneath the speedometer and dimmed the dash lights all the way to nothing. The only light that couldn't be extinguished was the green light that came from the information on the Motorola radio console between them, like a nightlight.

"They're coming in from the flanks," Tipton said. He leaned back in the passenger seat to prepare to spend the shift in wait.

Layne realized he was referring to the escalation in drive-through activity that the FOS had emphasized in Muster.

"I think they're sneaking in from way up here," Tipton clarified as he situated himself in his seat.

"You think?" Layne said.

"The trucks that are loaded have gotta be four-wheeling all the way up here to the highway, then driving from here into town. It's the only thing that makes sense," Tipton said. "Nobody is expecting them to come all the way up north way out here."

He leaned forward in his seat and was looking northeast down the highway where traffic heading to Douglas would come from. He explained, "Geronimo Trail and all the roads by the Port are too hot to take into town. So, they've gotta come all the way up here, then head southwest on the highway into town. No one's looking for it."

It made perfect sense. No one considered that the smugglers would four-wheel this far north and use the highway to reach town. Tipton went on to explain what he had been thinking. The cartels disabled every single light on the trucks they used—the taillights, the dome light, the dash, everything. This deep in the desert at night, even the light from a cellphone could be detected from a considerable distance. The drivers were clever and skilled. They were more familiar with the locations of the vehicle sensors than the agents were. Tipton speculated that they were crossing over the border and creeping north, gradually and patiently. It could take them several hours to make it all the way from the border six miles to the highway. But once they made it to the asphalt of Highway 80, they simply turned left and cruised into town doing the speed limit.

"I can't believe they drive on the highway with no headlights."

"They use night vision goggles—NVGs. You know that Supervisor named Starman? He left his truck unlocked on International Road one night and some guys from the south side came over the fence and stole all his crap out of his truck. They got his M4 too," Tipton said.

"How'd they do it before they had the goggles?"

"They would have a guy riding shotgun hang out the passenger side window, looking at the white line on the shoulder of the road to guide the driver. You know, 'Left a little, right a little, straight.'" Tipton explained.

"Going seventy on the highway?" Layne said.

"Yep, I think they're coming up to the highway somewhere around here."

"What's going on in town, then? Those drive-throughs that make everyone chase them?" Layne said.

"That's just a diversion so they can sneak in from out here. That's why the older guys don't even acknowledge them when they go by."

"I thought it was because they didn't want to get in trouble for breaking the rule against pursuit," Layne said.

"It's because they don't give a crap," Tipton said.

Besides giving up, the agents knew that the beds of trucks that drove wildly through the frontline zones were empty. A truck loaded with 1,000 pounds or more couldn't maneuver with such agility.

"Only the new guys and dumbasses get involved in that crazy rodeo. Even if they caught one, the U.S. Attorney wouldn't prosecute them without any dope," Tipton said.

"A thousand pounds seems like a lot of weight to be four-wheeling with," Layne said.

"The cartels have mechanics that reinforce the truck's rear suspension with leaf springs to handle the weight," Tipton said.

"I heard human smugglers do that to their vans, too," Layne said.

"Yeah, they're called overload springs. They do that so that we can't spot 'em. They ride low in the back with a lot of weight without those."

Layne visualized what he was talking about.

"The drive-through trucks also install sway bars under the bed so they can turn and high-tail it with 1,000 to 1,500 pounds in the back," Tipton said.

Layne checked his watch; by 1:00 a.m. they had seen only one or two cars pass by. Tipton barely glanced at the late night-travelers as the headlights grew bright, then faded away.

For Layne there had been no escape all week from his worry and anxiety until the Oral Board Exam was over. Even when he managed to fall asleep there was no solace. A nightmare about being unable to find his dress uniform tormented him. Another dream occurred so often that he could see it when something reminded him of it. He was at a Mexican wedding reception of some sort where Felina was on the dance floor, whirling in a red flamenco dress. Her glossy black hair was in a bun with a red flower, and she wore large gold hoop earrings. He was weaving through a crowd trying to catch up to her after watching her dance. But she had her back to him and was moving away in perpetuity, always unable to hear his voice desperately calling to her. His shouts were drowned out by the overwhelming music of trumpets and clarinets. Both dreams were so vivid they left him with sweat-soaked sheets and hair when he awoke.

By 2:00 a.m. he couldn't hold his expanding bladder any longer. "I gotta take a piss."

Tipton shrugged.

Layne opened the door carefully and stepped out. Just before he shut the door Tipton warned, "Don't turn on your Maglite."

The darkness was incredible this far away from town, and he could hear coyotes barking forty yards away as he unlatched his duty belt. The dirt lot was surrounded by mesquite trees, and Layne made his way to the other side from where they were parked. He looked directly upward at the vast blanket of stars above. It was like walking on the moon.

The seat was still warm when he climbed back in the Kilo. Tipton seemed to be bored, but not enough to admit their position was a bad idea. The only radio activity was intermittent sensor reports to the south, close to the Border Fence. Layne's mind began to wander as he continued staring east down the highway. He read a text message from Felina from earlier in the day. They had been in contact only through text messages since she canceled their plans. He missed the way she looked without makeup in the morning when her black hair was disheveled from sleep. She was self-conscious and wouldn't let him see her that way for very long. He hadn't known what to do with himself over the weekend by himself. He went to the grocery store on Saturday to buy one specific item and had left the store with multiple items except the one he had specifically made the trip for. He had passed through the liquor aisle but wasn't sure if it had been on purpose or by accident.

Eventually he decided to break the silence and tried to strike up a conversation to distract his mind from worrying, "What's the difference between a foot sensor and a vehicle sensor?"

Tipton looked pleased that Layne recognized his expertise. "Foot sensors are like a metal disk, about the size of a paper plate. The Sensor Unit buries them about a foot underground. They go off from pressure each time they're stepped on."

Tipton looked at Layne to see that he was absorbing the information, "Vehicle sensors are bigger, about the size of a manhole cover. They bury them a little deeper. They're magnetic, and they're tripped when the vehicle's chassis goes over them. That's why they never pick up animal traffic."

"Why do they change the sensor locations?" Layne said.

"After a while the south side knows where all the sensors are. It's dirty agents at our station that are leaking the locations as soon as we get a new sensor list. But mainly they go by trends in traffic. Out east they position them at rest stops and along trails. Remember that rest stop I took your group to out in 4-Alpha?"

"Oh, yeah. They put sensors in those places?" Layne said.

Tipton nodded. "Yeah, but experienced guides know better than to take a group through there. Usually, only people trying to make it on their own are dumb enough to follow a trail like that and walk right over a sensor."

Layne remembered checking the rest stop in the far east reaches of 4-Alpha deep in the night. It looked like a campground where nothing was disposed of. The scene was creepy in the beam of a flashlight. There was trash all over the place, hanging from mesquite branches. The trainees stepped on nasty things by accident, like used toilet paper and tampons.

"The thing I remember from that pay period with you was that woman who was trying to tell me her six-year-old son was eighteen," Layne said.

"I remember that; was that your group?"

"Yeah, I couldn't believe she brought that kid with her. I don't know how he kept up," Layne said.

"I've seen that a lot of times. Those women are so desperate they bring a kid like that with them. It's dangerous enough for women crossing the border with those border bandits down there. To bring a small kid is crazy," Tipton said.

"I searched her. She only had, like, forty dollars with her, and she came from way down south in Mexico. I always wondered what people like her do when they get deported back to A.P.? How do they have food and a place to sleep?"

"They don't. They sleep on the sidewalk, I guess. I don't think they have the Salvation Army or any kind of welfare in Mexico, like they do here."

"I wonder if she had to pay the guide for the kid or not?" Layne said.

"I don't know. That's why there's two kinds of illegal aliens that live in the United States. The ones who were brought over as kids and you have no idea that they're a wetback 'cause they talk just like us. Then there's the other kind that pick fruit because they can't speak English, or they talk with a heavy accent," Tipton said.

Layne stared in deep thought for a moment and opened his mouth to speak when the crackle of the radio coming to life interrupted him. The LECA's voice rang out, "Delta-226, 866, ten-eighteen."

"866, Delta-226, ten-nineteen."

Security check, Layne realized. It was intended to check the safety of each agent, also to wake up agents who were sleeping. Eventually after several minutes the LECA reached Layne's star number, "Delta-328, 866, ten-eighteen."

Layne already had the microphone to his mouth in anticipation, and he simply pushed the button, "866, Delta-328, ten-nineteen."

"Delta-328 what's your twenty?" the LECA asked.

Layne turned to look at Tipton with confusion, but he offered no explanation. He looked just as puzzled. Layne said, "I'm on the highway east at mile marker seven."

"Ten-four," The LECA responded.

"Why does she care where we're at?" Layne asked.

"I don't know," Tipton said.

Layne knew Escribano was hoping to torment him into resigning by putting him on Mids and forcing him to repeat Phase Four. If Layne quit Douglas, management wouldn't have to depend on headquarters to eliminate him. Layne suspected Escribano was behind the inquiry about his location. His attention returned to the night sky. He took notice of blinking red navigation lights from a high-altitude aircraft deep in Mexico. There were two-second intervals between the blinks.

The quiet and boredom stretched time, and when he looked at his watch again, he realized he hadn't seen a car pass by for over an hour. He bowed his neck with his chin over the steering wheel to look directly upward through the windshield, to marvel at the celestial canopy. He tried to identify the constellations he remembered from the planetarium as a child, Cassiopeia, the Seven Sisters, Orion, and the dippers. Suddenly, he sensed movement outside the Kilo on his left side. A vehicle was approaching from the east. He reasoned it was people traveling, coming from Lordsburg through the night. Out of nowhere, a lifeless truck passed by in front of them, cruising steadily like a locomotive somewhere around the speed limit. It was like an apparition; it had the presence of a ghost ship. Layne looked directly at its broadside in slow motion as it passed. It was a black four-wheel drive Chevrolet Silverado 1500. His first thought was the driver must have forgotten to turn the headlights on and there was nobody else on the road to flash their lights at him.

Tipton's torso sprung erect.

The truck's window tint was as black as its glossy paint and it was gone in a blink.

"What's that guy doing with his headlights off?" Layne said.

"Go, go, go, that's it!" Tipton shouted.

Layne froze, then, struggled to get the truck into gear. Frantically, he grabbed the handlebar on the steering column and overshot the D for drive, then undershot it when he tried to correct the mistake.

"Go! What are you waiting for?" Tipton yelled.

He made it into drive and stomped on the gas pedal and the tires broke loose on the gravel beneath them, spitting a rooster tail of dirt and rocks into the air as the truck fishtailed toward the asphalt. As the front tires stepped up onto the blacktop, he feathered the gas until he could feel the rear tires catch on the lip. He cramped the steering wheel right, to point the truck westbound then pushed the gas pedal until it met with the floorboard. The ball of his foot expanded over the sole of his boot and the engine erupted into a frenzy. He sank backwards into the seat, reaching forward to activate the bright headlights and the instrument lights against the force of acceleration.

The sound of the engine advancing was ferocious and forced Tipton to yell over the noise, "Turn on the emergency lights!"

Layne reached down and turned them on. He could see the red and blue lights begin flashing as the tachometer needle raged clockwise, then retreated just shy of redline as the engine exhausted the use of each gear.

The broken yellow line that divided the road rushed into a pulsating stream.

"He's got to have a quarter mile lead on me!" Layne said aloud.

"The driver is using NVGs, the passenger side window was rolled up!" Tipton shouted.

Layne had seen the excess edge of the tarp that covered the bed flapping in the wind. The broadside view was embedded in a snapshot memory. He began searching the road for the truck, straining to see the margin of light at the farthest reach of the high beams. The light from the instrument panel glowed like an orb within the cab as he glanced at the speedometer. "Ninety!" he shouted with uncertainty about what he was doing.

"It's okay," Tipton shouted back. "We gotta radio ahead!"

Tipton grabbed the microphone and as calmly as he could manage, he blurted, "866, Delta-162, we're behind the Delta Tango, heading westbound into town on the highway."

"Ten-four, Delta-162," the LECA replied. "All units on the east side, Delta Tango headed westbound on Highway 80."

Agents responded, one after another, "Ten-four," until Layne was confident that they were scrambling to assist him.

"Someone in town's gotta get out front and spike this son of a b—!" Tipton shouted.

The Kilo kicked when it shifted to the next gear. Layne was closing in on the truck. At the extent of the high beams' range he could just make out its tailgate. Thoughts arrived like the broken yellow lines in the road. This was crazy. The narrow width of the highway and the darkness unnerved him considering his speed. He visualized the Kilo rolling into a gymnastics routine just microseconds after he glimpsed a deer or a javelina enter the shallow field of his headlights. He would never get the chance to tell Felina he had passed the exam. He would fall short of ever being good enough for her.

The black truck disappeared then reappeared at the end of the light tunnel like a mirage at night. He could see the emergency lights reflecting off of its tailgate. They barreled toward a bend in the road and the Silverado pulled away, out of sight for a few seconds. Layne pressed the pedal back to the floorboard until the truck became visible again. It felt as if he were in a vacuum. The sound of his own hyperventilating drowned out the riot of engine RPMs and yelling.

"How's he driving like this with NVGs on?" Tipton yelled.

Fog from his own perspiration began to build on the windshield, and Layne was forced to lean forward with his nose a foot from the windshield to see. The speedometer read 105 miles per hour the last time he snapped a look at it. The transmission had ceased shifting gears, but the RPMs were continuing to climb relentlessly like a raging bull, spiraling, as out of control as his breathing.

Layne muttered an expletive then shouted, "I can't reel this guy in!"

"Stay on him!" Tipton shouted. "That's gotta be a million-dollar dope load!"

As Layne guided the speeding Kilo forward in the night, he felt like he was riding in the first car of a roller coaster or hanging on in a runaway train. It made him recall, fleetingly, his exchange with FTO Cruz and the admonition the FOS delivered in Muster not long ago. "You know that you're not supposed to chase them in a vehicle, right? For liability?" Cruz had reminded.

And Layne had confirmed his understanding: "If the vehicle doesn't yield to emergency lights, then you're supposed to break pursuit and turn around 180 degrees."

The warning the FOS had delivered played back, too: "If you crash into a minivan full of kids and screw yourself up chasing somebody, not only will you be sued, you'll be lying in a hospital bed with no pay and no health insurance because you'll be fired."

Just a few days ago, again during Muster, another FOS had said: "Remember the pursuit policy. I know you guys don't want anyone showing you up, but don't forget rule number one."

Finally, Layne voiced his concern. "But we aren't supposed to be chasing anyone!"

"We aren't chasing him!" Tipton yelled. "We're probing him!"

The lights of the city were growing larger like a sunrise. In under ten seconds they would reach Leslie Canyon Road and the east side where the truck could disappear into a labyrinth of residential streets and back alleys. The engine roared as they entered the final stretch before town. It was incredible that the driver could manage to evade them while looking at an electronic green image of the road through night vision goggles.

"When he hits the city lights, he's gonna throw those goggles off and he's gone!" Tipton shouted.

Layne couldn't respond.

The Kilo roared toward a dogleg left, just before the gates of the city. The turn pulled their bodies to the right from centrifugal force, and his foot instinctively relieved pressure from the pedal. He anticipated agents ahead blocking the road with stop sticks and guns drawn, surrounding the vehicle, yelling. But streetlamps were now zooming by and the city was upon them. In an instant, a cloud of dust filled the air like volcanic ash. His foot abandoned the pedal and the friction of the engine withdrawing applied pressure to his chest through the seatbelt harness. He looked desperately in every direction but saw only dust lingering through the light from the streetlamps like cigar smoke. The ghost ship had vanished into the same black magic from which it had arrived.

Layne's head swiveled in search of a clue to the truck's whereabouts as he decelerated. He searched with his fingers for the switch to roll the window down. "Where'd he go?"

"He's gone," Tipton said.

"Where is everybody? I thought there'd be a roadblock."

Tipton said nothing and returned to his arms-crossed position.

Layne turned left on Leslie Canyon to enter the easternmost residential neighborhood of Douglas where the dust trail appeared to lead. He looked around for a telltale sign of where the truck had gone, but dust seemed to linger everywhere. He plugged in his cutting light and extended his arm out the window to aim the beam into the alleys between houses. He scanned slowly, the smell of dirt and burnt oil strong with the window down. Each dirt alley he penetrated with the light beam revealed only trash cans, the reflective eyes of stray animals and waving sheets of floating particles. The Delta Tango seemed to have scaled every foot of a city block on its way, completely confusing its followers. The rotating flash of emergency lights from other units was perceptible several blocks away in every direction, but the radio was silent. There was no update on the vehicle's location.

"Where's the 5-Alpha MIT?" Layne said with confusion. "They had enough time to get in front of it."

Tipton seemed to be sulking while Layne combed the streets in search of any hints as to where the vehicle had gone.

Approaching from ahead, Agent Mendez, an MIT from 5-Bravo, pulled his Kilo up next to Layne, facing the opposite direction. Mendez wasn't alarmed. He behaved as if he were pulling up to ask for directions. His left arm was straight, resting on the steering wheel. He was wearing his search gloves and short sleeves. Mendez glanced at Layne then began speaking across him to Tipton in the passenger seat.

"You guys were behind it?" Mendez said, no hint of panic or defeat in his voice.

"Yeah, I took him to lay-in at mile marker seven and it drove right past us," Tipton replied. They spoke as if Layne were invisible.

"Black Silverado?"

"Yep," Tipton said.

Mendez looked straight ahead again, pausing for a moment as he nodded slowly, thinking. Then he looked back at Tipton and said, "Screw it," and drove off.

Layne scanned the houses on either side of the street they were traveling. There was a four-wheel drive truck in every other carport. It was hopeless. The smuggling operation seemed to be automatic; it functioned so efficiently. He reviewed the chase in his mind as he continued searching from block to block. "Dang!" he cried, for having reacted so foolishly. If only he would've called it out over the radio sooner someone might have been able to get out in front to block it from getting into town. Everyone would've been so impressed with him. Such an accomplishment might have saved him. Word would reach headquarters, and Escribano would appear nonsensical trying to blackball a trainee who had caught a drive-through.

Tipton remained silent, looking straight ahead with his arms crossed. It was obvious he was angry. But Layne knew that if he was critical of Layne's performance he would've said so. He realized Tipton was mad about the lack of effort by certain agents on the east side. They had allowed the truck to reach its destination as if they had been expecting it.

(26)

LAYNE STARED AT THE bars on Escribano's collar this time to avoid eye contact with him. He couldn't stomach looking at the pictures of him with his family anymore. Muster for Thursday's Day Shift was in progress. The voice of the FOS addressing his units reached into the hallway amidst the silence of the office. Escribano was pretending to organize paperwork again while Layne waited for him to reveal the purpose of the summons. Eventually the silence became too great and Escribano looked at Layne for a split second, then glanced over his shoulder at the door to his office and said, "He should be here in a minute." Then he resumed with his fake busywork.

The wall clock showed mercy and only a few moments passed before the door cracked opened behind Layne and Tipton peeked in. "You wanted to see me, sir?"

"Yeah, come on in and have a seat," Escribano said as he put the stack of papers that he was handling in a wire desk tray. He looked relieved to be able to look at someone while he spoke. His eyes remained trained on Tipton as he took a seat in the chair next to the wall on Layne's right.

Escribano finally looked at Layne and said, "Mr. Sheppard, how did last night's shift go?"

"Pretty good," Layne said.

"Did you forget to shave today?" Escribano said.

"No, sir, I've been getting ingrown hairs," Layne said.

"That's okay, I get them, too. Down to business. Someone on Mids said that you had an encounter with a drive-through vehicle last night." Layne was amazed at how quickly his snitch network exchanged information. One of Escribano's minions must have called and told him what happened while he was on his way to the station to start his shift.

"Yes sir, I did." Layne said after realizing what had transpired. He continued to speculate. Escribano must have called the station and had the LECA radio Tipton and tell him to bring his trainee to the office before he left for the day. Tipton had been as confused by the call as he was about the LECA requesting Layne's location five hours earlier.

"What happened?" Escribano asked. His braces were visible when he wasn't consciously trying to hide them by closing his lips.

Layne chose his words carefully, like a politician. "We went to lay-in out east on Highway 80 because of the drive-through that happened on Swings, and one of them drove right past us."

"And you chased him?" Escribano asked.

"No, I was monitoring him," Layne said.

"How fast were you going?" Escribano asked.

Layne carefully thought through his answer and acted candid. "I don't know. I never looked at the speedometer, about the speed limit, I guess."

"The agents in 5-Alpha said you got there right after the drive-through did," Escribano said.

"That's right sir. I couldn't catch up to him without breaking the speed limit," Layne said, doing his best to improvise.

"But you said you didn't know how fast you were going," Escribano said.

"It felt like I was going about sixty-five miles per hour. That's what I meant," Layne said.

"You can tell how fast you are going without looking at the speedometer?" Escribano probed.

"Yes, that's about how fast I drive on Highway 80 to work every day. I'm used to that speed," Layne said. It was the only answer he could come up with in a few seconds.

Escribano sighed. "Did you turn on your emergency lights?"

"Yes," Layne said. He glanced at Tipton, who looked stunned. Layne felt guilty for involving him. It was a routine night for Tipton, and he never expected to be answering questions about procedure.

"Then, why didn't you turn around when the vehicle didn't yield?" Escribano asked.

"Because he was too far ahead of us. I don't think he ever saw my lights," Layne said instantly. He had anticipated the question when he realized that Escribano was trying to cross him up.

"You're aware of the rule against pursuit then?" Escribano asked.

"Yes, I'm supposed to turn around and face the opposite direction if the vehicle doesn't yield to my emergency lights. But we were stationary, and he passed by us. So, by the time I got on the road to follow him he was at least a quarter mile ahead of me," Layne said.

"And you don't think he could've seen your lights from a quarter mile away in the dark?" Escribano asked.

"I don't know. If we had been right behind him and he hadn't yielded, I would have pulled over and done a U-turn then radioed ahead to advise on his course," Layne answered.

"How close did you come to catching up to him?" Escribano asked. Layne glanced at Tipton, who continued to look straight ahead, too spooked to assist him. He was afraid to incriminate himself.

Layne turned back to Escribano. "I don't know, sir, not close enough to see him, so there's no way to know."

"You said a quarter-mile," Escribano said.

"I'm just estimating by how much time that went by from when he passed us to when I got going the speed limit," Layne claimed.

"So, you never got close enough to see him?" Escribano couldn't maintain eye contact and began thumbing through the paperwork in Layne's file.

"Only when he drove right past us, but once we were moving, no, I never came within range to see his license plates or anything," Layne said.

Escribano turned to Tipton, seeking collaboration from him. "Is he making any improvement?"

Tipton opened his mouth slowly. "I haven't read any of his previous evaluations, but I'll submit my evaluation to you tomorrow, sir."

Escribano looked Layne in the eye briefly and nodded. "Fair enough; that'll be all. Mr. Sheppard, I need you to write a memo about what happened last night and have it on my desk by the end of the day."

Tipton stood up from his chair and made his way to the door to leave without looking at either one of them. Escribano returned documents to the manila folder as Layne stood up to follow Tipton out of the office.

After the door closed behind them, Layne attempted to speak with Tipton and address the situation with an innocent apology. But Tipton looked disturbed by the meeting. As he put his hat back on, he said, "I didn't realize you had this much heat on you. Good luck on the Oral Board tomorrow."

Then he walked in the direction of the locker room. It was evident by his body language that he didn't want Layne to follow him.

ABOUT THE AUTHOR

Sherryl and Christopher LaGrone

Sherryl LaGrone is the mother of the late Christopher LaGrone and daughter Aimee Hestera. She is a retired high school teacher who now enjoys being a "snowbird" in Mesa, Arizona, which is a couple hundred miles to the north of the setting of *The Delta Tango Trilogy*. Sherryl and her life partner spend their summers in the mountain town of Grand Lake, Colorado.

For more information about *The Delta Tango Trilogy*, please go to www.deltatangotrilogy.com, email us at Deltatangotrilogy@gmail.com, or follow us on Instagram or Facebook, searching for Delta Tango Trilogy.

A free ebook edition is available with the purchase of this book.

To claim your free ebook edition:

1. Visit MorganJamesBOGO.com
2. Sign your name CLEARLY in the space
3. Complete the form and submit a photo of the entire copyright page
4. You or your friend can download the ebook to your preferred device

Print & Digital Together Forever.

Snap a photo   Free ebook   Read anywhere

CPSIA information can be obtained
at www.ICGtesting.com
Printed in the USA
JSHW031451310721
17438JS00001B/96